WOLVES OF THE EMPIRE

THE LAST VIKING, VOLUME 4

JC DUNCAN

Boldwood

First published in Great Britain in 2025 by Boldwood Books Ltd.

Copyright © JC Duncan, 2025

Cover Design by Colin Thomas

Cover Images: Colin Thomas, iStock and Shutterstock

Map Designed by Flintlock Covers

The moral right of JC Duncan to be identified as the author of this work has been asserted in accordance with the Copyright, Designs and Patents Act 1988.

All rights reserved. No part of this book may be reproduced in any form or by any electronic or mechanical means, including information storage and retrieval systems, without written permission from the author, except for the use of brief quotations in a book review. This book is a work of fiction and, except in the case of historical fact, any resemblance to actual persons, living or dead, is purely coincidental.

Every effort has been made to obtain the necessary permissions with reference to copyright material, both illustrative and quoted. We apologise for any omissions in this respect and will be pleased to make the appropriate acknowledgements in any future edition.

A CIP catalogue record for this book is available from the British Library.

Paperback ISBN 978-1-80549-838-4

Large Print ISBN 978-1-80549-839-1

Hardback ISBN 978-1-80549-840-7

Ebook ISBN 978-1-80549-841-4

Kindle ISBN 978-1-80549-837-7

Audio CD ISBN 978-1-80549-832-2

MP3 CD ISBN 978-1-80549-833-9

Digital audio download ISBN 978-1-80549-836-0

This book is printed on certified sustainable paper. Boldwood Books is dedicated to putting sustainability at the heart of our business. For more information please visit https://www.boldwoodbooks.com/about-us/sustainability/

Boldwood Books Ltd, 23 Bowerdean Street, London, SW6 3TN

www.boldwoodbooks.com

CAST OF CHARACTERS

The Kingdoms of Norway, Sweden and Denmark

Afra the Constant: Elder of the bandit brothers, known for his persistence.
Eric 'Sveitungr' Alvarsson: The narrator, Harald's closest companion and follower.
Harald 'Hardrada' Sigurdsson: King of Norway 1046-1066, half-brother of King Olaf, and claimant to Danish and English thrones.
Halldor Snorrasson: One of Harald's Varangians, cousin of Ulfr.
Hrolf: Varangian and Ulfr's topoteretes, his second in command.
Ingvarr Hakonsson: Son of Hakon.
Jarl Hakon: Petty jarl, on his way to join King Magnus barefoot in his campaign to the Southern Isles.
Jarl Halfdan: Lord of Tinghaugen.
Jarl Torvald: Petty jarl, friend of Hakon.
Magnus: Illegitimate son of King Olaf.
Olaf: King of Norway.
Rurik: Varangian guardsman, follower of Harald since Stiklestad.
Sigurd: Varangian guardsman, and Eric's topoteretes (second in command)
Sveneld: Varangian guardsman.

Thorir the Cuckoo: Younger of the bandit brothers. Known for his thievery and disguises.
Ulfr Ospaksson: Varangian with Harald Hardrada, one of his senior warriors.

The Kyivan Rus

Yaroslav the Wise: Grand Prince of the Kyivan Rus.

The Byzantine Empire

Alexios: Young guardsman, Greek born to a Varangian father.
Andronikos Skleros: Domestikos of the Schools of the West: Commander of the Western armies.
Georgios Maniakes: Byzantine nobleman and general.
Hypatia: Handmaid to Empress Zoe.
John the Parakoimomenos: Eunuch and close advisor to Emperor Michael IV.
Maria Arantios: Byzantine noblewoman.
Michael IV the Paphlagonian: Emperor of The Romans.
Michael V: Successor of Michael IV as emperor.
Nikephoros Aspietes: Megas Domestikos, supreme general of the Byzantine military.
Petar Delyan: Bulgarian rebel and self-proclaimed emperor.
Petros: Leader of the Scholai scouts.
Stephen: Brother-in-law of John, father of Michael V, and admiral of the Imperial fleet.
Styrbjorn the Goat: komes of the fourteenth bandon of the Varangians; the Warborn.
Sveinn: A Swedish member of the Varangian guard.
Theodora Porphyrogenita: Sister of, and perpetual rebel and plotter against Empress Zoe.
Theophilos Dalassenos: Magister of the Scholai.
Zoe Porphyrogenita: Empress consort, wife of Emperor Romanos Argyros and then Michael IV.

PREFACE

At the conclusion of *Emperor's Axe* in the spring of 1041 AD, Harald Sigurdsson was a denuded force in the Eastern Roman empire, returning from a long, tenacious, but ultimately failed campaign in Sicily and Italy only to find the palace consumed in his absence by conflict and corruption.

In defeating an attempted armed coup in the palace, conducted by hired mercenaries led by his old rival, the Greek mercenary Bardas, Harald managed to secure his position, at least temporarily, and twisted the situation to his advantage to secure the trust of the ailing emperor Michael IV, at the cost of the emperor's brother and true power behind the throne: the eunuch John the Parakoimomenos.

Although managing to retain his position as the commander of the Varangian guard he was sent overseas to remove him from court, then tarnished by defeats in Sicily and Italy that, while arguably not his fault, would have degraded his standing with the people and the political players, nonetheless.

Not that many of the empire's elites would have been upset to see Harald's star fade. The defeats in the far western reaches of the empire were not important to those fighting for power in the capital, more focused on their own successes than the health of the empire they were supposed to govern. The bringing down of a powerful outsider, a man who held rather too much sway over the Emperor Michael and the Empress Zoe for the liking of many in the ruling class, would have been cause for outright celebration to many.

For Harald, this diminishment of his reputation and position would have been completely unacceptable. He had saved the emperor's life and his own titles, and defeated two of his key enemies in the palace, but none of that was what truly mattered to him. Harald Hardrada was in Constantinople for one clear purpose: To gild the path back to the Norwegian throne. He needed to build a reputation as a formidable leader, and obtain wealth with which to buy the men and influence to retake his half-brother Olaf's lost crown.

Harald dearly wanted to return home, but his last campaign being a failure, his last battle being a defeat, cannot be the way he left the empire. Peace may have come at last to the palace, but the storm of war is what Harald seeks. He needs the riches and renown of battle to realise his ambitions and his ambitions will not be contained.

Enemies of the empire should beware. Harald will be seeking a chance to wash away the stains of his recent past, and he would be happiest to raise the imperial banners of war and do it in a biblical torrent of someone else's blood.

PART I
OATHSWORN

1

TINGHAUGEN, NORWAY; SPRING 1098 AD

'The king is here! The king is here!'

Ingvarr looked up in surprise as a boy, younger than himself, ran past their temporary camp on the outskirts of Tinghaugen in the middle of the afternoon, shouting his message for all to hear, repeating it again and again as he went down the long field of tents.

The boy was gleeful as he ran and shouted, almost hopping in excitement. And exciting it was indeed, for every man there had gathered in that place to hear the words of King Magnus, to know if he planned to go on campaign, and to receive his judgement on a hundred different matters of law and dispute.

'I thought he was not due until tomorrow?' Ingvarr's father Jarl Hakon said to the other men sitting around with them in the glorious afternoon sun.

'I heard that too,' one of the others said with a shrug.

'It is unusual for the king to arrive so early, the Thing is not for two more days.'

'The weather is good, the roads are hard and the sea is calm. Perhaps his journey was simply better than expected, like ours was.'

Hakon grunted his assent at that, the logic could not be denied. 'Well, let's be up and go and greet him. We do not want to be noted as lacking in presence or enthusiasm.'

His small hird sprang into action, leaving the rest of their meal where it sat and strapping on their sword belts. The jarl hurried to put on his finest tunic, one he had reserved for this very moment, and for the days of the Thing, the great regional meeting, itself. It was a rich work, a deep red with gold thread woven into serpentine patterns at the neck and cuffs.

Ingvarr thought it was fitting, making him look every inch the wealthy lord, and he smiled at his father in pride.

'Come on, boy,' Hakon said with a wink and a thump on the shoulder. 'It's time to go and meet your king. If you are lucky, at some point during the Thing you might be introduced to him. That would be quite something.'

'I will swear my loyalty to him!' said Ingvarr eagerly, but Hakon frowned and stopped him with a firm hand on his shoulder.

'No, you will not. You are not a lord to give such an oath to the king. I have sworn my loyalty to him, and you to me. That is our way. You would embarrass me if you did something so foolish. Tell me you will contain yourself and respect our customs.'

Ingvarr bit his tongue, face going red in shame. He lowered his eyes and nodded. 'I am sorry, Father. I know the laws.'

Hakon laughed. 'Good lad. I know you are just over-excited, but a man of strength is calm and controlled at all times, especially in front of his king.'

'I understand, Father.'

'Good, then let's go! I want a good spot by the road.'

* * *

Hakon led his men out of the now bustling camp towards the road into town. The boy running through the camp was no accident; the king would have sent messengers ahead to make sure his people had time to welcome him properly. Nothing would be more embarrassing than to arrive unseen and unheralded, and not receive the adulation and respect of his people. Such a thing might cause him to turn about and leave, or punish whoever had failed to organise a reception.

Hakon secured them a good position along the side of the main square just outside the doors of the hall as other jarls jostled into position around the entire space and lined the road beyond.

Hakon stood proudly in front of his hird, arranged in organised ranks to show themselves as the warriors they were. Hakon gave a friendly nod to his friend Jarl Torvald, who was standing with his own contingent just a few paces away.

'Don't you look fine, Jarl Hakon,' Torvald called out with a grin. 'That red dress is almost as pretty as any my three daughters own!'

Hakon laughed a little too loudly at the quip, and Ingvarr could feel his prickle of annoyance.

'You have three daughters, Jarl Torvald? I thought you had two goats and a son!' Hakon called back, to a ripple of laughter around the square.

Such words might have led to blows between enemies, but Hakon and Torvald walked towards each other, both beaming broadly, and embraced to make sure everyone knew there was no steel in their words.

'Your father is a sharp man. Is he as good with a sword as with his tongue?' rasped a voice from behind Ingvarr, where he stood at the side of his father's men, and Ingvarr looked back in surprise to see Eric Sveitungr standing behind him, peering over his shoulder into the square.

The old Varangian gave Ingvarr a cheeky smile.

'Eric, uh...' Despite the old man's friendliness to him, Ingvarr still felt very awkward and did not know how to reply. Eric was a famous man, a companion of kings, and as such many men might call him 'lord' or show him great deference, but here he was lurking in the background and joking with Ingvarr as if he was a friend.

'Ah, your tongue is not so quick as your father's then,' Eric said with a soft chuckle, and Ingvarr flushed again in embarrassment. 'Don't worry, I have that effect from time to time.'

'I'm sorry, why are you here?' Ingvarr whispered.

'For the same reason as you, to see the king.'

'Yes, but... I meant here, with us. Surely you should be with Jarl Halfdan, on the steps of the hall.'

Eric looked towards the great hall's doors almost curiously, just a couple of dozen paces away, as if he had not thought about it. Jarl Halfdan was just appearing with his large entourage, spreading out to occupy all the space along the hall's front. 'I suppose so. I have not been invited to stand with him but he would not refuse me.' He winked. 'But perhaps I would be more comfortable here, unseen.'

'Eric!' Jarl Hakon called out uncomfortably loudly, causing Eric to wince slightly, before smiling politely and bowing his head fractionally to the jarl, who was walking back to his men and had caught sight of his son and the old warrior.

'Jarl Hakon,' Eric replied.

'What gives us the honour of your company here? Is my son bothering you?'

'Your son does not bother me, as you know, Jarl Hakon.'

'Good, good!' Hakon came over and gave Eric an enthusiastic arm-clasp and stood back, looking around. 'Come, come and stand at the fore of my men, in a place of respect.'

Eric gave Ingvarr a sideways glance and a subtle roll of his eyes, but quickly banished both and nodded. 'That is very generous of you.'

* * *

Hakon shuffled a few men out of the way to make a path and gestured at Ingvarr to follow. They made their way into the front rank and stood there while Hakon fussed over the rest of his men, finally satisfied and taking his place once more at their head.

Eric leaned in close to Ingvarr. 'Enjoy the proceedings, my boy – the king likes to put on a show.'

Ingvarr's attention was dragged away by a commotion from the street leading out of town and everyone around the space craned their heads to look for the source of the sound, the sound of marching men.

Even to Ingvarr's ears that sound was unmistakable. Armed, armoured men marching together make a certain sound unlike any other. Wood and metal, rattling and scraping and slapping together in a unique cacophony.

Sure enough, the first ranks of armoured warriors soon appeared, marching in a column four men across with their shields on their backs and spears in their hands. For any other lord arriving so armed, they would have been preceded by a man carrying a green branch to show they meant no hostility, but no such man led them.

The king did not have to show he had no hostile intent in his own kingdom. Violence was his right, marching with his men armed for war wherever they wanted was his right alone. It was intimidating, as it was meant to be. The column, now visibly at least a hundred strong, were outnumbered hugely by the waiting crowd. But in formation, in maille and shining helmets and with spear points waving above their heads like a forest of deadly saplings, they dominated the square.

Then King Magnus came into view, riding languidly on a huge, dark stallion, a dozen other mounted men, his closest advisors and family, following behind.

He was a young man still, the king. Perhaps only twenty-five years old but already a respected leader and warrior. The first years of his reign had been troubled. The northern jarls had rejected him, rallying around another king and descendant of Hardrada called Haakon Magnusson, who not only shared Ingvarr's father's name, but had been his uncle by marriage.

This was the root of Ingvarr's father's intense desire to show his loyalty. For just four years ago, he had come here to Tinghaugen, along with most of the lords of the north, to pledge their loyalty to King Haakon Magnusson, and to oppose the young King Magnus.

Magnus had avoided war, and shrewdly built his position politically, isolating his rival king, provoking him and embarrassing him until the pretender had conveniently died in a hunting accident.

Everyone knew Magnus had arranged it, Magnus wanted everyone to know it. With a single death he had secured the entire kingdom for himself, and his first move had been to graciously pardon everyone who quickly moved to support him, and then ruthlessly destroy those few foolish enough to hesitate.

Ingvarr had been too young to witness the events, still at home with his mother, but his father had kissed the new king's sword and became a forgiven man and a vocal supporter. Ingvarr felt no shame over it; everyone said Magnus was a king worthy of loyalty. And they quietly forgot the time when they had nearly been deadly enemies.

'Hail, King Magnus!' someone shouted, and there was a roar of noise as everyone else along the road joined in. The king, serene and unmoved, simply looked around with his back straight and chin high, soaking in the display of loyalty and respect.

The armoured men split in two as they entered the square ahead of the king, and they moved to line both sides, a single rank deep, facing inwards towards the king, symbolically surrounding him in a ring of steel. The disloyalty of the north may have been over, but the king made sure to subtly remind them that it was not completely forgotten.

King Magnus rode into that protected space and smartly dismounted, casually handing the reins over to one of his men, looking around and finally acknowledging the crowd with a soft and confident smile.

At the entrance to the hall, Jarl Halfdan stepped forwards to greet him. 'Welcome to Tinghaugen, King Magnus. The town and the people are ready to heed your call for the Thing, and to receive your wisdom and your judgement. My hall is open for you and your people. For as long as you are here, it is your home.'

Magnus walked forward almost languidly, soaking up the moment, and then he offered his arm to the lord of Tinghaugen to clasp with a grin. 'I thank you for your welcome, Jarl Halfdan, and for the warmth of your hearth. I look forwards to addressing the Thing, and hearing the council of my most respected subjects.'

Halfdan glowed at the praise, and inclined his head, gesturing the king to take pride of place on the steps of the hall, where he would be able to address the crowd.

Magnus walked up the half dozen steps and turned, one hand on his sword, and waited for the crowd to fall still and silent.

'It is my honour and pleasure to come here, to hear the words of the bravest men of Norway, and to let them hear mine.'

There was a roar of appreciation from the gathered men, and the king quickly held up his hand for quiet again.

'I am moved to see the display of duty and service you have put forth today, and I, in return, will perform my duty and service to you. I will hear your pleadings for justice and judgement and render it fairly for all men to see. I know that you all seek strength and wealth for our people, and I will present my plans to achieve that, to once more lead the unified men of Norway to the heights of glory and all that it brings!'

The whoops and cheers of appreciation were ever louder around the square and the king let the clamour of the crowd go on for a while before holding his hand up again. They all fell silent, leaning in, listening, hoping and expecting the king would announce his plan for a great campaign. Ingvarr could feel the excitement and tension like a living thing.

The king held that moment, then smiled, sweeping his arm wide. 'I am forgetting myself, for the Thing has not yet begun. The time for speeches is later, the time for drinking and celebration is now!'

Then he signalled to his men, who broke their formation up, and drifted in to gather as a group, allowing the rest of the crowd to fill the square. The king turned to speak to Jarl Halfdan, signalling that he was done. The gathering broke into excited conversation and laughter as the king spoke with the lord of the town.

'He is a very clever young man,' Eric said in amusement.

Ingvarr turned to him. 'In what way?'

'What he just did, testing the waters, whetting our interest in the campaign and then avoiding announcing it. It will be all anyone can talk about now, and he will be able to judge exactly how to propose it. A good politician, our young king. It is even more important than being a great warrior.'

Ingvarr nodded seriously, thinking about it. He had almost no experience with politics, even less than he had with war, but Eric's words made sense to him.

His father came over and gently took Eric's arm.

'I shall take you to stand at Jarl Halfdan's side! The king should see you.' Hakon nodded forcefully.

'Ah, I suppose so. Lead on, Jarl Hakon,' said Eric with subtle reluctance that Ingvarr saw but his father missed.

Then he was gone, whisked away by the excited Hakon, who was doubtless thrilled with the perceived chance to be seen as close to Eric, and witnessed by all to be escorting him to the great hall. Ingvarr followed behind, careful to keep his distance, remembering his father's warning.

Jarl Halfdan saw the two men come over and gave Eric a polite smile and greeting. Ingvarr could not hear the words that were spoken, but Halfdan gestured to his right, and his men made space for Eric to stand near him as the king spoke to other nobles.

Eric wore a faint look of amusement as he stood there in line among the Jarls and warriors, waiting his turn.

Hakon gestured furtively for Ingvarr to come and stand behind him, and he did, standing there and watching as the king greeted each man in turn, before coming to Eric.

Magnus looked at Eric curiously, then Halfdan leaned in to whisper in his ear, and the young king nodded sagely.

'Eric Sveitungr, I am pleased to finally meet you. My father spoke of you many times.'

'He did?' Eric looked surprised.

'Of course! He had great respect for you, and the service you did for my grandfather.'

Eric bowed. 'I am honoured.'

'You have been a great servant of my family, yet we have never met. Where have you been all these years?'

Eric smiled sadly. 'I was not in favour after your grandfather's tragic death. I went to raise my children and farm my land, and leave the troubles of rule to the younger men.'

'Not in favour? Nonsense, you would always have had a place in my father's court, and mine.'

Eric bowed his head again. 'I am deeply honoured to hear that, Lord Magnus, but I rather enjoyed my quiet life these last years.'

'Understandable. So what brings you here? I hear you have been telling the story of my grandfather's life.'

Eric nodded a little nervously. 'I came to show my support and offer advice if it was asked for. But a young warrior asked me a question about King Harald, and I answered. I accept some might claim that my answer has been a little long-winded,' Eric said with a self-effacing laugh. 'I first meant to tell the story to him alone, but a few men gathered, and then a few more...' Eric spread his hands helplessly.

'And now he has the whole hall listening every afternoon into the night!' Halfdan said with a wry smile.

Eric shrugged helplessly. 'Many men wanted to hear the story, it turns out. But the rest can be told another time, I will not disturb your council.'

Magnus shook his head. 'Nonsense. The Thing has not yet begun, and I would love to hear the story of my grandfather told by one who was there. I have never heard it from anyone who shared his time in the east. Come, sit with me in the hall and speak to me of my family's past, it would please me.'

Then the king looked around at the crowd. 'And anyone else who wishes to hear it.'

Eric flushed. 'You honour me, my king, but I do not wish to intrude.'

'Nonsense! There will be several hundred angry men if I do not allow it,' said Magnus, and Ingvarr detected the first hint of an edge in the king's words.

Eric surrendered. 'As you wish, my lord.'

'Continue with this tale to the one who asked, and, with your permission, I will join you.'

Magnus gave a good-natured smile and started into the hall. 'Come then, I need a seat and some ale. My journey was long and boring and I wish to hear the tales of the glory of my ancestor.'

They followed Magnus up to the head of the hall and Hakon and Ingvarr held back a bit, angling towards one end of the long table, not presuming to sit close to the king. That space was reserved for the great lords of the north, the king's closest and most powerful allies.

But Magnus offered a seat just a few spaces down from himself to Eric, and then snapped his fingers at Hakon, pointing at the benches much nearer to himself than they had chosen.

'Here, Jarl Hakon. Sit with us to enjoy this tale.'

'This is an enormous honour,' Ingvarr's father whispered in his ear. 'Do not shame us.'

'No, Father.'

Hakon went to the proffered bench, sitting between one of the jarls of Lade and the king's cousin, nodding to both proudly. Ingvarr slotted in next to Eric when the old man waved him over.

'Come then, Eric,' said the king as a silver-chased mug of ale was offered to him and the rest of the hall started to fill in. 'Where were you with the story?'

Eric coughed and thought about it, then nodded. The great hall started to fall silent as his old eyes drifted away, his mind moving back to his time all those long decades ago, when he had been a young man in the service of the empire.

2

CONSTANTINOPLE; SPRING 1041 AD

'Harald!' I shouted, banging on the door to his quarters. I was in my full ceremonial kit, brightly coloured cloak over my maille, helmet and spear polished to a bright sheen.

Harald should have been too. He should have been outside at the head of his men ready to march to the palace gate and escort the imperial family to the Hagia Sophia for the service of blessing. But he was not there.

I was furious, it was unlike Harald to be late for anything, to slacken in his duties. He never got drunk, he never lounged late in bed. I had twin fears, either that he had snuck out to be in Empress Zoe's bed, or that he had been poisoned.

The implications of him being caught in Zoe's bed, on that day of all days, were so dire that I was actively hoping he had been poisoned.

'Harald!' I said again, banging mercilessly on the door.

I kicked at it furiously, even as it opened and Harald appeared in his full regalia.

I lowered my foot with a scowl. 'I had assumed you were dead.'

Harald looked at me nonchalantly. 'And did that bring you joy?'

'More joy than trying to explain to the men why their commander is late for such an important event.'

I heard a shuffle behind him, and my brows creased. 'Do you have a woman in there? You are neglecting your duties for a woman?'

I felt a sudden, insane fear that it was the empress. Would either of them be so stupid as to have her snuck into the Varangian barracks? No, surely not.

My fear overcoming my sense, I barged in and saw the source of the noise and froze, feeling foolish. It was Thorir, who was folding some notes and slipping them into his robe. They had clearly been having a quiet meeting about something.

'Are you satisfied?' Harald asked coldly.

I stepped back with a grunt.

'Good, then let's go. I don't wish you to make me late,' Harald added acidly.

I glared at Thorir as if it was his fault, and Harald's quiet and tame bandit just gave me a small shrug that was devoid of any sympathy.

Harald set off without saying anything else, and I followed him down the shaded veranda outside his quarters in annoyed silence.

'Aren't you going to ask me what I am doing with Thorir?' Harald asked.

I sighed. 'No. If you wished to tell me, you would. I hope only that it doesn't cause me some intense trouble later, although I am sure that it will.'

Harald shrugged, his broad shoulders expressive even under his armour, tunic and cloak of office.

The curiosity needled at me as we walked down the stairs and into the main barracks yard.

'Well, what are you planning with him then?' I finally said.

'Oh, I am not going to tell you yet.'

'Then why ask me if I was going to ask you!' I said, exasperated.

Harald looked back with a smile. 'You are so easily riled up these days, Eric. You need to calm yourself and trust me to conduct my business and know what you need to know and when. How can you get back to your old self? You know, I think you need a woman.'

I cursed under my breath. Not least because it was true on most counts, perhaps all counts. But I had reason to be so on edge and nervous. It was only a month since the attack on the palace and our narrow defeat of it, a month since we had buried nearly two hundred of our own men, men who died at their posts defending the palace, betrayed by the very woman they were charged to defend.

Zoe had confessed to Harald that she had organised mercenaries and traitors to attack the palace and kill her husband, and tried to ensure we had not been there to defend him. And we wouldn't have been there if Harald had been less bull-headed about everything.

I had not forgiven her, even if Harald had forced me to accept it. Forced me to accept that we could not punish her, could not tell her secret. I was bitter every day, and nothing would assuage it. I was only made more bitter that Harald seemingly had forgiven her. Not only forgiven her but become her lover. He claimed it was only to keep her close, to ensure she didn't dispose of us and to keep an eye on her actions.

But I knew better than that. I knew the empress had a hold on him beyond politics and power. I had seen it before in Harald. He was ensorcelled by powerful, ambitious, beautiful women. And Zoe was the paragon of all three.

I feared for him, I was angry with him, I was extremely unpleasant to be around and I knew it. Now of course I see that my concerns were perhaps small and petty, while his were vast in scale and pragmatic. But to a man who still clung to the notion that he was good, that he was not just a mercenary killing for gold but a noble man with a God-given mission of duty and sacrifice, Harald's choices and orders were a terrible burden.

But you have seen before, and you will see again: that is why he was a great king, and I was merely a follower.

Regardless of my bitter mood, I would not let it affect my duties. In that I was resolute. So I put my sour face away and I marched out into the great central path of the palace with my head held high as I beheld the massed ranks of Harald's Varangians.

Ah, the memory of that sight still warms my cold, old blood today. We had long been a fearsome fighting force, but the campaign in Sicily, the battles in Italy and the defeat of the coup had honed us like a well-cared-for sword. Veterans, almost all of us – many of us had fallen but those who remained were paramount soldiers, battle-hardened and tested, and loyal to a fever pitch that defies the retelling.

They did not know that Zoe had betrayed us. They only knew that we had stood and fought when traitors turned and cowards fled. They knew that when the palace halls had filled with blood it had been their blades that did the spilling, and their veins that flowed our precious red life force so that our oaths of duty would remain unbroken.

God, my pride in them is impossible to fully name. It is in the beating heart of me and it will be until the day I finally join them in the soil, that magnificent company of my brothers.

They were standing there in the blazing sun, in all their glory, and Harald and I walked to their head and he smiled at them, for he used their lives like coin, but he loved them too, I know that he did.

'What are you waiting for? We have a ceremony to attend!'

The men laughed, then put their helmets back on and hoisted their shields onto arms and axes onto shoulders ready to move out as the other detachments of the imperial guard stomped down the path to join us, shining in their perfect unity and matching step.

We did not march in perfect formation like the other palace guards. No, that was the Roman way, to process in locked step like one man copied a thousand times. We marched like real warriors, like the killers we were, and we were known for it.

The Greeks of course looked down on us, said we were too rough and barbarous to be fully trained, but we laughed at their ignorance. We walked our own steps because we had the strength and pride to do so. We were not toy soldiers, we were Varangians.

We were joined by the Royal family in the Hippodrome to mount their magnificent, shaded chariots, pulled by white stallions who were deafened and blinkered so as to remain calm and docile. The emperor was weaker and more sickly than ever. He did not stand; instead, he was propped up on a cleverly disguised stool such that it seemed he was merely wearing a billowing set of robes, while two attendants stood behind him to support him should he need it.

Empress Zoe, on the other hand, looked magnificent as she always did, and stepped serenely into her chariot with effortless grace up the gilded steps laid out for her, taking her place on the raised, shaded platform behind the driver and smiling around at the guard.

They loved her, and it grated at me. She took every opportunity to thank and praise them for their actions in saving her and her husband. She lavished them with honours and gifts, and the generosity of her personal appearances, and they adored her for it.

Bah, let me move on from such a bitter draught before I become consumed by it.

* * *

We marched out behind the perfect block of the Vigla tagma, and in front of the riders of the Scholai, and we went through the great gates of the Hippodrome and the crowd cheered at the sight of us.

The emperor rode first, Zoe behind, but it was noticeable to us, marching all around the imperial family like an armoured box, that the cheers were far louder as the empress passed.

She had captured the people with the same charm and radiance as she had captured my men, and the emperor, while liked, simply could not rival the devotion the people showed her.

We were headed towards the Mese, the great road that went from the outer city walls to the magnificent Chalke Gate of the palace, through all of the great forums and public spaces.

Now, of course, we didn't need to take that longer route to escort the imperial family to the Hagia Sophia. They could have left the palace at the Chalke Gate and crossed a mere hundred paces to the cathedral, but the purpose of them going to this service was to be *seen* going, and to follow the lengthy and complex protocols of these events and festivals.

Bah, I shall not relate them all to you – it is as boring now as it was then. Suffice it to say we had an army of officials and palace aides to make sure everything went according to the rules of the ceremonies.

The way was laid with flowers and rushes that were ground into the cobbles by our feet, and streamers of colour and petals were thrown over us as we passed, until the canopies above the imperials were littered with them.

I mused, as we marched, that those canopies were there precisely for that reason – not to keep off the sun so much as stop the ruler's magnificent clothes becoming covered in the enthusiastic detritus of flowers and coloured cloth.

We passed the great baths that the nobility built for themselves on the peak of the hill, and the nobles gathered there to watch did so with much more restrained and muted enthusiasm than the rest of the people on the road behind us, and there it was, the Hagia Sophia, the greatest building of the world, standing proud with its soaring dome and brooding towers.

At Harald's shouted orders we spread out crisply into a three-sided box around the entrance, protecting the imperials from all sides while they dismounted their chariots and acknowledged the crowd before heading inside the cathedral with the first bandon.

Harald came over to me. 'You and the fourteenth bandon can take the inside watch with the first, I will have the seventh and second guard the perimeter.'

'As you command, Protospatharios.'

'Fourteenth! On me!' I said, turning to shout at the formation led by Styrbjorn the Goat, who smiled as I looked at him.

'We are going in?'

'We are going in,' I confirmed. He had his men quickly line up and march in by the side entrance, separating and filtering out to take up positions all around the magnificent interior, adding to the constant presence of the first bandon, the Emperor's Shields, who never left the imperial family's side.

Having another entire bandon guard them while inside the cathedral was superfluous in many ways, but since the attempted assassination, Harald took no chances, and the newly reformed first bandon, who had been almost entirely annihilated while holding their positions in the attack on the inner palace, were still short of men.

Afra, who was once more their komes, nodded to me and smiled. 'Lucky you, eh, getting to stand in here with the real men.'

'There are real men in here? Where?' I asked, looking around dumbly.

He laughed and patted me on the shoulder as we stood on the upper balcony, leaning heavily on the marble railing. His old leg injury was troubling him more and more as he aged. He was well past the point most soldiers would have been quietly retired. But Harald was not going to retire Afra the Constant, the old bandit turned spymaster. There was no one else he trusted enough.

I looked down over the balcony at the gathering nobility of the empire massing in the space below for the service. The imperial family were taking their places on the second level beyond us, behind the ornate carved marble doors, where they could sit and watch proceedings in solitude and peace. Or, in Michael's case, quietly doze without anyone noticing.

Afra didn't need me to command him in his task. There was nothing for me to do but to stand there looking imposing. That was a large part of our task, by the way. I tell you tales of battles and intrigue, but most of our time in service was actually spent standing in one place or another. It was quite dull, but sometimes not unpleasant.

I don't remember which festival or service it was that day, and I shall not recount it to you as they were all the same to me. It was only what happened during it that made it of any interest. I walked over to Komes Styrbjorn, who was standing guard with a dozen men near the marble doorway, ready to respond to anything.

A guardsman came over from the passage leading downstairs.

'Message from the protospatharios. We have more guests coming to the imperial balcony. Make way for them and form a guard.'

Styrbjorn didn't even look curious. He was not a man to argue or question. It was one of the things Harald liked about the old veteran. His foot was badly injured from the campaign in Sicily, and he would likely never go on campaign again. But as a bandon commander he was unmatched in diligence and loyalty.

The komes quickly organised his men into an honour guard framing the doorway and had it unlocked and opened, then sent more men to line the curved balcony as far as the doorway that led down into the antechambers of the building.

The sound of marching steps brought a dozen Vigla guardsmen into view along the balcony, with a small cortege of finely dressed women following them serenely, with a robed nun in their midst.

I stared at them in curiosity, because they were veiled and I could not make out who they were.

They approached the marble door to the imperial balcony, and Styrbjorn opened it and stood aside to allow them through. The Vigla stopped. They were not permitted into the inner sanctum, part of the complex and interweaving layers of rules that governed the many imperial guard tagmata. The women swept through the open portal and, just as Styrbjorn was about to shut it, I motioned to him to wait a moment and followed through myself.

Strictly, I was not supposed to be in there, it was the preserve of the first bandon, but as Harald's standard bearer I could do almost as I wished within the guard and Styrbjorn just gave me a curious look and nodded, letting me pass before the ornate doors closed behind me.

The little party of women approached the twin thrones confidently, and neither Zoe nor Michael looked surprised. I stood at the railing, intrigued, as one of the women, plainly dressed in the habit of a nun, stepped forwards and bowed gently to the thrones. The bow was shallow, far shallower than should have been due to the emperor and empress, but no one from the crowd of courtiers and officials admonished her.

Then she turned, facing down into the open space of the great cathedral. I glanced down and saw that the entire audience was motionless, all eyes fixed upwards on the woman on the imperial balcony.

Everyone in that great church was a member of the nobility of the empire, the ruling class. They knew the customs of the ceremonies and ways of power far better than I, and would have been even more surprised to see a group of anonymous women in such fine clothing paraded into the royal balcony, late for the service, with a simple nun at their head being greeted by the empress herself.

Ah, something clicked in my mind there, you see. The woman was not late; she was exactly on time. She had arrived at a moment when it was certain she would be seen and noted by everyone, and clearly at the invitation of Zoe, who now rose to stand beside her, her magnificent smile upon her face.

The room waited in rapt silence as the two women stood there, and then the nun gracefully lifted her veil to show the audience her face, and I felt my breath catch in my throat as I saw who it was.

There were gasps and a wave of muttered shock from the audience as the traitor, the black sheep of the imperial family who had been exiled to spend the rest of her life in an island monastery outside the city, was revealed.

Theodora: the rebellious sister of Zoe, rumoured in the city to have been behind the recent attack on the palace. An attack that was officially denied, but which everyone in the city knew had happened. A battle in the palace had simply been too significant to hide.

Some of the empress's attendants brought forward an ornate chair from the back of the balcony, placing it to the side of Zoe's throne and just behind. The empress turned and kissed her sister three times on each cheek, and then graciously motioned to the newly placed chair.

There was a smattering of applause and appreciation from the crowd, which rapidly rose to a crescendo as the slower members of the audience realised that this was the required response to the carefully choreographed display.

I was still dumbstruck, so that I did not notice one of the women who had come in with Theodora sidle over to stand at my side.

'Hello, my darling Eric,' a voice purred in my ear, and I turned to see the soft smile of a woman I very much hated to see, for where she stepped, trouble always followed.

'Maria?'

3

'Isn't it lovely to see them reunited?' Maria said, looking towards the sisters with a smug smile.

'What are you doing here?' I growled.

My blood was seething, because the last time I had seen the woman was in the aftermath of the failed attack on the palace, where Maria was revealed to have been the one who Zoe used to covertly organise the attack by the traitor Bardas and his mercenaries.

'I'm Lady Theodora's personal attendant while she is in the city,' she replied, smiling brightly.

'A spy for the empress, then.'

'Oh, nothing that serious. But yes, I keep a close eye on her for Zoe. I watch her sister, others watch me. Everyone in the palace is watched now, Eric. Even you and Harald.' Maria looked at me sympathetically. 'But don't worry yourself about such things. The empress's safety is your only concern.'

'The emperor's and empress's safety,' I said, my cheeks tensing.

She glanced back at me nonchalantly. 'Yes, that's what I meant.'

'Then you had better not threaten it.'

Maria giggled softly. 'Threaten? Eric, your imagination runs wild. I am a loyal servant of the Empress Zoe.'

I had no answer to her infuriating smugness, and simply wished to be away from her. 'I have duties to attend to,' I lied.

'Of course you do,' Maria said with a wink, and I flushed and stormed away with as little sound as possible, slipping back through the marble doors and heading to my commander.

* * *

'Harald,' I said, striding towards him across the great public square outside the cathedral as the service droned on.

Harald looked up and I could see from his tired look that he knew exactly what I wanted.

'Do you know who is in there?' I asked.

'Of course I do.'

'Why!'

'Because the empress ordered it, and I obeyed.'

'Theodora is supposed to be imprisoned!'

'And she was, at the empress's order. And now she isn't, at the empress's order.'

I put my hands on my hips in outrage. 'But why! You know her mind, you...' I almost said 'you share her bed', but we were not alone and Harald's eyes burned with anger at the threat of those words. It was an open secret in the guard, but still a secret. It was not spoken out loud. Harald might have killed me for saying it. Zoe certainly would.

'It is not your business to know why, Eric, which is why I did not tell you.' Then his expression softened, and he gestured to me to follow him, away from the other guardsmen who were politely pretending to ignore our public argument.

I followed him across the paved square, to the base of the vast column of Justinian that dominated the space, with its bronze statue of the emperor on a horse. The statue had been recently cleaned, and it shone brightly in the sun, absent its usual green stains.

'What is she doing in the palace? Theodora is a traitor, three times over!'

'Yes, she is,' Harald agreed.

'And she is dangerous, she might rebel again.'

'Yes,' Harald said with an infuriating nod.

I was beyond perplexed and threw my arms up in frustration. 'So what is she doing here?'

Harald regarded me carefully, weighing what answer he should give. He stared at me harshly. 'Do you trust my judgement, Eric? I am starting to question it.'

I was hurt. I was hurt partly because my loyalty to Harald defined me, and partly because it was true. I did not trust him any more, not since he had sided with Zoe after her actions had been revealed.

'Of course,' I snapped. Lying, and furious with both of us for making me lie.

Harald's stare did not relent. 'Hmm. Well, Zoe is convinced Theodora will be used to inspire a rebellion again, and the empire cannot afford it. That is why she is here, close to the empress.'

I stammered to a halt, seeing it clearly. 'So, she is here so she can be more closely watched?'

Harald nodded and then tilted his head slightly. 'It's more than that.'

'What?'

Harald looked around uncomfortably.

'Zoe is securing herself against all possible future threats. The emperor is dying, you know that.'

'Yes.'

'When he dies, Zoe will have sole power, but she now believes the people will not accept that, even as popular as she is. There has never been a woman in sole power of the empire, not since its foundation a thousand years ago. The people, and John's faction, will expect her to take a new husband.'

I nodded. It was all as I understood it.

'She fears a nasty fight to take her hand in marriage. Zoe is getting old, anyone who can force their candidate into marriage with her will likely have power over the sole emperor before too long. So the competition for her hand will be ruthless and bitter. It might even lead to civil war.'

'Can't she choose her own husband?'

'She could try, but who could she trust? That is what she did with Michael – she chose her own and look how it went. He was merely a puppet for someone else. No, the problem is the same: no matter who the husband is, he could turn against her.' He looked off into the distance, his face drawn. 'She wanted someone she could truly trust and she only had one option.'

That's when it hit me. 'She asked you?'

Harald nodded.

'By the mother, she offered you the throne?'

'Yes.'

'And?' I said, terrified of the answer.

'I refused.'

My mouth hung open. 'You refused the throne of the empire?'

Harald's eyes narrowed. 'You are surprised? I thought you knew me better. I thought she did too.' He sighed sadly. 'I told her it was the wrong throne, I couldn't do it. I am also unsure how the people would take a foreign emperor, but that is another matter.'

'She must have been angry.'

'Furious does not begin to describe it,' Harald said with a grimace. 'She considered having me killed.'

My eyes widened. 'How do you know?'

'Because she discussed it while I was in the room.'

'And what made her change her mind? Her love for you?'

Harald scowled. 'Don't be childish, Eric. It was because she still needs me. If I help her secure power she will reward us richly. It is a great opportunity.'

The brutality of that calculation, that exchange, shocked me. Zoe and Harald were two of the coldest people I had ever met, as most great rulers are, but that they could discuss either marriage or execution as if they were deciding what to have for their evening meal, and still be allies afterwards, was simply incomprehensible to me. Ah, I was still a naive young man!

I furrowed my brow. 'So Zoe prepares to take sole power, bringing Theodora close to control her, positioning you to secure her rule. But there is a missing factor. Surely John's faction will not accept this outcome.'

Michael's brother, the eunuch John, was imprisoned in the palace, but his network of alliances in the empire was broad and powerful.

Harald shrugged. 'Of course, the throne will always have enemies, but without a legitimate challenger of imperial blood, they will have no credibility or support from the people.'

I thought about that. 'But Michael and John still have family. What if one of them makes a claim? One of his and John's brothers or nephews.'

Harald nodded guardedly. 'It is possible, but preparations are being made to guard against that,' he said with a stern look.

'What do you mean, preparations?' I asked, feeling a tingle of doubt.

'I have told you enough, Eric. You are not going to be involved in those plans, others are more suitable.'

I narrowed my eyes. 'Thorir. You were meeting with Thorir about it this morning.'

Harald did not answer, did not even blink. It was all the confirmation I needed.

'Dear God, you are going to have them all killed.'

Harald looked alarmed. 'Be quiet, Eric! Do not speak of such things out loud. This is why I feared letting you into my confidence. Are you going to disappoint me?'

'They are the emperor's family!' I hissed.

'Only when he is alive.' Harald stepped in towards me, face rigid as stone. 'This is the way things have to be done to keep the empire safe, Eric. More rebellions would see more of our brothers killed. I am saving them with these plans, distasteful as they may be. Can you accept it? Or perhaps you should step down, as you offered to do.'

I closed my eyes, pressing them tightly together, trying to master myself before I answered.

Finally I looked back at him, meeting his gaze. 'You think this will spare our men from more needless loss, and get us what you need?'

Harald nodded.

'Swear to me that is a true aim, Harald. That you value their lives, that they have meaning to you beyond their usefulness. Swear that to me and I will follow you in this and all other things.'

Harald had the decency to look a little hurt. And I believed he was hurt, I wanted to believe it, I needed to believe it.

'I swear it, Eric,' he said, without breaking eye contact.

I breathed a deep, deep sigh of relief, and looked away towards the great cathedral. 'Then I will trust you, Harald, and I will keep my oaths and my silence.'

And I could not meet his eye again because I was ashamed that I had given in so easily, and more ashamed how little it upset me to think of those innocents who would die because of it.

* * *

'The emperor has summoned me,' Harald said a few days later as he adjusted his finest cloak. He had called me to his office and told me to dress for court. It was a common enough thing to do; we had to attend various state functions as guardians and as Harald's standard bearer, I often went with him.

But this was different, and his tone made that clear.

'Summoned?'

'Yes.'

'For what?'

'I do not know.'

'That seems...'

'It's trouble. Whatever it is, it is trouble.'

My chin sank as I considered it.

'Have you checked on John recently?' he asked.

I nodded.

'Are you sure he is having no outside contact?'

'Yes. He tried to co-opt two of the gaolers, but they simply told Afra. They are more afraid of Afra than of John, it seems.'

'As they should be,' Harald said with a satisfied nod.

'Why ask?'

Harald shrugged. 'I assume whenever there is trouble that John is behind it. So that was my first thought, that maybe somehow he had communicated with his allies. They have been causing trouble, petitioning the emperor to see him.'

'And what has the emperor said?'

Harald looked bleak. 'I think his willpower is fading.'

I nodded. 'It is his brother.'

'John uses him as a puppet, there is no brotherly love there.'

'Michael is not so ruthless as John.'

'Oh, I am well aware of that. Come, let's go and see what he wants.'

'Why am I coming?'

'I need a witness and a second opinion.'

I met his eye as he gave me a pointed glance. He was doing me a favour and showing a token of his trust, and I appreciated it. The previous month we had been as far apart as we ever had been, and the wounds were hard to heal.

* * *

We went from the barracks and walked to the palace, passing the newly rebuilt gate that had been destroyed by the rebels, and the walls that had been smeared with their blood during their final stand.

Even the halls inside the palace, where bodies had fallen three deep and blood had run like water, were gleaming and unmarked. Walls had been smoothed and repainted to cover weapon scars, the damaged furnishings used to barricade hallways by desperate guardsmen replaced, like the fallen guardians themselves.

All was spotless and new, as if it had never happened, but I had to walk the halls where we had fought and my brothers had died, and nothing was left there to show of their courage or sacrifice, or the dishonour of those who had killed them.

I looked up, torn from my melancholy, to see Harald's sympathetic face looking back at me. 'I feel it too, Eric. I hear their shouts in these halls, when the night is quiet. I see them lying here.'

'Truly?'

'Truly. I am not made of stone.'

'Hmm.' I could not think of a reply, because that is exactly what I thought of him at times, my ruthless prince – that he was carved from granite.

We reached the emperor's quarters and were quickly ushered in. Long gone were the days of having to pass John's minions. Harald could walk freely wherever he wished, and no one stood in his way.

Michael was not in bed, which was unusual those days. He was sitting on the shaded private veranda in the spring morning air, a servant standing by with a fan, and a medicinal drink abandoned on the elegantly wrought table at his side.

He looked up and smiled weakly. 'Ah, Harald.'

'How can I serve, Basileus?'

'Sit down. I want your advice, and to ask you a favour. Come.' He gestured weakly at the chair opposite him.

Harald nodded courteously and took the seat offered. I stood guard in the doorway, pretending not to be there. The emperor didn't seem to mind.

'What troubles you, Basileus?'

'The imminency of my demise, Protospatharios.'

'Basileus, don't—' Harald tried to protest, but Michael cut him off with an irritated cough and a wave.

'Don't bother. Don't be like one of those fawning sycophants who tells me this medicine, or prayer, will save me.' He gestured to the ill-looking drink. 'I am dying and you all accepted it a long time before I did. Maybe I will cling to this world for another few years – I certainly hope so – but nothing more than that and you know it.' He gave Harald a look that dared him to argue.

Harald's gaze fell and he nodded softly. 'I will not argue then, Basileus.'

'Call me Michael, for God's sake. No one else does, give me that comfort. Emperor this, Basileus that,' Michael snapped irritably. 'Ten years ago I was simply a young courtier who fantasised about bedding the empress.' He gave Harald a sly look. 'Something you understand more than most.'

Harald stiffened, doing his best not to look nervous. Michael laughed so hard he triggered a bout of coughing. 'Oh, Harald, everyone knows. Don't worry, I don't hold it against you. I pity you. You have fallen into the spider's web as I once did and the size of it escapes your notice.'

'Basileus!'

'Michael! I damn well command you to call me Michael if you won't do it out of kindness!'

Harald swallowed. 'Michael, I intend you no disrespect or harm.'

'I know. I know you had no choice in the matter, because neither did I.' He laughed softly. 'I thought I did, at the time, but now I realise I was as helpless as a fly caught in that web. I hope you escape it more easily than I did,' he added bitterly.

Harald sat there looking deeply uncomfortable.

'The only matter is that it remains a quiet secret. If the people start mocking me for it, I will have to have you killed.' Michael gave Harald a sad shrug, as if it was nothing to him but a matter of small regret.

'I understand. I will resign and leave, if you wish.'

'I do not wish it, there is none other I trust, oddly. For despite our differences and your... indiscretions, I know Zoe has tried to persuade you to remove me, and I know you have refused. I know that if your friend over there pulled out his sword and came for me, you would protect me with your life.' He gestured lazily at me as he spoke. 'What man could I trust more than that?'

Harald nodded. 'As you say.'

'But here is the problem. Your loyalty to me, does it extend past the moment of my last breaths?'

Harald looked even more uncomfortable. He had clearly not been anticipating the way this conversation had gone at all. He did not reply.

'No? That is my concern; what happens after I die.' He tapped his fingers on the side of his chair. 'I am writing a public decree, to make my nephew, Michael, into my formal heir. Zoe will be forced by this to make a decision: to adopt him publicly as our son, or to refuse him. If she refuses him, it will be a public declaration that she intends to usurp my lineage, and it could cause a civil war.'

Harald listened intently, trying not to betray anything. Michael stared at him, watching for a reaction.

'So, what do you think?' Michael asked.

'I think it is none of my business, Michael. I will do as you command.'

'Rubbish. I command you to be honest. What do you think?'

Harald took a deep breath; he was in a very difficult situation. 'Zoe will take this as an attack on her.'

'I know. And she will need someone to guide her into not responding to it as such.'

Harald looked pained. 'Ah.'

'Yes, now you see the purpose of my calling you here.'

'You want me to contain her anger.'

'Exactly.'

Harald sat back, hands clasped together. 'That will not be easy.'

'I know, but I need my family to have very visible protection, in case Zoe makes plans to move against them when I die.'

He looked carefully at Harald, who showed no hint of reaction to the words beyond looking deeply uncomfortable. I held my breath. If Michael decided we were not trustworthy, or that we might allow Zoe to kill Michael's family, we would not leave the palace grounds alive.

'It is not my only concern,' Harald said smoothly, moving the conversation on. 'Michael is Admiral Stephen's son, and Stephen is...'

'Disgraced, an ex-dockworker,' said Michael with a nod.

'Well, yes. Will the people accept his son as emperor?'

'Not on his own, no. He will rule with Zoe until Zoe dies, or her soul finally shrivels up and abandons her husk, whichever happens first.'

Harald looked at Michael in surprise. 'You would leave your nephew to rule with Zoe, you would not try and have him rule alone?'

Michael smiled sadly. 'If I could remove her, I would. But I cannot. You would not allow it, the people would not tolerate it. So no, I must hope that he can hold his own against her.'

'How? Basileus, I don't know your nephew well, and he seems a bright and likeable lad but not strong enough. He is not ready for this.'

'No, he is not. And that is the second reason I have brought you here today. Michael will need a strong ally, one who can stand up to Zoe and balance the power in the palace, as it has been balanced for all these last years.'

Harald looked distraught. 'Basileus, I cannot be that ally. I cannot take one side or the other in that struggle.'

'I wasn't talking about you,' said Michael flatly, and Harald stopped.

'You mean your brother, John.'

'I do.'

'Basileus...'

'*Michael*,' said the emperor, pointing at Harald without humour.

'Michael... Your brother betrayed you, sought to use you and manipulate you. He is worse than Zoe, he will use that sweet, young man and destroy him.'

'I don't believe he will. He does not have children, cannot have children. He needs my nephew to be strong and thrive. I believe he will have learned a lesson from his misjudgements with me, and if he has not, I intend to spend the rest of my life, however long that is, ensuring he understands it.'

'What makes you believe that is possible?'

'He has no choice. He will understand it, or he will go back to his cell. I will limit his authority this time, employ some outside powers and allies to counterbalance him, and if he does his task properly, when Zoe dies he will be the advisor to the sole emperor, which should satisfy his craving for power and legacy.' Michael smiled softly. 'It is not a perfect solution, but it is the only one I have.'

Harald looked at the floor. 'I cannot dissuade you from this?'

'No. I have already written the decrees and set the plan into motion. All I needed from you was to hear me, and understand it, before I made it your duty. I don't need to question whether you will carry out my wishes, I know that you will. I just wanted to explain it to you first, man to man, not emperor to soldier.'

'You said you wanted my advice, but it seems you do not need it.'

Michael smiled. 'I know you, Harald, and I knew asking for your advice would make you more amenable than to sit you down and simply command you to listen.'

Harald let out a snort of laughter and shook his head. 'Am I so easily manipulated?'

'I can't let Zoe be the only one who can do so. Well, will you help me and my family, Harald? I could order you, but my orders die with my death. I just want to ensure my family doesn't. I want your promise, your treasured words of oath.'

Harald looked at Michael with a serious expression and nodded. 'My oath is to protect the emperor and the throne. If you decree that on the moment of your death, your adopted son becomes emperor in your place, then he has my oath and I will die in his service, if required, to protect him.'

Michael visibly relaxed, his hand shaking on the arm of his chair, and he smiled. 'Thank God for you and your kin, Harald. There isn't a Roman man in the empire who would see it the same way.'

'My oaths are iron, Michael. You have nothing to fear.'

'I know. I apologise, but I must ask you to leave now. My attendants are hovering behind you because it is time to bathe me, and trust me on this, you do not wish to be present for that.'

Harald stood smartly and saluted. 'I am at your service, Basileus.' He turned to leave.

'Protospatharios.'

Harald turned back. 'Yes?'

Michael gave a sad smile. 'Have my brother freed, and brought to me. Immediately. And don't inform the empress about any of this. I will do that myself shortly.'

Harald gave a stiff nod. 'As you will, Basileus.'

* * *

Harald didn't speak as we left the palace. He was deep in thought, his face clouded.

'How do we resolve this?' I finally asked. 'Your plans with Zoe and your oath to Michael will not survive each other.'

'I know.'

'Then why did you agree?'

'I had no choice. If I refused, we were leaving here dead or in chains. Besides, he is right – my oaths are clear. I must be loyal to his son and heir if he is legally appointed and recognised as such. Zoe did not anticipate this, being forced to adopt his nephew as their son. It changes everything.'

'So, what will you do? What will you tell Zoe? What will happen?'

Harald shook his head angrily and increased his pace. 'Eric, I just don't know. I don't know how she will react to Michael's message, or what she will do about her plans with me. I don't know how we are going to get out of this.'

Now, I tell you that scared me. He had never said anything like that before.

4

We went to the old storehouse behind the barracks where we kept John imprisoned.

'As soon as he is out, he will start planning to kill us,' I said as we walked down the shaded path and past the neatly manicured trees that lined the verges before turning off and going down the slope past our quarters.

'He will have been planning already.'

We were away from the main thoroughfare down the central spine of the palace ground's upper tier now, between the walls of our barracks and the barracks of the Scholai cavalrymen adjacent to it, away from prying ears.

I leaned in, my stomach a knot of concern. 'Perhaps this is the time for us to leave.'

'You know I cannot.'

'We have enough riches, surely.'

'Not nearly,' he said sternly.

'But we have sent boatloads to Kyiv!'

'Where Yaroslav takes his share, and our men took theirs. It is not a mere band of mercenaries we need to buy, Eric. We need enough to take a kingdom.' He grimaced. 'Besides, gold is not the only thing we lack. Men will follow me if they think I will win, and at the moment, we reek of defeat.' He spat the word as if it was poison, and to him, it was. 'Who will follow a man who fled from a eunuch, disgraced from four years of failed campaigning? Who?'

'But that is not the truth!'

He turned on me. 'You fool, Eric! The truth is whatever men believe it to be, and men say that we were defeated, that we fled not once but twice.' His mouth was twisted into a snarl and I recoiled from it, the hatred behind it, and in that moment I realised he believed it himself. My glorious prince hated himself for those failings, even though they were not his own. I realised in that moment he would never leave the empire until he had washed the stain of his shame, not from the eyes of those who looked upon him, but from his own mind: the small voice in his ear that told him he had failed.

I girded myself and nodded. 'Then how will we change that?'

Harald stared at me a moment more and then turned to walk again. 'By finding a great enemy to fight, and crushing them. You worry that John will try and kill us, that the emperor or empress will do the same. This is your failure of vision, Eric. Only with powerful enemies can we expect the chance of glory. You fear the danger we are in, but I welcome it. Peace is what scares me, for with peace will come nothing but the promise of failure.'

He smiled the predator's smile as I hurried to keep pace with him. 'Let our enemies gather and surround us, let them bring their forces to bear; I welcome it. Let men say that when all seemed lost and hopeless, that Harald Sigurdsson found a way to triumph.' He raised a finger. 'When that is what is told of us, that is when we will be ready to leave.'

'It is not enough to welcome the danger, we need a plan. If we are not ready for these attacks we will only end up dead!'

'Death is preferable to defeat, Eric. Besides, I never said that I did not have a plan. I just don't yet know what is going to happen, and therefore which one I am going to use.'

I scowled. 'You have already planned to deal with John's freedom?'

'Of course!'

'But the emperor only ordered it moments ago!'

Harald turned to me with an amused grin. 'It was inevitable, Eric. For one who is so good with a sword, you are finding predicting our opponents' next moves surprisingly difficult.'

It was a well-made point. Of course Harald would have considered what to do if John were freed. I had not; I had been too busy worrying about Harald and Zoe to consider anything else. Blind to other threats.

'It is easy to see what a man with a sword will do next; he gives clues in his feet and his shoulders, the flicking of his eyes,' I said sullenly.

'And this is the same. Why do you think I am going to free John myself? I could have just sent you.'

I furrowed my brows. I had not, in fact, considered it. But now it was obvious. 'You are going to see his reaction, gauge his next move.'

Harald nodded in satisfaction. 'And see the placement and angle of his feet, so to speak. Let him think that I am afraid. I hope to draw him into overreach.'

Now he was speaking in words I understood. I hated politics and subterfuge, but when it came for swords to be crossed, I knew well how to disguise a strong counterthrust behind a look of fear and surprise.

'Then let's see what clues he gives you,' I finally replied. 'I will trust your judgement.'

Harald grunted with a hint of contempt. 'There was a time when you didn't need to say that.'

* * *

We reached the makeshift prison behind the barracks and four of Afra's guardsmen were sitting around the entrance, playing at dice. They looked up in surprise and then stood sheepishly. They had been guarding the entrance for months and Harald had never visited, nor had the prisoner been let out. It was among the dullest of our great variety of very dull duties.

Harald gave them an annoyed glance that would have melted lead, but then it passed. He had greater concerns. 'Open it up. The prisoner is being released.'

The guilty-faced guardsmen knew better than to argue, and the door was promptly unlocked to let us in. We were led through the entrance chamber where stores were still piled around, and another, inner door was unlocked, leading into a single chamber, lit by small windows along the back wall and a triple-mouthed bronze lamp near the door.

A small figure looked up from the bed in surprise as Harald stopped and looked at him. He saw us and the two guards behind us, and the scroll that he had been reading fell from nerveless fingers.

'No,' he whimpered.

Harald said nothing, simply regarding John with a blank expression.

'No,' said John fearfully, shaking his head, clearly assuming that we were there to end his imprisonment with steel, not freedom. 'The emperor would not allow it!' he said, then his face darkened. 'Is he dead? Has my brother died?' His voice was tinged with desperation. Then his face screwed up in anger at Harald's silence. 'Tell me, you brute!'

'The emperor is alive and has ordered your freedom. We are to take you to him, now.'

John's mouth opened a little in shock, eyes flicking between Harald and the guards, not knowing what to believe. Then he swallowed and tried to recompose himself. 'Truly?'

'Yes.'

'Why? Why now and not before? What has happened? Is Zoe dead?' His confidence was returning as he took a half pace towards us, but he was still wary.

'The empress is well. I do not question why, I merely obey,' Harald said, watching John's every movement.

John suddenly became self-aware of his state, straightening the simple tunic that he was wearing and then tussling at his hair, trying futilely to smooth it into place. 'I must go and wash before I see the emperor. Take me to my old chambers. This state you keep me in is a disgrace!'

'My orders are to take you directly to your brother.' But Harald chewed his lip a little, thinking it over. 'But I expect a short detour to make yourself presentable is acceptable.'

John's eyes narrowed and then he smiled a little. 'No, you are right, guardsman. You obey. Obey my brother's command and take me to him directly. Let him see what you have done to me.'

Harald shrugged nonchalantly. 'As you wish. Come.'

John took two steps forwards, then stuttered to a halt as Harald did not move, leaving only a narrow gap between himself and the door. John eyed it, staring at the open doorway and the open air outside, but he was still afraid it was some sort of trick.

'You are many things, Harald, but I do not know you as dishonourable. Tell me true, am I really free? If this is a ruse to have me go to my death quietly just tell me, for I have prepared myself for death for months. This is a cruelty I do not deserve.'

Harald tilted his head slightly. 'Why did you prepare yourself for death?'

John glared at him. 'Because the moment my brother died Zoe would have ordered you to kill me, as you well know.'

Harald made a dismissive gesture. 'It is not my business to predict the commands I may be given.'

'Pish, you try and predict everything. It has been a most infuriating trait.' He looked at the open air outside, eyes squinting against the unaccustomed brightness that was taunting him. 'So tell me the truth,' he grated through half-bared teeth.

Harald gestured outside. 'It is as I said. You are free to go, John. What will you do with that freedom? Will you make the mistakes once more that led you to this place?'

John took another tentative pace forwards, peering around the corner of the door into the entrance chamber, seeing if anyone lay in wait, still afraid to go out... or, perhaps, like a beaten dog, too afraid to leave the perceived safety of the room that had been his home for unbroken months.

'I will do as my brother commands, like you.' John finally summoned the courage to squeeze past Harald and into the entrance, hurrying his pace and going outside, stopping dead when he found the two guards out there either side of him.

But they did not move as we followed John out, and he looked uncertainly around once more, shading his eyes with one hand against the bright sun.

'See that you do, John, and that it is not you who seeks to command him. It will not be tolerated again.'

'Who are you to make rules for me, guardsman?' John said with a sneer.

'I am the Emperor's axe, set to protect him and the empress against all threats, no matter their name or source.' Harald smiled softly. 'That includes any who would seek to usurp his rule.'

John gave Harald a final, spiteful look, and then he turned on his heel and started hurrying towards the palace, ridiculous in his worn and dirty robe, his hair unkempt and misshapen.

Harald jerked his head at me and we set off after the eunuch, Harald's long strides easily keeping pace with the smaller man as we headed up the hill.

* * *

The doors to Michael's chambers were already open when we arrived, and the emperor was at his ornate desk. He looked up as we escorted John in and could not disguise his shock at John's appearance.

'My brother, I am glad to see you are well,' Michael said.

'I am not well! Look at what these... dogs have done to me!'

Michael raised a hand. 'Enough. All that they did, they did at my command.'

John was taken aback by the strength of the emperor's statement.

'But, Brother...'

'Basileus,' Michael snapped. 'You will address me properly, or you will be returned to where you were held.'

John looked appalled but had the sense to bow his head slightly and back down. 'I apologise, Basileus.'

'Good. I am hoping your confinement gave you the time to learn humility and respect. Do not disappoint me, Brother. Things have changed in your absence. I have learned what your presence concealed, and what I was lacking while I relied on you.'

John looked on silently as Michael eyed him.

'But I also learned keenly what service you did for me, and how I missed your insights and your networks, and your comfort as my family by my side. I need you, John, but under my terms. Can you accept that?'

John looked up at his brother and nodded curtly. 'Of course, Basileus. I am at your command.'

Michael nodded in relief and then looked at Harald. 'Thank you, Protospatharios. You may go now. Remember what I said – I will speak to the empress about this first.'

I understood that the little speech to John had been for Harald's benefit as much as John's. The emperor wanted Harald to be reassured that John was not a threat, that he would be kept under control.

'I understand, Basileus,' Harald said, making his salute and turning to leave with me at his heels.

Once we were outside and away from prying ears, I looked at him with the question writ large on my face. 'So? Do you believe it? Can Michael keep John contained?'

Harald shook his head. 'Not in the slightest. To be clear, I believe in Michael's sincerity. I think he intends to govern John, but I do not believe for a moment he is capable of it. John is too smart and deceptive, and Michael is naive and ill. All he can do is slow John's plans down.'

I nodded; it is what my instincts told me too. 'And what of John, what did you take from him? He seemed genuinely afraid of you. Will it be enough?'

'No. He left his fear of me in that room, cast it like snakeskin. It is not important to him. What he truly fears is his brother's death, and what happens to him afterwards. He will do anything in his power to secure his position when Michael dies and Zoe takes the throne.'

'So he will try and remove you again,' I said with a tired sigh.

'No.'

'No? But I thought...'

'I am not his problem now. If he kills me, whoever takes my place will obey Zoe's order to kill him just as well. No. He will not waste his energy confronting us, it will be spent ensuring his position.'

'So we are safe from him?'

'For now. But when Michael dies and John secures his position, then he will come for me.'

I shook my head. 'Why? Once he is in power, why?'

'Because he hates me, and because I am close to Zoe, who he will seek to overthrow.'

I shook my head mirthlessly. 'You got this all from those two conversations with him and the emperor?'

'No. They only confirmed my beliefs.'

'How can you be so sure?'

Harald smiled. 'Because it is all exactly what I would do in his position.

Come, we will worry about John later. It is Zoe who is the threat now. She will not take this news well and there is nothing we can do about it.'

'You fear her, truly?'

Harald looked at me and his eyes narrowed. 'She is the greatest threat we have ever faced.'

I was taken aback. 'The greatest threat? I was starting to think you loved her.' I laughed.

Harald shrugged. 'I do.'

And then he lengthened his stride, powering ahead and ending the discussion, leaving me hurrying to keep up, mind roiling. Harald was trying to keep just ahead of where the next threat would be, while I looked behind, fearful for what was past. He could see where my eyes could not, and plan where my mind could not go. But yet, for all he could see these dangers before anyone else, he could never seem to avoid them.

That was my prince, you see: brilliance and contradiction. He was drawn to power and ambition, but there is nothing so dangerous as the powerful and ambitious, especially to one they see as a reflection of themselves. He and Zoe were cursed lovers, for their love was real, and their fear of each other's power razor sharp. As long as their goals intertwined, so would they be.

But now Harald had given me a new fear to burden me: that they were both already planning for the day their ambitions could no longer coexist, and they would be enemies.

Ahhh, I longed for the simplicity of battle in times like that, but I am a simple warrior, and Harald was born to be a king.

5

'The emperor and empress wish to spend the day at the summer palace tomorrow, to take in the sea air with their family. They command your presence.'

Harald looked up at Afra in confusion. 'The emperor and empress... together?'

Afra nodded. 'I know. I am as surprised as you.'

It had been three days since John was released, and we had not heard a word from the palace, not from Michael or Zoe, and Harald had been restless. He had been expecting Zoe to summon him immediately, but it had not happened and that worried him.

'Then that is what I will do. Do you need me to provide men?'

Afra nodded sheepishly. 'I am still short of the full complement in the first. Covering both the palace and the summer palace leaves me stretched thin.'

Harald nodded. 'I will assign fifty men from the seventh. They have nothing better to do. I will talk to Ulfr.'

The burly Icelander was still the komes of the seventh, Harald's old bandon and his favourite. Most of our men who had been with us since Norway were in its ranks, although there were few enough of us. Many of the rest had marched under Harald's direct command in the Holy Land,

and in Sicily and Italy, and they were fiercely loyal to him at a personal level.

'I appreciate that, Harald. But I can find Ulfr, no need to trouble yourself,' Afra said.

Ulfr had suffered from the absence of his cousin, Halldor, who had been as close to him as a brother, despite their wildly different natures. Halldor had been composed and careful where Ulfr was brash, outgoing and hot-headed. But without his cousin to spur him on, he had lost much of his amused and endlessly adventurous outlook on life.

Halldor had been terribly wounded in Sicily, and had left the guard to return home, wealthy beyond his wildest dreams, but scarred for life by his service. His place as komes of the tenth had been taken by his topoteretes, his second in command: Rurik, one of the blood-sworn who had been with us since Stiklestad. Rurik was a good man, careful and courageous, although he was outspoken in his desire that we return home to Norway.

But whatever the change in Ulfr's character, he was, if anything, an even more effective commander now that his childish streak had waned. Harald favoured him and his men, along with his friend Styrbjorn and his fearsome fourteenth bandon, the Warborn, who had spearheaded the guard so often during our battles in Sicily.

Afra ambled off, limping slightly as he always did. The old bandit was kept in service only by stubbornness, and his peculiar loyalty to Harald. It was long past the time where he could have taken his wealth and returned home with his brother, Thorir, but he never even talked about the possibility. Never appeared to consider it.

I suspect he loved his life as the guardian of the inner palace and Harald's spymaster too much to contemplate leaving it. It suited him perfectly, far more than returning to the cold north as an old and crippled outlaw.

Harald turned to me when we were alone again, his face drawn. 'I can't imagine what would have brought them together, unless it is to try and cast me aside again. I sense John's hand in this.'

'He has only been out for three days. Can he already be enforcing his will?'

'I do not believe there is anything we should assume he is incapable of.'

'So what do we do?'

Harald looked down at his food again. 'We obey.'

* * *

The next morning we assembled with fifty men of the seventh bandon and several dozen porters and attendants at the palace to escort the imperial couple down to the summer palace at the water's edge. It was only a few hundred paces away down the hill to the south, the older palace of Boukoleon, nestled against the side of the hill in a series of magnificently arched tiers overlooking the royal harbour.

Despite its proximity, it could be noticeably cooler down by the waterfront, and away from the stink and stagnation of the waters of the Golden Horn on the north side of the city. Down at the south, facing the broad inland sea, the waters were fresh and cool, and under the watchful eye of the Vigla guards on the walls and the great harbour tower, fishermen plied the waters and extracted their endless bounty.

But there were no nets and fish guts despoiling the imperial harbour. Its small docks were reserved for imperial business, and sometimes the use of the Varangian guard.

The emperor was the first to be escorted out into the heat of the day, appearing in a cloud of courtiers, family and attendants. He walked stiffly out into the yard dressed in exquisitely wrought, flowing light summer robes that hid his stooped back and swollen legs well. Harald gestured to guide him into the ornate waiting palanquin with its dozen porters.

Michael shook his head, waving Harald away. 'I shall walk. I need the invigoration.'

Harald lowered his hand, looking nervous. Michael did not look in a good state to walk anywhere, and the route to the harbour was steep and cut through much of the palace grounds. Hundreds of people would see him and the carefully guarded state he was in.

'Basileus, it might be preferable to allow us to bear you.'

'No, I wish to walk,' said Michael, and further argument was impossible in front of so many witnesses.

'As you command, Basileus,' Harald said with a bow.

There was a minor commotion and I turned to see another party of palace denizens, smaller than the emperor's leaving the palace gates. It was Zoe.

She smiled graciously at her husband, and gave an enquiring look at the pair of palanquins.

'I have decided to walk,' Michael said stiffly.

Zoe raised an eyebrow and then inclined her head. 'A good idea. I shall accompany you.' She swept over and proffered her hand to Michael, who looked surprised but took it in his own.

My eyes widened. It was the first time in years I had seen the two of them have any communication beyond attendance at formal events, or arguments in private, let alone touch. The entire operation of the palace revolved around keeping them apart on a daily basis.

'Then let us go,' Michael said in a strained voice, and he looked at Harald, who turned crisply and ordered the leading group of guardsmen to set off.

* * *

As we slowly processed through the palace I was chilled to see how much Michael was struggling. His steps were laboured and his face strained. Alongside him Zoe did her best to support him while merely appearing to hold his hand. The rest of their followers snaked down the hill behind.

As the imperial pair finally reached the doors of the Boukoleon the head of the palace household tried to greet them, but Michael shook his head in irritation and simply walked through, servants scurrying to clear the way. As the emperor passed I could see he was pale and sweating, and that Zoe looked drawn.

Harald walked past and gestured at me to follow as the emperor was led through the ancient but fabulous entrance hall, and through the vaulted interior to the great balcony overlooking the harbour where he slumped down in the large, comfortable chair that had been prepared for him.

Within moments attendants were bringing him iced water, and several were working large fans to cool him.

Zoe gave Harald a look that spoke of her annoyance and took her seat beside her husband.

The emperor's chamberlain, a powerful noble in his own right, quietly ordered the room to be cleared of all but close family and advisors.

Harald moved to leave with me at his heels, but a voice called out. 'Not you, Araltes.'

Harald turned on the spot and bowed, for that is what you did when the voice of the empress gave you an order in public.

I vacillated in indecision, unsure if I should leave, but no one asked me to or indicated that I should, so I remained by Harald's side.

Soon there were only a dozen people in the vast space, and the emperor visibly sagged back into the deep cushions of his seat, breathing hard and tearing the sweat-cloyed wrap from his head.

'A foolish mistake, to insist on walking,' said the empress in a tired voice.

'Perhaps, but I am tired of being carried everywhere.'

'You are carried because you need to be.'

'Perhaps I need to be because I am carried everywhere. I am still a man. Walking is good for a man's humours.'

Zoe bit her lip and held back any additional criticism, standing and moving to the marble railing that overlooked the harbour, basking in the cool sea breeze and the sunlight.

Michael gestured weakly to Harald to attend him, and Harald paced over to bend down and hear Michael's words. Standing next to the emperor was his nephew, and now adopted son, Michael. I know, I know – the Greeks have little imagination for naming in the powerful families. Like us, many kept reusing auspicious names, and much though I'd wager a cupful of good ale there are a fistful of Harald Haraldsson's in this room, there were plenty of Michael son of Michaels in Constantinople.

Ha! I see from the laughter at the back of the room that my wager is safe. Well, I shall call this royal nephew the younger Michael, so that you know of whom I speak.

I had not had cause to meet the younger Michael before, beyond in passing, and he was a notably fine-looking young man, although on the side of being overly thin and almost feminine, as is common with the Greek nobility. He was perhaps twenty years old, barely a man. He had a strong chin and nose, dark curly hair that I never saw tamed, and a bright, intelligent stare that was unnerving in its wildness and intensity.

But he was demure and pleasant, almost oddly so. I did not get from him any hint of the scheming and quiet aggression that so many of the elite of the city always displayed.

'Harald, have you been properly introduced to my son, Michael?'

Harald bowed. 'I have had the honour, Basileus.'

'Good, good. Well. Now that he is my heir I want you to get to know him well, for one day, God willing not so soon, you will guard him as you guard me.'

'I will do my duty, if that sad day comes.'

Michael snorted. 'That day races down on us and we need tell no lies here.' The emperor took the younger Michael's arm in a tight grip and looked up at the standing youth with a fierce emotion. 'No, he will need to learn from you, as I have learned from you. He will need your guidance.'

'He will have all the guidance of your allies and nobles, Basileus. I am but a soldier,' Harald said with a small smile.

'Oh, sheath your jokes, Harald. You are more of a politician than I ever was, and Michael needs advice from beyond the walls of this city, from one who has seen the world and its terrors. Things no swaddled son of nobility can teach him.'

Harald nodded. 'What did you have in mind?'

Michael let go of his son's arm and nodded. 'Well, for a start, you can teach him about military strategy, give him the lessons you have learned on your campaigns.'

'He is not tutored in the imperial treatise?'

'Of course, he can recite the Tactica from memory,' Michael replied, almost contemptuously. 'But real learning is not taken from pages, but from experience.'

Harald smiled a little more. 'That is true wisdom, Basileus.'

Michael smiled at the small compliment. 'Good. Then I expect you to keep close to his side from now on. You will help prepare him to do his duty, when the time comes.' Michael's gaze wandered away, out towards the sea, and his smile dissolved. 'However soon that might be.'

Then the emperor's attention snapped back and he gently pushed the younger Michael forwards. 'Begin now. We will be here for several days and I must rest. You will have ample opportunity to begin his instruction.' He looked up sternly at his adopted son. 'You will listen to Harald, for he is wise beyond his years. The empire would be in a better state if I had realised that sooner. Listen carefully, and consider his advice deeply.'

'I should do as he says, Father?'

Michael's brows furrowed. 'No,' he hissed. 'That is not what I said. A ruler does not do as anyone says; that is the path of weakness. I say to listen to him carefully, but then make your own judgements. You will let no man decide the contents of your words and the path of your actions. That is what it means to be emperor. Do you understand?'

The younger Michael looked chastened. 'I think so.'

'Good. Now I must rest. Go with him.'

Michael nodded enthusiastically and looked to Harald with almost pitiable respect. I felt it was a weakness; he seemed so desperate to please.

Harald smiled awkwardly – he must have felt it too – and gestured for the young prince of the empire to accompany him as he walked back to the edge of the balcony, away from the emperor, who had lain back in his chair, looking exhausted.

'Thank you for this, Harald,' said Michael with a nervous smile. 'I have heard so much about your campaigns, that you are a peerless warrior and leader. I am honoured to learn from you.'

Harald turned to regard him with a serious expression. 'Tell me now and tell me once, Michael. Do you wish me to be honest and forward with you, or do you wish to only hear what you want to hear from me? Consider your answer carefully, my prince.'

Michael looked taken aback at the harsh tone. The words were carefully phrased so that there was obviously only one good answer.

'I wish you to be honest, Harald.'

Harald nodded gravely. 'Then here is my first advice. Never thank a man for merely doing his duty. A man's duty to his emperor is the least that is expected of him. As emperor, you will need to be careful with praise. You will need men to seek it, value it, strive their entire lives to experience but a taste of it. Yet you thank me for walking five paces with you, to begin a simple task I was entrusted by the emperor.'

Michael stuttered. 'I...' He looked unsure what to say.

'And my second advice. Do not speak until you are certain what words you will form. All men wait to hear the emperor's words, and they must be strong and confident when they come. The world will be looking for a hint of weakness, and you must not show it.'

Michael looked overwhelmed, and then nodded, looking down.

Harald pursed his lips, disappointed at the softness of the boy. Harald gave me a look that I could read like a well-written scroll. *I have a lot of work to do with this one.*

I smiled back and nodded my head fractionally. *I know.*

* * *

Harald spent most of the middle of the day with the younger Michael, talking to him of his campaign in the Rus, taking care to go over each and every mistake he had made, and glossing over his successes. I will not repeat any of that; it is a long tale and most of you heard me relay it a few nights ago. But his purpose was clear: to break down the young man's idea that Harald was born an infallible warrior and try and teach him the lessons that Harald had learned the hard way.

The boy listened all day in rapt attention, which I took as a good sign, for Harald was a dry and tedious teller of stories, nothing like the master of words you find yourself listening to in this great hall today, eh? The man could make any battle sound boring, all about angles and distances and consideration of the firmness of a particular bit of terrain. Bah, that is why he was a great general. It is honestly an art of expertise in the boring and calculated details, not a skill of bravery and hot-headedness.

Zoe came and went, going with her ladies to bathe and be massaged while the emperor dozed and listened to the musicians brought in to entertain him. Sometime in the afternoon Admiral Stephen appeared, the younger Michael's true father, and brother to the emperor and John.

I had not seen him since the debacle in Sicily, where Maniakes had shouted him out of the camp and caused him to abandon us. I do not need to tell you, my opinion of the incompetent, petty little admiral could not have been much lower. I think I probably scowled at him, and I know he noticed it, for he swallowed hard and avoided my gaze. That is how much of a small man he was. I should have been taken outside and whipped for my rudeness to a member of the imperial family, but he did not even protest, just scurried past me like a rat avoiding a dog and headed to the emperor to greet him.

When Stephen was done speaking to his brother, he made his way over towards us, angling towards his erstwhile son and Harald, and studiously ignoring me.

'The emperor would like to speak to you, Michael,' Stephen said to his son.

Michael nodded, looking instinctively to Harald for permission he did not need, and receiving only a raised eyebrow in reply.

Michael grunted and took the hint, turning to leave. Stephen glanced once more at me as I tried to keep my face neutral, and then faced Harald.

'So, what do you think of my son?' Stephen winced as soon as he said it, for the boy was no longer his.

Harald ignored the awkwardness. 'He is eager to learn, but he is not ready, in his mind, for power.'

Stephen deflated a little and nodded. 'I know it. This whole thing... It was not my idea. He is an ambitious boy, and clever, but he did not grow up in palace politics nor does he have any experience of any of this.'

'He can be taught,' Harald said.

'Can he? Truly?'

'It is possible. He seems willing to learn.'

Stephen looked slightly relieved, but turned to look at his son, who was crouched down beside the emperor, listening.

'I know you think little of me, Harald, but I beg you – do not hold him responsible for it. He will need all the help he can receive to... well, to survive this.'

Harald mulled over his response carefully. 'Perhaps my view of you is not so dim as you assume.'

'Is it not?' said Stephen hopefully.

'I think you did what could be expected for a man of your experience, put into the position you were put into.' Harald was dancing around the truth, which was that Stephen's position as an admiral was completely unearned, and that perhaps he had been intended to fail in order to sabotage the campaign in Sicily.

'You mean all that a shipyard worker could be expected to do, when suddenly given command of a fleet?'

Harald inclined his head softly. 'If it helps you, I think how Maniakes treated you was wrong.'

Stephen lit up a little. 'Yes! It was unfair.'

'I do not speak of fairness, I speak of practicality. That is all that matters for men of power. He was right that you had failed in your duty, but instead of trying to correct your course of action he publicly admonished you for your failings, humiliating you, driving you into the inevitable act of rebelling against him. Maniakes is a great general, but a terrible politician. He made the same mistake with his other allies after his return, and it cost him an entire province and his reputation. He is a fool who should have known better, while you were a man who had no chance of doing what you were expected. So I hold you in better regard than I hold Maniakes.'

Stephen looked taken aback at the bluntness of Harald's assessment, and I almost laughed at how bold it was.

Stephen took a deep breath. 'And what of my son then, Harald? He is the son of a shipwright, but will now become emperor. Has he any chance at avoiding failure, unlike me?'

Harald considered it for a moment and nodded. 'If he wants to, and he learns quickly, yes. But if he was made emperor tomorrow?' Harald shook his head softly. 'He would be as helpless as you, when you were suddenly given the command of the fleet by your corrupt and devious brother.'

We both knew he was talking about John, not Michael, but it was still an extraordinary thing to say. Even the downtrodden Stephen looked angry.

'Are those words a guardsman should speak?'

'It depends, Stephen. I asked your son if he wanted me to speak the truth, or merely the words he wanted to hear. He chose the truth. I see that as a good sign. Would you want anything different?'

Again, he had made a question with only one acceptable answer, and Stephen swallowed his outrage and nodded curtly. 'You are right. It is better that someone is honest in this nest of liars and flatterers. It is what my son will need. He will have plenty of sycophants to polish his ears and oil his arse with praise.'

Harald smiled, the first true smile I had seen him give that day. 'I was right to rank you higher in my estimation than Maniakes. He was too weak to hear the truth, and too strong to believe he did not know it already.'

Stephen straightened slightly, returning the smile and then he laughed. 'I can see why my brother John hates you, and perhaps, why the emperor has learned not to. You truly have no fear of who you insult or what men think of you.'

Harald shook his head. 'You could not be more wrong, Stephen. What men think of me is almost all that I fear in this world. I just don't care if they like me. It only matters that they respect me and know my worth.'

Stephen sucked on his lip for a moment, considering it, and then he nodded slowly. 'I was worried, when my brother told me you were to guide my son. I thought that you were too hard for him, too coarse and foreign and violent. But perhaps you are exactly what he needs. He needs a little of your honesty and your steel. And above all he needs respect, and to learn how to gain it. A lesson I was never able to give him, having never learned it myself.' Stephen smiled sadly. 'I have no choice in the matter, but for what little it matters, I will support you in your service to him.'

Harald offered his hand to Stephen. 'It matters enough.'

The admiral took Harald's arm gladly and awkwardly, for it was not the Greek way to clasp arms as we do, and then he wandered off to rejoin his brother.

Harald watched the man go and I looked at him incredulously. 'Why were you so... nice to him? That worm abandoned us.'

Harald did not look at me. 'His abandonment of us is in the past and no longer matters. As the father of the next emperor I can secure his respect and support now and in the future. Perhaps it will matter at some point, and it cost me nothing to gain it beyond some careful words.'

Ah. That was Harald. I have said many times that he was not a great politician, but I think that I am lying to myself, because there were so many moments like that one where he proved just how great he was. He saved our lives with that conversation, although we could not know it at the time. But he had the foresight to see that it was possible, the coolness to embrace a man who had betrayed us, and the mind to work out what to say. Such is the way of the truly great men. I would never have been able to do the same.

But that is why I am the follower, and he was your king.

6

We spent days in the summer palace while Michael tried to relax and his doctors fussed around him. It was dull but pleasant, and I preferred it greatly to being in the upper palace or in the senate. The balcony overlooking the harbour was cool and breezy, designed cunningly to draw in the sea air, funnel it through the building, and let it flow out of the back.

Michael's condition seemed to improve away from the rigours of his public duties, and Harald was kept busy with his tutoring of the younger Michael who was both enthusiastic and eager to learn, which I could see quietly delighted Harald.

Maybe it was the fourth day when Zoe finally drew herself away from her ladies and sat down for a conference with the emperor. Theodora arrived. She had been in and out of the palace during the preceding days, splitting her time between her duties to God and sitting with her sister. To my displeasure John was also invited, and he appeared from the inner palace, studiously ignoring Harald beyond giving him one acidic glare.

Everyone except the imperial family's closest retainers was dismissed, even the younger Michael. Harald turned to tell me to leave, but Zoe shook her head. 'He needs to stay. If something happens to you, there needs to be another from the guard to hold up your commitments here.'

Harald raised a brow. 'Is something expected to happen to me?'

'God is sometimes kind,' muttered John.

'Be quiet, both of you,' snapped Zoe with a glare. 'You are a soldier, Harald. Untimely death is to be expected. Now sit, both of you.'

We all sat in the chairs that had been arranged in the open space near the balcony, completing a rough triangle with the emperor, John, several of his generals and his chamberlain on one side, the empress, Theodora and their chosen assistants on the second, and Harald and I on the third.

Michael was the only one there who looked calm. I think he was the only one who felt like he was in control. The rest of us were unwilling participants, perhaps even hostages.

Michael sat up, making an effort to straighten in his chair and look like an emperor. 'Thank you all for attending us here. I do not wish to speak for long, my doctors advise against it. Nor do I intend argument or debate. We are here to discuss one thing alone, the careful and peaceful transfer of the throne from myself to our son, Michael.'

'Why is Michael not here?' asked Theodora, looking around in confusion.

'It is not appropriate to discuss his future with him present. It avoids any attempts to flatter or manipulate. Until he is crowned, he will remain closely closeted to avoid even the suspicion of interference.'

'Except by you,' Zoe said.

Michael flushed. 'No. Do not begin this meeting in that spirit. He is my son and heir, and it is proper that I guide him, but I cannot manipulate him once I have died.'

The last word fell like lead, and even Zoe looked a little embarrassed at Michael's righteous anger. She just nodded to show her acceptance of the point.

'And what of Harald? He is getting inappropriately close to Michael, so I hear,' John protested.

The emperor turned to his brother. 'You hear? Brother, be less arrogant in revealing you have spies in my household. I might be driven to have them all replaced.'

We all knew what 'replaced' meant. Those who witnessed the emperor's inner life and secrets could never be allowed to leave it with a grudge.

Michael looked at Harald and continued. 'Harald is, by my instruction, educating Michael on the matters of war and strategy. It is entirely appropriate, and who better to do so than one who has proven his loyalty to both sides of this family, and his unwillingness to put one above the other?' He looked around to find disagreement, but saw none.

'I agree,' said Theodora. 'He served me well on my pilgrimage. Displayed both loyalty and bravery.' She inclined her head towards Harald, who bowed his own in return.

'And he defended both myself and my wife, numerous times,' said Michael to John with finality. 'His loyalty is beyond reproach.'

'He tried to kill me!'

'You deserved it,' replied Michael flatly. 'And I am well aware you did the same to him. I am not a fool, Brother.'

John squirmed a little in his seat but did not reply.

'And your petty feud is over, now, isn't it.' It was not a question, and Michael's eyes flicked from John to Harald.

Harald nodded. 'It is. Honour is satisfied, and the cause no longer exists.'

'So you admit it!' John said, looking at Harald with a sneer.

'Yes,' replied Harald emotionlessly.

John was taken aback by the carelessness of Harald's confession, and that no one in the room looked surprised, let alone outraged. He saw that he had no sympathy for his cause so he sat back in his chair, muttering to himself.

'It is over, isn't it?' Michael repeated, staring at his brother.

John looked at his brother angrily, but then nodded. 'It is. There is no benefit to me any more. You need the brute, and I support you.'

'Good,' Michael said with a smile. He ignored the obvious unspoken fact – that as soon as he died, so would John's reason for keeping the peace with Harald.

'So, let us move on from this unpleasantness, and consider the future and avoidance of any further conflict inside the palace.' He looked at Zoe. 'You fear that you can be removed, leaving me or my successors in sole power over the empire.'

Zoe inclined her head fractionally.

'So, Theodora is now alongside you to quench that threat. No one could get away with removing you both, no one can outmatch the combined power, support or popularity of you as a pair, and anyone who acted against you would simply be replacing you with your sister, and thus condemning themselves to a terrible fate. Correct?'

Zoe acknowledged the point with another reluctant nod.

'On my side, I fear the same, that I will be removed and your family will have sole control. John and I do not have nearly the network of support in the elite class as you, nor the popularity with the people. So, to protect myself, I have made Michael my heir. Removing me would only lead to ascending him to continue my legacy.'

Michael sat back a little, spreading his hands with satisfaction. 'So, by this balance, are we united in enforced peace? Thus can we focus on the good of the empire alone?'

He was obviously very pleased with his political solution, but I thought it weak and with more holes than a rammed galley. He had announced a race to seek control of the younger Michael, and everyone sitting there knew it. That hapless, nervous young man was now the key to the empire.

'We tried establishing peace once before, but we enforced it with strength and threats instead of mutual interest and balanced power.' He nodded towards Harald. 'We thought that having a strong outsider to enforce the peace through his own power would be enough, a foolish theory, in that he simply became the target of the conflict.' Michael shook his head sadly.

It was also a complete lie. He tried to make it seem as if it had been his idea, not that Harald had dragged the royal couple kicking and screaming into a tenuous agreement not to kill each other on his watch. It had, as Michael said, been an arrangement destined to fail. Both of them had turned on Harald and sought to weaken and remove him so they could strike at the other, at enormous cost to the empire.

But then, an emperor could hardly admit the truth of what Harald had done to them.

'I know, as you all do, that I am entering the last years of my rule. My doctors are positive that if I follow their regimes, and frequently rest in the sea air, I might yet live to be an old man. But I think they lie to please me, and from your looks, so do all of you.' He swept a sad smile around the gathering of guilty-looking people, almost all of whom were actively hoping for his death. 'I find your care touching,' he added drily.

'We all pray that your doctors are correct, Basileus, and will support you in your duties so that you may follow their instructions and recover,' said Theodora with such vehemence that I believe she meant it.

'As do I, of course, my husband,' said Zoe, putting on a less convincing display.

Everyone else in the circle was shamed into adding their own display of support, except Harald, who remained silent. I thought that was odd, but then Harald was not a man of performative display. He had made his oath and done his duty, and to him that alone was all he needed to prove himself.

Michael flushed, looking relieved and touched by the affirmations, and he smiled contentedly and sat back. 'Then I am pleased we have found our peace. The empire needs us, it needs our strength and unity, or we are doomed to fall alongside it.'

Zoe smiled affectionately and stood, walking gracefully over to crouch at her husband's side, reaching to hold his hand. 'It is a noble and worthy gesture, husband, to set aside our differences and give us all the security we need, rather than to continue this needless factionalism.'

Michael's face lit up at the gentle touch of his wife. 'Will it be enough to keep the peace? Not just with you, but with all of your allies?'

'My supporters will be entirely satisfied with it, I assure you.'

Michael shifted in his seat, his smile breaking out into its full radiance, for he was still a handsome man, despite the veil of his illness. 'I would be so pleased, my wife, for I think nothing has added to my ill health more than the toll of this constant strife. It is not too late, you and I can lift this empire to new heights, and leave it better for our son to rule.'

She clasped his hand tighter and nodded, staring into his eyes. 'I agree.' Then she leant down and tenderly kissed his hand before meeting his eyes again. Finally her smile faded into a nervous expression. 'But can you ensure the same, that there are no more plots, manoeuvrings or ploys for power? You know how some of my supporters suffered at the hands of those who ruled in your stead.'

She was talking about John, not naming him, but speaking of him as if he were not there.

Michael nodded softly. 'There will be no more of that. My will is clear, and everyone will follow it. Even John.'

John looked like he had swallowed a thorn, but resisted saying anything. Zoe smiled and rose. 'Then, husband, I say that we have an agreement.'

'That makes me happier than you can imagine.'

'Then why was he here? What is his purpose in this?' said John, waving irritably at Harald.

Michael looked at my prince and nodded. 'He is here to witness this secret accord, for no one else can be trusted to have knowledge of how it came to be or the struggles we have been through. He is also here to understand that he no longer has power to enforce peace on either of us as he once did,' Michael stated. 'We are the rulers of Rome, and we keep our own peace.'

The words were scolding, but the tone was not. Michael was not admonishing Harald, merely making sure his place was understood.

Harald bowed. 'Nothing makes me happier than not to be concerned with trouble within the palace, so that I can focus on external threats.'

'Good. But your purpose will also be to enforce this peace on the rest of the palace and indeed the city itself. Because the empress and I have agreed to end all plotting and fractiousness, any plots or ploys for power are therefore not of us, not sanctioned by us, and subject to immediate and summary punishment as treason against the throne without exception.

'You are hereby given supremacy over all other commanders of the guard tagmata. You will have the added responsibility to monitor and extinguish any such plotting, subterfuge or corruption, wherever in the palace you should find it. Any person who stands in your way shall answer to the empress and I, and the answer shall be swift and final. We stand at the precipice. Nothing will be allowed to oppose our will, and only one whose loyalty is so far beyond doubt can be trusted to enforce it.'

Zoe stiffened a little, and John looked up in renewed interest as Harald digested that decree. This was clever, this was the final reveal of Michael's plan. Harald would be free to clamp down on anyone committing or plotting malfeasance in the palace, and because the emperor, John and Zoe had affirmed to each other that it would not be them doing it, none of them could object, nor stand in his way.

Harald stood, only so that he could bend to one knee on the cool, hard marble floor, bowing his head deeply to the emperor and empress. 'As you command, Basileus, I will obey.'

'I know you will, Protospatharios. That is why I have chosen you.' Michael gestured at Harald to rise, and he stood proudly. He looked surprisingly calm to me, considering that Michael had just made him one of the most powerful men in the empire, with the entirety of the imperial guard system at his command, and an emperor's decree to crush all subversion and dissent. He had been first sword of the Varangians; now he was the first guardsman of the empire.

The room was silent as they digested the severity of Michael's decree, and how he had enforced it in a way that simply allowed no dissent. I had thought him weak when Zoe knelt beside him to pour honey in his ear, but now she was trapped in its sticky embrace. She would be immune to Harald's oversight, but no one working covertly or independently in her service would share that protection.

John still looked like he had swallowed a thorn, tapping his fingers feverishly on the arm of his chair.

Michael gazed around the room, his expression calm and satisfied, and then he nodded with finality. 'I must be taken to see my doctors so they may conduct their treatments. I thank you all for your support. John, you will come with me. My wife, Lady Theodora, please excuse me.'

His two attendants helped him to his feet and the emperor was escorted carefully from the room while Zoe stood immobile and watched.

Theodora smiled brightly. She alone seemed unimpeded by the weight of what had occurred. Perhaps she simply didn't understand.

'I must go to prayers, sister,' she said, kissing Zoe twice on each cheek.

'Of course,' Zoe said with a taut smile, as her sister took her attendant and left.

Then we were alone in the room with Zoe and her ever-watchful attendant, Hypatia. Zoe looked at Harald thoughtfully, and Harald bowed. 'I should attend to my duties, Basilissa.'

'You shall not escape so easily. No.'

Harald shifted uncomfortably but did not argue.

'Did you know about this before?' Zoe said, waving her hand at the emperor's seat.

'I did not, Basilissa,' he said truthfully and awkwardly. Or at least, I think that was the truth.

'So you are as manipulated as I am, then.'

'I merely serve.'

'Oh, quiet that now. It is just us so respect me with honesty. This new power is more in your own interests than mine.'

'It is possible, but I am not so sure.'

'Why?'

'It makes me a target.'

Zoe laughed. 'I thought that is what you liked, Harald – being a target. You certainly have a knack for making enemies. Why do you do it so often if you are not so fond of it?'

Harald considered that, and I remembered what he had said to me on that very subject.

'A great man needs enemies, it is true. A man with no enemies has either killed them all, or achieved nothing of note.'

'Indeed. But a great man also needs allies, and I'm not sure you have any, which makes having this power now so dangerous.'

'It was not my choice.'

'No, I believe you. But you will conduct the duty faithfully, won't you?'

'I will.'

Zoe sighed and walked over to the marble balcony. 'Your infuriating honour, Harald, it will be the death of us both.'

'I will not allow that, Basilissa.'

'You cannot stop it! You must know, Harald, what will happen now. Michael may lie to himself and us with claims that he will live to see the empire renewed, but we both know it is not true.'

Harald said nothing, he just stared at the waters outside the harbour, deep in thought.

'What do you think will happen when he dies, if power is so divided and there is no one to secure it?' Zoe asked.

'Civil war, Basilissa. Or at least open conflict between your supporters and John's.'

'Exactly. Michael thinks he is clever for binding us in these chains of peace, but he is a fool who thinks he will live long enough to benefit from it or secure the power himself. He is dying, Araltes, and the empire must be prepared for what happens when he does.'

'Your son Michael will take the throne alongside you. He is the chance to prevent war.'

'And you think he is ready?'

Harald pursed his lips. 'I think he has a chance of growing into the role, noble birth or not.'

Zoe looked at him dubiously. 'You really think so? And who will control him? He has no understanding of the complexities of this empire or how to play the game of politics, despite my husband's naive attempts to educate him in a hurry. God above, Araltes, he is a commoner's boy!' Zoe looked furious. 'No, he will at best be a conduit for the true ruler, so who will that be?'

Harald grunted. 'It can only be you.'

Zoe smiled. 'Good, so you understand. The choice is between me and John. Either one of us will gain control of him, or neither of us will and there will be a war for the throne.'

'Yes. John will seek to influence him, gain control of him.'

'I will also try to sway him to my side, of course, but I have no leverage over him. The longer John has to dig his claws into Michael, the more likely it is we will face a war, or even immediate defeat, when my husband dies. The longer he lives, the worse things will be.'

She said it softly, carefully, and its meaning was deathly clear.

Harald stiffened. 'I will not discuss what you are thinking. It is my most sacred oath.'

'You know that if he survives for too long it may condemn us both to death!' she whispered urgently.

'And you know I am oathsworn to protect him!' Harald said, hissing to avoid raising his voice. 'I will not allow anyone to threaten him, even you!'

'Damn you and your honour!' Zoe said, throwing her hands up in exasperation and turning away. 'It will be the doom of both of us.' She was silent for a while as she composed herself, but then continued in a calm voice. 'But if you will not stand aside while I do what needs to be done, perhaps there is another way to assuage your honour.'

'What are you saying? I will not be part of any plot against him, I will not allow any plot against him to exist, no matter how cunningly you construct it,' growled Harald.

Zoe turned back, setting her flinty gaze on him. 'No but you obey his commands.'

Harald looked suspicious 'Yes...'

'Then there is an answer, one that serves all our purposes.'

'I do not understand.'

'The rebels led by the false Bulgarian emperor Delyan, in the west. They need to be eradicated. They are a deadly threat to the empire.'

'They are.'

'And you would love nothing more than to be the one who dealt with them, to expunge your recent failures?'

Harald bristled, but nodded.

'And the emperor wants to secure his legacy, to be known as one who strengthened and brought glory to the empire.'

Harald nodded again.

Zoe shrugged. 'What better way to do that than to lead his armies into the field and crush the rebellion, with his loyal commander Araltes as his sword-hand?'

Harald froze, his eyes flicking as he considered it. 'Going on campaign could kill him, through sickness or battle.'

'Only God knows if that is true, Araltes,' Zoe replied casually, dancing around the issue. 'But if he goes on campaign, then we will find out God's will directly. All I would need you to do is help me persuade him. I alone cannot do it. He will turn to you for advice, and he is weak so he will do what you recommend.' She tilted her head as she looked at Harald. 'That is all you need to do, Harald: advise your emperor to do his duty, secure his legacy, and end this rebellion himself. If that effort claims his life, so be it. Such is the risk of greatness.'

'I would not just allow him to die, nor do anything to speed his end.'

Zoe shook her head. 'Of course not, I cannot expect you to. But, perhaps, you would allow him to risk his life for the glory of his nation. Is that not something you believe in, Araltes?' she said, looking at him accusingly.

'You know it is.'

She stepped over to him slowly, placing a finger on Harald's chest. 'This is the only way we can both get what we want and ensure our safety, and you know it. Your treacherous heart has probably already considered it, weakened you with the dishonour of the thought.' She ran that finger up his chest, tracing her painted nail up the hollow of his throat and into his beard before holding it under his chin, forcing him to stare into her eyes with its touch.

'All you have to do is help me convince him that going on campaign is the best thing for him and the empire. And you don't even have to risk your precious honour, Araltes, because it's the truth.'

Harald swallowed, his throat moving against the back of the finger that Zoe was using to fix him so gently and forcefully in place.

'It is,' he finally said.

Zoe smiled, taking her finger away with a flick. 'Then do your duty, Araltes. Go with my husband to end the rebel threat, stand by his side, protect him, be merciless to his enemies and let God decide the rest.'

Harald nodded slowly.

'If you secure my control of the throne when my husband dies, I will make you the wealthiest man in the empire. I know that is what you truly desire. Oh, and help me convince my new son not to let John have me killed?' she asked, with a sweet, almost casual smile. 'I would appreciate that.'

'I will not let that happen, whatever else occurs.'

'I pray that you are alive to have the choice, Araltes.' She shrugged. 'Dead men wield no swords. Be careful, my love.'

Leaving those last words hanging, she turned and elegantly swept from the room, leaving me in stunned silence as Harald stared at the sea, his face roiling.

Finally he turned to me, and I raised an eyebrow in question.

'So we are going to war,' Harald finally said, his blue eyes full of turmoil, but his mind clearly made up.

'Again?' I asked, less sure of everything. 'After what happened to us the last time?'

Harald put one hand on my shoulder. 'Again, and for the last time, we will march for the empire, and earn our reward.'

Then he walked past me, heading for the closed doors leading to the inner palace.

'And then what?' I called after him.

Harald did not break his stride.

'Then we take our riches and go home.'

7

The imperial family left the seaside palace a few days later, when Michael felt strong enough to move back to the palace. Harald set about covertly preparing the guard for war again, and as part of that, our regime of training between our guard duties intensified in the days that followed.

I was in the broad training square practising with men of the seventh bandon when I saw Harald coming down from his quarters dressed in a simple tunic, making a direct line towards me.

I was relieved to see that tunic, because it meant we were not going to the palace. I hated going to the palace; we never went there for good reasons.

'Come with me. I need to go and see the magister of the Scholai. I am told he is down at the stables,' he said.

I looked at my opponent, a young guardsman who had been worryingly close to besting me, and nodded while trying to hide my relief. 'Yes, Protospatharios.'

'I will return to finish you,' I said to the guardsman with a tired grin.

The junior man had the sense not to retort or mock me as I heaved to get air into my tortured lungs, he simply took my training weapons and went away to find another opponent, looking as if he had made no effort at all.

'You are getting slower,' said Harald bluntly as we walked away.

'I am not!' I retorted, lying through my teeth.

It was true, though. I was thirty-one years old, and I could feel that I had lost a moment of speed, even if my strength had never been greater. I hated it, I hated it more than anything else. Not being young any more burned at me for I had once felt my youth would never fade, but then it was gone before I had fully experienced it.

'I was watching you for a while. He was going to beat you, this man I don't even recognise.'

'Nonsense. I had a plan,' I lied again.

'Was your plan to die of heat exhaustion while he stood over you?'

'What do you know? When was the last time you swung a sword?' I protested.

'Recently enough to know you are not quite the swordsman you once were, old man,' Harald said with a concerned look.

I bristled. I would have snapped the head off any other man who had said something like that to me. 'I was not at my best today, that does not mean I am losing my edge.'

'You were once perhaps the best swordsman in the guard, now you are labouring against a man whose name I don't even know.'

'Alexios. His name is Alexios. He joined while we were away in Sicily. He shows great promise,' I replied in a surly tone.

'Alexios?' said Harald, looking at me in confusion. 'What is a man with that name doing in the guard?'

His confusion was understandable. To join the guard you had to be a man of the North, and Alexios was as Greek a name as they come.

'He was born in this city, but his father was a guardsman and his mother a local woman. They gave him a Greek name so that he could make a life here outside the guard. He ignored them and joined anyway when we ran short of recruits and relaxed the rules. So we have an Alexios in the ranks now.'

The relaxing of the rules had been inevitable, you see. The guard had taken significant casualties during our time there and had been understrength even before that. We were desperate to fill the ranks again and the rules had widened to allow any warriors with ancestry from the North and the Rus, even those who had been born in the empire to parents from those places.

And, in honesty, we bent the rules even further than that. There was even a Saxon of England in the fourteenth bandon, and a few others in the other banda. A Saxon! Can you believe it, hah! Our blood enemies for ten generations served alongside us! Now of course any among you who know of the guard now will not be surprised, because there are more English in the guard than Norsemen these days. They fled there seeking service after William of Normandy took their land. Good soldiers too, as you know already. Anyway, the guard was already changing in my time, a herald of things to come.

'Hmm, I see. Well, Alexios is faster than you,' Harald said with distaste.

'It is not all about speed, Harald. I have experience and battle skill that is not best shown with blunt swords and heavy shields.'

'I know it. You are still a superb warrior, and you miss my meaning, Eric. I am not chastising you, I am making a point about how long we have been here. It will not be long before I too have seen my thirtieth year, and I mean to do so at home, on the throne. I must do that before the vigour of my youth is gone, as yours is fleeing you.'

I stopped and glared at my prince, and he turned around looking surprised at my reaction. My fingers clenched and unclenched as I tried to master my emotions. 'You know, Harald, you are an utter prick sometimes,' I finally said, which was a lot less harshly worded than I wanted.

Harald looked at me equally furiously for a moment. 'You know, anyone other than you I might kill them for such disrespect.'

'And I the same to anyone who called me old and slow!' I said, puffing my chest out.

We stared at each other for a few moments, me breathing hard and Harald's eyes blazing, and then Harald's face broke into a little smile and he laughed, and I laughed too, because I was still blowing like a chariot horse at the end of a long race and the ridiculousness of my pride was too much to take seriously.

He walked back and slapped an arm around my shoulders. 'You are still the greatest swordsman of your generation,' he said as a compromise. Then I felt him shrug. 'It's just that some of your generation are plucking their silver hairs to hide them, and seeing their first grandchildren born.'

'And whose fault is it that I am still here at this age!' I snorted.

Harald stopped again and looked at me sadly. 'It's mine.' He let go of me and looked ahead, down the path towards the training field of the Scholai, cold again. 'Come, I need the magister on good terms with me. I think he will not have taken my elevation above him well.'

Then he walked off and I was forced to jog to keep up with him, still out of breath.

* * *

We went down the terraces near the eastern shore of the palace, to the stables and field where the Scholai kept some of their horses, always ready if the emperor needed them. Those days it was requirements for escort or parade that mostly occupied them, but once they had been a unit who struck terror into their enemies in the field; the armoured fist of the emperors.

Most of that role had been taken over by the Varangians, and the Scholai were seen by us as little more than spoilt sons of the elite class, who served a few years in the guard as part of their journey up the social ladder, not as a true act of service. Bah! We were all such hypocrites.

A dozen or so men were exercising horses in the field, and a servant sweeping the path directed us to a low building at one end when we asked where the magister was. We went over to find him and came across him saddling a horse. Magister Theophilos Dalassenos was a middle-aged man with short cropped greying hair and a trim beard. He was sun-weathered but fit, and his body betrayed no sign of easy living and excess. His hands were rough and gnarled like a labourer's. This was a man who had spent his life at duty, not ease.

He looked up and gave Harald a brief, searching look. 'What do you need?' he said casually, continuing to work on his horse.

Harald looked annoyed at the informality of the reception, and unsure what to do. 'You have heard what the emperor has commanded me to do?' he said.

Theophilos smiled softly. 'Oh yes, I have been informed.'

Harald nodded stiffly. 'Well, I wanted to come down and meet you, properly.'

'Really? I see. All these years you have been here, I have been here, and now you want to meet me properly?' He gave Harald a raised eyebrow and a crooked smile.

Harald bristled. 'We have met before, at many events.'

'Oh, we have stood next to each other at parades, it is true, but as you say, not met properly.'

'I have hardly been in the city.'

'So I hear!' the magister chuckled. 'Sounds like you have had quite the adventures.'

He finished adjusting the buckles on his horse's saddle and whistled to some of the other men in the stable, gesturing at another pair of horses.

'Well, I am here now,' said Harald, trying to remain calm as the magister continued about his work.

'Can you ride?' Theophilos asked us suddenly with an open smile.

'What?'

'Can you ride?' The magister's brows furrowed. 'You must know how to ride a horse, yes?' He gestured to the men who were bringing two saddled horses over.

'Of course,' Harald snapped, starting to lose his composure. 'But I did not come here to ride, I came here to talk.'

'Well, I am in the middle of my duties, and my duties involve riding. So if you wish to talk to me, it will be from horseback. Come.'

Harald was given the reins to one of the horses by a well-dressed young cavalryman, and I almost laughed at his barely controlled outrage. Perhaps I would have laughed if another man had not pressed the second horse's reins into my hand.

Let me tell you, I was not then, and have never been since, a competent horseman. Harald had been born noble enough to ride when he was a child, and I had not. This is important for you to know by way of excusing myself, before I relay what happened next.

'Oh God, I hate horses,' I muttered to Harald as I stood there awkwardly holding the reins, trying to stay in front of my horse as it circled, eyeing me indignantly with its big brown eyes, ears flicking and head dipping suddenly as if it were about to strike me.

I scurried backwards to avoid it lashing out and a gnarled hand grabbed mine and steadied me.

'No man who knows horses hates them. Your hate is only ignorance and fear. They are the most magnificent of God's creatures, as long as you know how to manage them,' the magister said. He stepped around me and approached the horse from its front, cooing at it gently, and placing a calming hand on its snout, before running the hand lovingly down its neck and patting its shoulder, letting the horse smell the side of his head.

The horse calmed and pawed gently at the ground.

The magister turned to me with a smile. 'You must let the horse know you, and feel your confidence. Don't dance around behind its shoulder where it can hardly see you but can still feel your nerves. It thinks you are a threat if you behave like one. They are not clever animals, Varangian, not like dogs, but they have a depth of emotion and a feel for our fears and desires that puts any dog to shame. Let the horse feel your confidence, and they will have confidence in you also.'

'But I have no confidence,' I said, approaching the horse carefully.

The magister laughed. 'Then this will be fun indeed. Like I said, they are quite stupid, so you must pretend you do. Now, up you go!' Then he bent down without warning and grabbed my leg, shoving my left foot into the stirrup, leaving me no choice but to grab hold of the saddle and then push off with my right to mount it, lest I be toppled and dragged around the stable.

'Virgin spare me!' I exclaimed as I nearly went over the other side of the horse's back, and the animal shivered and moved underneath me, whinnying nervously.

'Easy there! Take the reins but let them lie loose until you need them. You have done this before?'

'Perhaps twice,' I said, trying to settle into a good position. 'But not for years.'

'Good! Twice is good! It is three times better than none at all,' he added cheerfully, and with dubious mathematical veracity. 'Let's go, then.' He turned and vaulted onto his own horse with absurd ease, and I braved looking away from my own mount for long enough to see Harald had mounted and was looking at me embarrassing myself with a scathing expression.

The magister clicked at his horse, who started walking out of the stable without him even appearing to touch the reins. Harald pulled his mount around to follow. I looked down at my own beast, who had twisted its head around to stare at me balefully with one eye.

'I don't like this any more than you do,' I reassured the horse. 'Now let's go.' I wiggled my heels and pulled on the reins.

The horse didn't move. I tapped with my heels a little more, and the horse started off with an irritated grunt, but not towards the exit. I pulled on the left rein, and the horse turned its head but not its body.

'What is wrong with you!' I hissed at the dumb animal, and pulled harder on the rein.

'The reins are for direction, not for forcing,' said one of the cavalrymen, watching me as he and his comrade wore ear-to-ear grins. 'He is bigger than you, so you will not win a contest of strength. You must merely guide. You are leaning forwards, over his neck, so he goes forwards as he is trained. Sit up straight, push your feet forwards, then pull back and up on the rein and pressure with your leg to turn him, inwards, not outwards.'

I struggled to keep up with what the man was saying, feeling terribly unbalanced as I straightened in the saddle, gently putting tension on the left rein and pressing in with my leg. It felt horrible, but the horse started turning and I almost whooped with joy. I looked up to see Harald staring at me in disappointment, and the magister in amusement, as I finally got my mount headed over to join them.

'You are a natural!' said the magister.

'Really?'

'No. Come.'

I swore under my breath and lumbered after them, struggling to keep my balance. The magister deftly diverted his horse past a large rack of long spears and plucked one as he passed. The spear was a plain shaft with a round head of padded linen and stuffing.

'Land a touch on me with your spear and we will talk, Varangian. End up on your back, and you can come back and find me later,' shouted the magister at Harald as he whooped and urged his horse into a canter down the field.

Harald cursed and swerved over to fumble for one of the spears, narrowly avoiding coming out of his saddle as it got caught on another practice weapon in the rack.

He hefted the odd spear and gave me a filthy look. 'You best just stay out of the way,' he commanded me, before he looked around and set off after the magister, spear wobbling comically.

I had never been happier to obey an order, so I guided my horse to the side of the field and when it got to roughly where I intended, I simply let it stand.

The magister had reached the other end of the field and turned, his horse's hooves throwing up spurts of dry earth. Harald was barrelling after him, pushing his horse hard, and was going far too quickly to adjust and follow the magister's change of direction, sawing on the reins as his confused mount slewed and tried to slow, missing his target by a dozen paces.

The magister, already through his turn, thumped his padded spear mockingly against Harald's back as he passed, and set off again down the field.

Other cavalrymen continued with their exercises and training, practising their own bouts as Harald finally got his horse turned and spear up ready to try again. He made another thunderous charge, and this time the magister met him at an angle, on his right side, smacking Harald's spear aside and bouncing his own off Harald's leg.

I saw Harald's anger, but he did not give up. He turned again to face his tormenter. But this time, instead of charging, he watched another pair of riders make a pass, and how they both used their spears, and he urged his horse forwards, much more slowly this time.

Theophilos rode around Harald in a wide circle, and then with a twist of his knees and leaning forwards, swooped in for an attack. Harald spurred his own horse forwards, breaking the magister's intended angle and forcing him to slow to turn, bringing him into the line of Harald's weapon.

Harald raised his arm and thrust forwards with his spear towards the magister's open side, but the older man swept his own weapon around at impossible speed, parrying Harald's blow aside and thumping Harald in the side of the head with the shaft as he passed, visibly dazing him.

'Oh, that was good,' one of the cavalrymen watching near me said with a whistle.

'Of course it is good, he is the magister of the Scholai and we do not fight on horseback!' I said angrily, leaping to Harald's defence.

The Greek noble smiled at me and shook his head. 'You misunderstand me, I was not talking about the magister. Your commander forced him to overcommit, it was unexpected and done well,' he said with a respectful nod.

'But the magister still parried his attack and hit him?'

'Yes, but only with the shaft. A poor blow done in haste.'

I looked back at the two men with renewed interest, suddenly hopeful that Harald was not going to be humiliated. The magister was walking his horse now, watching Harald carefully. Harald did the same, so that the men circled each other like dogs, thirty paces apart. All the other men training on the field had stopped now to watch, sensing something significant was happening.

Harald made the first move, suddenly turning his horse in and running across the angle, closing the distance fast and bringing his spear into line, leaving the magister little time to react or counter-charge.

The magister, instead of turning to meet the charge, pirouetted his horse the other way and wrongfooted Harald, who desperately leant in and tried to drag his own mount around without losing too much speed. Harald's horse half-stumbled, and dirt sprayed, but he managed to make the turn and the magister, barely having got going, kicked his horse into a motion to meet the oncoming spear with a shout and a cloud of dust.

The two horses passed with a clatter as the spears met. I whooped as Harald's spearhead bounced off Theophilos's shoulder, a whoop that died in my throat as the magister's own spear hit Harald square in the chest, folding him over.

Harald's horse was going far too fast for Harald to keep his seat, and he tumbled over the back of his saddle in a spray of limbs, thudding down in the dust that then completely obscured him from view.

'Fuck!' I shouted, grabbing haplessly at my reins and kicking my horse into action. The animal simply protested and tried to buck me, so I threw down the reins with a curse and jumped awkwardly from the saddle, abandoning it and sprinting out across the field to where I could see Harald's prostrate form in the swirling dust.

The magister had circled back around too, pulling up alongside as another cavalryman collected Harald's loose and panicked mount. Theophilos dropped down off his horse while I was still only halfway there, and leaned down to look at the body in the dust.

My heart dropped into my stomach; I had seen far less serious falls kill men. The magister leant down into the dust haze and reached out an arm. And Harald's arm rose from the dust to grab it.

I arrived, huffing and panting, as Theophilos pulled a filthy Harald to his feet with a grin.

'Well struck, Varangian,' the magister said, shaking his arm. 'I did not expect that at all.'

Harald coughed, his face red and dirt griming his watering eyes. Then he spat a mixture of dust, spittle and blood to the side.

'I was going to win the next one,' Harald said with a lopsided grin.

'Not next time, but perhaps with a few weeks' training. You have the mind for it, but your use of the reins makes my eyes hurt. Come, let's go back. I said if you touched me with your spear I would meet with you. I didn't expect you to, but you earned it.'

'Do you make everyone who wants a meeting do this?' Harald said with a raised eyebrow.

'No, only when I think I can get away with it,' the magister replied with a smile.

The cavalryman who had secured Harald's horse arrived and proffered the reins. Harald looked at the beast with discomfort, but wasn't about to be embarrassed by refusing, so he hauled himself painfully back into the saddle as the magister vaulted back onto his like a boy.

They both looked at me, and then the magister gave a confused look at my mount, which was alone, cropping grass by the side of the field.

'Who knocked you down?' he asked.

'Who? No one... I got off to come here.'

The magister looked at me as if I were an idiot. 'It would have been faster to ride. Come. Back to the stables. I will have refreshments brought.'

Then he clicked at his horse and set off at a trot with Harald, leaving me standing there. I looked back across at my horse, who stared back with that big dumb brown eye while it nonchalantly chewed a mouthful of grass.

I swore furiously, decided I was not brave enough to try the beast again, and set off to the stable at a run.

8

By the time I arrived at the stable, huffing and panting again, Harald and the magister were already sitting at a sturdy table that was covered in bits of half disassembled tack and items being repaired. The magister carefully moved some to one side and was just done talking to one of the stable boys when I reached him, sending the boy off on an errand.

'So, Protospatharios, you have my ears. What can I do for you?' he said with a genial smile as I slumped down next to Harald.

'I'm not here to ask for a favour, Magister. I'm here to agree on how we can work together.'

'A fine sentiment, but it is the same thing, I think?'

Harald shook his head forcefully. 'It is not. I have been ordered to take oversight of the guard tagmata. I did not seek but it is the emperor's command, and I obey. It does not mean I need you to serve me, but it does mean I must ensure we work together.'

Theophilos smiled. 'Good. I am glad to hear it. Every couple of years some new powdered ass is set above me, to grow rich while pretending to command me. They are nothing but a nuisance. Having a real man of war giving me orders will be a pleasant change.'

Harald smirked. 'I know the men you are speaking of. Well, I am not in command of the army, just the security in the city. The domestikos of the West still commands on campaign,' said Harald, referring to the emperor's most senior general in that half of the empire.

'What happens in the city is all that matters to me,' Theophilos replied. 'We have not been sent to war since emperor Basil was on the throne.'

Harald frowned. 'Truly?'

'Yes,' Theophilos said sadly, then gestured around. 'We are nothing but parade soldiers now, neglected for decades.'

'Why?' Harald looked bemused.

'They were afraid of us, afraid of our power.'

'The same thing I heard of for the Excubitors.'

'Exactly.' The magister sighed and leaned in, lowering his voice. 'All of the recruits here are sons of the great families. They are here to learn a little discipline, a little skill at arms, and to burnish their credentials before moving on to more lofty and profitable things. Sending them to war would give them the opportunity for fame and glory, and some of them might think themselves capable of taking the throne for themselves, or joining those who would. It's happened before. So, they are given no real opportunity. They join for a few years, look good on parade, impress their families, attract the daughter of a wealthy family and then leave.' Theophilos shrugged sadly. 'That is how it is.'

Harald leaned in, looking confused. 'But it seems like you train them hard. Why?'

'Why?' The magister's sun-worn face creased with amusement. 'Because it is my duty!' He looked out the door affectionately at the cavalrymen who were still out riding on the field. 'And because I think it is important. I take these spoilt boys and I make men of them, if I can. I put some steel in the spine of the elite of this city. Even if it is just a little, it matters. Without that steel, the spine would collapse. In the old days, every nobleman was a warrior, bound to defend the city and the empire. But now?' He shook his head. 'Now I barely get a fraction of them through my stables. Most of the noble class consider themselves above such things, and their weakness is the empire's weakness.'

Harald nodded vigorously. 'That is the way of my people. Every man who seeks to command another must be able to take his place in the wall, or none will respect him.'

'I know, that is why I like you long-haired barbarians,' Theophilos said with a grin. 'You are still warriors at heart, even if civilisation is alien to you.'

Harald raised an eyebrow. 'You think civilisation is alien to us?'

The magister's smile broadened. 'Our stables would be your palaces, would they not?'

I felt personally attacked by the comment, but then looked around and could not deny the truth. The stable we were in was built of finely crafted limestone, taller, broader and longer than any northern hall. It was, without a doubt, a finer building than the one we sit in today and I mean no insult by it. And that was an unremarkable building in the grounds of the great palace. Drab, even.

Harald knew the truth of it too, and he huffed a little. 'Our uncivilised barbarians are the only thing that keeps your precious buildings safe.'

Theophilos nodded sadly. 'I know it. We are people weakened by our own wealth, and I pray it is not a sickness that will destroy us.'

'Well, perhaps I can help change it. How many men do you have?'

Theophilos considered it for a moment. 'About two hundred.'

'So few? I knew it was bad but... only one bandon?'

'Five banda, in fact. Although one of them only has seventeen men in it. Every year it is fewer.'

Harald looked outraged. 'Why?'

'Few enough of the youth even want to join the guard any more, and I cannot compel them. It used to be a position of great honour and prestige, to call yourself a man of the Scholai. But now... It is barely noteworthy.' He sat up. 'Even if I could get more men, I cannot get enough funds for the equipment or the horses to supply them.' He pointed out at the field. 'I have been fighting for ten years just to keep this training area. You cannot imagine how many greedy eyes in the palace are set on having this space. About fifteen years ago I almost lost it – the empress was going to build another wing of the palace here when she first ascended to the throne.'

'What stopped her?' Harald asked.

Theophilos smiled coyly. 'I was very persuasive.'

Harald's eyes widened and Theophilos laughed deeply. 'I was once a young, handsome man like you, and an influential member of Romanos's court. What, come now, you think you are the first?' I gulped. Harald's secret was clearly not a secret at all. We never stopped finding people who knew. That was the way of the palace, and I should not have been surprised. The only currency of the servants and eunuchs was whispers.

Harald tensed. 'It is not suitable to speak of the empress like this.'

'It is far less suitable to curry her favour the way we both have, but, we do what we must,' he said with a joyful smile. 'Regardless, this is the only space in the entire palace quarter where our horses can be stabled and the men can have a little space to train. It is essential, but it is only a matter of time until someone decides it is of more use as yet another gilded hall.'

'You seem to have a lot of contempt for those you serve,' Harald said carefully.

'Really? I disagree, Araltes. Who do I serve?'

'The emperor and empress.'

'Hmm, I say I serve the throne, and by extension the people of this city and the empire. You have only been here a few years, Araltes. I have served seven rulers. They come and go like the tides, but the city stands resolute as it has done for six hundred years. The city is what matters, not those who rule it for such short lives.'

Theophilos leaned in, his face calm and clear. 'I protect the emperor and empress, Araltes, and I do so loyally, but I serve the empire. Are you truly different?'

Harald stared at the magister for a moment and then nodded. 'No, our oaths are similar.'

'Good, then you understand. Sometimes the rulers are idiots, many of their decisions are terrible. I would fight for them regardless, but I will disagree with their stupidity when it occurs.'

'You are remarkably open with that disagreement. Men have been killed for less.'

Theophilos's smile widened. 'I am not an easy man to kill.'

'Who are you, then? You berate these noble boys, you disparage the royal family, but how did you end up in charge of the Scholai? Are you so different to them?'

Theophilos laughed. 'Different? Lord no, I am one of them. In a different world I might have been emperor myself, if I had been foolish enough to try. I am the last scion of the family Dalassenos, one of the most powerful clans in the empire.'

Harald's brows knitted. 'I have never heard of them.'

'You wouldn't have, Protospatharios.' His smile faded a little, his eyes creasing with some deep, heartfelt pain. 'They became too powerful, too greedy for power, and were cast from favour, exiled or worse. I am the last that remains.'

Harald's eyes widened in understanding. 'I see.'

'So I serve the empire, and I try and train the arrogance out of my boys, so that they avoid the mistakes my family made.'

'A worthy duty.'

'I think so,' said Theophilos. 'Now, I have those boys to train, so tell me, Araltes – what do you wish from me?'

Harald tapped his fingers on the table, thinking. 'If you were called to go to war again, would you be ready?'

Theophilos looked interested. 'Is war coming?'

'War is always coming to the empire.'

'True, but we ourselves are rarely needed. What is different this time? What do you know that I don't?'

Harald waved the question away brusquely. 'It doesn't matter. You will know soon enough. All I need to know is if you will be ready to march, and I need you to have more than two hundred men. Can you recruit more?'

Theophilos huffed. 'It is difficult without a good reason. If we are going to war soon, and I see from your words that it is likely, I have no time to train green men. I need experienced riders, preferably those who have served before. It is true there are hundreds of such men in the city, but to attract them back without a specific reason?' He spread his hands. 'It will be difficult.'

'Gold?'

Theophilos barked a single disparaging laugh. 'Gold? These men piss gold, they care nothing for financial reward. No, and I will need equipment, especially horses.'

'I will make sure it is all supplied.'

'With respect, Protospatharios, you don't have a clue what to get or where to get them. Find me the gold, and I will supply myself. What? You think I will steal it?'

'It is what everyone else here does,' Harald grouched.

'True, but I have been commander here for over twenty years, and I am not wealthy. What does that tell you?'

Harald nodded. It was a point well made. 'That you are not corrupt, or you are a terrible gambler.'

'It should reassure you then that I am excellent at dice.'

'How are you excellent?' I interjected, curiosity getting the better of me.

Those wise eyes turned to me and he smiled softly. 'I don't play.'

Harald laughed. 'Now that is true wisdom. If I get you the gold, how many men could you field in two months' time?'

Theophilos pursed his lips and thought about it. 'Four hundred? Five, if I am lucky and your cause is persuasive.'

'Do better than that. I will promise your riders a campaign that will grant them reputation and glory, and privileges in the city. I will reintroduce them into the inner palace guard and give them power in security in the city alongside my men. They will ride the streets in uniform, with the signs of office on their chests, and men will make way for them wherever they go. I'll put up a fucking statue in their honour with each of their names at the base, as long as they come and serve.'

Theophilos nodded softly. 'So you do understand what the nobility want.'

Harald nodded curtly and stood. 'I was a spoiled brat of nobility too, Magister. If you let Eric here talk for too long, he will say I still am. Thank you. I want six hundred of the best cavalrymen in the empire ready to ride by summer in the emperor's name. If you need anything else to make that happen, just come and tell me.'

Theophilos stood too, and clasped arms with Harald. 'Deliver what you have promised, and it will be done. Ahh, I did not know it until now, but I long to ride under the banners once again.'

'We will ride together.' Harald smiled and turned to me, patting me on the shoulder. 'Eric will probably walk.'

* * *

As we headed back up to the barracks, I asked Harald the question that had been burning in my mind.

'Why are you so determined to have the Scholai come with us on campaign? The thematic forces will provide heavy cavalry, far more than five hundred. We've seen how good they are before, in the east.'

He nodded. 'Yes, and I won't know them or their commanders. I will have no control over them, no ties of friendship.'

'Ah, I see. You need a cavalry force you can control. But on campaign they will be commanded by the domestikos, and he won't listen to you.'

'That is true, but you remember Sicily – I had no command over William and his Normans, not formally, but was my alliance with him not essential to our survival?'

'True enough. Although it didn't end well.' I trailed off, for William had ended up being our enemy, even defeating us.

'And that is exactly why I am choosing my ally more carefully this time, Eric. Theophilos cannot turn against us, that was the true purpose of our conversation. I needed to know who he was, whether and why he was loyal. I need an ally like the Normans who will remain our ally, no matter what. Theophilos and the Scholai can be that ally, but not with only two hundred men.' He shook his head. 'The short-sighted fools that let them whittle down to such a stub.'

I laughed and he gave me a dirty look.

'What amuses you?'

'You were angry when the magister said he serves the throne, not the fools who sometimes sit on it. But now you curse those fools yourself without reflection.'

Harald snorted and turned back to the path, silent for a dozen paces before he spoke again. 'You are not right very often, Eric, but it is infuriating when it happens.'

My grin only broadened. That was a great victory for me.

'So, do we go and speak to the Vigla now?'

'No, men of the Vigla turned on us in the battle in the palace. They are not worthy to stand beside us.'

'True, but it was Zoe who turned them, and others died alongside our men. Is it not better to have them as allies too?'

Harald turned on me and his eyes were livid. 'That some of them stood on one side and some on the other is the worst condemnation of their nature. They have no loyalty even to themselves. Can you imagine men of the guard standing against each other?'

I shook my head sheepishly. 'No.'

'Exactly. Something is rotten inside the Vigla that cannot be fixed so quickly. I will never trust them until it is purged, and the purging would take years. They can stay here and guard the walls. Even that I cannot trust them with, but I have no alternatives.'

'As you say,' I mumbled.

'I do need to go to the Optimatoi however, and make sure they are ready for campaign. If the emperor is coming with us, his provision and support must be excellent.'

I nodded. The Optimatoi were the imperial storemasters and guardians of the emperor's baggage train. On campaign, they built his personal camp, guarded it and ensured he, his guard tagmata and his household were properly fed, sheltered and equipped. They were a truly professional unit, part of the unpraised core of the imperial army's success. Wherever the emperor's army marched, even detached guard units, it was the Optimatoi that allowed them to stay in the field long and well-supplied enough to secure victory.

They had a final, more secretive task too: ensuring that outside of the palace grounds no one could assassinate the emperor with poison or other subterfuge.

'But to visit them, I must sail across to the south to their barracks. That will have to wait, I cannot leave the city at the moment.'

We were arriving back at the barracks and I saw a gathering of palace attendants outside the gate, remonstrating with a bored-looking guardsman. One of the attendants saw us and pointed, and I felt Harald sigh as much as heard him.

One of them strode over to us, and I recognised him as one of the emperor's assistants.

'You are summoned, Protospatharios. The emperor requires you to meet with him.'

Harald nodded and forced a smile. 'I will attend him imminently.'

'Now, Protospatharios,' said the humourless man, who turned around giving us no choice but to follow.

'This can't be good,' I muttered.

'It does get tiresome,' Harald replied in our own tongue, earning us a suspicious look from the official.

9

'Harald, good. Why did it take you so long? Doesn't matter.' Michael waved the question away as soon as he had asked it, gesturing for Harald to join him. He was sitting in a padded chair in the war room, alone but for a few of his ever-present attendants.

'I apologise, Basileus, I was not in the barracks.'

'Fine.' Michael was unusually animated, perhaps nervous or excited, it was hard to tell. 'I have called you to ask your advice on a military matter.'

Harald nodded. 'I will help as best I can.'

'The empress has presented me with a plan, a plan to take the imperial army and march again to the west and defeat the rebellion there. She is concerned, as I am, that the enemy might march towards us and threaten the city itself. Is that possible?'

Harald sucked in a breath through his teeth. 'It would be difficult. The Thracian and Macedonian themes are very strongly garrisoned, but then so were the themes of Hellas and Thessaly, so I hear, and they were defeated.'

'They were betrayed, undermined by traitors within. They could not have been defeated by force alone by such a rabble,' said Michael irritably. His irritation was understandable; he had been present the year before when the army had been defeated near Thessaloniki.

'As you say, Basileus,' Harald answered, not interested in arguing.

'But it is possible that it could happen again,' Michael mused softly to himself. 'And regardless, we cannot allow this rebellion to take root and become accepted. No, Hellas is a crucial part of our land, the core of our empire. It is unacceptable to allow it to be held by this man, this rebel who styles himself as emperor.'

'Petar Delyan?' Harald asked innocently, softly goading the emperor.

'Yes! That filth, the Bulgarian ingrate. A traitor, a man who used to be a commander in our forces, turned against us!' Michael almost shook with anger. 'No, it cannot be allowed.'

'So you intend to send your armies to end the rebellion?'

'Yes, that must be done, but... but the empress, she thinks I should lead them.'

Harald nodded slowly and remained silent, not wanting to appear to reflexively take Zoe's side.

'Is it foolish, Harald, to consider it? My generals are appalled, I can tell. They think I should remain in the city while they take care of it.'

'And get all the credit,' Harald said nonchalantly.

'Exactly!' said Michael, pointing a finger at Harald. 'I knew you would understand. I will be remembered as the emperor who was defeated by this rebel and had to send my generals to finish them. That is what they will say. It is shameful.'

'But you are reluctant to go yourself?'

Michael looked defensively at Harald. 'I am not afraid to do it, Harald. It is only...' He shifted uncomfortably in his chair. 'In my condition, the campaign may be too hard on me.' His face screwed up and he looked distraught. 'Curse this illness! It has taken my youth, my vigour, my manhood. Soon it will take my life.'

'I thought you were feeling better, Basileus,' Harald said, with unfeigned sympathy.

'Yes, a little, but it is clear to me it is temporary. I tell everyone I am recovering, of course I must. They would be circling my bed like vultures if they knew the truth,' Michael muttered. 'All that is left to me is to determine how men speak of my rule. I am not a fool, Harald, even if you may have thought so,' Michael said, giving Harald a fearful look.

'I never did think that, Basileus.' Harald paused, unsure of himself.

'What?' asked the emperor.

'May I speak honestly, Basileus?'

'I demand it,' said Michael emphatically.

'I thought you naive, at first. But you have grown into your throne. Sadly, life has not given you the chance to become the emperor you could have been, but I see the potential in you.'

Michael looked at Harald in sad delight. 'Truly?'

'Truly. I see how you care for the empire's status, and for peace and prosperity. I saw how you manipulated the empress to your will, and that is no easy feat.'

Michael smiled softly. 'I was pleased with that.'

'And you should be. You ask me, Basileus, whether you should go on campaign. I ask you instead, what do you care about? Is it remaining alive, or living well? Is it being emperor, or being a leader?'

Michael clenched his fist. 'I want to be known as an emperor who succeeded, Harald. I want men to speak of me well, long after I am gone.'

Harald nodded. 'I understand. That is what I would want.'

'Then what would you do, Harald, in my position?'

'I would go to war,' Harald said, without hesitation.

'So sure of yourself,' Michael replied in wonder. 'Why? You would risk it all? The final act of my rule might then be defeat by these rebels as a vain, dying man who should have stayed at home. Defeat that might end the empire's power forever. You would risk that?'

'I would, Basileus.'

'Why?'

Harald straightened a little, his eyes wandering to the great map on the wall of the war room. He swept his hand across it. 'None of this was earned without risk, and none of it can be kept without risk, either. Great men are not those who avoid risk, but those who calculate it carefully and seize it at the perfect moment. I do not advise you to fall headlong into war, and I do not think we shall lose. Quite the opposite. If we prepare well, our victory should be all but guaranteed.'

'Hah, such confidence. You have not seen this enemy. They have defeated us again and again. Why will this be different?'

Harald smiled and looked back at the emperor. 'Last time you merely joined the local forces, avoiding risking the true power of the empire. But that strategy merely wastes it one part at a time. No, you should march with all the power of the empire behind you. Risk it all, put it all on the field. Then you will have a just victory.'

Michael nodded slowly, his nervous fidgeting falling away. 'You are so certain of yourself, Harald. I wish I had your confidence.'

'You will have it, Basileus. I will march at your side, and all the power of the imperial guard with us. We will sweep this rebellion from the land and the people will remember your victory.'

'And yours?' Michael said softly.

Harald nodded curtly. 'I also need to purge the stain of defeat.'

'I know, and my brother says you would use me to do that. That you would risk my life to elevate yours. Is it true, Harald?'

Harald looked hurt, and he shook his head. 'If I did not think this was what was best for you, I would not recommend it. I would tell you to send me with your generals and keep yourself safe. I would share the glory with them and come home bearing the heads of your enemies to lay at your feet, safe here in the palace with your brother.' Harald breathed deeply. 'But that is not the way of great men. So, Basileus, command me as you wish, and I will do it.'

Michael smiled slowly. 'I have been lucky to inherit you, Harald, among all the terrible things this throne has brought me. I have resented you, suspected you and, when I first heard of the rumours about you and Zoe, despised you.'

Harald straightened and looked ashamed, staring at the wall behind the emperor.

Michael laughed, a low, sickly laugh that ended in a cough. 'I cannot hate you for it any more, Harald. I did exactly the same thing, with exactly the same woman. I know as well as you that she is impossible to refuse.'

'I apologise, Basileus, for any hurt I have done to you.'

'I thought great men like us did not apologise to each other, Harald?'

Harald smiled softly. 'Not all of my actions are worthy of greatness.'

'Well said. Now, we come to the last question. I am not a fool, and I know Zoe's reasons for suggesting this campaign are not pure.'

Harald met the emperor's gaze again, hardly moving.

'She hopes that I will die there, doesn't she? I assume she trusts you enough to have confided that in you.'

Harald was in a terrible position. He could admit to what amounted to treason, or he could lie. But a lie would be very hard to believe, given the conversation so far and Harald's stony expression. The truth might see him die in that room, if the emperor wished it.

'I suspect it, Basileus. But she has not said it directly.'

Harald gambled, as he had advised the emperor to do, risking it all on a single move. His entire fate, his very life, depended on Michael's reaction to his words, his deception. I felt myself almost melting under the tension of it.

Michael put a hand under his chin and regarded Harald carefully. 'If you suspect the empress wishes me to die out there, why would you possibly allow it?'

'Because it is not her choice or mine, Basileus. It is yours. I will put my life, and the lives of every man in the guard, between you and danger. Zoe's wishes cannot harm you, nor dictate the outcome of the campaign. It is true, she may want you to go and she may hope you die there, but all that matters is if it is the right decision for you – the emperor of Rome.' Harald smiled softly. 'You could spite her by surviving in victory.'

Michael smiled too. 'That would be glorious, would it not?'

'Is glory what you seek, Basileus?'

Michael put his hands on the arms of his chair and levered himself up, struggling and snapping at his assistants to back away when they tried to help. 'Yes, Harald,' he said, glaring across the table. 'Damn my wife, damn my generals and my doctors. If I am truly to die, I want to achieve something before the end. Let us wipe this rebel filth from my empire's borders and celebrate together in my wife's spiteful gaze.'

Harald walked over to the emperor and stood before him. 'Then raise your banners. Do not argue with men or generals; they are all yours to command and we all serve you. With one word you can send the empire to war. Simply give the command, and it will be done.'

Michael raised his chin and a triumphant glare spread across his features. I prayed he didn't realise how pathetic he looked, barely able to stand on his own, speaking of war and glory, but reeking of fear and pride.

But he was beyond seeing that, only smelling the sweet, alluring scent of greatness that he so desperately wished for.

'Then I command it, Protospatharios,' he said with as much force as he could muster. 'Summon my generals. We are going to plan for war.'

Harald bowed, fully and slowly, in the Greek style. 'As you command, Basileus.' Then he backed away and turned to leave the room with me on his heels.

* * *

We went through the palace to the office of the domestikos of the West, the chief commander of the empire's military in the western themes, an old, experienced officer of the imperial army called Nikephoros Aspietes who had served as a general under the Emperor Basil. He was standing in his office, deep in discussion with a general called Andronikos Skleros, who then held the rank of stratopedarches, one of the most senior men in the Byzantine army and Nikephoros's second in command.

Both men looked up at Harald with terse expressions when we were brought in by Nikephoros's guards.

'Protospatharios,' the commander said with a cold look.

'The emperor requests your presence, my lords,' Harald said in a demure tone. There was no gloating or pride. Harald needed to avoid upsetting these men as much as possible.

'And why did he send you to get us?'

'He did not say.'

'Hmm, so, did you manage to persuade him on this foolish endeavour? God alone knows why he values the opinion of the commander who lost us Sicily and half of Italy in a single year,' Andronikos sneered. The stratopedarches was younger than the supreme commander, perhaps in his forties, and one of the wealthiest and most powerful men in the empire. He was fit, good-looking and ruthlessly ambitious. Like all greedy, arrogant men he could not abide the presence of another who might threaten his position and in Harald he clearly saw such a threat. The dislike between them was instant, like two wolves of different packs meeting in a forest.

'You are mistaken, my lord. I was neither the commander in Sicily nor in Italy,' Harald replied evenly. 'Then, as now, I was simply obeying orders.'

'And what did the emperor decide?' Nikephoros said with a glance of annoyance at his younger companion.

'That is not for me to say, my lord,' Harald said with a small shrug.

'Listen, fool...'

'Enough, Andronikos,' said Nikephoros with a raised hand. 'He is correct. The emperor's words are for the emperor to deliver. We will go and hear them ourselves.'

With the bristling Andronikos following him, they walked out of the room with their attendants in tow. Harald motioned at me to follow, and we went behind them.

We followed the procession down the corridor back to the war room and the doors were opened for the generals. Harald was about to follow in, when Andronikos turned and put a palm in his chest. 'Not you, Varangian. You are not a general, you are not a Roman, so you do not participate in planning our strategy or campaigns. Go and guard something, for that is your only role. These doors, perhaps.'

'It is not you who commands me in this palace, Stratopedarches. Only the emperor's word directs me here,' Harald said with an edge in his voice.

'And did the emperor command you to return?' the general asked with raised eyebrows.

Harald's lip curled, but he relaxed back half a step.

'He did not, then? So guard the door, Northman.' The Byzantine nobleman gave Harald a nasty smile and went into the room, which an apologetic looking guardsman shut behind him, studiously avoiding Harald's eye.

Harald huffed at the door in fury for a few moments, then turned on his heel. 'If we are called for, we will be in the courtyard down there,' he said to the guardsman as we strode away.

'Yes, Protospatharios.'

* * *

'So we are committed,' I said, breathing freely at last as we walked out of the corridor that led away from the war room and into the garden.

'It appears so. I think the emperor's mind will not be changed, even without me in the room.'

I looked around uncomfortably. 'He certainly seems to believe you are supporting him in this for his own good.'

'I am,' said Harald carefully. 'It is in his best interests.'

'So you say. And Zoe also thinks it is in her best interests.'

'She does.'

'And you have convinced me that it is in our best interests too.' Harald nodded, and I looked at him carefully. 'Tell me, Harald, which of them is true? You have everyone convinced that you are acting for them, that you prioritise their interests, but it cannot be true for all of them. I admit, I don't even know myself any more. Who will truly benefit from this? The emperor, you, or Zoe?'

Harald looked at me with those calculating blue eyes. 'If you are not sure yourself, then I have achieved what I wanted to. And why do you not consider that all will benefit, despite each believing it will only be them? Whoever sits on the throne, it is in their interest that the empire is strong and secure. Perhaps I have merely forced them to focus on that, and thinking it gained them personal advantage was only the lure.'

I stared at him for a moment longer and then shook my head. 'I truly don't know if you believe that or not.'

Harald smiled softly. 'Good. Let us leave it that way.'

'What have you done, traitor?' a voice snapped at us from the shaded portico that flanked one of the courtyards inside the palace.

I looked up and saw John striding towards us, flanked by half a dozen of his staff.

Harald put his hand to his sword at the ambush, but then, looking around at the unarmed men, realised there was not a threat and let his hand drift away.

'You should have some evidence before using that word, eunuch.'

'Evidence? You have plotted to take your emperor on a campaign that will lead to his death, overriding all his advisors and generals. You are adept at appealing to his weaknesses, but this is a betrayal nonetheless!'

'I have done nothing except what the emperor orders, and you be careful how you slander the emperor's reputation in my presence.'

John screwed up his nostrils in fury. 'You and Zoe will pay for this, Varangian. If my brother is killed, I will have you hunted until the ends of the earth!'

'And that hunt will be swift!' shouted Harald in return, advancing on the eunuch. 'For if he is slain in battle you will find my body at his side, as I will have died in his defence!'

Several guards rushed into the courtyard at the sudden shouting, and some passing palace staff peered out in alarm. John looked around nervously at the sudden audience, while Harald was to all appearance oblivious, staring John down without so much as blinking.

'And if sickness takes him?' John asked, his anger equal to Harald's but his voice lower.

Harald breathed hard, and I saw a flicker of guilt in his face. 'Sickness can take a man in his bed as easily as on campaign. But only one of those deaths is worthy of greatness.'

'I assure you, Harald, sickness will not be what takes you.'

'I assure you, John, not for one moment in my life have I expected it to be.' Harald turned on his heel and stormed off, leaving John fuming behind him in impotent fear and rage.

I stood a moment longer, staring at the eunuch, my anger barely controlled at what John had said. Not because I was outraged, but because I had the sickly fear that it was the truth. That all of it was true.

'You should follow your master, dog,' John said.

'You should hope I am not his dog, you cockless worm, or one day he is likely to set me on you and I will tear out your throat.'

I smiled and stepped in to John as I spoke, close enough that he could smell my breath, and he backed down a little at my mad grin. I was a killer, you see, and all men can sense it in you, just beneath the surface. Few can stand up to that fear that you might just let the killer out at any moment when you show it to them.

'But I am not his dog, eunuch, none of us are. We are not so tamed or cowed. We are the wolves that keep the empire's foes at bay, always looking for the next enemy to set upon. Pray we are never unleashed on you, as I pray that we are.'

'You are both going to pay for this,' John croaked.

'Not to you, we aren't,' I retorted, and I gave him a little shoulder as I turned to follow my master, scattering the small crowd of perplexed palace denizens whose normally quiet day had been interrupted by the confrontation.

'When the time comes, let me kill that one,' I said as I caught up to Harald outside on the path back to the barracks. 'I will really enjoy it.'

Harald looked at me blankly and then nodded. 'If the time comes.'

'You think there is any other outcome?'

'Yes,' Harald replied without hesitating. 'I wonder if it will be him standing over us with the knife.'

That dampened my mood. I could not countenance the idea we would lose to John, but he was perhaps the most dangerous man we knew, despite not truly being one.

'What do we do now?' I asked.

'We get the guard ready for war.'

'When do you think we will march?'

'It will take several months to prepare the imperial army for campaign, especially with the emperor accompanying it. So not until summer.'

'It won't leave us long to complete the victory before winter.'

'Winter means little here. If we need to fight through the winter months, we will.'

'Winter in the mountains of Hellas would not be good for the emperor.'

Harald paused. 'You are right, I had let that slip from my mind. We will have to finish the rebels quickly then and return to the city before the end of the year.'

'So what do you want me to do?'

'Send word to every Varangian barracks and outpost. They are to return to the city immediately. I want every guardsman in the empire here within the month. I will prepare orders for the local fleet commanders to assist if our ships are not sufficient.'

'Every single one?'

Harald looked at me and nodded. 'This is it, Eric. This is for everything. We succeed or we die.'

'And then we go home? Truly?'

He put an arm on my shoulder and smiled. 'Then we go home.'

PART II
BULGAR BURNER

10

TINGHAUGEN, NORWAY; 1098 AD

Eric looked up from the table as the doors to the great hall opened and a party of warriors walked in. The man at their head stopped in confusion as he looked at the mass of quiet men in the benches, and he stopped hesitantly, looking to the king for some kind of reassurance that he was not interrupting.

King Magnus waved the men in with a smile. 'Jarl Olav, welcome. Come up here. Do not fear the silence; we were being told the story of my grandfather.'

Olav nodded and smiled, trying to regain his composure as the eyes of hundreds of men were upon him.

'Another past enemy of the king, now become his supporter,' Eric whispered to Ingvarr with a wink.

'My hearing is better than yours, old man,' said the king with a wry smile, and Ingvarr looked up in a kind of panic to see the king looking their way. But Eric just chortled softly and held up his hands a little from the table in surrender, and the king did not seem upset.

The king's eyes wandered to Ingvarr's panicked expression and his smile widened. 'Making friends of your enemies is a high achievement, young man. While Eric is teaching you, let me add that lesson.'

Ingvarr nodded, not daring to reply and swallowing despite the painful dryness in his throat.

'He is quite correct,' Eric said with a nod, and then Olav had arrived at the table.

'My lord Magnus, I was not expecting you to be here yet. I am ashamed to have arrived behind you. I meant no disrespect by it.'

'And none is taken, Jarl Olav. My journey was merely easier than expected. The hall is quite full, but I expect you can find some space over there, by the side.'

It was a calculated admonishment, and even Ingvarr could sense it, although Olav tried hard not to show any offence. He just looked around for somewhere for his men and him to sit, and saw some benches along the wall, not even at a table. Benches that perhaps thralls or servants might usually use.

'What is happening, for so many to be gathered here in the hall while the sun is still high?' Olav looked deeply unsettled.

Magnus gestured to Eric. 'We are blessed by the presence of Eric Sveitungr, who was my grandfather's companion throughout his journeys to the east. He is telling the story of his life to pass the time before the feast this evening.' Olav looked over with a raised eyebrow.

'Eric, is that you? By God, I haven't seen you for, it must be a dozen years or more. I am surprised...' Olav tailed off.

'Oh, about twenty years I suspect, since I last attended a Thing,' Eric said with a nod. 'And yes, I am more surprised to still be alive than you are to find me so,' he added, and raised his mug of ale in salute.

Olav winced in embarrassment, but Magnus stepped in to save some of his dignity. 'Eric, give me a moment to speak to my old friend Olav, then I wish to hear of my grandfather's battles against the Bulgars. I have not heard it told by one who was there since I was a boy.'

'As you command, I obey, my king,' Eric said with a stiff bow of his head.

'A true Varangian,' Magnus replied, and then stood to go and speak with Olav in private at the back of the hall.

Chatter broke out instantly around the hall as the king moved off the dais and Ingvarr's father Jarl Hakon looked at Eric thoughtfully. 'You make much of King Hardrada's honour, but it sounds like he was breaking his oath to the emperor. Do you truly feel he was not?'

Eric looked at Hakon carefully. 'I thought so too, at the time, and occasionally afterwards. But no, I do not think he broke his oath to the emperor. I think he came as close to it as he could, which was a great skill of his. He took his oaths very seriously, more so than almost any man I have ever met, but he was adept at finding ways of interpreting them to better his interests. His oath was essentially to protect the emperor, and nothing was mentioned about preventing him from putting himself in danger. I know that it is a thin argument, but correct, in my opinion.'

Hakon gazed at Eric in deep contemplation. 'I think that if an oath is to be broken down and argued like that, it loses much of its meaning.'

Eric smiled. 'I used to think that too. But my experiences have taught me differently. I think deciphering the deeper intent of an oath is what gives it meaning. It is why we have laws, not just an oath everyone takes to be good and honest. Tell me, Hakon, would taking an oath to be good and honest be enough for you to avoid breaking what we now know as our laws?'

Hakon bristled. 'Of course. I would not steal, I would not lie, I would not kill men for no reason.'

Eric nodded solemnly. 'All noble intents, undoubtedly. But tell me, Hakon, if your son here was yet a child, and starving, would you not steal a lamb to feed him, or lie about future payment to a shepherd when you had no coin? Tell me, what is truly good, to save the life of your son, or let him die while remaining unspoiled by sin?'

'I am not a thief,' Hakon said angrily.

'You are not a thief because you have never needed to be one. Perhaps, if faced with the need, you still would not be, but be honest with yourself, Hakon, if the only thing holding you back was an oath to be good and honest, what would you do?'

Hakon looked at Ingvarr guiltily and he deflated a little. 'I would save my son. A good father looks after his family.'

Eric smiled. 'So an oath is not enough. Men would argue over what both good and honest truly meant. That is why we need laws that specify it exactly. That was the weakness of the system that constrained Harald. His oaths allowed him some room to decide exactly what they meant. He decided that our oath to protect the throne meant protecting its power and interests, which meant protecting the empire. In order for the empire to flourish, the rebellion needed to be defeated and the emperor would benefit in his own way by accomplishing that personally. It is what, after all, Harald would have done himself.'

Eric sipped his ale again nonchalantly. 'But I am just telling the story, you are the audience. Tell me, do you think Harald was wrong?'

Hakon quailed from the implications of the question. 'I will not pass judgement on the king, it is not my place. I merely wanted to understand what you were saying.'

'A sensible position.' Eric turned his gaze on Ingvarr. 'What about you, lad? You like to speak your mind. What do you think? Were Harald's actions correct?'

Ingvarr considered it. 'You have not told us what oath he took, exactly. So we cannot know.'

Eric nodded. 'True. But then, do you think them honourable?'

'Be careful, Ingvarr,' said his father, giving him a stern look. Ingvarr looked from his father to Eric and back, trying and failing to keep his tongue in check.

His passion won over and he shook his head. 'He did what he did knowing it was the intent of those who wanted the emperor to die. It was wrong.'

Eric raised an eyebrow. 'Does that, alone, make it dishonourable? Do the intentions of others matter more than his?'

Ingvarr screwed his eyes up to think about it, foot tapping on the floor. 'Maybe, well…'

Eric gestured to his left, where the king's empty seat was. 'If it was the intention of the king's enemies to kill him in battle, would his oathmen be dishonourable to encourage him to meet his enemy on the field and defeat them, knowing that it might lead to his death and the victory of his enemy? Or would it be dishonourable to advise him not to accept battle, saving his life but losing his throne?'

Ingvarr looked down at the table. 'You are right. It is the intent of his oathmen and the king's best interests that matter more, not the intent of his enemies. He should meet them in battle and save his throne, even at the risk of his life.'

Eric smiled broadly. 'Then you understand. It is true that Harald manipulated the situation to his advantage, and put the emperor at risk, but it was in the emperor's best interests to take that risk.'

'And in the empress's, too,' Hakon said.

Eric nodded softly. 'A convenient arrangement, to allow him to placate both of them. Rare, too.' He gave them all a satisfied look and stood up. 'I must go and attend to my own business.'

'Oh, how long will you be?' said Ingvarr, missing Eric's meaning.

The old man laughed. 'Well, the older I get, the less certain it is how long this business will take me. But pray for my swift success. Lord knows I frequently do.' And with a laugh he wandered off, leaving Ingvarr red-faced again as he realised.

'You do often concern yourself with the pissing habits of other men, Ingvarr,' Jarl Torvald said with a mischievous grin. 'I also need to go. I will make sure to regale you with the details when I return.'

Ingvarr just looked away as the men around the table laughed at his expense.

* * *

Eric returned not long before the king, and was just sitting down when Magnus came back to the table.

The king did not spare the jarl a glance, and the older man looked pale and shaken as he quietly went back to his seat at the side of the hall.

Magnus let all eyes in the hall linger on him as he casually took his seat, and then turned to Eric. 'If you are ready, Eric, you may continue.'

Eric, trying to ignore the tension between the king and Jarl Olav, nodded and straightened himself in his chair. 'If you are inconvenienced, my lord, I can save my tale for another day.'

'Not at all, Eric. I would like to hear more of your tale. But let us get to the campaign. No doubt I will need more time for audiences with my jarls before the sun has set.'

'As you wish, my lord,' replied Eric, with the closest thing to nervousness

Ingvarr had seen him show. Then he cleared his throat as the eyes of the room locked on him again, and he began to speak.

* * *

Well, let me speed my tale by simply telling you that the preparations for the campaign took months, and were not particularly interesting, as such things rarely are. We recruited men, trained, readied our equipment and performed all of our normal duties in the palace. Harald was good to his promise to the magister of the Scholai, securing a significant sum of gold from the treasury to help them rearm and recruit. The emperor was spending money like water on the upcoming campaign, for he depended on its success so dearly.

In the palace Zoe and John both vied to build a relationship with the younger Michael, as did Harald, who used his frequent sessions tutoring the boy to grow closer to him and earn his trust. There were no great plots or attacks, no attempted assassinations. On the surface, the city was quiet. Underneath, there was a furious struggle to control the future.

Well, I was not part of it. I worked relentlessly with sword, spear and shield, trying to force my aging body to rediscover its youth. To some extent, I succeeded, and the endless exercise and practice hardened my soft body and mind again. I remember that fondly, you see, because it was the last time I was ever truly ready for war. How miserable I would become, in later years, when attaining that state became impossible, before I realised that there are other things in life worth pursuing for men who are no longer young.

Sorry, my old mind wanders again, and you do not care for the faded longings of my life. Well, it was June of 1041 before the emperor gave the command for us to join the gathering army to the west. Now, when the emperor of the Romans leaves the city to go to war, a war that might decide the fate of the empire, it is no small thing. The entire force of imperial guard tagmata was assembled to escort him from the city in a magnificent procession.

Much of the citizenry of the city tried to come and watch, filling every forum, lining every street corner ten ranks deep and hanging from every available window and balcony, all for a glimpse of their emperor going to war.

As soon as we were out of the city the emperor was taken from his chariot and put aboard a ship to sail to Mosynopolis, the city in the west of the Macedonian theme where the army of the empire was assembling.

And what an army it was. Nearly forty thousand men, not farm-boys and levies, no. Every man in the army a real soldier, twice the magnificent force we had fought with in the east six years before.

And at their core were the imperial guard. Harald had scrounged two thousand Varangian guardsmen, leaving only two banda in the city under Afra, who had not tried to hide his relief at not going on campaign.

The imperial court and family were left behind. To Harald's dismay, the younger Michael was not brought on campaign; the emperor was not willing to risk it. Harald had argued that the boy needed real experience of war, but John had strongly advised against it, and had won. 'Don't worry, Harald, I will take good care of him here,' the smug little man had said, while Harald tried to contain his anger.

We had hoped to start marching west as soon as we arrived at the army, but the empire does nothing that it does not do slowly. Such a serious campaign, with a sickly emperor in tow, moved with the pace of a snail and the urgency of a bad-tempered mule. Before leaving there were ceremonies to perform, meetings of every kind, organisation of supplies and marching orders... The emperor even founded a new church there as an offering to some saint or other for success in the campaign. He had been founding churches those last months the way a dog finds new places to piss – everywhere he damn well could.

He had decided that along with a military legacy, he wanted to be remembered for great piety and service to the church. He raised churches and lavished Patriarch Alexius with gifts purely to buy love, and it worked. By the time he left the city for the campaign people were already starting to talk about his future sainthood.

We finally set out westwards in perfect order after all the preparations. For all you will hear of my dislike of them, those Greek generals knew how to organise an army, and I have never before or since seen it done so well. Forty thousand men who largely did not know each other gathered together and set out on the roads west in parade-ground precision, each with all the horses, supplies, servants, support forces and equipment they needed. All told, there were nearly a hundred thousand people on the march, an entire city on the move.

We marched slowly but steadily west along the Egnatia, the great road that cut across all of Northern Greece from Constantinople right through the heartlands of the rebellion. We marched a little over ten miles a day, because that was all that was possible with such a large army, and such a slow-moving emperor. All of this was in lands we were told were still loyal, protected by the shadow of the fortress city of Thessaloniki to the west that still held out for the emperor. But we knew everything beyond that was in rebel control and we were cautious.

In two weeks we had reached the walls of Thessaloniki and found the emperor's standard flying high over the battlements and the people rapturously happy to greet us. They had been under constant harassment and degradation for over a year, trapped within their walls and unable to farm the lands around, nor freely trade.

It was in the camp outside Thessaloniki that the scale of Michael's disability became apparent. The emperor was in considerable pain, and travelling ten miles per day was a significant trial for him, even in his padded carriage. He rested for three days at the city before he would consider moving again.

Finally he called his senior commanders in to meet, and Harald and I went to his fabulous tent in the centre of the sprawling camp, larger even than the nearby city.

'We need to get moving,' grumbled Harald as we walked through the neat encampment. 'This is exactly why they were defeated last time; they sat here until the rebels came and attacked them.'

'The emperor is going to be hard to get moving, and never as fast as you would like,' I said to him with a sad nod.

'Indeed, but I have a plan to present to the emperor and his generals.'

'Harald, why do you even believe they will hear it? You are not a general here. They only call you to this meeting because you are responsible for the emperor's safety and need to know what is happening.'

'I know, but once I am in the meeting, I think they will hear me. They always do.'

'That is true enough. Well, I expect to be appalled.'

'That is why I am not telling you what it is first,' said Harald with a nod. 'So you don't have time to argue.'

We reached the tent and were ushered through to the emperor's presence, finding the two generals already there and in conversation with him, pointing at a large map laid out on a table in front of Michael.

They barely gave Harald a glance as he went to stand at their side.

'From there, we can either move on Dyrrhachium or Sophia, depending on where the enemy is located,' Domestikos Nikephoros said, pointing at two cities on the map, located in the east and west of Bulgaria.

'Or perhaps Belgrade,' Andronikos said, pointing at the extreme north of the rebel Bulgarian realm, where the capital of the Bulgarians, and the birthplace of Delyan's rebellion, was located.

'No, we could be too easily cut off there, too close to winter. If they move there, we consolidate the rest of the rebel lands, and deal with their capital in the spring,' Nikephoros said firmly.

Andronikos looked perturbed but grunted his assent.

Michael, who looked pale and puffy, nodded nervously, and then turned his eyes to Harald. 'What do you think, Harald?'

Harald leaned in over the map, studying the markings and scribbles indicating scouts' reports and the knowledge of the local forces. 'You intend to capture Skopje first, Domestikos?' he asked, looking at Nikephoros.

Nikephoros looked annoyed to be questioned, but nodded. 'Yes. It is central and a strong position. Once we hold it, we can split the rebel lands into parts.'

'With respect, Basileus, we do not need to justify our plans to the Varangian,' Andronikos protested.

'Yet, I wish to hear his opinion,' Michael said dismissively, and the general fell to fuming silence again.

Harald continued as if the general had not spoken. 'How long might it take to capture Skopje? I have never been there, I have no idea of its defences.'

'Perhaps a month.'

'So we will need to be supplied along this road through the mountains while we do it, which will require thousands of men to patrol and guard.'

'Yes, but we have the men. We have planned this out, you should not be surprised to know,' Andronikos scowled.

'I know that you have, Stratopedarches, but how many men must we leave as garrison once we capture the city?'

'Perhaps ten thousand.'

'Ten thousand? So, along with the men we will lose in the siege and leave to guard the road, we will lose nearly half our army before we move on again to those two other cities.'

'We will bring in more men to replace them.'

'And how long will that take?' Harald said, looking at the general with a dubious expression.

Nikephoros sighed. 'Not long. We have already notified the themes who will be required to send them. We have the men available in the empire, Varangian.'

'I know we do, Domestikos, but I am concerned that we do not have the time, and I am also concerned with what the enemy will do with that time.'

'It is only June. We have at least four months of campaign, easily enough to take Skopje and whichever of the other two cities we choose.'

'And then? We wait until the spring to finish the campaign?'

'Yes.'

Harald stood up and looked at the emperor with concern. 'That is a long time.'

Michael looked queasy. I am sure his generals did not understand how serious Michael's condition was. In fact, preventing the elites of the empire from knowing his full weakness was a core concern for the ailing emperor.

'This plan will work, it does not have to be quick. We will grind them down, city by city, using overwhelming force until they are forced to fight or surrender. Either way, we will be victorious,' Andronikos said. 'This is our way of war. I don't expect a foreigner to understand.'

'I do understand, Strategos. I saw your way of war in the east, and again in Sicily. Taking few risks, defeating the enemy in every battle and avoiding those that cannot be won.'

Andronikos smiled ruthlessly. 'Exactly.'

'But we took two years to capture an area this size. And it was all lost again, despite winning every battle. Then, sensing weakness, rebels seized much of Italy too.'

Andronikos's smile faded and he put a hand on the table. 'That was not a failure of military strategy,' he growled.

'No,' Harald said, shaking his head. 'It was caused by other factors which were ignored in the military strategy. We fought as if time and showing our strength and resolve were not important, but they were. And are here, too.'

'Why? Why is time so vital?'

Harald paused a moment, looking at the emperor and then the two generals. 'Other factors.'

'What? Don't speak in riddles, Protospatharios. You are not in command here. Your duty is to protect the emperor while we conduct the campaign. If you will not even detail your concerns I have no interest in considering them,' the domestikos said, dismissing Harald with a wave. 'Basileus, our plan gives the best chance of victory,' he continued, giving Michael a confident smile.

Michael looked nervously between the three men and then shook his head. 'The protospatharios is correct. We must defeat the rebellion more quickly. I did not anticipate it requiring another year. No, a quick victory, Domestikos,' Michael said, nodding.

'A quick victory? Basileus, we all pray for such, but how? The enemy must be brought to battle and utterly defeated, but they can simply hide from us. Rebels are perfidious, Basileus. We cannot chase them to ground so easily. That is what the Varangian does not understand, and why should he, he has no experience of this,' Nikephoros protested.

Harald snorted derisively. 'Do I not?'

The domestikos turned on him with real anger. 'You need to learn your place. What is the largest army you have commanded, Guardsman? A thousand men? You have no business deciding what we do with the imperial army, no experience of our enemy.'

Harald remained composed. 'You are right, Domestikos, I have no experience commanding an army this size. A couple of thousand men is all I have held power over alone.'

Nikephoros stood up, smug in his victory. 'Good. Then we are finished here.'

'But fighting rebels, moving quickly, forcing my enemy into battle, finding victory when none expect it? Those things I have been doing my whole life.'

'Hollow boasts,' Andronikos derided. 'This is madness. Basileus, you must trust us – we are following the methods our ancestors have used to make this empire last a thousand years. This barbarian knows nothing of our ways.'

'Then find a way to do what he suggests. Find a way of quick victory.'

Nikephoros blanched. 'Basileus, there is no quick and easy victory. We must secure our line of supply, we must remove the enemy strongholds, and they are unlikely to face us in the field until they are forced to. It could take a year, it could take two, but we will be victorious.'

'That is not acceptable,' Michael suddenly snapped. 'So listen to Harald.'

Nikephoros looked stunned at the emperor's anger and was unable to reply. Andronikos pointed at Harald. 'He does not have a plan, only complaints.'

'I *do* have a plan,' Harald said confidently. Everyone in the room turned to look at him, Michael with hope, Andronikos with anger and surprise.

Harald looked meekly at the emperor, gesturing to the map. 'Basileus, may I?'

Michael waved him on impatiently, leaning forwards in keen interest.

Harald stepped forwards, the furious and reluctant Andronikos making way for him at the table.

'As the generals say, the enemy strongholds are essential to their strength against an invasion by a large army such as this. And, as they say, we cannot force the enemy to fight unless they want to. They can march twice as fast as us, and be supplied far more freely. They know this too, which is why they are so brazen. They will know exactly what we intend, for they also understand the empire's way of war. So I expect they anticipate drawing us into the mountains, allowing us to waste our strength taking a fortress or two and securing ever longer lines of supply. Then, they will start attacking those lines of supply. They will start threatening the cities we have captured, forcing us to march to and fro, ponderously, whittling us down all the time.' Harald stood up from the map with a sad shake of his head. 'Eventually, one of two things will happen. Either we will, as the generals say, finally flush them out of their hiding places at great expense in time and men, or we will be weakened sufficiently that they can gather their forces and fight us.'

'That is ridiculous. They will not defeat this army!' Andronikos sputtered. 'And how can you claim to know so much about the rebel intentions?' he asked, pointing at Harald accusingly.

Harald shrugged, not looking bothered by the accusing stare. 'Because like the rebels I too have read your manuals, and that is what I would do to defeat you. I would take my time and wear you down, hoping for an opportunity, or as you said, for other factors to come into play.'

'This is outrageous, listen—'

'Enough,' Nikephoros said, holding up a hand to restrain his fiery deputy. 'He is right. No plan is without risk and he has outlined the risks of this one correctly. I do not agree with the scale of the risk, but Basileus, if you think time is a greater problem than I anticipated, then perhaps I am wrong.' The older general gave Harald a careful look and a small nod, which Harald returned, relaxing a little.

'Nikephoros, please,' Andronikos said, trying to reason with his superior.

'No. I will hear him out. What would you do, Varangian?'

Harald smiled and leaned over the table. 'I would make it look like we were doing as expected. March on Skopje with the army. If we act as expected, the enemy will too.'

'Then what?'

'Then, instead of wearing them down, you force them to come to us at Skopje.'

'How? Besieging the city won't achieve that. They will simply wait for an opportunity to take it back.'

'Skopje is an important city, yes?'

The general nodded. 'It is.'

'And the people there and in the surrounding towns are loyal to the rebels?'

Nikephoros stiffened, but nodded. 'Some of them are, more than we expected.'

Harald shrugged. 'Then it is not the city that is the key. It is the people. Without people, a rebellion has nothing. You already admit this Delyan cares nothing for holding land. But he has to care about his people.'

Nikephoros's brows narrowed. 'So?'

'So,' said Harald, pointing at the city on the map, 'we take every town and village between here and there, and destroy everything, kill them all.'

The general looked confused. 'Who? The rebel leaders?'

Harald looked at him and shook his head. 'No. All of them. Everyone, everything, complete destruction.'

'You can't be serious,' Nikephoros said, appalled. 'Those are imperial citizens.'

'They are traitors and rebels, or harbouring them,' Harald said, raising his voice. 'And what do you think the citizens of Skopje will do, when you arrive there, and they know both that we will kill them all if Delyan cannot defend them?'

Andronikos looked at Harald thoughtfully, his finger on his lips. 'They will do anything to avoid that fate,' he said.

'Exactly, Strategos,' Harald said with a ruthless smile. 'Exactly. We force Skopje to surrender or we take it by force and put them all to fire and sword. And then we send messages to every other rebel city that they either turn on the rebels, or we will do the same to them all in turn.'

'They might still refuse, especially at first.'

'Perhaps, but what will Delyan do, knowing that we will advance on them regardless? Imagine the panic his people will feel, the pressure they will put on him to act?'

'He will be forced to come and confront us, with all his strength.'

'Precisely. We don't have to go to these other places, the threat is enough. Delyan cannot stand by while his people are slaughtered – they will abandon him or turn against him.'

'Our citizens will hear of this barbarity against our own people. There will be disquiet, perhaps even protest.'

Harald shrugged. 'Good. Everyone in the empire will hear of what we did to the rebels here, that there is no mercy, that the price of treason is death, not forgiveness. Show your people, both those loyal and those disloyal, your strength and resolve. Let those who would not turn on you now be reassured that your defence of the empire is resolute, and those who would consider it know the price if they do. You spoke to me of legacy, Basileus. Let it be that you brought unity to the empire, by strength.'

Harald stood up straight, and Michael was nodding rapidly, even as Nikephoros looked deeply uncomfortable.

'It will take us a long time to go around subduing these towns one at a time,' Andronikos said carefully.

Harald shook his head, looking at the emperor. 'No. The strategos said I was nothing but your dog, Basileus.'

'I spoke in anger, Protospatharios,' the general said with a touch of shame.

Harald stilled him with a gesture and stared at the emperor. 'No. Your strategos had a point; I am not a commander of armies, merely a guardsman. But we Norsemen are not just guard dogs. In our own lands we are wolves; hunters and killers.' He looked at me with a grin. I did not realise that he had heard my little speech to John some weeks before, but now it was clear he had.

'So let us be your wolves of war. Unleash us, set us on these rebels. My men can march twenty-five miles a day in terrain a horse and cart cannot pass at all. We can go where the enemy do not expect us, take towns and forts by surprise and subterfuge. We can defeat any force small enough to confront us, and run from any large enough to defeat us.'

He turned to Andronikos. 'You asked what my experience leading men at war was, and this is it, Strategos. This is what I did to the rebels in Anatolia five years ago. They say I took forty fortresses in three months, although it may only have been twenty, and I did it with five hundred men. I did the same in Sicily, taking towns an entire army could not.'

Harald raised a clenched fist to Michael, his eyes alight. 'Unleash me, Basileus, and I will be a terror to your enemies, and when your generals arrive at Skopje with this fine army of yours, the enemy will be rushing to come and meet you to end my depredations. If you are worried about the politics of this action, as Nikephoros is, you can always say it was your untamed wolves of war who did it, not good Roman men.'

Andronikos snorted in laughter. 'That is true enough.'

Michael looked wide-eyed at Harald, excited and nervous. 'And this will be quick?'

Harald nodded firmly. 'One way or the other, this will be over within a month or two.'

Nikephoros spoke up. 'You seem to be forgetting your duty, Varangian. If you and your men are gone, who will guard the emperor?'

'Do not mistake me, I will not be taking all of my men – just half. The other half will continue their duties of guarding the emperor and are more than sufficient along with the Scholai and the Optimatoi. There will be no danger, I assure you.'

The emperor looked to his two generals for confirmation. Nikephoros looked like he was feeling ill. Andronikos was just smiling, looking down at the map. 'I misjudged your guardsman, Basileus, and I am not too proud to admit it. I thought he was trying to seize control of the army for his own ends, to risk everything to gain power. But this risks almost nothing except him. If it goes wrong and he is killed, we can still continue with our original plan and blame him for his own failing.'

'Nikephoros?' the emperor asked, looking at the older general.

The domestikos looked nervous, but he surrendered. 'As the stratopedarches says, we have little to lose by trying. Pity the citizens of the Bulgarian theme, they will not forgive us for this.'

Harald looked at the old general coldly. 'Do not worry, Domestikos. Dead men hold no grudges.'

11

THESSALONIKI, JUNE; 1041 AD

'You aren't taking me and the fourteenth?' Styrbjorn said, his mouth wide open with indignation.

'No,' Harald said, shaking his head firmly.

'But the fourteenth are one of your best, most loyal banda!'

'That is precisely why I am leaving you in charge of the emperor's security,' Harald countered to his aghast subordinate. Then Harald glanced at Styrbjorn's leg, but said nothing. It was a very telling look, and Styrbjorn saw it and clamped his mouth shut with obvious anger.

Styrbjorn had lost two toes in Sicily, and walked with a noticeable limp. He pretended it did not bother him to march on the crippled foot, but it was obvious how much he was hiding his discomfort and struggling with it. The punishing pace we would be setting on our long raids might not be manageable to him, and although Harald was kind enough not to say it outright, he wanted Styrbjorn to know it.

'I see,' Styrbjorn muttered.

'Do not be so angry, Styrbjorn. You have seen enough action for a dozen lifetimes, and will again before this campaign is over. It is not glory we are marching to, but infamy.'

'So you claim,' the veteran komes grumbled.

'I will leave you with seven banda, they are not all at full strength, but it will be nearly a thousand men. I will take the rest.'

'Which ones?'

Harald glanced at me; I had been checking their availability and numbers and preparing the list.

'Second, seventh, eighth, tenth, twelfth, sixteenth and nineteenth are coming with us,' I recited.

Styrbjorn glowered. 'Most of the veterans of Sicily; the best men.'

'The ones I can trust to do what I need them to do. You are paid too well to whinge this much, Styrbjorn. You are being left in charge of a thousand Varangians to guard your emperor in the field. It is an honour men would kill each other for. Am I leaving the right man in charge?' Harald said, losing patience.

Styrbjorn stiffened. 'Yes, Protospatharios.'

'Good. Eric, come. We will gather the komes who are coming with us. Styrbjorn, you do the same with yours. Until I return, you have absolute authority over the guard.'

'Aye, Harald.'

Harald nodded and set off without another word, clearly still annoyed with Styrbjorn's complaints.

'You know why he is upset,' I said, chiding.

'To be left guarding the emperor? It is a great honour.'

'No. He assumes men will think he is being left behind because of his foot, that it is weakness, that he is a cripple not fit for war. That is what he fears men will think.'

Harald's brows furrowed a little. 'But it is true. He is not fit for the kind of marching we are setting out to do. Those who cannot keep up will be left behind. I did him a mercy by offering him command here instead.'

I sighed. 'Well, maybe he doesn't see it that way. Would you, if someone offered to let you look weak as a mercy?'

Harald ruminated over it. 'Well, what should I have done differently?'

'You are right that he cannot come with us and he knows it, but you didn't have to stare at his leg to make sure he knows what you think of him. And let him complain a little without thinking less of him. He has earned that.'

'You are too friendly with them, Eric. Their pride is not my foremost concern, but their duty.' He pointed down a side path. 'Come, I need to talk to Theophilos. I need some of his men.'

'I thought we were going where cavalry could not?'

'Heavy cavalry, no. I want some light horsemen who can scout for us. I'm sure he has some.'

* * *

'Araltes. What is this I hear, you are leaving the army?'

Harald looked surprised. 'You are well informed, Magister. I have barely left the meeting where that was decided.'

Theophilos smiled softly. 'I know everyone in the army, Araltes. Everyone worth knowing, anyway. Words travel fast if you know the right people.'

'That does not fill me with confidence about the emperor's security,' Harald rumbled. 'Have you corrupted the emperor's aides?'

'Don't worry – Andronikos and I are old friends, and he just left.'

'Ah, I see. Then this will be quick. I need a dozen mounted scouts. Can you do that for me? The terrain will be very difficult. I need good riders on light horses.'

'I only have good riders, Protospatharios,' the magister said with an amused grin. 'But don't worry. I have a lot of good Greek boys, they grew up riding in these hills and hills like these. They can go almost anywhere you can go on foot, and twice as fast. I will give you two dozen.'

'I only want one dozen.'

'No, you think that is what you need, but you will need messengers, some horses will go lame, some will die. Soon you will have no scouts.' The magister nodded to himself. 'I will give you two dozen.'

'I might not be able to find food for two dozen horses.'

'Four dozen horses, Araltes. Each scout takes two so they have a spare. But don't worry, they find their own fodder. It's part of their training.'

'Forty-eight?' Harald grimaced. 'I only wanted a handful of horses, not a baggage train.'

'Have you ever campaigned in this country?'

Harald shook his head reluctantly.

'Good. It is nothing like Sicily. You need more than a handful. Sicily is a nubile young thing compared to northern Hellas, smooth and soft and welcoming. This land is ancient – the womb of the world, and it is old and wrinkled and angry all the time.' Theophilos nodded smugly. 'You will grow to know her, and learn you need two dozen scouts with two horses each.'

'Fine,' Harald sighed. 'But if they cause me too much trouble they get left behind.'

'You will find it hard to leave men behind who know the land and travel twice as fast as you.'

'Please, enough!' I said with a roll of my eyes, earning an annoyed glare from Harald and an amused look from Theophilos. 'Magister, just send their leader to me. I will organise the rest.'

The magister bowed his head with teasing depth. 'As you command, Strategos.'

* * *

As we walked away back to the section of the camp where the bandoa were quartered, Harald glared at me. 'Don't do that. Don't undermine me in front of others. You know better.'

'I have a lot to do before we leave, and had no time for that contest of pride,' I said defiantly, but Harald's look was dangerous, and I relented. 'I apologise. I will remember not to.'

'Hmm,' Harald said, and I cursed myself inwardly because he did not easily let go of such things.

'Go and get your equipment ready and organise those scouts when they come.'

'You do not want me to come with you to tell the komes our plans?' I asked.

'No,' Harald said curtly, and strode off without me.

You see, he was already punishing me.

* * *

The next day we set off at the first light of dawn, headed away from the army in a tight column of a thousand men, led by the little bands of scouts. We had no baggage train, no tents, no servants or followers. Each man carried enough food for three days, water for one, his fighting equipment, a blanket roll and a cloak.

That was it. We were heading out into the hills of Greece to raid in the old way, to live off the land and the stores of our enemies, to survive or die by our wits and our blades, with no one to come and aid us. It was a foreign way of war to the meticulously organised Roman army, but for us it was the way of our ancestors. We were going Viking in the heart of our enemies' lands.

It was an exhilarating prospect, I admit it. I was excited! Even after so many years of war, I was thrilled to once again be going out on our own under Harald's command, with no scheming Greek officers to ruin things, no incompetent admirals or generals to mess things up, no slow-moving imperial forces to bog us down and tie us to the roads.

Within a day we had left the Egnatia road, and headed across the wide plain north-west of Thessaloniki towards the broad maze of valleys and hills that lay in the shadow of the great mountains of ancient Macedonia. The main army would follow the road, capturing the first major rebel town of Vodena that guarded the low passes into the Macedonian mountains, while we skirted it to the north and went over them.

The Macedonians were long gone, but the Roman histories tell that they were a great race of warriors who were born in those hills and went on to conquer the world. They are revered by the Greeks that live there now, although no trace of them yet exists upon the face of the earth other than a few low ruins. They sound a little like us, and their mountains reminded me somewhat of our own here at home. Perhaps that is why they were such great warriors, because the land hardened them.

Or perhaps it has no bearing, because the men who lived there when we marched upon them were weak and scattered. Bah, who knows. Regardless, it was not long before we came across the first large town, nestled at the edge of those foothills.

They did not see us coming until the last moment, our speed and distance from the road ensured that. Bravely, or foolishly, their men armed themselves and drew themselves up to defend the approach to their unwalled town.

Shall I describe the fight? No, I need to move as fast through this tale as we did through those mountains, and it was not a fight worthy of note. It was mere practice to get our men back into the habit of war. We shattered the five hundred poorly armed men who dared to oppose us, fools and rebels whose names are lost to time and who do not deserve the glory of remembrance. We slaughtered them, we killed those who pleaded for mercy, and we marched quickly onwards to the town, intent on looting it before they had time to flee.

As we got to the edge of the town the mounted scouts spread out around on either side to warn us of any reinforcement, and Harald stood at the front of our formation, blood darkening on his armour, and he glared at us, his face a mask of bloodlust and anger.

'Our mission here is not one of mercy, or salvation. Our task here is revenge and fear. We will kill everything in this town, every man, woman and child, every animal of the field and beast of burden. We will burn this place to ashes and leave its dead beneath them. Take only the food and water we need, not even silver to weigh us down.' He paused. 'What gold you find, is yours to keep.'

The men around him roared their appreciation, as simple soldiers with their blood up will always do at such a prospect.

'We kill everything?' Ulfr, komes of the seventh bandon, the Storm Ravens, asked with a surprised look. 'Even the dogs?' He was looking at the town, and I could hear dogs barking, sensing the intrusion and conflict the way they always do.

Harald looked at the town, hearing it too. 'Not the dogs,' he finally said. 'I like dogs. They are loyal creatures, and they will help eat the carcasses of the livestock we leave behind. Kill everything else.'

Ulfr nodded and shouted his orders at his waiting men, who raised their shields and marched into the town in disciplined blocks, with Rurik's tenth bandon close behind them, and the others spreading out to make sure the entire town was cleansed.

The seventh bandon had been Harald's old command, years ago before he had been raised to commander of the whole guard. They still bore the name he had given them, the Storm Ravens, and marched under his chosen banner, the black raven on a red field. That banner stood proud and menacing over the seventh as they marched into the town, and it disappeared into its streets just as the screaming began.

* * *

Harald walked into town near the back of the column after making sure everyone had their orders clearly understood. We went to the central square and found a church there, a tired, dusty place with a terrified old priest who was shielding several dozen people inside. Even our men, under Harald's orders, were reluctant to kill a priest and storm a church. The whirlwind of carnage was ripping through the town around us, with the sounds of death and terror everywhere, but Harald walked up to that shaking priest at the door to his church calm and aloof.

'Who are you hiding in there, priest?'

'Innocent people. Mercy please, Strategos, mercy!'

'Bring out someone to speak for them.'

'I can speak for them,' the man said, his voice wavering.

'You cannot, Father. Send out whoever speaks for them.'

The priest nodded fearfully and ducked inside the door. Rurik of the tenth bandon, whose men were surrounding the church, came over, looking nervous and a little ashamed. 'I'm sorry, Protospatharios. I heard your orders, but...' He waved his hand helplessly at the building. 'But a church?'

'No, you did the right thing, and I had not considered it. We will not be burning churches, nor massacring those inside them. Some things are inviolable to good Christian men.'

Rurik looked hugely relieved, despite the fact that half of our men were not, in fact, Christians, even if they pretended to be in order to be allowed to serve. There were many hammer amulets hanging around Varangian necks at that time, although I doubt there still are.

The priest came back out with an ageing man who looked forlornly around at the town, hearing the sounds of the ongoing massacre with horror. Harald snapped his fingers at two guardsmen and then at the man, and he was roughly dragged over and forced to kneel at Harald's feet.

'Who are you, imperial soldiers? Why are you doing this? What is this outrage?' he wailed.

'Why did you fight us when we arrived?' Harald asked coldly.

The old man quailed. 'Someone brought word of armed men coming this way, and the leaders decided to fight.' He shook his head. 'It was not my decision.'

'Why did this town recognise the false emperor, the rebel?'

The man gulped. 'We... we had no choice. They came here with overwhelming force, and we could not resist them!'

'Like you resisted us?'

The old man's mouth fell open, and then he flinched as a building somewhere collapsed, fire having eaten away its structure.

'How many of your people died fighting the rebels when they came?' Harald asked, his face impassive.

'None,' the old man whimpered.

'How many died fighting them since then?'

'None,' said the old man, lowering his head. 'Please, I beg you.'

'Begging will not help you. You betrayed your emperor. Justice has come.'

'If we had resisted we would all have died!' the old man whined.

'That would have been better,' Harald said, then he drew his sword and beheaded the old man with a single, sudden strike. The priest shouted in fear and then scuttled back inside the church.

'I have heard enough. These people are cowards and traitors. What we do here is justice. Finish up quickly and then we move on.'

'What about the people in the church?' Rurik said, jerking his thumb at the structure.

'Leave them. We need someone to survive and tell of what happens to traitors and rebels.'

Rurik nodded, relieved. He turned to his men. 'Leave them alone. Move on through the town. Let's go! Don't want those bastards in the twelfth taking all the gold now, do we?'

I looked at the beheaded man with curiosity as the tenth moved off at a run.

'So they were only rebels out of fear, not belief. What do we do now?'

'We ensure they learn to fear us more than they fear the rebels. We remind them what the empire truly means, and how terrible its vengeance can be.'

'It is that simple?'

Harald nodded. 'It is that simple. Come, I want to leave this place behind before sunset and move on. This fire will draw any enemy force within twenty miles, and we should not be here if they arrive.'

* * *

We burned that town and left, as Harald had ordered. I do not even remember its name, and I do not know if it was ever rebuilt, so thoroughly did we destroy it. Perhaps that dusty old church is still there, standing forlorn among the overgrown ruins. I don't know.

We marched onwards through the foothills, and we burned every village we came to, killed everything and everyone we could, although some always escaped and we did not try too hard to stop them. Harald needed the word of what we were doing to spread. And spread it did.

In the next four or five days we burned another two towns, fought three victorious skirmishes and ran from a large force that was marching through the hills towards us. Was it looking for us? We did not know, but we had no interest in finding out. Breaking the rebel's military force was the task of the emperor's army. We were there to destroy their people's will to fight.

It rankled with some of our men, of course, to flee from our enemy.

'We could have beaten them,' Ulfr grumbled.

'Yes, but it would have been a hard fight. We would have lost enough men, taken enough wounded, that we would have to have headed home,' I said. Harald was at another campfire, and Ulfr felt free to raise his grievances with me.

'I know,' muttered the Icelander. 'Still, men will say we fled to avoid losing, but we could have beaten them.'

'I know,' I said with a sympathetic nod. 'We will have our time to prove ourselves in battle.'

'This is not honourable work,' Ulfr said, giving me a grim look. 'Killing unarmed people and fleeing from those who can defend themselves.'

'I know that too,' I said with a sigh. 'But Harald and the emperor deem it necessary.'

'Not honourable work,' muttered Ulfr again, as if I had not spoken, looking away into the darkness. 'Not at all.'

I looked at him thoughtfully as he stared glumly into the darkness. Ulfr had once been so full of mischief and joy. The longer he was apart from his cousin Halldor, the less of that was shown to the world. It worried me. He was still a fine leader and a fearless warrior, but those things that can eat at the inside of a man's mind can kill them just as surely as any steel, and far more insidiously.

'We are doing all this to force them into a fight. There doesn't seem to be another way,' I said, trying to bring the man around to see Harald's reasoning, but Ulfr just shrugged.

'The reason doesn't change what men will think.'

Well, I didn't have an answer for that. It was true.

'This won't be for long, Ulfr. Soon we will be back to the real war, and it will be all the easier for having destroyed their support first.'

Ulfr sighed and got to his feet, preparing to go to his bedroll. He patted me on the shoulder as he passed me. 'Sounds very glorious, Eric. Glorious indeed.'

I looked at him with a troubled expression as he walked away, but he had been through a lot, and I supposed I just needed to give him space for his anger.

12

I think the sense of excitement we had all felt when we set off on our raid died as quickly as the few rebels who dared to face us.

Ulfr was right, although he was one of the few who dared to speak it. That campaign felt wrong. Dirty. Cowardly. Those people we were cleansing from the land were not some foreign enemy, and we had no hatred for them nor any reason to want them to die. They seemed almost the same as the people we lived alongside in the city – Greeks, mostly, although some were Bulgars and other people I was not so familiar with.

But mostly, they were just terrified farmers and herders who woke up one morning to find us in their villages with steel and fire and death.

To run from every real fight while we did that sapped at the men's souls, and I could see it. Some were unaffected by it, especially the older men who had been to war many times before and become inured to its horrors, but there were others who started to look sullen and detached, or were less than diligent in their new murderous duties.

It didn't change our progress noticeably. For every man who was half-hearted, there were plenty of others willing to enforce Harald's destruction of the land, even if they no longer whooped and cheered as they did it.

We burned a swath through those hills and valleys, leaving desolation in our wake. A mess of burned villages, slaughtered flocks, and weeping survivors who crept from the hills and bushes after we were gone to try and find their kin in the ashes.

Many of those places meld together in my mind, because I did not wish to remember them, but one in particular stands out to me. We were clearing a broad valley, root to tip, the banda spread out in a broad line several miles across, burning a crescent swath up through the farms and villages while the scouts watched our flanks.

There was no one to oppose us in that valley, just farmers and herders, but the rebels relied on those farmers and herders for food, so they had to die, and their crops and animals had to be destroyed.

So destroy them we did.

By the end of the afternoon we had cleared all the way to the top of the valley, and Harald gathered us, ready to send us down into the next valley the following day. No respite could be given to the people, no time to run away with their precious animals and supplies.

As we rested in the late sun, I was taking Harald's orders around the banda and I went to where the seventh was gathered but Ulfr was nowhere to be found. One of his men pointed me nervously down the ridgeline, and I saw a solitary figure standing by some rocks, gazing out over the next valley. I went over to see him, and found him motionless, his bloodied hands knitted across his chest.

'Ulfr?'

He started a little and turned to me, and I saw that he had been weeping. I turned away, not wanting to shame him by acknowledging it, but I was horrified. Not just at the display of weakness, but mostly that it had got so bad without me noticing. I had seen it before; even the bravest warriors can eventually be broken by war, by losing friends or those they loved.

'Don't turn away from me, Eric,' he said angrily. 'Gaze upon the dutiful guardsman who has done the emperor's will today.'

I looked at him again, confused at his anger.

'I don't understand. What are you saying?'

'I have done as you said, I have continued in my duties, because you say the emperor needs it, and Harald commands it.'

'Yes, it is true.'

'Well, that is what I told myself today. But you know, Eric, I don't believe it. I don't believe that the people I killed today were a threat to the emperor.'

'They were,' I said, trying to sound confident.

'Really?' He looked at me with wide, challenging eyes. 'That family that I found hiding in a barn with their goats. Were they a threat to the emperor?'

'Yes. Their goats feed the rebels and their army.'

'Ah, well, I killed the goats, so the emperor can sleep safely tonight!'

'Ulfr...' I said, starting to get worried and a little angry. His behaviour was bordering on dangerous.

'And the goatherd, of course, I killed him so he cannot herd dangerous goats again,' Ulfr said, looking down at the valley below us, where smoke still rose in curls and fires flickered in the late afternoon shadows.

'He, at least, tried to fight me.' Ulfr laughed, a mirthless, barking laugh that contained no humour. 'He only had an eating knife! But still, at least he held something sharp in his hands while I gutted him.'

I swallowed, seeing the depth of pain in the way Ulfr's hands wrung together, flakes of dried blood cracking off and falling from them like he was trying to rub away the memory.

'But the wife and young daughter? Were they threats to the emperor?' Ulfr looked at me, and his eyes were full of anguish.

I winced, guiltily, and could not meet his fierce gaze. 'I'm sorry.'

'Harald said to kill them all, did he not? Including the women and children?'

'Yes.'

'So I was doing my duty then, when I killed them. Have you killed many children in these past few days, Eric? Have you done your duty too?'

I looked down at the dusty ground, too ashamed to answer.

'What, you cannot even face me, Eric?'

I winced at the accusation and forced myself to meet his eye again. 'No.' I muttered. 'I have been with Harald.'

'Ah, I see. Yes, too important to kill the children. An easy task, nothing to bother yourselves with.' He held a finger up, eyes still ablaze with anger. 'Except it's not so easy, Eric. That young goatherd's wife, barely a woman, she made it difficult for me. She sheltered her daughter behind her, you see. As I moved from her dying husband to her.' He breathed hard and steadied himself, and a fresh tear appeared on his cheek.

'She had no weapons, and I had just killed her husband in front of her, so do you know what she did, Eric?'

I shook my head mutely. 'She begged me. She spoke no language I understood, of course, but I didn't need to know her words. She begged me, and then she offered herself to me. Can you believe that, Eric? She offered herself to me to spare her child. She tore open her tunic and bared her little tits at me, spread her legs, and showed her womanhood to me, imploring me with her eyes and her body to take that, not her child's life.' I closed my eyes at the horror and shame of it, and Ulfr's voice shook.

'And she wasn't crying, she wasn't screaming. The body of her husband was lying next to her, and she was defiant! She judged me with her eyes, she tempted me with her cunny, and she shielded her child from me with her body.' He shook his head. 'She showed more courage in those moments than we have showed in a dozen years of war.'

I felt sick, but I opened my eyes and looked at him, questioning.

'Oh, don't worry, Eric,' Ulfr said with a sneer, stepping to me. 'I did my duty to the emperor, and I cut that brave young woman's neck from shoulder to shoulder and then I fished her daughter out from behind her dying body and I delivered the emperor's justice to her too.'

He leaned in, spiteful and angry, spittle flying in my ear. 'I hope the emperor sleeps safe tonight, knowing that we are slaying brave young women, and running from armed rebels. Us, the mighty Varangians, the wolves of the empire. Look at me, Eric. Look what it has done to us. Look at the price of our victory over these people.'

I did look at him, and it was the most difficult thing I had ever done, because everything he was saying was the truth, and we were shameful for it. And what could I say to my grieving friend? I knew he was not truly angry with me, except that he was angry with everyone and everything. He had watched us lose men for a dozen years of war to protect the emperor and accepted it. Losing his beloved cousin had taken the joy from him, and that brave young mother had taken his honour. Looking into his red-rimmed eyes, I could see he had nothing left but anger – anger and the bonds of oaths and duty. I could only hope the latter were strong enough to last until we returned to the city.

'I will rest your bandon tomorrow,' I said weakly. 'I will make sure you don't have to do that again.'

'Oh no, Eric. Do not spare me. Don't make others do it instead of me. I will do my duty and don't you fucking dare doubt it,' he said, pointing a finger right in my face, and then he stormed off, a lonely, hunched figure on that barren ridge, leaving me churning and miserable in his wake.

* * *

The next day we moved into the next two valleys, and we brought the same destruction and death as before, and I saw with my eyes now open how many men were hiding their anger and shame like Ulfr was, but what could I do? Harald was set on his course and nothing would turn him from it. So like the coward I knew I was, I said nothing, I did nothing, I simply hoped we would be out of those miserable, corpse-ridden places as soon as we could be.

* * *

After a few days the scouts, who were excellent beyond my expectations, told us we were approaching another large town, nestled in a broad, hidden plain in the hills to the north, right below the largest of the mountains.

We marched on that town at speed during the night, and in the morning we saw it properly, spread out in front of us. It was large, home to five thousand people at least, more than large enough to raise a force to defend itself, but none came out to meet us.

We marched towards the town carefully and quickly, expecting an ambush or trap, but none revealed itself. Instead, as Ulfr led the seventh to the edge of town at the head of our attacking columns under his red raven banner, a small party of unarmed men hurried nervously out to come and face us, gathered together like cattle under a tree in the rain.

Harald had them brought to us, at the same time sending three banda to surround the town. 'Who is your leader?' he asked impassively.

One of them, a middle-aged man who was almost completely bald, but carried himself with dignity, stepped forwards. He almost looked unafraid, which impressed me, because he surely knew what was going to happen.

'I am.'

Harald looked at him. 'Where is your army? Where are your fighting men?'

'They are away,' he said regretfully.

'Where?'

The man paused, regarding Harald carefully. 'Looking for you, I believe.'

Harald's brows knotted. 'Looking for me? Do you know who I am?'

The man shook his head. 'No. But I've heard of you and your blood-red banner, the Land-Waster, the black bird of death and despair.'

Harald furrowed his brows and then turned to look at the seventh bandon's banner, which was fluttering proudly in the light breeze, the black raven stark on the red background. He looked at it thoughtfully for a moment and then turned back to the old man. 'So why did you come out and talk to me?'

'To offer our surrender.'

'Do you think no one has tried that before?'

'I know they have.'

'And what have you heard happened?'

'You destroyed them regardless.'

Harald nodded. 'So why are you different?'

'This town is large, rich, important. The empire needs it intact. You should spare us. We will come peacefully, and we will help you. We can offer food and aid.'

'Nothing I cannot take for myself.'

The old man's eyes fell tiredly. It had been a desperate hope, a weak offer. I felt nothing but sympathy for him.

'You offer surrender, but you sent your army out to fight us. So your surrender is meaningless, an act of desperation.'

'We had no choice.'

'Ah... choice. I hear this all the time recently. Humour me, old man. Why did you have no choice?'

'The rebels sent a force out here to hunt you, two thousand men, and they demanded we send our young men with them.'

Harald looked at the old man with an almost tired expression. 'And why did you not fight them?'

'Because we had less than a thousand, and we would have lost.'

'But you could have fought them, you *did* have a choice.'

The old man breathed heavily, then nodded. 'Yes, we had that choice, but it would have failed. We would have died for nothing.'

'But you were hoping the rebels would kill us and thus you would be safe.'

'Yes.'

Harald sighed and nodded. 'You see, this is the problem. You considered only what would keep your people safe.'

'Of course.'

'Not duty, not honour, not loyalty to your emperor. Do those things mean nothing?'

The old man just stared at Harald.

'You think you can surrender to any armed force when they arrive and pretend loyalty to whoever has the most spears levelled at your chest. Do you see why this is a problem for the empire?'

Harald stepped forwards slightly, looking past the old man at the town. 'An empire must be ruled by more than a convenience of violence. An empire needs loyalty. You could have fought them, and yes, perhaps you would have lost, but you might have hurt the rebels so badly they were forced to retreat or made them easier prey for my men, a victory for the empire.'

Harald put his hand on the man's shoulder.

'Tell me, old man, if I forgive you, and your town was threatened by a foreign army in the future, would you expect the empire to raise its mighty hand and send men here to protect you?'

The old man looked fearful, trapped, but he nodded weakly. 'Yes.'

'You expect us to come and die for you, but you are not willing to die for us? Do I understand that correctly?'

The man didn't answer, his shoulders just slumped.

'I see. You are unwilling to raise your hand in defence of the empire, but you expect our mercy for raising it against us out of fear.'

The man shivered a little.

'You know what my answer will be, don't you?' Harald said, almost conversationally.

'Yes,' the man whimpered. 'But please.'

'But please nothing. You are lucky. I am going to let you live, you and some of your people. You may go out and seek shelter somewhere else and warn them of the consequences of betraying the empire. The rest of your people and possessions will face the emperor's justice.'

The man quailed and backed away, bowing, given sudden hope by his unexpected reprieve. 'I understand. I thank you for your wisdom.'

Harald snapped out a hand and grabbed the man by his wrist. 'Ah, not so fast. Justice must still be done. You refused to raise your hand in defence of the empire, so it is forfeit. Eric?' He turned his icy blue eyes on me, and I gulped. I knew what he wanted me to do, and I knew I could not betray him by refusing, but my hand shook as I stepped forwards and fumbled drawing my sword.

Harald saw it and scowled, but I got the blade out and Harald stretched the wailing man's arm out for me, proffering his bared forearm.

'The emperor's justice will always be served,' Harald said, and I brought my blade down hard on the poor man's wrist.

* * *

Then we cleared the town. The shame of Ulfr's words drove me to take part. I did my share of the duty. I brought the emperor's terrible justice to young and old alike and my hands ran red with the blood of the weak and the innocent.

Harald rounded up a hundred or so of the town's men and had all their right hands cut off and their wounds tied, then drove them, weak and stumbling, from the town.

'Why?' I asked, almost forlorn, as I watched the weeping and maimed people staggering out of town, clutching their hastily bandaged stumps, or falling to pass out at the roadside. 'Why do we need to perform such cruelty?'

'Because others will hear of it. They will all seek shelter with their people, and tell of what we did.'

He turned and waved to the head of the scouts, a young man named

Petros. The Greek trotted over, seemingly unbothered by the devastation around us. Three women lay dead at the roadside nearby, slaughtered as they fled.

'I want you to try and find the force that is supposed to be hunting us. They cannot be far behind. Be back here by midday tomorrow.'

Petros inclined his head. 'As you command.' He neatly turned his horse and trotted off again towards a gaggle of his men who were feeding their horses at a looted stable building.

'As for the rest of us, we will stay in town for a day to rest, and burn it when we leave. Let's get the men a deserved night's sleep in real beds, and tomorrow we can eat real food, get our strength back.'

'I wish you had told us that sooner,' Sveinn said with a sigh. 'We could have taken all the people outside before we killed them.'

I shook my head, tired and dispirited. Sveinn was not one of those who was bothered by what we were doing.

* * *

I found some corpse-free houses for Harald and our little command group and set myself to sleep once guards had been set around the town. I was woken what seemed like moments later by a rough hand.

'Eric, Eric, you must come,' a voice whispered urgently.

I sat bolt upright, my worst fears materialised. 'Are we under attack?'

The enemy must have appeared during the night. It's what Harald would have done. I cursed myself as I jumped from my bed. We had got lazy.

'No,' the guardsman whispered. 'It's Ulfr. He's drunk.'

I peered at the figure in the darkness. 'What?'

'Komes Ulfr, he has gone mad, ranting and screaming in the street. I wanted to tell you before...' The man's voice was frantic, and I understood.

'Before Harald found out.'

If Harald found Ulfr in that state the komes' career might be over, or worse. The guardsman wasn't reporting Ulfr to get him punished, he was trying to save him.

'Take me to him,' I urged, trying to keep my voice low. Harald was in the adjoining building.

I hurried out into the open, but the guardsman needn't have given me directions, for I could hear a commotion down the street. I ran like I was running towards a fire, full of panic for my friend, and found him shouting wildly at a half dozen guardsmen, brandishing a sword at them. In the flickering shadows I could see he was hiding someone behind himself.

'Get away!' he shouted shrilly as a guardsman remonstrated with him.

'What is going on here?' I hissed, trying to keep my voice down, futile though that might have been.

The men looked at me, and one of them was bleeding from a cut on his forehead.

'We are trying to calm him, he has lost his senses,' the cut man said.

'The fool is drunk,' another said angrily, and one of his fellows elbowed him into silence.

'Ulfr? What are you doing? Who is that?' I said, pointing at the figure he was sheltering behind him.

'Fuck you, Eric!' he gurgled.

'It is a boy he found hiding in a house. Apparently, he had run out of looted wine and was looking for more. Found this rat instead.'

'Looted wine? Getting drunk on campaign – are you insane, Ulfr?'

'I couldn't sleep,' Ulfr sobbed. 'I haven't slept for days. All I can see is her, Eric. I just wanted to sleep.'

'Then what are you doing with this boy?'

'I won't let you kill him. I'm releasing him,' Ulfr muttered, his eyes and feet unsteady, his sword waving about.

'We found him like this, dragging the boy through the street, ranting about the emperor.'

'The emperor is a cunt and a coward for ordering this,' Ulfr mumbled.

I stepped forwards in a flash and knocked the drunken man's sword aside, seizing him by the throat. Getting drunk while on campaign would see him being demoted and lashed at best; insulting the emperor like that meant death.

'Be silent, you fool,' I hissed in his face. He went limp, his eyes dead and despairing as he looked at me.

'I can't let him die. I need him to live,' Ulfr whispered to me, almost sobbing.

'Fuck him, we need to get you out of the street.'

'What is this?' barked a familiar voice from behind, and I slumped in misery. It was Harald.

'What the fuck is this noise in the middle of the night?'

I let go of Ulfr and turned guiltily towards our commander. 'I'm seeing to it. It won't continue.'

'Is that Ulfr?'

'Yes, it is,' said Ulfr, stepping forwards unsteadily with a spiteful hiss in his voice.

'Are you... drunk?' Harald said in outrage.

'I am.'

'What insanity is this? On campaign, in enemy lands, and one of my officers is drunk?'

'Don't worry,' said Ulfr, waving his sword vaguely. 'I can kill children when I am drunk. I could kill them in my sleep.' He paused, considering it. 'I think it would be easier, perhaps.'

Harald turned to me, fury coming off him in waves. 'How long has this been happening?'

'This is the first time,' I said. 'Harald, please, we can deal with this quietly. He is a loyal servant of the emperor.'

'Yes, I am!' slurred Ulfr. 'Loyal, me. I will protect the emperor from all threats. Kill all of his enemies. Crawling babes, one-legged old women, deadly foes like that.' He stopped, spreading his arms in exaggerated question. 'Maybe I can strangle some cats for him. Dangerous creatures, cats.'

'Shut your mouth, you fool,' I hissed.

'I'll kill anything for him, and for you. Except armed men who can fight back, apparently.' Ulfr shook his head in confusion. 'Not allowed to kill them for some reason.'

'What is happening here, Eric?' Harald asked me, softly and with a dangerous rumble in his throat.

'He is suffering. His cousin's wound, and then this campaign... Something is gone in his mind. Please, we can deal with this quietly.'

'I think the time for that has passed,' Harald said, then he pointed to the men around Ulfr. 'Seize him. And who the fuck is that boy?'

'A local,' one of the men said while four others pounced on Ulfr, who was too slow to react beyond an outraged yelp.

'A local? Why is he still alive? Get rid of him.'

'Yes, Protospatharios.'

'*No!*' Ulfr roared, suddenly squirming with unreasonable strength against the men holding him, managing to rip one arm free and punch one of them on the nose with a wild swipe. 'He is mine!'

Harald looked on in consternation. 'Has he taken that boy as his drunken lover? What is going on here?'

'What? No, he just wanted to save him. He needed to. Please, just let him go. It doesn't matter, one boy.'

Harald scowled. 'It doesn't matter? Eric, you are blind sometimes.' He walked away from me towards the struggling, howling Ulfr. I looked around and saw dozens of men were in the street now, watching the spectacle.

Harald got up to Ulfr and swung, hard, punching him across the jaw and stilling him, reducing him to a soft moaning. Then he beckoned to the boy, who was cringing against a wall in fear. The boy did not move at first, but Harald held out his hand and motioned to him. The boy, surrounded and with little choice, timidly moved away from the wall and took Harald's hand.

Harald drew his knife with his other hand and swept it across the boy's throat, so fast in the darkness I don't think the boy even saw it. He just suddenly stopped in confusion, his other hand reaching up to his throat to grab at the sudden pain, before blood exploded through his fingers and he sank to the ground, twitching and coughing.

'*No!*' Ulfr wailed, struggling against the powerful hands that restrained him.

Harald looked at the wailing komes and shook his head. 'Bind him. I will deal with him in the morning.' Then he looked around the crowd, scowling. 'All of you, back to your beds.'

Guardsmen scurried to obey, clearing the street as four of Ulfr's men dragged him away, his resistance gone other than for a quiet sobbing.

Harald walked back towards me. 'Come with me, now!'

I went up the street with Harald. 'Why didn't you let the boy live?'

My prince turned on me, his anger raw and powerful. 'And what lesson would that teach – that disobeying my orders works? And what if the boy did return to his people and told them of our weakness and indiscipline? How would that help our cause, Eric? How many more villages would have to die to erase the seeds of doubt that story would plant? You are a fool sometimes. You are too close to some of these men.'

'Some of these men? You mean my friends, the men I have served and lived with for years? You think I am too close to them!'

'Yes! They are not our friends, Eric, they are our soldiers. We do not befriend them, we *command* them. That weakness of friendship is what allows this to happen.' He stepped into me, almost nose to nose. 'Tell me, were you aware of this problem with Ulfr before tonight?'

I gulped, and he saw the hesitation and guilt in my eyes. He nodded and stepped back. 'I thought so. For how long?'

'A few days ago, he told me... It doesn't matter. He showed me disrespect, questioned our duty. I thought...' I shrugged helplessly. 'I thought punishing him would only make it worse, that he needed time.'

'And you did nothing about it? Why? Because you think he is your friend. Now look what your weakness has caused. We have lost him.' Harald almost spat the last words. 'We have lost one of our best men because you did not do your duty.'

'What do you mean, lost him?' I asked, my voice trembling. 'What will you do, Harald?'

He looked down the street and his face regained his stony composure. 'I will restore discipline. And I'm starting with you. You are no longer my second and my standard bearer; it is a position of trust you no longer deserve. Sveinn will replace you as my formal second in command. He has proven capable of it.'

I think my legs almost failed me then, and the breath caught in my chest. But I could not speak. I had given my life to Harald, and I had failed him. He was not a man that tolerated failure.

'You will take over as komes of the seventh from Ulfr. Clean up this mess of shame and indiscipline that you have allowed to form. And you will return my raven banner to me and make your own. I won't let my flag be stained by Ulfr's shame. Perhaps you will have the chance to show me that you are a leader of men, and that you have learned what it takes to achieve what we are trying to achieve.' Then he shrugged. 'Or perhaps you will not.'

Then he turned and stalked away into the darkness, leaving me on the verge of weeping at my shame and bereavement.

I had made my life's duty to support Harald, to protect him and follow him, and after more than ten years I had been cast aside. I had wavered in the strength required to stand by his side, and he could not tolerate weakness in the scale of his ambitions.

You see, you all think it is an insult that men call me 'the follower', that it shows that I was weak or that I lived off the scraps of his glory, but you could not be more wrong. Following Harald was the most supreme test of strength and fortitude. It required sacrifices that seemed unbearable, and devotion that seemed impossible.

They call me Eric the Follower, and damn you, through blood and sacrifice you cannot imagine, I earned that name.

13

In the morning I had not slept, but I made sure I was up before the first light. I went to find the seventh and roused them. Ulfr was unconscious, and the rest of the men were subdued, on edge. They all knew what was likely to happen to the man.

'I am your komes now,' I said as I gathered them. I knew many of them well; I had served in the seventh for several years from when we first joined the guard. Most of the surviving blood-marked, the men who had stood with Harald at Stiklestad and remained with us ever since, were in the seventh. It is true, many of the rest were new faces since then, replacing men lost on various campaigns, but we had always kept the seventh close as Harald trusted them, and I knew many of the new men too.

I think that was the insidious part of Harald's punishment. He had put me in charge of my friends, the men I knew best. He was seeing if I had the strength to command them, to discipline them... to order them to their deaths. He was a cold bastard like that.

I looked at the gathered men in the street, thinking it over. I made my choice. 'Sigurd, you will be my topoteretes.' I nodded to one of the blood-marked, a solid warrior who I had never much liked. The choice was quite deliberate. I didn't want to be dealing with a friend.

'Eric, I was Ulfr's second,' protested Hrolf.

'And his failure is also yours,' I said with a scowl. Hrolf was a good man, kind and fierce, and I liked him well. The hurt and humiliation on his face hurt me, but I forced the pain away.

'We are all punished by this. Do not think that I was sent here to honour me. I was sent here because like all of you, I let my friend Ulfr destroy himself, and I must atone for it.'

There was a mixture of shock, fury and shame in the men in front of me, but I did not let my demeanour slip into any form of sympathy.

'We have lost our reputation, our honour and...' I flicked my fingers towards the flag-bearer, who was standing holding the rolled-up standard that never left his side. 'We have lost our flag and name. Harald reclaims it for his own.'

There were moans and muttering at that proclamation, and I turned towards the loudest. 'Do you wish to show you have learned nothing by complaining about our commander's order?'

The guardsman's mouth curled in anger, but he had the good sense not to speak.

I had been considering what to call the seventh during my sleepless night and had made my decision. 'We will bear a new name and banner when we earn it, and not before.'

Some of them looked away from me in disgust, as if I was dishonouring them. But we had all caused this, and we would have to share the pain.

'And what of Ulfr?' Hrolf asked.

'We will prepare him to face Harald's justice, and that he is courageous is all that we can hope for,' I said with a firm glare. 'Sober him up as best you can, and we will go to the central square.'

'Is that it? You will do nothing to save your friend? You are so close to Harald, can't you convince him?' Hrolf asked.

'My opportunity to save my friend passed unnoticed, as it clearly did for all of us. Now I must do my duty to my subordinate, and hope Harald shows him justice and mercy. Either way, we will not complain. Whatever happens has been earned, and only the weak would oppose that. Nothing I can say will change what Harald will decide, and it would shame us further to try.'

Hrolf turned away in disgust, but he and a few of the others went to get Ulfr.

The offender was brought out from the house in his tunic, looking sick and dishevelled. He stopped in front of me, his hands still bound in front of him, and gave me a look of shame and regret.

'I am sorry, Eric. I let you down. I let you all down.'

'So did we all. I should have acted before it was too late, as should your men.'

'They were afraid of me, and ashamed.'

'Cowardice is no excuse for not doing what is right.'

He shook his head slowly. 'They are not cowards.'

'Not in battle, no. But all of us who let it get to this did so because we were afraid to stop it. We all share your shame, if not your punishment.'

Ulfr swallowed and looked at me intently with his hollow eyes. 'What will Harald do to me?'

'What would *you* do?' I asked softly, and he just nodded, straightening his back. 'I will try to face it like a man, but gods I feel sick.'

'Well, do that now if you must. The whole guard is gathering for your trial. You don't want to shame yourself in front of them.'

'Anything that was in me left me during the night, I assure you. It is just the feeling that remains. My body betraying me.' He sniffed, breathing hard to try and steady himself. 'I hope it's quick. Maybe he will grant me that mercy.'

I nodded curtly, although I was not so hopeful. Harald did not seem to be in a merciful mood.

'Come on, no sense waiting. It will only anger him.'

* * *

We marched up to the main square, where the rest of the men not on guard duty were assembling in their hundreds, leaving an open space in front of the town's large church. I had ordered the seventh not to arm or armour themselves. We went in our tunics as penitents, not as warriors, dressed the same way as Ulfr as a symbol of solidarity, for what little that was worth.

We gathered at the side of the space and waited as the rest of the men of the guard assembled and Harald came out to stand in the open before the ranks.

The whole assembly fell to silence, waiting for him to speak.

'Ulfr Ospaksson, stand forwards,' Harald called out in his battlefield voice, and Ulfr took a deep breath and walked forwards with me holding one of his arms, and Sigurd the other. We stopped in the centre of the open space and faced Harald in silence.

'You are accused of being drunk while on campaign, disobeying orders, sheltering an enemy, and, most seriously, of disrespecting the emperor,' Harald shouted so that all who were there could hear him.

Ulfr was shaking slightly in my grasp, and I tightened my grip to try and steady him, praying he would not collapse or weep.

'There is no need to hear testimony. I myself witnessed the first three of these crimes, and your guilt is undoubted.' Harald stared at Ulfr. 'On the accusation of disrespecting the emperor, I believe it was a misunderstanding, and that you meant no disrespect,' Harald said, loudly and pointedly.

I had been there, and Ulfr had undoubtedly disrespected the emperor, as Harald well knew, but I understood that he wanted to quash that crime, as it would be terrible for the guard when word reached the army that a guardsman had been found guilty of it.

It did not matter either, as the other crimes were so serious as to lead to only one outcome.

'What do you say, Ulfr?'

Ulfr's chin rose. 'I admit my three crimes,' he called out, his voice almost cracking. 'But I did not intend disrespect to the emperor. I serve him in life, and if needed with my death, as is my oath.'

Harald nodded sombrely, clearly satisfied with the answer.

'Ulfr, you have disgraced yourself and all of us with your conduct in the face of the enemy. You have admitted your crimes, and the punishment must be appropriately severe.' He turned and motioned to some men behind him and they appeared from the crowd with a wooden frame, nailed and tied together from parts of a dismantled wagon. Sveinn was at their head.

The frame had three upright legs, spaced apart in a triangle, and on one canted side, a cross-piece at the height of a man's shoulders.

It was a lashing frame. Mutters and murmurs spread around the audience.

'Dear Mary have mercy,' Ulfr whispered to himself as he saw it. He had surely been expecting simply execution, as I had, but that would have been clean. Instead he might be faced with a large number of lashes first. It was not unheard of, for serious crimes, to be lashed and still then beheaded or beaten to death.

'Be strong, Ulfr,' I hissed, leaning in to put my mouth near his ear.

The two men set up the lashing frame in front of us, so that the crossbeam faced Ulfr, and two others came to get him.

'Tell my cousin some clever lie, Eric. Don't let him know what happened to me,' Ulfr said, panic in his voice. 'Don't let my family know this.'

'I promise,' I choked, as the two men of Harald's personal guard took Ulfr's arms and cut the rope that bound his wrists. They led him towards the frame.

Harald spoke again, almost shouting. 'Ulfr Ospaksson, your sentence is to receive one hundred lashes. May God have mercy on you, and see you washed clean of your sin.'

There was a ripple of shock and almost outrage in the massed ranks of guardsmen around the square, and Ulfr stumbled as he heard it, his mouth opened in horror.

'Harald, no,' I whispered, staring at him in fury.

A hundred lashes was an execution by torture, not a punishment. Six lashes was a normal punishment, sometimes as much as ten. Twenty would ruin a man for life, and anything more than that could kill. No one survived the effects of fifty. Fifty lashes would rip all the flesh from a criminal's back, down to the ribs, leaving them to die in agony over days or weeks.

But a hundred? A hundred was a performance of cruelty, designed to send a message. It would take a very long time to administer and Ulfr might linger in horrific agony even after it was over. I stared at Harald and felt true hatred for him for the first time in my life. He was going to torture our friend to death to make a point. Worst of all, he was probably doing it in part to punish me and my failings, because that had disappointed him more than Ulfr's.

Ulfr was silent and shaking as the guardsmen took off his tunic, pulled his arms to the sides and lashed them to the crosspiece, and then lashed his feet to the poles, spreading him helpless against the frame. He turned his head to look at me with terrified eyes as a grim-faced guardsman put a folded piece of thick leather between his teeth. A small token of mercy.

Then one of the four guardsmen brought out the whip, the thin, stiffened, weighted leather strip used for punishment. He stood to one side and looked at Harald. Harald stared at Ulfr, who was shivering, barebacked and vulnerable in the square with hundreds of eyes on him. He drew the moment out as I stood there in helpless anger, and then he nodded.

'One,' Sveinn called out.

The guardsman with the whip stretched out his arm and took his stance, feet apart, and brought his arm forwards in a wide arc.

The whip flicked and cracked into Ulfr's back with a noise that hurt me in my bones. Ulfr went stiff as if he had been stabbed, veins bulging, eyes and mouth clamped closed, head back as he arched his back against the intense pain, trying not to make a noise. I urged him on in my mind to stay brave, but I felt utter heartache as I knew that soon, the pain of the lashing would become unbearable, and he would cry out, and then scream, and with time he would be begging and babbling. It happened to all men who faced such a large number of lashes.

The guardsman reset himself, and Sveinn called out, 'Two.'

The guardsman leant into another blow, landing just below the first one, and Ulfr spasmed again, rocking his head back and forwards as a cut appeared all the way across his back, blood from the first one running over it and mingling together to run down his spine into the small of his back.

'Three,' Sveinn called out in his monotone, and the lash landed again, Ulfr's hands and feet wriggling against the unyielding bonds as he tried to contain the agony.

'Four.'

Ulfr was breathing like a blown horse now, spittle frothing past the leather pad clamped in his mouth, moans of pain escaping his lips.

I tore my gaze from Ulfr and looked at Harald, and found that he was staring right at me. That discovery unleashed a wave of pure anger in me.

'Five,' Sveinn called.

Ulfr's back was already a mess; five stripes, some crossing each other, were showing in the flesh. Bleeding red welts marked their passage, and in several places the cuts were deep enough that the white of the fat beneath his skin showed.

'Six.'

The lash landed again and Ulfr cried out a little for the first time, the impact driving it from him even as he leant his forehead on the frame and tried to hold it in.

'Fuck this,' I muttered, glaring at Harald.

I wasn't going to allow this. I wasn't going to witness it. I had failed Ulfr, I had seen his torment and done nothing, and I could not stand there and watch him be torn to pieces to satisfy Harald's thirst for control.

I stepped forwards and walked past Sveinn, who called out in anger.

'Get back!'

I ignored him and shoved aside the guardsman who half-heartedly tried to stop me. I reached out my hands to Ulfr's wrists, and two guardsmen, spurred into action to stop me releasing the captive, grabbed hold of me.

But I did not untie Ulfr's wrists, I just placed myself over his back, looping my fingers into the ropes that tied him.

'I will take the rest of his punishment,' I shouted, glaring over Ulfr's shoulder at Harald, visible between the legs of the top part of the frame. Harald frowned, but he did not move.

The men who had grabbed me stopped pulling at me, confused by what to do.

Ulfr spat the leather pad out weakly, breathing hard, wincing as my chest pressed into his wounds. 'What the fuck are you doing?' he panted.

'I don't know,' I said. 'Maybe he'll stop this.'

'He won't,' Ulfr said, shaking his head slightly. 'Are you mad?'

'Yes,' I said, and Ulfr actually laughed a little, before groaning at the pain it caused.

Sveinn stepped forwards. 'Eric, stand back.'

'No.'

'Stand back or my men will remove you.'

'You can't give me orders, Komes. Only Harald can,' I said. 'I insist on taking the rest of the punishment.'

Sveinn sighed but stood back uncertainly, looking at Harald.

I stared at my prince too, challenging him with my eyes, daring him to stand there and watch me be torn to pieces, to betray his brother's last wishes.

Oh, how little I knew Harald, even then. In what madness did I think he would change his course just because I made a scene? It is ridiculous to me now, to think that, and as I watched Harald's face through that frame I realised the depth of my mistake. He wasn't going to stop, he wasn't even going to consider it.

Sveinn leant in again. 'Eric, step back. You've made your point. This will kill you.'

I was horrified, staring at Harald in disbelief. I could not believe he would let it continue. I had not actually expected to be lashed to death when I stepped forwards or, honestly, I would not have moved. No one voluntarily allows that. I was suddenly, desperately hoping he would change his mind.

'I'll allow it,' Harald's voice called out. 'He can take as many as he chooses, and when he gives up or falls, then finish the sentence on the prisoner.'

My muscles relaxed in shock. What?

Sveinn grumbled in my ear. 'Eric, this is a death sentence.'

I was too far gone to back down now. I had cornered myself. I just laughed manically. 'It's not the first time he has sentenced me to die,' I said.

'Last chance, Eric. I'm going to continue,' Sveinn said.

'Do your duty, Komes,' I grated, panic rising. 'I'm going to do mine.'

'Get off me, you idiot,' Ulfr huffed. 'You are just making this worse.'

'I'm sorry, Ulfr, I always seem to.'

'Seven!' shouted Sveinn, and I clamped my teeth together, my whole body tensing for the impact.

I cannot describe the lash; you cannot understand it until you have felt it. An impact like a hammer-blow, but along a trail of white-hot fire that only got worse after the initial shock was gone. The bones in my spine ground together as all my muscles tensed more tightly than I could ever make them myself, and I felt something click and pop. My fingers strained at the ropes to hold myself in place. I knew I would not be able to hold myself there for long, but I stared at Harald with white-hot hatred and my stubbornness did not allow me to let go.

'Eight.'

The lash landed again, indescribable agony layering on top of the first one. My teeth ground together and I bit my cheek and tasted blood even as I felt more of it running down my back.

'Eric! Get the fuck off me, we don't both need to die,' moaned Ulfr, who was suffering almost as much as me from the way I was grinding into his back. I backed up a little, removing my chest from his back, just grasping tightly with my hands.

'I'm sorry, Ulfr,' was all I could mutter.

'Nine!'

My left knee buckled as that one landed, the impact numbing my whole leg and sending lightning up and down my spine in furious waves of agony.

I cried out in pain – I couldn't stop myself – but with all the willpower I possessed I dragged myself upright again, slowly but surely, and repositioned myself, glaring at Harald through the frame.

I prepared myself in terror for the next lash as there was a commotion behind me, and then hands took my right wrist.

'Fuck off, Sveinn! Get on with it, you bastard!' I snarled, turning my head to look.

But Sveinn was not there – it was Hrolf, and he smiled at me softly and nodded his head. 'My turn, Eric.'

'What?' I asked groggily.

'I am guilty too. I was his second. You've done enough.'

I saw, dumbly, that he was stripped to the waist, and he gently prised my fingers out of the lashings and firmly pushed me aside, replacing me, putting his body over the spreadeagled form of Ulfr.

I staggered gratefully to the side, not really understanding what was happening, and Sveinn looked to Harald for advice. Harald just nodded.

'Ten!' Sveinn called, and the lash landed on Hrolf, who tensed and growled angrily, but left his back proffered for the next strike. Now I didn't know what to do. My back was on fire, lines of agony etched in my skin that burned and refused to fade. I realised I did not have the courage to go back to the frame and face it again now that I was free, but nor could I leave Hrolf there alone with Ulfr.

'Eleven.'

Hrolf grunted again as the blow landed, and from the corner of my eye I saw a flash of movement, a flash that became a wave, as the men of the seventh started stripping their tunics and walking forwards, first just Sigurd and a pair of his comrades, and then whole groups and finally the entire mass.

'Twelve,' called Sveinn uncertainly, eyeing the advancing men with obvious nervousness.

But Sigurd did not try and stop him, did not display any threat – he simply went to Hrolf's side and whispered in his ear. The panting warrior just nodded gratefully, and stepped aside, letting Sigurd take his place.

And the men of the seventh formed a line beside him.

The bastards queued in perfect ranks, backs bare in the morning sun, to take the place of their comrades, one after the other. Not a single man remained behind.

I watched in a daze as they stepped forwards, again and again, placing their bodies over Ulfr's to take his blows while the Icelander wept freely on the frame.

One by one they took their lashes and moved over to stand behind me in wincing, panting, bleeding ranks.

Time dragged on as the punishment continued, until finally Sveinn called out, 'One hundred.' The tired guardsmen taking turns with the lash looked relieved. The man who had taken the last lash stepped gratefully away while Ulfr was untied and led over to us, his eyes red and his face twisted with pain and shame.

'Thank you, brothers,' he said, barely holding it together. And I pulled him into a painful embrace.

Alexios, the bright young swordsman, had been the next in line to take the lashes, and he looked at Sveinn in indignation.

'It is done,' Sveinn said, waving the waiting men away.

'Horseshit is it done, Komes. I want my turn! I'm as guilty as any of my brothers.'

Sveinn's brows knotted. 'The punishment the commander assigned is over. You will obey.'

'I'll not be called a coward for letting my brothers take it while I didn't!' Alexios complained, and he stepped forwards, placing himself against the frame.

Sveinn looked lost, and he spread his arms at Harald questioningly.

'It's done,' Harald boomed across the square.

Sveinn looked completely exasperated as he shoved Alexios away. 'Madmen.'

'That we are,' said Alexios with a small grin, and he walked over to join us with an apologetic shrug as the rest of the bandon gathered around, clasping arms and gingerly thumping shoulders as they congratulated and commiserated each other. They didn't have the look of punished men, but of victors of a hard battle, as their blood dripped into the dusty ground.

I felt an intense surge of pride for them and I looked over at Harald's emotionless face.

I had beaten him. I had turned his merciless punishment into a badge of honour, and he wasn't even looking at me any more. The pain from my back subsided into the background as the glow of pleasure from it spread through me.

14

We walked back to our chosen part of the town in a painful but happy gaggle. Ulfr had had the worst of it, and he went to lie down and have his wounds tended while the rest of us who had been lashed washed around a well, taking turns to carefully clean the nasty cuts the whips had left.

When I was done, I stood on a low wall. 'Listen to me carefully,' I called out, and the seventh all turned to look at me.

'I'm proud of you,' I said with a smile. 'We showed today that duty is important, but that our bonds to each other matter also. Neither can be abandoned.'

'Aye,' Sigurd said, nodding vigorously. And many of them sounded their agreement.

'But be careful,' I cautioned them with a raised hand. 'Whatever we may feel, this cannot be an act of disobedience. We are not going to break the discipline of the guard. We were given fair punishment, and we deserved it. Do not use this as an excuse for disobedience or arrogance, for the next time one of us defies Harald's orders, they will take their lashes alone. Understood?'

They all nodded and called out their assent, reluctant though it seemed to some.

'Good. Now get ready to leave, and keep those wounds clean. It will not go well for anyone who falls sick on the march.'

I stepped down and went to pick up my ruined tunic, looking at it thoughtfully. The back had three broad bloodstained stripes across it where the lash had cut through it. It looked like the claw mark of some giant beast. I had an idea that brought a smile to my face.

I looked up and found Sigurd, waving him over. I held up the tunic for him to see. He looked confused at the bloody garment and my grin. 'What?'

'I have found our new banner, Sigurd.'

Sigurd raised an eyebrow and then looked at the tunic appraisingly. He nodded slowly and gave me an appreciative look. 'It's good, it has meaning.'

'Get someone to find a square of cloth and paint it properly. There must be something in this town we can use.'

'Aye, Komes,' Sigurd said, and then he handed the tunic back to me, not letting go for a moment as I took hold, looking at me carefully. 'It was a mad thing, what you did. It shouldn't have worked.'

I grinned. 'It didn't work, Sigurd. I was hoping Harald would back down.'

Sigurd's brows creased. 'Why would you think that? That was never going to happen.'

'No, I see that now. But thank you, you all saved me from my stupidity.'

'Well, we were happy to do so, after you saved Ulfr from his.' He leaned in. 'Just don't make a habit of it, yes?'

'I don't intend to, Sigurd, I swear to you.'

The big man smiled and patted me on the shoulder, eliciting a shiver of pain that ran through my back. 'Good. Welcome to the Blood Claws, Eric.'

I met his eye. 'The Blood Claws?'

Sigurd nodded seriously. 'You chose the banner, I chose the name. We will lead them together.'

I stared into his eyes, trying to decide if he was testing me or provoking me, and deciding it was simply a gesture of respect I took his free arm in mine.

'The Blood Claws. It is a strong name, Topoteretes.'

'It has to be, it is a strong bandon.'

I thumped him on the shoulder. 'Good. Now let's get them ready to go.'

***

When we were ready I sent Sigurd off with the bandon to join the others gathering outside the city walls. They did their best to hide it, but marching in tunics and maille with the fresh wounds was murder. I know, because I was doing it too.

I took Alexios with me to the meeting Harald had called. I had chosen him as the seventh's standard bearer, a position he had been thrilled to accept.

I was nervous about seeing Harald, but excited to face him in victory. My anger had subsided a little but still caused heat to run through my veins whenever I thought about what had happened.

When I gathered together with the other komes and senior officers, Harald annoyed me by simply ignoring me. I thought perhaps his pride was too badly hurt to acknowledge my presence beyond scanning the group of us.

'Good. Listen in. Petros and his scouts say the enemy is coming, they will arrive by this evening. So we must be long gone, and the town burned behind us. We will march north-west to cut across the mountains. There is a pass up there leading into the inland areas.'

He beckoned to his new standard bearer, a notably tall veteran called Sveneld who had been in the guard since before we arrived. Harald had chosen him wisely, I begrudgingly acknowledged. He was well-respected and knowledgeable, and would be a useful assistant to Sveinn, who was now Harald's official second in command.

Sveneld came over with a large, wrapped banner on a pole far taller than a man. 'It is time the guard marched under our own banner, alongside the emperor's, especially when we are separated from him,' Harald said, and, taking the banner, unrolled it with a flourish, showing it to the group.

I stiffened. It was a newly painted, larger version of the seventh's old banner, the black raven on a red background. A banner I had once carried for him.

'Apparently the people here recognise this banner, know who we are from it and thus what it means.' He grinned at us wolfishly. 'They call it Land-Waster. I like the name. I have taken it from them as we take everything else. This is now the banner we will march under through these lands, and everywhere it is seen they will know what it means and fear us. Before long, I expect they will flee or throw themselves at our feet at the mere rumour of it. Then we will know we have succeeded.'

He handed the banner back to Sveneld, who carefully wrapped it again.

'Petros's messengers back from the army tell us they are preparing to besiege Vodena, and expect it to fall quickly. But before they take it and open the road inland we will be alone and cut off, so be ready. Take all the food we can from this town, and do not let your men weigh themselves down with loot.'

'This is a wealthy town, it will be hard to persuade the men to abandon its riches,' Rurik said.

'I don't care. After today's events, if they disobey an order it should be clear there will be no mercy. All punishments in future will be given to the accused men alone.' His eyes finally flicked up to mine. 'No more leaning on my generous nature for reprieve.'

There was a dry laugh from the men assembled, since they all knew that was not the truth of it, but no one argued further.

'Good. You all have your orders. I want to leave before the sun passes over the church tower. Go.' The meeting broke up quickly, but Harald pointed at me. 'You stay a moment, Komes.'

I went to stand in front of him, rigid and defiant.

'Are your men fit to fight and march after their little display this morning?' He asked calmly.

'Of course, Protospatharios. I am sorry if their actions upset you. If you feel the need to punish anyone further, it should be me, not them.'

Harald looked at me questioningly. 'Eric, why do you think I would punish you for what you did?' He smiled and put a hand gently on my shoulder. 'It was the first real leadership I've seen from you in years.'

I straightened a little at the praise, and the warmth with which it was given. Damn him, my anger washed away like sand in a flood, and I felt the keen desire for his praise, to be loved and respected by him. Ahhh, how he induced that in men was a wonder.

'I thought you would be angry that your punishment was ruined?'

'It was not ruined. You and your men set an example the entire guard will aspire to follow. You saved a comrade, you accepted responsibility, you showed unity and a spirit that could not be broken.'

I looked at him, trying to see if he was lying to salvage pride, but I saw nothing like that in his face. 'But you would have let Ulfr die.'

'Yes, he deserved it.'

'And... would you have let me die?' I asked, my eyes begging him to say no, that he would have stopped it.

'If you were brave enough to stand there for long enough for it to kill you? Yes,' he said without shame or concern. 'I let you make your own choice, Eric, and I let the men see it too. Besides, the outcome was better than I could have hoped for.' He winked at me. 'But I still need to pretend I am angry for the others. Can't have them thinking they can change my mind or question my orders now, can I?'

I nodded gratefully, racked with emotion. I had come expecting a furious commander, and been welcomed joyfully by an old friend. He cared about me, you see. He almost never showed it, but he did, even when he was sentencing me to death. That was Harald.

'I understand.'

'Good. Go and be with your men, Komes, and don't ruin that healthy streak of resentment they have for me. As long as they respect me and follow my orders, a little anger and a desire to prove themselves can be a good thing.'

'You're a bastard, Harald,' I said, but I hung my head and laughed.

Harald chuckled. 'I know, and you're a good man. But all true leaders are bastards. It's just part of what we have to do.'

15

We left the town burning behind us. We set fire to the olive groves as best we could, although they are very resistant to being fired and we had learned that the result was not worth the effort. It was not yet harvest time, and we burned the town's fields with their standing crops. The barns and fodder stores we lit, and all the livestock were killed too.

Even if people returned to that valley, it would be impossible to live there for several years without outside help.

That is what we did everywhere. Our scouts reported the enemy force were desperately chasing us, but they did not have our speed, nor our food supply, and we left them behind us to futilely march in anger and parching heat.

I don't need to describe the next weeks, for everything was the same. We went through those hills under our red and black raven banner and we laid waste to the land and the people in it with ruthless efficiency. Fortunately, for men like Ulfr at least, the locals became so scared of the threat of us that when we arrived at towns we usually found the locals had already fled at the mere rumour of our arrival, taking whatever they could carry, leaving the rest for us to burn. The entire region depopulated as they fled from the very rumour of our coming.

We got news from the army that Vodena had fallen, and they were marching north into the interior plain of Macedonia, with Skopje their next target, two weeks' march away.

'That is where we are going too,' said Harald at a gathering of the banda leaders one night. We were south-east of Skopje, in the range of hills on the edge of the broad Macedonian plain. 'We are done with these hills. It is time to go down into the plain and to Skopje. We could be there in five days, even taking our time.'

'We are not headed to join the army?' Rurik asked.

That caused some consternation among the officers. Skopje was fifty miles to the north-west, through untouched rebel lands. And this was not the fringes of captured Greek settlements like those that we had been passing – Skopje was inside the old Bulgarian empire, the heartlands of the rebellion.

Harald looked at our discomfort with something approaching amusement. 'I feel your disagreement, but I do not hear it spoken. Why?'

'We will be far from support, Protospatharios,' Sveinn said. 'We could meet the army on the road, three days' march west, instead of going alone into the rebel heartland.'

'Yes we will be alone, but also where the enemy does not expect us to be. As we have done so far, we will outmarch anyone we cannot fight.'

'That will not be so easy down in the plains – if they have a significant force of horsemen.' Sveinn looked nervous, which was very unusual for him.

'Any significant force of horsemen will be called to their army to face the emperor, not spent chasing after a raiding force that, regardless, is not where they expect it to be. No, it is a small risk.' He smiled. 'I have been chased by horsemen before and survived.'

I knew what he meant, as did some of the others. We had once defeated a warband of the Pecheneg that had hunted us across the flatlands of the southern Kyivan Rus. Although, he failed to mention, it had cost us hundreds of men.

'Then what is the point of this, of taking this risk to arrive at Skopje first?' Rurik asked.

Harald swung his bright gaze onto the confused Varangian officer. 'Because I'm going to force them to surrender, and men will know that it was me and not those arrogant generals who did it.'

We looked at each other in surprise. This had not been the plan, not been our orders, but no one was going to argue with him. We might as well have demanded that rain cease to fall.

* * *

We marched out into the Macedonian plain the next day. It is a broad area of good farmland and rich towns, surrounded on all sides by mountains and hills in the distance. We kept near to its edges, so that if forced to, we could flee into the highlands. It was the one concession Harald made to Sveinn's concerns about being cornered by a large enemy force.

But we did not see one. Our scouts rode freely across the plain and reported nothing but fat towns and villages, and a total state of panic at our coming. Many tried to flee, but far from all were able to, and once again we slaughtered and burned our away across the plain, which was far richer and more populated than the hills we had.

We drove a wave of survivors in front of us, herding them like sheep towards Skopje, a deliberate ploy by Harald, who wanted the city overwhelmed with the terrified survivors of our depredations.

No one who has gone on campaign is a stranger to the terrible deeds that happen when the town of a hated foe is captured, or how you feel about them after a battle where many of your own have died. But these people had barely killed a dozen of us, and those in desperate defence. We pitied them far more than we hated them.

Nor do I think Harald hated them, despite his ruthless pursuit of their destruction. In fact, what was most chilling to me is that I knew with certainty that he did not hate them at all. Those people were nothing to him, in the most absolute way. The trail we left of tens of thousands of dead was merely a path towards his ambitions that he required them to pave with their bodies. God, what a terrible foe he was for any man.

We burned everything. We cut a swath through the plain at twenty miles a day, and because no real force tried to stop us, we spread out and burned three times as much as we could have managed in the confines of the mountains. A dozen great towns were reduced to ashes, and three times as many villages, in less than a week.

We found from prisoners we took that the reason no one opposed us was, indeed, that the fighting men had been called west, to prepare to face the imperial army.

We finally crossed the low range of hills that separated the Macedonian plain from the broad valley where Skopje nestled and Harald ordered us to spread out all along the ridgelines that evening and set everything we could find aflame, from villages down to shepherd's huts and piles of brushwood.

It was a brilliant ploy. That night, as darkness fell, we looked down on the twinkling lights of Skopje's watchfires, and they looked up at a vision of hell to their south-east, as the entire range of hills overlooking the city was wreathed in flame, spitting streams and columns of smoke that covered the horizon and reached up into the heavens themselves.

They did not know that half of those fires were just brush burning, set purely to make a scene. The city was stuffed with refugees telling of the horrors that were coming from the south, of massacres and towns reduced to ashes, and weeping, mourning one-armed men who had met the ruthless leader who led the oncoming host, the man who stood under the red and black raven flag: the Land-Waster.

In the morning we could see Skopje clearly at last as we gathered together and marched down out of the smoke-wreathed hills. It was a fine city, with good, high walls and a river that ran beside it along its southern side. At one corner of the walled city, a great fortress stood on the north bank of the river, new and gleaming in the sun, Byzantine-built only a few years ago and it was strong and well-sited.

It would clearly be a difficult city to besiege, even for the siege-masters of the empire.

Harald sent the scouts away to the north-east, circling around Skopje, and then we marched down towards the city all through the morning and stayed on the southern bank of the river, opposite the city. It was into the late afternoon before we arrived at the single stone bridge that spanned the river, and Harald drew us up near its end and went forwards with the large imperial standard to plant it in the ground near the crossing.

And then we waited.

It was not long before the gate of the city across the river opened, and a small party of horsemen came out, tentatively riding across the bridge to halt before they reached the end, uncertain if it was safe to leave its protection.

But Harald stood there by the imperial standard, immobile, and finally the enemy group summoned the courage to come and meet us.

There were perhaps twenty of them, about half were armed and armoured, and the others mostly richly dressed older men.

Most of them dismounted, including all the unarmed ones, and then a few of the richly dressed ones came over to Harald, who was regarding them blankly, giving nothing away.

Our opponents stopped a couple of paces away, unnerved by everything, and surely by Harald's impassiveness and the fact he had not spoken. There were imperial protocols for conducting negotiations, and we were not following any of them. We had no herald, no assembly of generals or officers. It was just Harald standing under the banner with his hands at his waist, and all of us arrayed behind him.

'Who are you?' one of them finally asked in an indignant tone. 'Who commands your army?'

Harald tilted his head slightly to look at the one who spoke, like a hawk might spy a rabbit, and then strode forwards, walking straight past the man, who flinched in surprise and shrank to the side, before walking over to inspect the horses they had ridden across on. He patted one's flank, a fine white stallion, and inspected its tack. Then took the reins from a man who just stared at him, open-mouthed.

'I thank you for your gifts. I have marched hundreds of miles, and my feet are sore. It makes me look more favourably on your offer of surrender,' he said, without even looking at the man who had spoken.

The rebel leader stuttered, completely unmoored. 'What? These are not gifts. Surrendering?' He nervously looked at our ranks again. 'You think we came here to surrender to you, with what, only a thousand men? You cannot take our city with this!'

Harald did not turn, just continued stroking the white stallion's flank. 'Only a thousand men here. Do not fool yourself into thinking I would show you my whole force. And do you see the banner I was standing under? Do you know what it is?'

The man glanced up. 'Yes,' he snapped. 'It is the banner of our former overlords, ones we are now free of.'

Harald shook his head slightly, still smiling at the beautiful horse and running his hand along its nose. 'That is the standard of your emperor, your lawful ruler. There will be no siege. You have seen how few men I have and yet you still came out to talk. That means your garrison has been stripped half bare to be sent to your usurper, the man who calls himself emperor of the Bulgarians. If you had enough men, you would have marched them out here to destroy me, or ignored me.'

Harald turned, still gently holding the reins of the stallion, looking at the man for the first time. 'But instead you came out to treat with me, and confirmed to me your weakness.'

The man looked stunned, and two of the others near him remonstrated with him furiously. Clearly they had not thought going out to meet us was a good idea. He argued with them briefly in their odd tongue and then he turned to Harald with a furious expression.

'What do you want, then?'

Harald nodded, his smile fading. 'Finally, the correct question. You have until tomorrow morning to raise the imperial standard over your citadel. If you do not, we will take this city and I will raise my raven banner over its ashes.'

'Immediate surrender? To you and this paltry band of mercenary dogs?' the first man spat, seething with outrage. 'Are you insane? Why would we do that? We know who you are, barbarian. We know what you have been doing!'

Harald let go of the horse and stalked forwards, staring at the smaller, unarmed man. 'You have heard who I am, and what I do, but you think it wise to defy me?'

'This is not some defenceless village, you scum. We will hang your corpse from our walls!'

Harald stopped, and his mouth turned down into a little frown of anger. He stared at the first man, whose fellows, aghast, separated themselves slightly from him as Harald stood there with his hands on his waist, regarding the man in darkening silence.

Then Harald's blade flashed from his scabbard and through the enemy leader's throat before anyone had time to react. There were gasps of horror from the rest of the delegation, who tried to back away, but Harald was between them and their guards, so they only backed towards our ranks.

'This is a negotiation! You cannot do violence!' one of them shouted in anger, and the guards readied their weapons behind Harald, staring wide eyed as a thousand Varangians raised their own in response.

'Hold!' roared Harald, raising his hand into the air. And everyone did, even the enemy guards.

He slowly lowered his hand, and walked unhurriedly towards the delegation, stepping over the body of the man who had threatened him. 'I did not offer you a negotiation. You are not in a position to negotiate as I do not recognise your authority nor your status. I did not call you to talks. I offered you no terms of safety and no promises of any kind,' he said with a sneer. 'I merely stood here, a servant of the emperor in the empire's rightful lands, and this fool decided to approach and threaten me.'

He paused, raising his eyebrows as he looked over the huddled group. 'Now, if any of you wish to live, tell those men behind me to put their weapons away before my guardsmen decide they are a threat.'

The second man stared fixedly at Harald, breathing hard, but then nodded and looked over Harald's shoulder at the dozen or so mounted guards. 'Put your weapons away,' he said in a remarkably calm voice, and the horrendously outnumbered guards were only too happy to comply.

The second man looked at Harald. 'I am—'

'I do not care who you are, I do not care for your name. I care only for your compliance,' Harald rumbled.

The man stopped and took a deep breath, then shrugged helplessly. 'You cannot seriously expect us to surrender the city to you and your men.'

'I insist that you do. I am the emperor's legal authority here. You will either surrender, or...' Harald paused and pointed towards our ranks. 'I will consider you enemies of the emperor and raise that banner.'

The delegation looked, and I did too, seeing Harald's new standard bearer stepping forwards with the rolled raven banner. He held it across his body on its staff. The bright blood red of the banner was clear, as was the black edges of a raven's wing.

The man visibly paled.

'You will raise the imperial banner over your city, or I will raise that one over its ashes. I will kill every living thing, your families will be slaughtered in front of you, I will cut your limbs off and pile you like cordwood to burn while you are still alive.'

Harald let the corners of his mouth rise in his nasty, predatory smile. 'It doesn't matter when, it doesn't matter if I have to wait for the emperor's army to crack open your walls. When that banner enters the city, you and your people will face its justice, and it has no mercy. So ask yourselves very carefully. Do you really trust your walls and your false emperor so well as to risk that?'

The man's mouth hung open, and I saw the fear, true fear, flood through him.

I smiled. I admit it. Harald was a master, and this poor man was helpless.

The man looked aghast and started to speak. 'We can—'

'Silence!' Harald thundered, and the man stammered to a halt. 'You forget, again, that this is not a negotiation, you are not adversaries or equals. I have delivered the terms of your judgement. You will comply, or you will not. The emperor's decrees are not subject to your opinion. If you comply I will not even enter the city, I will simply leave. If the rebels return you will close your gates against them and treat them as the enemy that they are.'

Harald nodded slowly to himself. 'I will leave men to watch you. If you refuse my commands in any way, if you lower that banner again for even one moment, the last thing you will see through the flames that consume you will be my face, and the ashes of this city will lie for the rest of time as an example to those who would defy their duty and their emperor. Go, now, and make your decision. Anyone who speaks another word will be cut down,' he added with a snarl before turning to collect his new horse and walking it back to our foreboding ranks.

The rebel delegation gathered together, looking at us in fear and anger, before they set off across the bridge in an undignified gaggle.

'I don't understand why you didn't force their compliance now. How are you so certain they will comply and not resist, or merely flee?' I said to Harald.

He smiled, looking past the city at the hills beyond. 'They won't flee. When the darkness comes, they will realise they cannot.'

I furrowed my brows but did not dare question him further. I followed his gaze up to the hills beyond the city, but saw nothing that helped me understand.

'We will make camp here!' Harald called, and Sveinn started allocating duties.

16

We made a hastily fortified camp near the end of the bridge and put a strong guard on it overnight, but the enemy garrison did not dare try and attack us during the darkness.

Harald's ruse was soon visible, all along the hills behind the city. As evening fell fires sprang up there, all along the northern flank, an arc of flames in the evening sunlight that burned brightly deep into the night, cutting off the city from the lands beyond.

I worked out, of course, that it was just Petros and his two dozen scouts, riding along the hills and setting fires as fast as they could. But the people in the city could not know that. They would only see the fires and realise that they were surrounded by the men who marched under the raven banner, and know the fires were coming for them unless they surrendered in the morning.

I went to bed with a smile on my face once more, because I trusted that Harald was right.

* * *

When morning came Harald assembled us again at the end of the bridge and we watched the first light of the sun hit the hills behind the city, glowing in the drifting smoke still rising all along the horizon, and saw the gates standing there, closed and resolute. Just as I was starting to think the enemy had somehow summoned the courage to resist, the blazing gold of the imperial banner was hauled up on a crossbar at the top of the highest tower in the citadel, and our men cheered at the sight of it.

Harald just stood there smiling as an entire city capitulated to the power of his will without a drop of blood being shed.

* * *

We set off immediately back towards the army, heading south to meet them on the road. It was two days before we reached their vanguard, and Andronikos himself rode out to see us when Harald sent a message with what had happened.

'What nonsense are you trying to claim?' he asked Harald from atop his horse.

'The rebels have surrendered the city to us.'

'How? When?'

'Two days ago.'

'What? Your orders were to raze the lands around and then meet us here when we besieged the city.'

Harald shrugged nonchalantly. 'I miscalculated the distances perhaps, and arrived there in advance. The city agreed to surrender and their garrison is now holding the city for the emperor.'

Andronikos bristled but controlled himself; there were a lot of men watching, and he could not afford to look petty, despite Harald standing there in front of him, smugly claiming the prize that the general had expected to take himself.

'Well, I see. I commend you for your actions. I will send word to the emperor,' he finally said.

'I will come with you, to make sure everything is reported correctly,' Harald said with a smile, mounting his white stallion with a friendly grin on his face.

Harald followed as Andronikos wheeled his horse and rode away with his guard, leaving us standing there with the banda.

***

It was not long before Harald rode back and dismounted by our anxious gaggle of officers.

'What are the orders, Protospatharios?' Sveinn asked nervously.

'The army is turning around. We are heading west to engage the rebel forces directly. They were expecting us to besiege the city, and we could not have gone after them without securing it to our rear, they would merely have retreated. Now, though, they will be forced to try and defeat us, knowing that their cities will capitulate without even putting up a fight.'

Harald smiled, horrifyingly pleased with himself. 'Come on, let's go and catch up with the rest of the guard. We will be making camp soon.'

***

We made camp for the night not long afterwards, reuniting with the rest of the guard. Styrbjorn came over to us with a broad, joyful smile on his face. 'You glorious bastard,' he said, giving Harald a vicious embrace.

Harald was less enthusiastic, giving the big man a look of rebuke for his behaviour in public that Styrbjorn saw and completely ignored.

'How was the campaign with the army? Any problems?' Harald asked.

'Boring as an empty whorehouse,' Styrbjorn spat. 'None of us even got to fight, not once. You even stole our fight at Skopje! I was looking forward to a good sacking.'

'I was hoping for a more complete report than that, Komes,' Harald said drily.

Styrbjorn gave him a wink. 'You picked the wrong man to leave in charge then, Commander.'

'No threats to the emperor, no trouble?'

'Nothing.'

'Well, that is good at least,' Sveinn said, regarding Styrbjorn coldly. They were about as different as two Varangian officers could be, Styrbjorn and Sveinn. Styrbjorn was all power of presence and brooding violence, who was cowed by nothing and gave his respect only grudgingly. Sveinn, on the other hand, was cold and calculating, ruthless and meticulous in his duties. I wondered why Harald valued and trusted them in particular so much, but perhaps it was because if you put both of them together, you would get something approximating Harald himself. He had Styrbjorn's wild fearlessness, but tempered with Sveinn's calm courage. He had the passion and fire of one, the dominating personality, but refined and projected in a far more precise and careful manner like the other.

I realised that they suited him far better than I. I did almost nothing but worry and tell Harald not to do the things he was considering. I was not decisive, I was not a particularly good battle leader although I was, as I may have mentioned once or twice, perhaps the greatest swordsman in the guard. Nor was I very popular or well-liked, even if my record in battle was respected.

I think, as I stood there watching Harald listen to Sveinn as he dragged a more detailed report out of Styrbjorn, that I feared I had nothing left to offer Harald. He had not removed me from his side because I had failed him, but because I had reached the limit of my usefulness to him. He needed something I could not give him, more than just loyalty. He needed a true second in command, a position he had never actually granted me, although many had treated me as such. I was never really fit to be his second, his replacement if he fell. How could I be? How could I stand in the footprints of Hardrada and hope to do even a measure of what he did? No, that was not my true purpose, and we had all been flattering me with the pretence of it for all those years.

With that sad realisation a brooding weight of expectation was lifted from me, and I was somehow freed and lightened by it. I was not downcast, I just felt that I finally understood who I was. I was a loyal follower and there was nothing dishonourable or wrong with that, but I was not a leader of men, not like any of those three. I turned away unseen to go about my duties getting my bandon's section of the camp ready for nightfall, and behind me, the true leaders of the guard continued their discussions.

*   *   *

'The emperor has given his orders. The army will march again west,' Harald said, rolling out a parchment map of the area that the scouts had prepared.

'The enemy is hurrying to gather their army fifty miles to the west, near a lake. Their preparations will not be complete. We assume they expected to have many months to wear us down before facing us in the field. Significant enemy forces have come down from the Bulgarian rebel heartlands to the north and east and moved to join the false emperor, Delyan. More are still coming.' His finger swept around the map as he spoke.

'We will move west to strike this gathering army before they are too numerous for us to have the advantage.' He looked at us with grim satisfaction. 'One way or another, I believe this will all be resolved within a week.'

'You don't sound too excited by that prospect, Protospatharios,' I said, looking at him curiously.

Harald nodded slowly. 'The enemy forces that are gathering are larger than expected, so the stratopedarches' scouts report.' He smiled mirthlessly. 'Apparently, our campaign has inspired a great thirst for revenge, and their forces swelled dramatically.'

I felt my stomach sink. 'How many?'

'They are already at least equal to our numbers,' Harald said quietly.

There was a collective intake of breath. Our army was vast. Meeting another force that size so soon showed the rebellion had more support than expected. Perhaps, I thought for the first time, insurmountable support. No wonder we had faced no threats on the plains in our campaign of destruction. The rebels must have stripped every fighting man for a hundred miles in every direction.

'So, gather your men, prepare your equipment. We will be marching immediately.'

The meeting broke up and Harald gestured to me. I nodded and went over. 'Protospatharios,' I said.

He gave me an irritated look. 'Stop doing that. Since when have you stopped using my name?'

I shrugged. 'It seemed appropriate for my position.'

'Stop sulking, Eric, it does not become you,' he said with a small shake of his head. 'Now, I need you and the seventh to come with me and replace the fourteenth as the emperor's personal guard. Styrbjorn insists it is his turn to join the vanguard, and I cannot hear his complaints any longer. It will give your men a rest from the worst of the campaign.'

I looked at him and nodded, seeing this as the peace offering it was intended to be. Our men would be spared the rampaging progress of the vanguard, and men like Ulfr would see a little peace and easy duties.

'As you command, Harald,' I said, with a little nod.

'Be happier, Eric. This is a position of immense honour. You will be the personal guardian of the emperor.'

I smiled. 'I've done too much of that sort of duty to think of it as a boon, Harald.'

He laughed. 'Well, if it helps, I don't care what you think about it. Come, let's go and meet with the other guard commanders to plan the march.'

* * *

The army set off quickly, by imperial standards, anyway. Styrbjorn took five banda with the vanguard along with a large formation of cavalry, clearing the road for the army while scouts ranged out ahead looking for threats and selecting campsites.

I marched with the seventh arrayed in a box formation around the emperor's large, covered wagon, with the tenth in a block behind us and the twelfth in front, near the head of the main body of the army to reduce the dust stirred up in the emperor's way. Banda of the Scholai cavalry ranged in the fields either side of us, and at the head and tail of our little column. The emperor was constantly surrounded by a ring of flesh and steel no less than four men thick, and that was not including the entire army strung out behind us on the road. He was, perhaps, the safest man in Christendom.

We marched for four days westwards, rejoining the Egnatia road that lead like an arrow towards Dyrrhachium.

Finally word came back about the main enemy army being sighted, marching towards us along the road near the lake ahead of us. I was with the emperor as the messengers talked in hasty tones to the generals who rode ahead of his wagon, and then when Harald appeared.

The two senior generals and Harald came hurrying over to the emperor's carriage. He motioned to me, and I moved the emperor's concealing curtain aside and bowed.

'Basileus,' Nikephoros said, bowing and looking at the emperor, who rose from his padded seat a little to look at his generals.

'What is your report, Domestikos?'

'We have found the enemy army, Basileus.'

Michael looked relieved. 'Good. When shall we meet them?'

'If we continue like this, in a day's time, just past the lake that we are approaching on the south side of the road.' He pointed at the lake, the corner of which could just be seen glittering in the near distance.

'Will they give battle?'

'It appears that they intend to,' Nikephoros confirmed.

Michael nodded. 'Good. Then continue.' He lay back on his cushions and waved at me to close the curtain again.

* * *

So we continued the march, camping just before the lake, and setting off again in the morning. We marched all day into the afternoon, until our vanguard caught sight of the enemy's leading forces near the town of Ostrovo which sat on the shore of the lake.

The army had been marching hard. The emperor rode his horse that day so that the army could see him. It pained him terribly, we could all see that, and at each halt he moaned in agony as we helped him dismount, and his legs were swollen and discoloured. It made the few of us close enough to see it feel horrified at the suffering he was going through, and the risk of his weakness becoming widely known.

But every time we moved again, that poor man got back atop his horse, white with the pain and exertion of it, and I gained respect for him that I had never had before.

Generals Andronikos and Nikephoros came to consult with the emperor. Harald rode back on his fabulous new horse; he had ridden off with a few men to scout the flank of the march although he did not say why.

The generals looked at each other nervously. 'The enemy are greater in number than we expected.'

Michael's smile faded. 'How large is their army?'

'Perhaps twenty thousand men more than us, we think.'

'So what do we do?'

'We retreat immediately. We cannot advance into this danger any further.

If we turn around now, perhaps we can get back to Vodena in time, and send for more forces,' the domestikos said with an embarrassed tone.

'We will not make it to Vodena in time if the enemy chooses to attack. We must stand and face them,' Harald said.

'You have done enough harm, Varangian. Be silent,' Nikephoros said. 'I warned you we should have followed the well-established strategy of the army, but you insisted on a rash course of action that has riled the enemy up beyond reason, and rushed us ill-prepared into a trap.'

'We all agreed to it,' Andronikos said with a sigh.

The domestikos looked at him bitterly. The old man's fear and shame were writ clearly on his face. 'More fool me for being so deceived.' He turned to the emperor. 'Listen not to this foreigner who has got us into this position, Basileus. I beg you. We can set a rearguard and retreat.'

'We should fight them here, as we intended,' Harald said firmly.

Andronikos's brows creased although I could see he was conflicted. He did not share his senior's certainty that retreat was the only path.

Harald came over and bowed, fully to one knee, in front of the emperor. 'Basileus, I beg you, let me speak. You have trusted me before with your life, trust me now one final time.'

'Do not listen to this man, Basileus, he has led us into this trouble,' Nikephoros insisted.

'And I will show you the way out,' Harald said firmly, never taking his eyes of Michael, who looked desperate to believe him.

'He will speak,' Michael said shrilly, and Harald bowed deeply again in thanks as Nikephoros screwed his face up in anger.

Harald gestured to the senior general. 'The domestikos is correct. We could sacrifice one part of the army to allow the rest to attempt an escape, but the risk is high. If the enemy catches us in the open lands that lie behind us we will be at a heavy disadvantage with that part of the army lost.'

'What is the alternative?'

Harald gestured at the hill beside us. 'We fight them right here, this very afternoon.'

Nikephoros looked at Harald as if he were mad. 'Here? This is no battlefield, this place is not suitable for our army! If we stop here to face them we will merely be trapped, unable to retreat while they send men around behind us to finish the task. This is madness!'

I could see his point. The place where we stood on the road was a narrow valley floor, only a few hundred paces across, and on the south side broken ground leading down to the lake. On the north side of the road were a series of small ravines and hilly slopes leading up towards an impassable ridgeline. It was horrendous terrain to try and manoeuvre an army in.

Harald was not dissuaded. 'Basileus, please. I have scouted the rising ground above us, and although it looks unsuitable from here, I assure you, it is very different once you see it from above. This could be the ideal place to give battle, one they will not expect. And with their greater numbers the narrowness of the field would only be to our advantage.'

'Our cavalry is our greatest strength, and they would be useless on that hillside!' Nikephoros said in outrage.

'I know,' Harald said, raising a calming hand to the general. 'But please, let me show you.' He looked at the emperor, pleading in a way I do not think I had seen before. 'Basileus, can you ride up the hill a little way with me? Let me show you that we can fight here, and not only that, I believe we will have victory. If I cannot convince you, there will still be time to retreat as your commander advises.'

'Perhaps it is worth hearing him,' Andronikos said, gaining a look of furious rebuke from the older general, and his eyes flicked up to the hill while Harald's stayed fixed on the emperor, imploring him.

Harald's certainty and Andronikos's support finally won Michael over. He nodded. 'Show me, Protospatharios. And God forgive you if you are misleading me.'

Harald let out a breath of relief. 'Thank you, Basileus.' He turned to me. 'Eric, fifty men of the seventh to come with us and protect the emperor's party.'

* * *

Harald carefully led the emperor's horse up the treacherous, uneven hillside of rocky soil and scrubby brush. He took us up a minor ridgeline about halfway up towards the summit and then stopped on a small area of flat ground in a spot where we could overlook the entire army.

In the distance we could see the dust and flashes of the vanguard as they skirmished with the tip of the enemy forces, and behind them down the road, the dark mass of the main rebel army, just a few miles away.

'So what is your plan, Varangian? Be quick,' Andronikos growled.

Harald pointed down towards the road. 'Array the army along behind this ridgeline, with the road as our left flank.' He turned and pointed up the hill. 'Use the peak as an anchor on our right flank that cannot be turned. The enemy will have no choice but to form up opposing us down in this ground in front of us.'

I could see, now that we were up there, that the ground in front of us was a little lower, and more broken. The position Harald had chosen had the advantage, although it was not obvious from the road.

'Protospatharios, we need space on our flanks for the cavalry to manoeuvre! This ground is hopeless, we will barely be able to move. Our formations will be shattered before we even make contact!' Nikephoros said.

'Yes, but the enemy will know this. They will know we can only put all our cavalry on the left flank, along the road, so they will fear that and focus their largest and best forces there to oppose them.'

Andronikos shook his head. 'This is stupidity. If you confine our entire cavalry force to that narrow valley on the left flank, the enemy will easily block it.'

'Correct. And that will make them bold, and they will not see the true threat, which will come from up there on the right.' He pointed up above us, nearer the peak, where the ground was the worst – steep, broken and uneven.

'The right? Our men cannot make a serious attack across that ground. What are you talking about?'

Harald smiled confidently. 'No, yours cannot. But mine can.'

Andronikos's eyes narrowed. 'Yours? You intend to make the flanking attack with some of the guard?'

'All of the guard,' Harald said, and the officers and attendants muttered in shock.

Nikephoros steadied himself against his anger. 'Protospatharios, you have lost your mind in your desperation. The role of the Varangians is to protect the emperor. In battle you form up around him as a reserve in case of threat. Especially in a battle so desperate as this one would be. How can you have forgotten that?'

'I have not,' Harald said, overriding the general, 'but neither will the enemy. Many of them used to be soldiers in the imperial army, their leaders were imperial officers, correct?'

Andronikos bristled at the shamefulness of that, but he nodded.

'Then they too will know or believe everything the domestikos has just said. They will believe this position is bad for us, they will know we are forced to put our entire cavalry on that narrow strip on the left flank, they will know our best troops are reserved to guard the emperor and most importantly, they will know we cannot attack from the right. So what will be their weakness?'

Nikephoros was shaking his head in despair, but Andronikos's eyes were flicking back and forth, calculating. Harald held his attention by a thread, but perhaps a thread was enough.

'Their weakness will be to an attack on our right flank, from our reserves, which they cannot expect to be on our right flank,' the general said.

Harald nodded vehemently. 'Exactly. They will deploy to face our main line. They will put their greatest strength down there, near the road, and only enough up here to hold us. They will let us attack on the left flank and, when that attack is defeated, they will attack our main line, accepting the casualties, until they overwhelm us with sheer numbers.'

'That does not sound... like a victory,' Michael said, sounding confused and concerned.

Harald turned to the emperor. 'We do as they expect – we make ourselves look desperate. We attack on the left as they anticipate, but then, as they move their strength to counter it, we attack in the centre. That will unbalance them, because it is not what the manuals would advise.'

'For good reason,' Nikephoros said, but Harald ignored him.

'Then, as the main line in the centre diverts their attention, and the cavalry diverts their strength, my Varangians make the true attack, up there on the right.' He pointed again above them. 'It will be a complete surprise. We are slightly higher up here on this crest, not easy to notice from below, but by enough that I can hide several thousand men in that gully near the top. They will never see us until we appear out of it, and then it will be too late.'

Andronikos's expression had changed. He was looking up and down the battlefield carefully, analysing it, working it out in his mind. 'Your attack will reach their line before they can move any men from lower down the hill to face it.'

'Exactly,' Harald said, nodding vigorously.

Andronikos muttered, holding a hand up to his chin. 'But still, how will that win the battle? Their forces will mostly be intact, and ours fully committed. A small victory on this far flank will mean little.'

Harald nodded again. 'General, if you were the enemy commander, where would you position yourself?'

Andronikos looked out again, assessing the likely enemy positions. Finally he smiled, and pointed at a raised area of flat ground on the opposing ridgeline, nearly three quarters of the way up the hillside. 'There.'

Harald grinned, the final aspect of his plan revealed. 'That is what I assume too. Nearly opposite our right flank. It is the only ground on their side where they can see the entire battlefield. That little knoll is where their commanders and their false emperor will stand, I am sure of it. They will feel safe there, knowing we cannot attack from the right, and with all our most dangerous forces down in the valley below.'

'So you don't intend to defeat their flank, you intend to go through it.'

'Yes,' said Harald. 'I will burst through like a spear, and head straight for their command position. We will kill or scatter their commanders, and they will collapse.'

Andronikos laughed a little and shook his head. 'By God, you are mad. And if you fail to capture that knoll, or the enemy flees but maintains command? You and your men will be the wrong side of tens of thousands of rebels, with nothing we can do to help you.'

'Then you will be rid of a troublesome barbarian,' said Harald with a manic grin.

Andronikos laughed and nodded, putting his hands on his hips. 'Certainly that would be comforting.' He looked at the domestikos and the emperor, who both looked deeply unsure. Everything Harald was suggesting was against their lifetimes of training and experience.

'Will it work?' Michael asked hesitantly, looking at Nikephoros.

'I... I don't believe it, Basileus. It is all wrong. We should not abandon five hundred years of hard-won experience and risk everything like this. We should retreat,' he ended emphatically.

Michael turned his gaze to the more junior general. 'And what of you, Stratopedarches?'

'It might work, but it is close to insanity,' Andronikos said.

'It is more likely to work than trying to flee across fifty miles of open plains with that on our heels,' Harald said, pointing at the vast shadow of the enemy army. 'But here, on this hillside, we might surprise them, and if we succeed we could end this rebellion by sunset. This is the chance, Basileus. This is the gamble that greatness turns on. If we did not look desperate, by the Lord if we were not desperate, our enemy would never even offer us the opportunity. This is our chance for a great victory for the empire, and no great victory comes without great risk.'

Harald stood staring at the emperor, and his utter conviction was clear to everyone. Michael looked at Andronikos, who was still looking bemused, and at Nikephoros, who looked sick.

'I need the commander of this army to have confidence of victory. Do you have confidence?'

'I do not, Basileus,' Nikephoros said, shaking his head.

'Then Domestikos Nikephoros is no longer in command,' Michael said, his eyes glittering, pointing at Andronikos. 'Can you win this battle, Stratopedarches?'

Andronikos looked in surprise at the emperor and the appalled domestikos, and then at the field in front of them.

'Do you really believe your men can punch through the rebel army, across this terrain, and reach that knoll in time?' Andronikos asked Harald.

'Magister, my men are the only ones in the world who could.'

There was silence around the group as we waited for the general to make his decision, even the emperor staring at him with bated breath.

Finally Andronikos took his hands from his hips and turned to the emperor. 'I believe it can work, Basileus, but there is no time to debate. If you wish me to command this battle, with your permission I will begin immediately.'

Michael nodded quickly, his hands fidgeting on his reins. 'Do it, Stratopedarches. I appoint you as the new Domestikos of the West.' He looked at Nikephoros, who was visibly distraught. 'You have served the empire well, but it is time to pass your duties to someone younger and bolder.'

Nikephoros bowed his head miserably. 'As you command, Basileus.' He then turned and staggered back from the knoll.

Andronikos turned to his officers, setting his feet and puffing out his chest, the gold and silver of his fabulous scale armour and inlaid helmet shining in the pale sun. 'Bring the imperial banners up here and set them on this ground! This is where we will stand and, God willing, this is where we will triumph in his name.'

I looked at Harald as the officers made the imperial salute and shouted back their assent. I caught his eye and he gave me that little smile, the upturned corner of his mouth that I had seen before.

I loved that smile, it was the hunter's smile, the predator's smile.

I feared that smile. It was the foreshadowing of battle and the spectre of death.

17

All of the leaders of the army's units were summoned to receive their orders. The emperor stayed where he was; he had no intent or ability to ride back down the hill and then up again. He looked uneasy even just sitting on his horse, but did his best to look regal for any close enough to see him.

Magister Theophilos of the Scholai came over in his magnificent, gilded scale armour, holding his helmet under one arm, looking at Harald with a strange expression on his face.

'It seems to me that for a guardsman, whose life is dedicated to the safety and security of our rulers, you have a curious insatiability for danger and death, Aralthes of the North.'

Harald smiled at him. 'I do not intend to die today.'

'No one ever does, but you certainly intend for there to be a great deal of dying at your behest.'

'We fight the emperor's enemies. Death is the tool by which victory over them is achieved, do you not think?'

Theophilos tilted his head. 'I think if every problem the empire faced was solved with slaughter, there would be no empire left to protect. How many times could we risk everything to win, and still hope to be triumphant?'

'I have done it many times, and I am still here. Are you afraid to risk it all for the empire, Magister?'

Theophilos did not get drawn by the barbed comment. He pursed his lips and stared at Harald carefully. 'I have lived long enough, and through enough wars, to know that those who seek the glory of battle eventually end up on the wrong end of the blade. I fight when I have to, Varangian, and at no other time.'

'Would you not say today is a day where we must fight?' Harald asked.

Theophilos smiled. 'You have very cleverly ensured that it is so, Aralted. So yes, today I ride for the emperor.' His face turned serious, and he nodded his head respectfully. 'I hope you find what you are seeking.'

'Victory, Magister. I seek victory.'

Theophilos inclined his head and half turned away. 'Victory is not a thing to seek, Aralted. Victory merely divides the path between death and ambition. For all of our boys who die today, I hope your ambition is worth it. Good luck, Protospatharios. I will watch for your banners on the field,' the magister said, and then crunched away down the rocky slope after the rest of the cavalry officers.

'He is an odd man,' Harald said, watching the magister go with a smile. 'I like him.' He patted Sveinn on the shoulder. 'Come, it is time to prepare our men.'

* * *

Andronikos arrayed the army as Harald had suggested, and we left the emperor and his generals on his ridge and moved into the dead ground up near the ridgeline, lowering our standards to the ground and hiding from view as the infantry of the imperial host lined up along the crest in front of us.

Harald and the rest of us officers stood at the top, watching, as the rearguard retreated in the face of the enemy, and the vast rebel host poured into the ground in front of us.

And it was vast, far beyond our numbers. Fifty thousand perhaps, and we had little more than thirty left with us to face them. The rest were guarding Vodena or patrolling the road, or had been lost to the fighting, injury or disease.

But Harald did not seem troubled. He had known the enemy numbers when we chose this fight. The enemy seemed uncertain at first as our vanguard retreated away from them and our position on the hillside became clear. Their whole mass ground to a disorganised halt, and Harald smiled. 'You see, they are not truly one army.'

'No,' said Rurik drily. 'They are at least two armies.'

'Their numbers will matter little in this terrain. Their ability to organise and react is everything.'

'I agree with your theory, Harald. I only hope fate and the enemy are kind enough to allow it.'

'I do not intend to give them the choice,' Harald said, turning away from the enemy and looking down across our army to see if they were ready.

The main line was already well-formed, strung along the ridge. Our cavalry formed massed ranks down in the flat and narrow valley floor astride the road with a thick formation of infantry in front of them, warding off any attempt the enemy might make to simply push down the road.

But the rebel force, after a period of some confusion, started unrolling up the hillside, blocks of infantry coalescing to face off against ours, lining up on the gentle crest opposite us that Harald had predicted. The enemy cavalry, which was significant in number but mostly composed of light horsemen, milled about on the valley floor opposite ours.

The enemy numbers were so great that they formed a second line, thick down at the valley floor but opposite us, near the top of the ridge, the enemy only had a much lighter force – skirmishers in the broken ground, a main line of heavy infantry six ranks deep and some less well-organised light infantry behind.

Harald watched with intense interest as a parade of horsemen picked their way up the hillside under unfamiliar banners.

'Come on,' he muttered, watching their progress. 'Come on.'

The group, which was clearly the enemy commanders, moved up level with the knoll and then stopped before dismounting and occupying it.

'Ha!' Harald said with wild delight. 'Praise the rigid thinking of the empire's sons,' he exclaimed. 'Our plan stands. Komes, go and brief your men. You know what to do.' He came to each of us in turn and embraced us, coming to me last of all. 'Good luck, Eric.'

'I should be at your side. It is my duty.'

'Your duty is to your men, Komes,' Harald said with a warm, generous smile. 'They will need you more than I. But make sure you are right on my heels.'

I felt sick to my stomach. I had never willingly let Harald out of my sight in battle. Not once. It had been a promise I had kept to my long dead King Olaf for over a decade.

I felt ashamed, and I felt angry, but I nodded and saluted my prince. 'God protect you, Prince Harald.'

'God does not protect us, Eric, otherwise how would you explain my brother's death?'

I looked down. I had merely meant it as a votive of fortune, but Harald had clearly thought about the subject before. 'God must have had more need for him than we did,' I finally offered.

Harald smiled and nodded. 'I like that. Well, let us hope his need for us is neither imminent nor great. Go now, make sure the Blood Claws are ready for battle.'

I saluted and went at a jog towards my bandon, who were sitting in ranks twenty paces away, waiting patiently and catching every moment of rest they could like true veterans do.

I thumped Sigurd on the shoulder. 'The men are ready?'

'And already bored,' said Sigurd with a smile.

'Good. We will wait here for the order to advance. Formation will be arrowhead with the second in the centre with Harald, and we will stay on their right and slightly behind. The fourteenth will be on the left, everyone else will follow in behind us.' I looked up at the ranks of my men who were watching and listening intently. 'We are not going to fight their line, we will not deploy into line ourselves until we have pierced it. Our duty is to smash a hole fifty men wide into the enemy flank and pour through it. Once we are through, we will storm their command position.' I gestured with my fist, thrusting it with my fingers outstretched towards my other hand.

'And once we are behind their army, what then?' someone asked.

'We kill everything in that command position and hold it until the rest of the army arrives.'

'And if the rest of the army does not arrive?' Hrolf said, looking dubious.

'Then we will be holding it for a very long time,' I said with a confidence I did not feel. 'Speed will be everything, we stop for nothing. The dead will lie where they fall.' I added with a serious expression.

'And the wounded?' Sigurd asked.

I gave him a stern gaze. 'The same. If we stop, we all die. If we fail, we will all die. There is nothing to do but push through and trust the army to come to us.'

'Sounds like fun,' Alexios said with a grin, and there was some nervous laughter.

I smiled at him. 'No showing off, boy – stay with the formation, keep your discipline.'

'There is no need for me to show off, Komes. Everyone has already seen that I am the best.'

I wagged my finger at him. 'It is quite another thing in battle. You must impress me here now.'

'And how will I do that?' he said with a mocking expression. 'Shall we compare how many men we kill?'

'By doing your duty and surviving.'

Alexios's grin faded a little and he looked a little embarrassed as the man next to him elbowed him in the ribs to be quiet.

It made me nervous. I had been a young man like him once, full of fire and desperate to prove my skill. Only luck had seen me survive that.

'All of you,' I said, looking around at them. 'Keep moving, do your duty, and do not waste your lives. That is all I expect of you.'

'Aye, Komes.'

I nodded and straightened up. 'Now sit here, and don't let yourselves be seen. The attack will be soon.'

I walked back up to the crest and looked over. The skirmishers from both armies were already advancing, filling the open ground between the lines with their little battles, prowling and scampering in the rough, rocky terrain. It was merely the opening moves of the imperial dance of war.

I looked up at the sky. It was mercifully cloudy for that time of year, and cool on that exposed hillside. I was not wearing the heavy outer layer of my armour, the klivanion. Few of us were. It was too heavy and too hot to go mountaineering like a goat while wearing it. I just had my chainmail hauberk on, what the Greeks called the lorikion. It is very similar to what we wear here, but with slightly smaller, finer rings.

I was carrying a good shield and my sword was at my waist. I carried a short spear too, although I expected to lose it quickly. If I got it stuck in someone there would be no time to retrieve it. In fact, I was considering throwing it during the first charge, just to try and help break the shield wall in front of me.

Many of the men behind me were carrying the long axes the guard was famous for in the east, but I never favoured the axe – using it sacrificed your shield and it was less precise than a spear, although more devastating.

I checked all of my equipment again as I watched the opening stages of the battle, going through my ritual as my hands ran over every strap and buckle. Everything was in its place and done up correctly, as it had been the last three times I had checked, and would be when I checked again. The ritual was not for checking equipment, it was for focusing the mind.

The enemy were not goaded into an advance by our skirmishers, as the commanders had expected they would not be. They could defeat us merely by waiting on their ground and they knew it.

The lines of skirmishers expended their missiles and retreated, carrying their wounded and leaving the dead. Down in the valley on the left, at the end of the long line of the main body of the army standing patiently in its serried ranks, a series of horns blew, and I saw the glittering masses of the imperial heavy cavalry shudder as they moved into action.

There was no subtlety to their advance, no room for manoeuvring or flanking, no subterfuge by which they could hide their advance. They were going to ride into the teeth of the enemy defenders and I knew they would suffer serious losses, and so did their leaders.

Not that it changed anything for those brave men. They rode forwards, knee to knee in flowing, fluttering ranks that stretched as they sped up, moving like a loosely woven fabric across the valley floor.

It was the largest charge of cavalry I ever saw. It dwarfed the devastating charges of the Normans in Sicily or Italy, or the imperial cavalry attack at Edessa. Over four thousand heavy horsemen, the full might of the armies of the western empire, spread out three hundred horses wide and fifteen deep, swept across the floor of the valley like a brightly coloured flood and even up there on our hillside we could hear the rumble over the sound of the horns.

The enemy had left a wall of infantry in front of them but I think they crumbled before the leading ranks of horsemen hit. Can I blame them? I think we might have stood firm, but it would have turned my bowels to water to face such an attack and we would have paid a horrendous price for doing so.

The enemy line simply disappeared into the flow of dust and glitter as the imperial cavalry rode over them, but that enemy line did the job their commander required of them, they slowed the flood down as the wave of horses crashed over them, disrupted their ranks, ate into their momentum as the horsemen had to cut their way through the disintegrating masses.

The enemy made their retort as the imperial horsemen tried to reform, and several thousand rebel horsemen swept down in a counter-charge, hitting the disrupted ranks like a hammer on an anvil, turning the whole fight into a churning, swirling mess that was quickly lost to sight in the dust-cloud that erupted from tens of thousands of churning hooves.

Harald watched, intently, how the rest of the rebel army reacted. The dust cloud seemed to edge towards the rebel side as the weight of numbers on ours overwhelmed the initial shock of the rebel counter charge.

More infantry units from both sides were sent into the melee, one to exploit the advance, the other to try and stem it, but then we saw clumps and trails of horsemen fleeing the melee, fleeing towards the rebel side.

'Yes!' Harald said, thumping one hand onto his thigh, then sweeping his gaze to the huge block of the rebel reserves and the enemy commanders on the knoll.

'Do it!' Harald urged.

Perhaps the words carried like a whisper to the rebel commander's ear, or perhaps he saw, as we did even from that distance, that the fight in the valley was inexorably pushing backwards, curling around the rebel flank and threatening it.

Flags were waved, horns sounded, and the mass of the enemy reserve started shifting and moving down the hill.

As soon as he saw that, Andronikos launched the main attack, what normally would have been the killing blow, and the main central force of the imperial army on the shallow lower slopes moved forwards to the bray of horns.

The thick enemy main line prepared themselves to meet the attack, and some enemy reserves diverted to support them.

Harald watched with excitement for a few moments longer, and then turned and crouched, looking down at the massed ranks of the guard in the low ground below him and the wolfish gaze was on his face, eyes sharp and teeth bared. He drew his sword.

'Now is the time, Varangians. They called us defeated, they called us fallen and cowards, but now the moment of our glory comes. I am going to fight my way to the false emperor and plant our standard in his corpse for all the world to see! All the empire will know what happened here and say that we, the Varangian tagma, risked it all to save the emperor and the empire. We will stop for nothing but death, for death or immortality are the only fates we seek. Come with me, men of the guard, let the world see who we are and fear us!'

Two thousand Varangians rose to their feet with a roar, and Harald gestured to Sveneld. The tall standard-bearer raised his pole, and I and the others around me gasped when we saw it unfurl and that it was not the imperial battle flag, as it should have been, but the black raven on the field of red, the harbinger of death: Land-Waster.

'Forwards, Varangians!' shouted Harald, and the first three banda leapt into action, running up the short slope behind the bright-red banner as Harald strode over the crest, shouting at the officers of the imperial unit in front of us that the moment had come.

As we crossed the ridge the imperial troops in front of us parted to allow us through, scampering out of the way as fifty files of Varangian guardsmen scrambled down the shallow slope, scattering dirt and stones in our armoured steps.

We burst through the hole in the thin imperial flank and poured forth in a single column, running down into the shallow ravine that separated the two armies.

We leapt, scampered and jogged through the broken ground, parting like water to flow around boulders and avoid sudden pits or impenetrable patches of brush.

We passed first the bodies of imperial skirmishers and then, climbing the far slope, the bodies of the rebels in turn. We slowed a little as we climbed, the uncertain footing causing some men to tumble, but we kept the arrowhead of our formation intact, flexing and reforming as we went, the bright banner at its tip alongside Harald.

We did not roar and scream as we ran; all our breath was for our lungs alone, drawing it in and spewing it out as fast as we could, legs burning from the climb.

Arrows started falling among us but it was a desultory shower, for the enemy had few enough men standing ready to face an attack they did not expect. We were only fifty paces from their line now, hidden on the flat of the ridge above us. All I could see was their banners flying above them as we passed the steepest part of the slope and started to approach the top.

First the tips of their spears came into view, then a line of worried faces under helmets, then shields and levelled weapons as the distance closed to two dozen paces and I felt the pressure of my brothers either side of me supporting me, urging me on.

Then we let out our war cry, bellowing madness at the waiting enemy ranks, mouths open and beards flowing, eyes wide with the rush of battle-rage.

I sighted on my enemy, the man whose death I had chosen, whose shield hung too low and whose spear wavered in indecision as he tried to work out who to defend himself against.

I flipped my spear into an overhand grip even as I ran, planting my foot on a higher patch of rock, bending my back and half twisting, landing with my left as I whipped my arm over my head and threw.

All around me other missiles arced forwards, and the Varangian guard charged into the waiting enemy ranks.

The great battle Harald had dreamed of, fought for, manipulated an empire into committing to, had finally begun.

18

My sword was already leaving my scabbard as my spear impaled the enemy I had chosen, and as he fell, my next opponent was revealed, unready, unsure, shocked by the speed of the roaring armoured ranks that were suddenly bearing down on him from the quiet valley he had been posted to guard.

I jumped into him, crashing his spear aside as I punched him in the face with the hilt of my sword, not wanting to be slowed by dragging it from his corpse. I felt bones break, I felt him fall under my feet but I did not stop, I left him to be trampled to death by the men that followed.

A Varangian axe crunched through the forehead of the next rebel who came into my view, and someone knocked me aside as they wrenched it free, screaming their challenge at the next foes. I did not slow, I did not stop. I smashed into the next two men in front of me, desperately trying to keep my feet as we all tangled together.

I lashed out with an elbow and my shield, shoving forwards, always forwards, and they shrank away from me only to be cut down by guardsmen who pushed past me either side.

I cut another man with a vicious downswing and swept at another with the back-cut, forcing him to leap back where Alexios skewered him with a beautiful thrust to the chest and a whoop of glee.

He ripped his sword free from the dying man as he passed him to get to my right shoulder. He looked at me with a grin and I shook my head at his wild need to prove himself.

The last rank of enemy were backing away, but Alexios and I lanced into them, scattering them like wolves into a flock, swords flashing and thrusting, competing for kills like we were children.

And then we were through their line, and I was jogging over open ground. As I looked left and right, bloodied Varangians were bursting through the back of the disintegrating enemy line everywhere. Sigurd was on my left and his face was a twisted snarl.

'Keep going!' I shouted.

If we stopped, the bandon behind us would have nowhere to advance to, and the enemy would have time to gather and stop us.

I ran forwards myself, seeing the raven banner on my left pushing forwards with Harald at its base in a clutch of men of the second.

We jogged forwards, reforming as best we could, because the second line was just in front of us and they had seen what was coming.

Ha! They were skirmishers and light troops, barely trained militia, utterly unsure what to do about us. We crashed into their masses and we slaughtered them, spreading out a little and slowing, such were their numbers. The enemy had put their worst troops up there in the safest position. These were farm boys and cowards, men who were not ready for war, let alone for the armoured wolves of hell that bounded through the first line and came after them with such terrifying speed.

We put them to flight, but inevitably tired and slowed, spreading out to kill ever more of them as their second line sagged and fractured.

Behind us I saw more and more banda coming through the gap. The tenth and the fourteenth, the eighteenth and the sixth, their flags flying as they followed us across the rough ground in the rear of the enemy.

But even as we poured through the first line, we had only punctured it, not shattered it, and large numbers of the enemy still stood firm on either side of the break.

Their commanders were reacting now, turning blocks of men inwards by the hundreds, rushing to stem the terrible stab wound we had pierced through their army. If we stayed to fight, to widen that gap, we were still in danger of being stopped and then overwhelmed.

'Keep going!' I roared at my men, for there was nothing we could do but go forwards, and I turned to look for Harald and found that he had turned the second bandon and stopped them, letting us reform the other banda on his flanks, now in a broader line three hundred men wide, ready to sweep down the hillside. Ahead of him, I saw his target: the enemy command position on the knoll five hundred paces away. There was nothing between us and it apart from a small, shallow valley filled with scattered and fleeing enemy.

The imperial forces at our rear were moving in behind us, attacking on the right flank to pin the enemy first line in place and stop them turning around to crush us. With our rear secure for the moment, Harald raised his sword and pointed it at the enemy commanders, and we set off down the slope of the final valley with a cheer.

My lungs were raw now. I could taste blood in my throat, but it did not matter. We were so close to our goal. There was panic in the gaggle of guards, attendants and messengers around the enemy leaders in front of us as we swept down towards the knoll and they finally realised the full insanity of our plan, that they were the target.

We got down into the bottom of that shallow valley and it was only two hundred paces now. My legs were shaking but I would make it, I would not be left behind.

There were shouts of alarm and I looked up, seeing to my shock that there were hundreds of enemy, thousands of them, appearing from behind the commander's position and deploying onto the crest to face us.

'Where did they come from?' Sigurd shouted in panic.

I looked at them in horror, feeling all the wild thrill of victory flee my exhausted body. The enemy had kept a surprise behind, hiding their own reserve force in the next ravine. They could not have known our plan but they had kept a hidden reserve anyway, by luck or cunning.

I looked behind us, and saw that the second line of the enemy main force had turned and was advancing down the previous slope towards us, chasing the tail end of our last bandon. The entire guard was now in the ravine, with enemy in front of us and behind. We were utterly trapped.

'Keep going!' roared Harald, pointing up the hill, and our exhausted front line manfully tried to push up against the thick mass of enemy who came over the crest and hammered down at us.

There was a sudden and vicious battle on the uneven slope as our men scrambled to overcome the fresh defenders. Alexios to my right, fresher and younger than most of us, howled in rage and threw himself at the enemy, cutting the ankles from under one and then thrusting his sword up beneath the maille of another.

But someone hammered a sword into the top of his helmet and another kicked him in the stomach, sending him sprawling down the hill in a tangle of limbs.

'Stay in line!' I shouted furiously over the din, swearing at the foolish young warrior as I pushed my way over to see if he lived, disrupting our ranks.

I found him crumpled under the legs of the men who were pushing past and grabbed his sleeve, hauling on him and cursing.

'Get up, you stupid sack of shit!' I yelled at him, and his dazed eyes fixed on me drunkenly, one of them blinking away the blood that was trickling down from under his helmet.

I got him unsteadily to his feet and tried to lead him back through the ranks.

'Leave him!' Sigurd shouted, grabbing me and giving me a furious glare. 'Your duty is the bandon, lead them! The wounded will deal with themselves.'

I bristled at being talked to that way, almost lashing out, but Sigurd was right and I felt a hot spear of shame. I was not used to leading so many men in battle. I gave Alexios the prideful fool one more shove towards the empty centre of the circle that the guard was now forming, and looked around to work out what to do next.

The rearmost banda of the guard had turned around to face the enemy there, and the two sides clashed in a fury of steel and wood. But the enemy were coming at us in two lines, overlapping our hurried circle, and they closed in rapidly on all sides until, in a few moments, we were completely surrounded in the base of the valley.

Banda mixed together as men forced themselves into the line wherever they could to ensure we covered every angle, and there was a chaotic din that no orders could be heard over from more than a few paces away as our entire guard was engaged in every direction, three or four ranks deep in our ragged circle.

The enemy, who were above us on almost every side, pressed in fresh and giddy with the sense of victory over our beleaguered attack. I swept my eyes around the perimeter, trying to find something, anything, that gave me an idea. I looked back at the men around Harald, hoping that somehow, against all sense, they had managed to force their way up that final slope against the enemy reserves. But they had not.

My brave comrades, exhausted and outnumbered, were being inexorably pushed back down the incline by the weight of enemy numbers. There were few weapons even being used; the press was too great for that. It was just two lines of desperate men shoving and cursing at each other over their shields, feet scrabbling for purchase.

The wolfhound banner of the second, Sveinn's men, wobbled as its bearer was shoved back, and then it toppled, falling into the open ground in our circle. No one even went to retrieve it; every single man was already in the desperate and deadly press on the slope.

The din of battle was drowned out by the thumping of my heart in my chest and the rasping of the breath in my desperate lungs as I stood there, bewildered, and looked around at the ruin of Harald's plans.

I felt a crushing, overwhelming sadness at the irreplaceable men of the guard, who stood shoulder to shoulder and defied the enemy with their weapons and their voices, who raged and hacked and gave ground... step by step.

There was nowhere for us to go, no force in reserve to come and save us. I knew we were going to die in that valley, and all around me, as the competition of shoving ground to a halt and the weapons started rising and slashing, my weary brothers were already being felled.

I shoved myself back into the press of the fighting, feeling helpless to give my bandon orders, for there were none to give. Every man was already doing what he needed to do – to fight until he could fight no more and cover the open side of the guardsman next to him.

We took from that enemy so much more than they did from us, but they had far more to give. Reinforcements flooded into the back of their constricting noose while every man we lost could never be replaced, and, as we tired, our losses only kept mounting.

Maille-armoured bodies were sinking to the ground, bloodied helmets were being knocked from broken heads, battered swords were falling from nerveless fingers, even as our famous axes reaped the enemy like summer wheat.

As I pressed into the back of the line, all around me the guard was dying, one cut at a time. I knew it would take a long time to kill us all, but there was no comfort in that.

I shoved men aside, clawing my way through my own ranks recklessly to get to the front, to put myself in harm's way so that I could take the place of just one of my men, to prolong their defiance just a little longer even if at the cost of my own blood.

I jammed myself into the mess and put the rim of my shield into an enemy's mouth, smashing teeth and spraying droplets of blood. The head snapped back and I jammed my sword into the exposed neck. An arm appeared holding a spear, too far from the protection of a shield. I half-severed it with a vicious up-swing. But the pressure on me while I swung was too great, and I took a step back.

My next opponent slipped on the body of his friend and I hacked into the back of his neck, splitting his spine. He flopped into me, limp and helpless, and pushed me another two steps back. Another tried to come at me over the body and I killed him too, ignoring the blows I took in response. It was all so easy, so slow, so inevitable.

They weren't running out of bodies, but we were running out of space.

A sword hammered into my helmet from some unseen foe, and robbed my eyes of sight as the pain of the impact rattled around inside my head, nearly knocking me senseless entirely.

Someone pulled me back, took my place in the line even as my arms screamed and my breath burned. I stumbled back, the rage that had powered me failing as the age in my body betrayed me, and my head was swimming with pain and confusion. Whoever owned the hand that withdrew me saw me about to fall, and dragged me back before the enemy dragged me down.

Bless his soul, for I never knew his face or name.

I turned, blood-soaked and numb, and saw with blurry eyes that the space in the centre of our circle of defiance was shrunken, and the ground was littered with the dying and the wounded.

A generation of the Varangians lay around me as I staggered, and I looked up and saw the black raven banner over me against the dim sky and I went to it. I was going to die beside Harald. Nothing else was left in me. Fate had always decreed that I would, and fate could not be ignored.

I found him under the standard, with Sveinn and Styrbjorn beside him. Had he given in? You know that he had not, he did not know how. He was scanning the circle of our men, calculating, assessing, trying to decipher where blood could be spent to save the day, even as the stocks of that blood were torn from loyal men.

'Tell me you have a plan,' I muttered at him, hands by my side. My shield was gone. I don't know when I lost it and I cannot tell you to this day. It had been stripped from my hand by the chaos. Only my sword remained.

My sword was all I truly needed.

He looked at me with those fierce blue eyes. 'We wear them down. They cannot stand this much longer.'

'Can *we* stand it?'

'We must.'

'We break back through to the main line,' Styrbjorn said, putting his hand on Harald's shoulder.

Harald shook his head violently. 'That is no sanctuary, only a temporary respite.'

'What then?' Sveinn asked, imploring.

'The only way out is forwards,' Harald said, pointing up the slope towards the enemy command position, where, even now, a gaggle of well-dressed men, the enemy command group, watched us in dread fascination, fifty paces away, the wrong side of six ranks of the enemy soldiers.

'We can still do this.'

'Retreat while you can, Harald,' I begged him. 'Perhaps some of the men can be saved.'

He rounded on me, snarling. 'Nothing can be saved except victory.'

Harald looked at Styrbjorn. 'Gather a hundred men. Give them a moment's rest from the fighting, and then we lead them up that slope, straight through them. That is the only way.'

Styrbjorn swallowed hard and then nodded, his face strained. 'The guard obeys.'

He turned and walked away, shouting orders to half a dozen men at a time over the tumult of battle.

Harald turned to talk to Sveinn, but I could not hear them, I could not hear much at all. But I could feel something. My head pounded, my old injury from a decade before in the Rus blurring my thoughts, dulling my ears and my eyes and making my thoughts swim.

My head pounded, it thrummed and pulsed. The sensation was not noise, but... I could feel it, over the din of battle – the pounding of feet and... hooves.

Hooves?

I looked up, begging my eyes to focus properly, Harald looked at me in confusion as I held my empty hand to my temple, trying to force my mind to obey me.

Hooves. I was sure of it. I could feel it in the soles of my feet.

I stared over the fighting beyond Harald and a banner broke the skyline of the downhill crest, fluttering, weaving, jerking with the movement of the unseen wielder below. Spear-tips appeared, and the thundering of the wound in my mind opened further, threatening to burst. Then the spear-tips dipped, dipped in a line even as the bright helmets swarmed into view beneath them, helmets and glistening golden armour atop thundering heavy horses, all under the battle flag of the emperor.

Harald looked at me in confusion, and Styrbjorn came back, wide-eyed, staring up the slope.

'The Scholai! The Scholai are here!'

Harald swung around, staring over the tumult of his wavering lines, as a hundred guardsmen of the tagma Scholai surged over the crest in a ragged line, down into the gully, and pounded into the back of our enemy.

The impact shook the entire battle. The enemy line in the base of the gully was crushed into us by the clash, and the shockwave spread around the ring like a ripple in water as our men looked up and saw salvation, and the enemy paused in their grinding attack and felt the cold hand of panic.

Harald did not stand in shock and stare, as I stood in shock and stared. He slapped Sveneld on the back and turned to Styrbjorn, waving him onwards. 'Now! Forwards, Varangians!' He gestured at the unbroken line between us and the knoll, a quarter way around the circle from the melee where the Scholai cavalry had crushed a section of the enemy attack and were, even then, wheeling and hacking, trying to cut a clean path through to us.

'Harald!' I shouted, grabbing at his cloak. 'They have bought us a way free, back to safety!' I yelled, pleading with my eyes, begging him to see sense and to push us through the line where it was weakened, down the gully and back to our army.

He grabbed his cloak to pull against me. 'The only freedom is in victory. The only way is forwards.' He ripped the cloth away from me and raised his sword to the men Styrbjorn had gathered. 'Victory or death!'

The bastards cheered him. They surged up the slope into the hesitant enemy ranks, into the jaws of certain death, to waste the gift of life the Scholai had brought us, and I did not have the strength to go with them, so terrible was the weakness in my head, the crushing pain of my old wound reopened by the blow I had taken.

I saw Sveneld surging up the scree with the raven banner held high, a spearhead of his brothers forging a path into the ranks of the enemy even as the foe nervously looked to their flank and the swirling, pounding riders of the Scholai.

I saw Harald pushing up with Sveinn under the banner, laying his sword about him and shouting his challenge at the sky. I saw Styrbjorn the Goat, screaming encouragement at his comrades, scamper up the slope as if his injured foot was nothing, clambering up a rock and slaying two enemy, before ripping another from the line, casting him down to be killed below.

I saw the enemy spear lance forwards, bursting through his chest, emerging from his back like an angry serpent, and I saw his arms go limp and his weapons drop as he shuddered and started to fall.

Styrbjorn fell slowly backwards off the rock like a toppling statue, grim against the grey sky, and crashed to the ground below with a spray of dirt and stones.

I screamed, I raved, and tears of rage flooded my eyes as I scrambled over to find him lying there on his back, blood in his beard and hands trembling at the spear that had pierced him and stood like a flagpole from his breast.

I fell to my knees beside him as dozens of our brothers pushed past us, clambering up the rock that Styrbjorn had won, following the red raven banner without question or fear. I grabbed for his hand, taking it in mine, and I looked down at his confused, flickering eyes.

'Take me to the North, Eric,' he said, looking at me in confusion, his voice high and strained, his mind not understanding where he was or what had happened. 'I always wanted to see the North.'

And then he ceased. His breath ceased, and his hand went loose in mine as his eyes lost focus on this mortal realm.

I lifted my head and howled at the sky, broken, waves of pain lashing my skull and unchecked fury seizing my soul. I gripped his dead hand so hard I felt bones crackle and slip as something died in me. The death of hope and fear.

I rocked back on my knees, and I saw the black and red raven banner surging up the slope with my friends underneath it. They were doing the impossible, that little band. They were forcing their way up the hill into the teeth of the enemy's finest, and the rebels were looking over their shoulders, edging away from the fury and the death that could not be stopped.

Men on both sides were dying unchecked, all semblance of a shield-wall gone. I saw Sveneld take a cut across the neck even as he parried another with his sword, and he roared, spraying blood, and cut down the man who had given him his death blow. Then the tall guardsman fell to one knee, jamming the spiked base of Land-Waster into the ground, clinging to it for support as his head sagged and his life fled his body in a red river.

And a hand seized the pole, a living hand even as the dying one lost its grip, and Harald took Land-Waster and he raised it himself and surged forwards unrelenting, just a few paces from the crest. He beat men aside with the pole, and speared its base into their bodies, always rising, always pushing forwards as his men fought to remain at his side, carrying him up with their desperate violence.

Now, I know that perhaps you will not believe me, that you will hear the ravings of a shamed old man who knelt while others fought, but at that moment the clouds parted, just a little, and the sun broke through as Harald climbed inexorably towards the crest.

The rays of that heavenly light lit the red banner up like fire and shone on Harald's metal and his fury. The men around him gleamed red and white in the harsh light of the hidden sun and my eyes hurt to behold its glory. I felt, as I had never felt before, and have never felt since, the close, overwhelming presence of the Lord our God as those absurd men reached the top of that impossible crest, casting aside all who would stop them.

Harald broke clear, scattering the last of the terrified foe in the light of his anger and the Lord's judgement, and he carried Land-Waster over the crest and onto the knoll.

There was a howl, a wild, feral cheer from the armoured ranks of the guard, for all of them could see the bright banner glowing in the light at the summit of the enemy's position and all knew what it meant: death had come, death had come to claim the foes of Harald Sigurdsson, and nothing could stand in his way.

I felt the power too, I felt it fizzle through my bones and refill my broken soul. I gave poor Styrbjorn's hand a last squeeze and I rose. I rose to my feet and I joined them. I went up the hill to join that banner in a flood of my brothers and my friends, and we rendered the last of the enemy reserves into the dying and broken.

They fell back before us as Harald fought alone on the summit for long moments with one hand on the banner and the other wielding his sword. Standing proud in the bright light of the sun with the raven rippling in the air above him as he resisted the last desperate attempts to push him back.

I tell you, it was the pinnacle of his glory. In all the years I followed him, in all the battles and desperate fights, nothing he ever did, before or since, could touch the perfection of that moment in the sun. The enemy fought back desperately, but our brothers clawed and hacked and howled their battle madness, tearing a bloody wound into the last ranks of the enemy, with Harald inviolable at their head, immovable from the ground that he had claimed.

And then he put the last enemy to flight and, with Sveinn and a half dozen men at his side, he ran into the panicking dregs of the enemy command position and he scattered them too.

I lost sight of him for a few moments as I pounded up the hill, desperate to get back to his side. When I reached the top the enemy had fled or died, and there was almost no one on the knoll that was not one of ours. Harald was grabbing a terrified figure in gold and red finery and dragging him towards the centre of the space.

It was the blind and false emperor, Petar Delyan, who had been unable to flee, unable to see what was happening, and had been abandoned by his faithless supporters.

Harald threw the gaudy, babbling emperor to the ground and with one swift strike he killed him.

The rebellion died in that stroke. It did not have the strength to survive the falling of its false ruler. Harald planted Land-Waster in the ground next to the body in the bright sunlight and as I looked around I saw that the enemy army was already disintegrating before our eyes.

The entire battlefield could be seen from where we were, and they could see us in turn. They could see the raven banner supreme behind them in a pillar of sunlight, and all of them knew what that blood-red banner meant. The heart was ripped from their army, units and blocks collapsing one by one as the determined imperial attacks pushed on.

None of them tried to come and save their leader. That is the great weakness of a rebel, you see. They had no loyalty to Delyan. He was just a figurehead, a tool for their petty ambitions. And when that figurehead was ripped from their army they had nothing to bind them together, no deeper bond or structure to take over amongst their hastily gathered ranks.

As we watched, exhausted and stunned standing atop that knoll, the enemy line shattered and broke, fleeing en masse, diverting like water to flow around either side of our position, and we were too tired to try and stop them.

Down below us, in the valley on the road, the mass of the imperial cavalry burst free from the fetters of the enemy defence and, bloodied and vengeful, started riding down the fleeing army.

A trio of horsemen, mounts white and pink with foamed sweat and spattered with gore, slowly rode up the gentler side of the knoll, coming over towards Harald. He turned to look at them and I saw that Theophilos was at their head. The magister of the Scholai reined in near Harald and shook his head.

'There is something quite wrong about you, Araltes of the North. I came to save you, to bring you back from your insanity, but you merely continued your attack.'

'The path to victory lay ahead,' Harald said, as if the magister had made no sense.

Theophilos laughed. 'Yes, I see that it did.' He gestured at the body near Harald's feet.

'Is that him?'

Harald nodded nonchalantly. 'I think so. He is an overdressed blind man with no sword. Who else could it be?' He gave the magister a thoughtful look. 'How did you come to be up here, so far from the rest of your men?'

The magister smiled. 'I saw your banner trapped in that gully, and I made a decision I was sure I would regret. I am not usually one for disobeying orders, but I couldn't let another guard tagma fight alone and be destroyed.'

Harald walked over, reaching up to take the magister's hand. 'Thank you, Magister. This is also your victory now.'

Theophilos nodded tiredly. He leant forwards on his mount and took Harald's hand. 'No one will think that, Protospatharios, and if they did I would deny it. Glory is a young man's game, and I have no wish for the attention and power that comes with it.' He let go of Harald's hand and straightened, giving him a stern look. 'Be careful, Araltes. The rulers of the empire always need an enemy; a powerful threat for the people to fear and oppose. You think you just killed that enemy, but I fear you may have simply become him.'

Harald nodded, his face contemplative. 'Thank you, Magister, for your help and your advice. I am glad for both. Thank your men for me too. They were...' He shrugged, trying to find the words he wanted. 'Magnificent.'

Theophilos smiled slightly, touched his fingers to his brow and bowed his head, then turned his horse with a deft touch and walked the exhausted beast back down the hill, towards where the men of the Scholai were harrying the fleeing rebels.

I staggered over to Harald, my legs barely willing to work.

We exchanged no words, we made no gestures. We just stood there in silence and looked out over the terrible vastness of his triumph.

PART III
OATH-BREAKER

19

TINGHAUGEN, NORWAY; 1098 AD

Eric stopped his recounting, staring down at his hands, and the room was silent around him. Finally the king spoke.

'I have never heard the tale of that battle before from one who was there, Eric Sveitungr, and I must admit, your telling of it is not what I expected.'

'What did you expect, my lord?' Eric said, his voice tired.

King Magnus tapped his fingers on the arm of his chair, deep in thought. 'I did not expect to hear such a tone of what sounds like regret over such a magnificent victory.'

'It was not the victory that I regretted, my king. It was the death around me and inside me.'

'Inside you?'

Eric nodded slowly. 'The warrior inside me died that day, you see. I am ashamed to admit it, ashamed to say it in front of all these men, but that was the last time I fought as a warrior, a true warrior, anyway. My body was losing its youth, that is true, but the real problem was in my mind and in my heart. That terrible blow I had taken long before during the siege in the Rus damaged something in my mind that never healed, and every time I was hit in the head again it only got worse. No helmet could stop it, no medicine could help me.'

He looked at his hands and they were shaking. 'The sword-blow broke my mind, but Styrbjorn's death broke my heart. He was the best of us; the perfect guardsman. Faultlessly loyal, fearsome and inspiring in battle, and loved by all in the barracks and the guard for his wit and his generosity. He was a man I just never imagined could die, for he was so utterly full of life.'

Eric looked at the king and his eyes were red. 'Seeing that even Styrbjorn could die drained the last of my warrior spirit. I had once enjoyed war, revelled in it, but after more than ten years of ceaseless fighting, I was finished.'

There was an uncomfortable muttering around the room and the king frowned. It was tantamount to admitting cowardice, what Eric was saying, and any other man might have been rousted from the hall for the display, but they had all heard what he had done, and there was no man there who could claim he was a coward. Jarl Hakon put a comforting hand on his shoulder, unsure what to say.

'I think, Eric, that you need some respite from your tale,' the king said, trying to salvage the previously happy mood in the hall. 'Maybe you can start again later, after the feast, when we have all had a little ale and merriment?'

Eric looked up and nodded gratefully. 'I apologise, my king. I did not mean to dampen the spirits of this great gathering. I did not know what recounting it would bring back to my tired, old mind.'

The king waved the apology away. 'Do not be concerned. No power on earth could dampen the spirits of these fine men gathered here today,' he said, rising to his feet and raising his silvered horn. 'For now it is time we drink and feast, and look forward to our own days of glory in the sun, skol!'

The men of the hall stood and raised their drinks back at the king, chanting and draining their cups, the damp cloud evaporating in a moment as they sat back down and the babble of conversation settled again over the hall.

The king gave Eric one last thoughtful look and then turned to say something to Jarl Torvald at his side.

Ingvarr looked at Eric in uncomfortable confusion. 'Were you not happy with the victory, Eric?'

Ingvarr's father gave him a warning look, but the boy ignored it. Eric smiled weakly. 'I was pleased with how many of my brothers survived it, although too many did not. We laid over three hundred of my comrades out in that blood-ridden gully, with Styrbjorn at their head. It was too far to take them home and the ground was too hard to bury them, so we burned them all together in the old way and piled the bones and ashes that remained.'

Eric shook his head at the pain of the memory. 'It is called the valley of the Varangians by the locals now. A small chapel was raised there on the knoll where Delyan died, in honour of their memory. I always wanted to go there to visit them, but I never had the chance. I hope it still stands, and I hope the spirits of my brothers still lie in the sun.' He took a shaky sip from his mug and then stared at it sadly. 'Styrbjorn is the last one who still comes to me, in my dreams. His face is gone, long forgotten, but I recognise him, nonetheless. Of all my fallen brothers, and there were so many of them, he is the one my mind cannot let go of, perhaps because he was there the day it was so badly broken.'

Ingvarr nodded, looking a little shocked, and he did not press the old man any further as the food started to come out and the table fell to small talk and jokes as the feast went on. But Ingvarr kept looking at Eric, and saw that the old man barely touched his food, just moved it around the plate and occasionally smiled and thanked men who came over to him to ask him something or thank him for his tales.

But those bright eyes were dark, and the smile never reached them, and Ingvarr was struck by it terribly because they showed nothing of the pride and glory that he had expected.

* * *

The feasting went on all the rest of the afternoon, and into the evening. Eventually men stood to tell jokes, or recount their own stories, but then one man stood and raised his cup. 'Let us hear the rest of Eric's tale!' he shouted, and men all around the hall banged their horns on the tables.

Eric looked up from his seat where he had been in his own little world, and he looked over towards the king, who ran his fingers over his beard, betraying a small look of annoyance before standing and waiting. The room fell quiet and the king held up a hand.

'Who am I to deny you?' he said, a broad smile cracking across his face.

He turned to Eric. 'Can you finish your tale of the empire, Eric, and give us time for the real drinking to start afterwards?'

Eric bowed his head. 'I can, my king, for there is not much left to say.'

'Then it would please these men to do so, and I command it!'

There was a cheer of appreciation, and the king sat, giving Eric a firm look before turning back to Jarl Halfdan to speak to the lord of Tinghaugen.

Eric hastily cleared his throat as quiet descended, men settling into their benches to hear the old voice speak.

* * *

Well, I shall move on from the sadness of the end of battle, for it does not need to be recounted. We did right by our fallen brothers, and I keep their memory alive for as long as I survive the ceaseless assault of time.

We took over twenty thousand prisoners. The battle had been short, and the fighting had barely begun along the main line by the time it was over, so the only significant casualties on either side before their lines broke had been down in the fight on the valley floor, and in our desperate fight for the knoll.

So the emperor was faced with the decision of what to do with tens of thousands of traitors. Most of the officers advised him to execute them as a warning to any others that would remain defiant.

But Harald counselled a different approach, one that surprised me as much as anyone else.

'Free them, Basileus. Free them all except their leaders,' he said.

'Free them?' Andronikos looked at Harald aghast. 'They are rebels and traitors!'

'And they are broken, Domestikos. Men who have been defeated so utterly as this, been overmatched so completely and expected to die will not easily rise again. Give them mercy, and they will remember it. Kill them, and this region will not recover for a generation and their children will grow up bitter and fatherless, ready to rebel again in turn one day.'

They all looked at Harald in amazement, but the emperor raised a shaking hand to silence the debate.

'That is what we will do. It is the holy virtue of mercy, and we will show it.

Let my people know that they have nothing to fear from me if they repent of their sins and give themselves up to the empire and the Lord.' He nodded at the new domestikos. 'See to it.'

I could see that Andronikos was annoyed. He had good reason to be. Everyone in the army credited Harald for the victory over the rebels, and it must have chafed at the new and ambitious domestikos sorely. But there was nothing he could do.

We took the leaders of the rebels in chains to be paraded in front of the people in the capital, and the rest of the rebels were disarmed and allowed to go back to their homes. Andronikos and most of the army moved on again northwards to clear out the last rebel strongholds and secure the rest of the land, but the emperor was desperately sick and weak. He could no longer stand unassisted, and the imperial guard escorted him home, racing to get back to the city before our ruler died.

* * *

Not many of us expected him to survive the journey, but somehow he did.

We returned to the city through the Golden Gate, parading in triumph through Constantinople with the emperor propped on a bed of cushions and inside a curtain screen so that he could barely be seen. But the people massed in crowds to see him, and tore their clothes and screamed out their love for him as we passed. I saw Michael's tears of joy as he weakly waved back at his people, being welcomed home as a conquering saviour.

We took him to the palace and an army of doctors descended upon him in his chambers, and there was nothing left we could do.

* * *

We settled back into our palace life, immediately back to the rota of guard duties, training and chores that defined our times in the city. Once again, as with the time after every campaign, the issue of recruitment to fill the ranks of the dead and badly wounded reared its unwelcome head.

Every time it was becoming more difficult. There are only so many of our kin who travel east and the empire had been spending their lives as if the stream would never run dry. Well, the guard was the smallest it had ever been. Once those too badly wounded to continue in service had left, and those who decided they had seen enough of war and adventure had too, the guard had less than fifteen hundred men fit to serve.

* * *

Several weeks passed as we settled back into our duties and the emperor was confined to his chambers and his doctors' ministrations. Harald pored over the bandon lists with us one afternoon, and we broke up some of the weaker banda and transferred their men, the strong ones. This was a delicate process; moving the wrong men would generate a never-ending grievance. Most men were fiercely loyal to their own banda and their comrades, but it was a task that had to be done.

'Eric, wait behind,' Harald said as he dismissed us. I raised an eyebrow but nodded as the rest filed out. Afra gave me a friendly wink.

Harald sat there in awkward silence for a moment or two, which was unlike him.

'How do you like being komes of the seventh?' he finally asked, and I could feel it was a pointed question.

'I don't,' I heard myself reply before I thought about it.

He looked up at me in surprise. 'You don't?'

I shrugged; there was no unspilling the words. 'I am not good at it, Harald.'

'You and your men fought well in the battle, and you seemed to have earned their respect.'

'In the battle I was helpless. I was too worried for those who were wounded and dead to pay attention to the living. I was not in control of my men, nor in command. Truly, I think Sigurd led them in my absence and they are too embarrassed to complain after...' I trailed off, a feeling of anger swelling in me. My back still hurt sometimes from the scars of the whipping.

'Yes,' said Harald thoughtfully. 'They would be inclined to give you some forgiveness after what you did for Ulfr.' He intertwined his fingers and leaned forwards on the desk. 'I am glad to hear it though.'

'What?' I was taken aback. 'You are glad to hear I failed in my duties and my men ignored it?'

Harald simply nodded. 'It makes what I wanted to do far easier.'

I sagged. 'Which is what?'

Harald rubbed his thumbs together. 'I think being komes is not right for you.'

I was heartbroken to hear him say it, I tell you. My head drooped and I stared at the floor, humiliated. I knew I was not a good komes, but to hear Harald say it... to feel the raw truth and feel so... relieved. Ah, you see, I was more relieved than anything else. I felt like a fraud all the time I was komes. I was only put in the position because I was close to Harald, not because I had earned it.

'The men all respect you as a warrior, Eric, and as a brother who is dedicated to them. There is no doubt about that. But I need someone with more...' He spread his hands, trying to find the words. 'More fearlessness, in command of them.'

I nodded dumbly, not looking up at him. 'I understand. I don't know how I will stand the humiliation of another demotion, but I can't disagree.' I finally looked up and met his eye. 'I just can't stand losing so many of our friends. There are so few of us left.'

He nodded softly. 'I know. Well, who should replace you. Ulfr?'

I thought about it and shook my head. 'He cannot come back from what happened. No, Sigurd would be excellent.'

'Your second in command?'

I nodded. 'When I was losing my head, in the valley, he held his calm and organised the men, kept them fighting. He is the only choice.'

'Good. That is best for everyone.'

'Thank you, Harald,' I said with a sigh.

'For what?' He looked at me carefully.

'For not doing this in front of the other officers. I didn't need them here while I was declared to be of no further use.' I laughed bitterly. 'I don't know if I am even that good with a sword any more. What should I do now?' I gave him a worried look. 'Do you wish me to leave the guard?'

Harald furrowed his brows in annoyance. 'I did not say I had no further use for you, Eric, nor would I abandon you so easily. I am irritated that you even think it.'

I stammered and straightened a little. 'Oh, I... Well, what do you want from me?'

Harald looked at me as if he were reconsidering, but then shook his head slightly and leaned back. 'You have always worried too much, Eric. About everything.' He held up a hand to forestall me speaking, and I closed my mouth.

'On its own, unchecked, it makes you a poor leader. But I have always found it helpful for I worry about too little. Hearing your concerns, picking through them, has always been useful to me and I have been lacking it since you left my side. Sveinn and Styrbjorn...' He paused when he spoke our dead comrade's name, and his face darkened a little. 'They are, they were, great leaders and warriors, but they rarely questioned me. You challenge me, Eric, on everything. Nine times you might be wrong, but the tenth...' He looked at me uncomfortably and pursed his lips as if the admission hurt him. 'The tenth time has saved me from myself on several occasions.'

I smiled a little, feeling a spark of pride because it was true. I had saved him before, and kept him from grievous mistakes.

'I need that again, Eric, if your mind is clear enough to do it.' He stood and walked to the back of the office, where the rolled standards of the guard were resting on a wooden rack.

He picked up Land-Waster, not with reverence or affection, for it was merely a tool to him, and carried it over. He proffered the flag to me with a stern look. 'I have need of a standard bearer again. A loyal man to accompany me in my palace duties, and carry the symbol of the guard in battle. Can you carry its burden, Eric? And I don't just mean...'

'I know what you mean, Harald,' I said, reaching out and taking hold of the rolled cloth on its crosspiece, gripping the fabric firmly and feeling a rush of pride from its touch. 'I can bear the burden of standing beside you once more, enduring your ambition and giving you my advice only to hear it ignored.' I smiled at him as he let go of the flag. 'I will content myself with the one time in ten when you finally heed me, if that is useful to you.'

He gave me a last assessing look and then nodded. 'It is done, then. You are now the standard bearer of the Varangian tagma, and will stand at my side once more.' He finally smiled. 'As my brother wished.'

I swallowed to clear my throat at the relief and happiness I felt at that. 'Thank you, Harald.'

He laughed softly. 'Don't thank me yet. And put our banner back, our first duty is not going to be a pleasant one.'

'Oh, why?'

He gave me a dark look. 'I have been called to see the empress.'

I sighed and looked at the banner, then shook my head and put it back in its rack. 'Nothing good will come from that. And I suppose you want me with you?'

'She is always calmer in front of a witness, and there are few I trust with her words other than you.'

'Afra?' I said hopefully.

'Afra is busy, so it will be you.' He gathered his magnificent cloak of office and then stopped, looking up at me. 'It's too late to regret your choice.'

I nodded ruefully. 'By a great number of years.'

* * *

We went to the palace and were let through into the empress's quarters where we were asked to wait in the gilded anteroom. We were there for quite some time, which we both understood was a measure of how irritated Zoe was with Harald.

Finally we were admitted by Hypatia, who looked at us as if we were street mongrels who had wandered into the palace, which only further confirmed it.

Zoe was standing by a window looking out over the gardens, one hand tapping impatiently on the windowsill.

'You kept me waiting, Protospatharios,' she said in a cold tone.

It seemed an outrageous lie, but you do not merely say that to the empress.

Harald bowed. 'My apologies, Basilissa. I came as soon as my duties allowed.'

'I am your duties, guardsman.'

Harald took a short, calming breath, but did not reply. Zoe was only expressing her anger. Finally she turned her icy glare on us. 'The emperor returns triumphant and alive.'

'As is my duty,' Harald said carefully.

She shook her head and laughed bitterly. 'You have killed me.'

'That will not be allowed to happen.'

'Bah, you have no idea. While you were gone John was rampant, aligning the entire palace behind my adopted son, readying him for power. Have you seen him yet?'

Harald looked nervous but shook his head. 'I have not had a chance to see the prince yet. But I am sure I can guide him once more.'

'No, it is too late. While you were away John sank his claws deep into the boy.' She shook her head bitterly. 'The real battle was here, and I lost. My husband didn't even have the decency to die. Instead he comes back here as a festering corpse, clinging to life like a stray dog to a scrap.'

The language was shocking, even for Zoe. I looked uncomfortably at the wall, trying to pretend I was not hearing it.

'What do you wish me to do, Basilissa?' Harald asked carefully.

She looked at him and there was real fear in her eyes, real sadness. 'It is too late for you to do what I wanted, Aralter. The emperor will die and my life will be forfeit the moment John can persuade Michael to decree it.'

Harald bristled. 'Have you any proof John is plotting against your life? I will end that, immediately.'

She laughed. 'Proof? No, of course not. I merely know it. It is what I would do.'

'Michael has promised to rule with you as co-empress.'

'And I am sure he will keep that pretence, for a while.'

'Basilissa, I will not let them harm you,' Harald said, stepping forwards with venom in his tone. I could tell he meant it, truly meant it. There was no warmth between them any more, if there ever truly had been, but Harald's duty to her was an iron bond in him that could not be broken, that much was beyond doubt.

'No, you can't. They will not come for me with swords, but with documents and whispers and votes. It might take weeks or months, but it will happen.' She looked at him and her anger collapsed into sadness. 'I have lost,

Araltes. Will you truly protect me when they order you to turn on me? I am too old and proud to flee, and there is nowhere I could hide.'

Harald inclined his head. 'I promise it.'

Zoe searched Harald's face for any sign of dishonesty, but appeared satisfied. 'Good. Then prepare yourself for the new emperor's rise. I have heard from my husband's doctors.' Her face set in a cold, neutral expression once more. 'I suspect it will not be long.'

* * *

We were ushered out of her quarters and went out into the palace. A familiar figure was waiting for us at the gate leading out, and I felt the heat coming off Harald at the sight of him.

'Harald,' John said with a venomous expression. 'The traitor who has killed my brother.'

Harald stopped, looking at him for a moment in worry. 'Surely the emperor still lives?'

'For a short time. He is breathing, that is all that can be claimed. His body is dead. Have you seen his leg, smelled it?'

We had, and we knew how bad it was.

'I helped your brother secure his legacy and the love of his people,' Harald said, trying to keep himself calm. 'As was his wish and command.'

'Yes, you do have so much more influence over him than I ever expected.' John's scowl melted into a more vicious, gleeful expression. 'But don't worry, I have ensured that won't happen again.' He tilted his head like a hawk, accentuating his odd, long nose and facial features.

'I made so much progress with my nephew's education, in your absence.'

'What do you know of military matters, eunuch?'

'Oh, nothing, but I paid for the finest tutors. Real Roman generals, not reckless barbarians. But I also schooled him in politics, governance, all the things he will need.' John smiled an oily, disgusting smile. 'And in loyalty, both to family and empire.'

Harald started walking again. 'I am bored of your gloating, eunuch. If you have nothing to say why waste my time with it.'

'Oh, I am trying to help you, Protospatharios,' John said, matching Harald's pace and walking alongside the much larger man.

'I cannot imagine how.'

'I want to save you from what is coming, and save me having to deal with you.'

Harald could not help but tense a little at that, and John saw it and smiled. 'Ah, yes, you have considered it. Leave with your gold and your life and leave the governance of Rome to the men who are tasked with it.' He shook his head. 'We don't need your meddling any more. Be gone now, before it is too late.'

Harald rounded on the smaller man, suddenly and with enough vigour that John instinctively leapt a pace back and his eyes went wide.

But Harald did not strike him. 'You think I will run from you, John? Abandon the empress and my duties? It is not worms like you who are the rightful rulers of the empire.' His lips curled into a furious sneer. 'A family of money-counters and shipyard workers, eunuchs and cowards. You are not the guardians of empire – you are the suckling parasites who cling to its belly. The empress is the daughter of royalty, born in the purple, and I am a prince of Norway. I will not run from you, maggot.'

Harald fizzled with anger, getting right in John's face, towering over him.

But the eunuch managed to stand his ground, even though his hand shook a little.

'Good,' he finally said with a victorious smile, before half turning and taking a step away. 'I so desperately look forward to seeing you brought down low and destroyed. It will be the greatest achievement of my life, and you cannot say I didn't warn you.'

And then he bowed and walked away.

Harald stood there, fuming, and footsteps came down the corridor, breaking his trance.

'Protospatharios!'

Harald looked up to see a guardsman of the first bandon.

'What?'

'It's the emperor,' said the guard with a grim expression. 'You are needed.'

'Shit,' muttered Harald. 'Not so soon.'

20

CONSTANTINOPLE; OCTOBER 1041 AD

We hurried to the emperor's quarters and Harald pushed his way past attendants and found a gaggle of the emperor's doctors around his bed. The air was heavy with the scents of fragrant oils and perfumes that could not hide the pungent smell of decay.

'Make way,' Harald snapped, and a couple of indignant men in white robes moved aside.

We reached the emperor's bedside and saw that he was alive, but pale and wasted. The blankets over his legs were tented by some sort of frame to keep the covers from touching them. His eyes sluggishly looked up at Harald. 'Ah... Harald. Good.'

Harald knelt down beside the bed to listen to him more closely. 'What is it, Basileus?'

'It seems... It seems I will not have time to enjoy our glory, Protospatharios.' He beckoned to an attendant and Harald looked at the chief doctor.

'What is happening?'

The old Greek man, who looked exhausted, nodded nervously. 'The emperor is reaching the end of his God-given duties on this earth.'

'There is nothing you can do?' Harald asked.

The old man shook his head.

Michael took a pair of scrolls from his attendant with shaking hands. 'I have some commands for you, Harald.'

'Yes, Basileus,' Harald said, taking the scrolls.

The emperor breathed hard with the effort of speaking, but he pointed at the first scroll. 'You have always had the interests of the empire at heart, Harald. And I charge you to keep the peace when I am gone. I am bestowing upon you the rank of spatharokandidatos.' The emperor closed his eyes a moment and swallowed, sweat beading on his brow. 'It is an old title, not often used any more, but the highest a non-Roman can receive. It is meant as a great honour, Harald, and I hope you receive it as such.'

Harald bowed his head. 'I do.'

'Good, but that is not why I am giving it to you.' The emperor paused again and a doctor fussed at his forehead with a cloth, which Michael weakly waved away. 'I need you to have authority to keep the peace.' He gestured to the second scroll. 'This will put every armed man within fifty miles at your command. It will prevent any usurper pitting one part of our forces against another, or against the palace. Use them wisely and honestly, Spatharokandidatos. There are good reasons why no single man is normally given this much power, and I trust you alone not to abuse it.'

'I will not,' Harald replied.

The emperor signalled for a drink from a hovering attendant, and he weakly sipped at an iced cup, coughing a little and then breathing hard to recover. 'I have to go now. I wish to remain at peace and so I also instruct that no one be allowed to visit.' He shut his eyes and sighed on the pillow, pain showing in his straining mouth and neck. 'No one should see the emperor like this.' Those once bright eyes looked at Harald again. 'It somewhat ruins the air of majesty.' And then he laughed, which turned into a crackling cough.

'Go where?' Harald said in confusion, looking around.

'The Monastery of the Stoudion,' the doctor said. 'There to rest and pray while he waits.'

Harald looked at the emperor in surprise. 'To simply wait?'

Michael nodded. 'Down by the sea, in peace, I will pray for salvation and perhaps if I am lucky, for I was a great sinner, receive it.' Then he groaned and shifted uncomfortably on the bed. 'That means this is our farewell,

Harald. I thank you for your service to me, and I am sorry to have left you with such burdens.'

'I am not abandoning my duties, Basileus,' Harald said with a little anger. 'I will still guard you.'

'You may guard the monastery as you see fit, Spatharokandidatos, but you will not disturb my solace. No one will. That is my wish and you will honour it.'

Harald looked deeply unhappy, but he nodded. 'As you command.'

'You must go now. The emperor needs his rest before we move him,' the doctor said, shooing Harald away with a look of distaste.

Harald saluted and we finally made our way out as the cloud of doctors descended upon Michael again like flies on a corpse.

As we walked away, I was shocked to see that Harald was almost in tears.

'I did not expect you to be so affected,' I said. 'You used to hold him in very low regard.'

'He has changed, as a man and as a leader, and he does not deserve this. It is undignified and unjust for this to happen in the moment of his victory.' He looked at me with deep sadness in his eyes. 'He was only just becoming the leader the empire needs, and now that potential is wasted.'

'Perhaps Zoe can be the leader the empire needs.'

He shook his head. 'I fear it is too late. But nor will I leave her in the clutches of the rat bastard John. Come with me, I need to make alternative plans.'

*   *   *

Afra looked up as we went into his small office in the first bandon's small barracks in the palace. He saw Harald's face and nodded grimly. 'So you have seen him.'

'We have. Do you know?'

'That he is leaving? Yes, we will be guarding him on the journey to the monastery, of course.'

Harald nodded slowly and Afra gave him an apologetic look. 'I'm sorry, my friend, there are some things I must keep secret, even from you. It was the emperor's command. He wanted to tell you himself.'

Harald waved it away. 'I am not angry with you, you are doing your duty. I have another task, however, one that requires equal secrecy.'

Afra raised an eyebrow. 'I hope it is not one that contradicts my other duties.'

'It is not. I need a ship and fifty or so men, mercenaries that can be trusted.'

Afra laughed, and then saw Harald was serious. 'You want mercenaries that can be trusted? Harald, you might ask me for a pig that shits gold, but I cannot work miracles. Why not use our own men?'

'We cannot. Not for this.'

Afra looked troubled. 'I will see what I can do. When and where?'

'Have them wait in the main docks on the south side of the city, not the Golden Horn, and I need them as soon as possible. Low visibility, not armed – keep their weapons and equipment in the ship. They will need them on the voyage and at their destination but not here. They will not be fighting in the city. They are transporting a precious cargo out of the city, that is all they need to know.'

Afra nodded slowly. 'And this precious cargo, it is ready to leave?'

Harald bit his lip. 'Not yet. We will send for them when it is.'

Afra looked at him with a concerned expression but then shrugged and nodded. 'I will find someone, and pay them well.'

'Not too well,' Harald said. 'It will raise suspicion.'

'As you say.' Afra stood with a wince; his leg was getting worse. 'I have arrangements to make for the emperor. I will come back when I can and tell you what I managed to get for you.'

Harald put his hand on Afra's shoulder and looked at him meaningfully. 'Thank you, Afra.'

'For what? I am just doing my duty.'

'For being more than men said you were.'

Afra smiled. 'I have always been what men say that I am, Harald. I am Afra the Constant, and, in your case, that means constantly loyal. In other cases...' He gave Harald a wink and said no more as he left the room.

* * *

The emperor left the palace the next day by boat, quietly and with no ceremony or fanfare, hidden completely in a plain and curtained palanquin as if he were just some visiting dignity.

We escorted the anonymous cargo to the ship and watched him go, knowing we would never likely see him again. It was a dark day.

His adopted son did not come down to see his father leave. Perhaps he was not even made aware of it. He had taken up residence in the Boukoleon Palace down by the harbour but he did not appear at its railing, and Harald noted that with dark disapproval.

'Let's go and see the future emperor,' he said once the ship had left.

We went up the stairs to the front entrance where the commander of a half dozen Vigla guardsmen attempted briefly to deny us permission.

'No unauthorised visitors are allowed, Protospatharios,' one of them said nervously.

Harald gave the soldier an icy glare. 'I am spatharokandidatos of the guard. I am the authority and no door is closed to me. Stand aside, now, or I will have you whipped until you die.'

The guardsman looked wide-eyed but then nodded and stepped aside, mumbling some sort of apology.

The doors were hurriedly opened for us and then we went through into the arched entrance hall and beyond, into the wide space with the open veranda where Michael had held the great peace conference earlier in the year, when he had hoped he might recover from his illness.

It was empty now, not a soul in sight, one curtain that had come loose from its ties blowing gently in the breeze.

There wasn't even anyone there to ask where Michael was.

Harald looked around in annoyance, but then we heard a muffled peal of laughter from behind the doors on the left, the doors that led to the private bathhouse. He turned and walked towards them, opening them with a crash and going through into the marble hallway that led into the various rooms of the baths.

He took us down the hall, following the sound of voices and the wafts of steam, and pushed through a curtain into the hot baths. I went through behind him as a peal of female laughter rang out and I saw the younger Michael sitting in the bath, naked, with one girl perched sideways on his lap and another sitting by his head, feeding him teasingly from a platter of grapes.

Harald stopped and we both stood there until there was a squeal as one of the girls saw us.

Michael looked up in surprise and then fear as he saw us. 'Harald?'

Harald bowed. 'My apologies, my prince, I did not mean to alarm you.'

The girl who had been feeding Michael grapes stood and backed away, but Harald held up a hand. 'Do not be alarmed, girl, you have nothing to fear.'

That was a ridiculous statement. We were two armoured giants standing in the steam room, fully armed, without warning. Even Michael looked afraid, although he had good reason to be. He would not have been the first prospective emperor to die in a bath at the hands of his own guards. In fact, I think that was almost a tradition in the empire.

The girl sitting on Michael's lap slipped into the water and floated beside him, leaving Michael embarrassed and exposed.

'My prince, I need to speak to you. I apologise for the circumstances, but it is rather urgent.'

'I see... Well, I was just... You know my uncle doesn't let me out of the palace and...'

Harald held up a hand, smiling reassuringly. 'There is no need to explain yourself, my prince. We were all young men once, and you may do as you wish. But perhaps the girls could return later?'

Michael looked relieved and nodded, gesturing to the girl in the pool next to him, who stared at Harald with beady, wary eyes. 'Do as he asks. I will call for you shortly.'

The girl bowed her head, a ridiculous gesture as she was up to her neck in the steaming water, and then dashed up the marble steps, water streaming from her as she padded away across the floor with wet slaps with her companion close behind her.

Finally we were alone, and Michael sat there awkwardly and exposed, waiting for Harald to speak. Harald did not ask him to dress and come to a different room, despite the fact that I knew he, like I, would soon be sweating profusely in our thick tunics, armour and cloaks.

'Do you know where the emperor is?' Harald asked.

Michael looked at him dumbly. 'In the palace?'

Harald shook his head. 'No, while you were... enjoying yourself, he was moved to the Monastery of the Stoudion, near the city walls.'

Michael looked surprised. 'What, why?'

'To pray for salvation, and await God's call,' said Harald icily. 'You were not told?'

Michael looked lost. 'I was not. My uncle told me that he would die in the palace, that I should be kept separate from everyone else for my own safety, and to avoid attempts to corrupt me.'

Harald nodded carefully. 'I am sure your uncle meant well.'

'He has prepared me well, in your absence, Harald,' Michael said brightly. 'He has brought me the best tutors and I have been studying the Tactica and the writings of the Emperor Basil. I am to study the Praecepta Militaria next.'

Harald nodded. 'That is good, it is good to have the proper military education, but perhaps in shielding the outside world from you, you are also being shielded from the outside world. It is important to know what is happening.' He pointed at the door through which the young women had disappeared. 'There is nothing wrong with a little relaxation, but your prime duty as emperor, which you will soon be, is to know what is happening, at all times, and at all levels. The emperor of Rome, your father, just passed by your window to travel to his deathbed, and you didn't know.' The last words were harsh, and Michael looked crestfallen.

'I... I wasn't told.'

'Sometimes leaders need not wait to be told, otherwise men will only let you hear what they want you to hear, and thus you will be their slaves.'

Michael nodded, suddenly ashamed, and he stood from the water and walked quickly over to grab a gold-trimmed white robe. He walked towards us around the bath.

'I am sorry, Harald. I will learn from this and be a better emperor, I promise you.'

Which was a worthy aim, if made slightly ridiculous by him being soaking wet and hurrying around with his manhood flopping about like a horse's tail while he fought with the delicate robe.

But he seemed oblivious to that and finally he got his sodden arms into it and closed it at the front. 'What do I need to do?'

Harald nodded gently. 'You need to prepare to become the emperor. Which means you need to call the important men of the city to meet you, get to know them, learn their intents and secure their loyalty.'

'But my uncle has done all of that, he knows them all. He can deal with them?'

'Your uncle is not going to be the emperor, is he?'

Michael blushed red. 'No, I am.'

'So you need to know them yourself, or they will not know you.'

'But my uncle told me not to see anyone. Tell me what to do?' he said, looking lost.

Harald's brows knitted together and he leant down to look at the young man carefully. 'Michael, you are the prince of the empire, the heir to the throne that will soon be yours. You can do whatever you want.' Harald put a hand on his shoulder. 'If you want to call those girls back in and fuck them, eat grapes and drink wine until you can't make your prick stand up any more, do so. You don't have to take instruction from anyone, not your uncle, and not me. We both live to serve at your command, not you to ours.'

He took his hand off Michael's shoulder as the boy nodded, wide-eyed. 'Yes, of course. God, I was being so stupid. I'm sorry, Harald.' He shook his head and put his hands over his face. 'I'm just not used to this. I want to be a great emperor, I really do. I want to be like you, a powerful man who men respect.'

Harald gave him a hard expression. 'Great men do not wish to be so, they merely are.'

Michael nodded. 'I understand. Thank you.' He paused, and I could see that he had been about to ask what he should do, but then he caught himself and raised his chin. 'Thank you for your visit, Harald. I will call for you when I need you next.' The words almost rose to indicate a question and Michael looked terribly nervous, as if he had just crossed a line, but Harald smiled broadly and took a step back before bowing.

'I am at your command, my prince.' He saluted and turned smartly to leave the hot, damp room, with me on his heels.

Getting out into the fresh air of the room with the veranda was a supreme blessing, and I breathed in deeply and flapped my cloak to try to air out my sodden tunic beneath my armour.

By the time we got out through the doors it was clear that effort was futile, and nothing but a complete change of clothes would save me so I gave up. I had suffered worse.

'That went well?' I asked cautiously.

'I think so,' Harald said. 'I wish I could be sure that John will not simply bring him to heel again. John is far stronger and smarter than that boy. I suspect I have won Michael only a temporary respite from his control. Time will tell. I will try and see him again, regularly.'

'So that you can control him instead?'

Harald looked at me as if I was simple. 'Of course. You don't think that scared, helpless child has a chance of deciding what to do by himself?'

I shook my head. 'No, I don't think he does.'

21

CONSTANTINOPLE; DECEMBER 1041 AD

'Harald!'

Harald looked up from our meal in the barracks as the voice called out. There were few enough people who would call for him by name and not title. Fewer still inside the barracks.

Thorir came through the door and saw us, and he ran over and leaned in to whisper in Harald's ear.

Harald went stiff and then nodded, abandoning his cutlery. He stood, gesturing for me to follow. I knew what it was, I didn't need to hear Thorir's whispers to know. There was only one piece of urgent news we were waiting for: the emperor was dead.

It was surprising to everyone how long the emperor had clung to life, through half of the autumn. We heard from Afra that Michael's legs had completely fallen to decay and the doctors had removed their lower halves in a desperate attempt to save him. Somehow, through sheer willpower, the emperor had survived that for another three weeks, although heavily drugged and insensate to the world.

The powerful players in the city had waited impatiently for Michael to finally give in, preparing their pieces in the great game to jostle for power as the new emperor came in.

Harald had played the game too, trying to spend as much time with the younger Michael as possible, but being cleverly rebuffed more often than not by John's or Michael's courtiers. The boy was always busy doing something else that precluded Harald's visits, and his trick of threatening his way past the Vigla guards did not work on Michael's courtiers, who were not his to command.

He had not spent a lot of time with the empress. She had secluded herself with her remaining allies and advisors, and it felt that she had finally given up on receiving any support from Harald. She had also travelled to the emperor's deathbed, begging to see him one final time, perhaps to try and extract some form of protection or decree, but Afra had firmly turned her away. We had not heard from her since.

Afra had found us a ship full of mercenaries, men from Italy and the Rus, and had them waiting quietly at one of the city's smaller harbours, ready when we called them.

Now we would find out who had prepared better, and where the pieces would fall.

'Who knows?' Harald asked Thorir as we moved out into the courtyard.

'John and his family were there at the bedside when he died.'

'Shit,' Harald cursed. 'So he will already be making his moves. Does the empress know?'

'Yes. John ordered that she not be told, but we ignored that. For the moment she is the only legal authority. She has demanded you go with her to the patriarch's palace; she is going to try and block Michael's ascension. If Patriarch Alexius declares Michael illegitimate, perhaps the empress can prevent him being crowned.'

'I cannot help her with that. I swore an oath to Michael that I would help his son secure the throne and rule. The guard does not get involved in politics.'

Thorir nodded. 'The empress said you would say that, but she doesn't want your help, she merely wants you to guard her while she travels to the patriarch. She says if you do not, she will go alone, naked, wearing all the jewellery she can carry.'

Harald looked at him in fury. 'She said what? God above, she might do it too. Fine, I will guard her while she travels, but no more. Where is Afra?'

'With the emperor's body. He will escort it back ready for the funeral services.'

'Eric, rouse the on-duty bandon and have them meet me outside the palace. We will escort the empress to the patriarch. Who is on duty?'

'The seventh.'

Harald nodded. 'Good luck for us then. Go, quickly.'

I nodded and ran to the guardroom where a detachment of armed and armoured guardsmen was always ready, waiting for any emergency.

Sigurd was there, idly carving at a small model of a ship while other men sat around a table of dice. They all looked up at me as I entered.

'Trouble?' Sigurd asked, dropping the carving. Everyone in the room went still.

'The emperor is dead,' I said, and there were grim faces all around.

'What do you need us to do?'

'The empress needs an escort through the city. I don't expect violence, but at a time like this anything is possible. Get your men ready to leave, immediately.'

Sigurd nodded. 'At once.' He and the rest of the men jumped into action, grabbing their helmets and weapons and filing out of the door into the courtyard as I followed.

The activity was noted immediately, and Rurik came over with a worried expression.

'What is it?'

'Find Sveinn, rouse all the banda who are in the barracks and be ready to move at a moment's notice.'

'Aye, Eric.' He paused. 'Is it...?'

'Just do it, Rurik,' I said with a nod. He understood.

'I will.' And then he turned away, shouting orders at the men who were watching.

The seventh bandon was assembling in the courtyard as Sigurd harangued them into place, veins pulsing, barking orders and directing men with the haft of his spear.

I smiled as I watched him work, watched the instant compliance he got from his guardsmen. I was happy with the decisions Harald and I had made. Sigurd was making a fine komes.

Before long they were all assembled, and Sigurd turned smartly to look to me for orders.

I cleared my throat. 'It is essential we avoid violence, but not at risk to the empress. If there is any threat to her we will cut our way free, even if it is through the people of this city. Let's move!'

We filed out of the barracks in a column four men wide and jogged to the palace, where Harald appeared with Zoe and a little gaggle of her attendants.

'There was no time for a palanquin,' he said.

'The empress goes on foot?'

Harald shook his head. 'No, I arranged for... Ah, here they are.'

There was the sound of hooves behind us and I turned and saw a dozen guards of the Scholai ride into the outer yard of the palace, with Theophilos at their head. He was leading a spare horse.

He bowed to Zoe. 'Basilissa.'

She smiled at him with genuine joy. 'Magister, I am pleased to see you.'

'If only it was under better circumstances, Basilissa. I mourn your loss.'

Zoe nodded politely. 'Thank you.' She moved towards the spare horse while two guardsmen moved to help her mount.

'I hope you remember my lessons, Basilissa,' Theophilos said with a coy smile.

Zoe turned her most charming gaze on him. 'I remember everything you taught me, Theophilos.'

The magister actually blushed as Zoe settled comfortably in the saddle, doing her best to arrange her gown which was not designed for riding. But there was no time for fussing over her lower legs being exposed.

'Let's go.' The magister looked at Harald and bowed a little. 'I hope your men are in good shape, Spatharokandidatos. I think we need to move fast.'

'Don't worry, Magister. These men are the best I have. Just don't get left behind.'

Some of the guardsmen laughed at that.

Harald turned to the assembled group. 'The route has not been cleared or prepared for us, and people will be filling the streets and surprised to see us. Stop for nothing but use your weapons only if you must and the threat is real. A massacre of the innocent could leave the city in flames.'

'Aye, Spatharokandidatos!' the men called in reply.

'Then we go!'

Harald set off at the head of the column, taking me and half of the seventh with him, and the magister followed with his column of horsemen with the empress hidden in their midst. The rest of the bandon brought up the rear.

We marched hard and fast, taking the underground passage through the basement of the Hippodrome and then out of its main gate into the streets near the Hagia Sophia.

People scattered as we broke into a jog, our equipment and the hooves of the horses making a rattle and din that could be heard from streets away.

'Make way!' Harald roared at the front, for there was no point in subtlety.

We plunged into the street that led down the hill from the cathedral towards the patriarch's palace, which was not more than half a mile away on the shore of the Golden Horn.

But half a mile is a long way to jog through crowded streets in full armour, and we were soon huffing and blowing and had to slow several times to give the packed streets time to clear. We moved down through the city towards the shoreline and reached the sea wall, heading along it until we got to the palace, lungs on fire and legs aching.

Harald, seemingly immune to such things, ran up the short flight of stairs and hammered on the door. It was opened immediately by a surprised-looking attendant.

'Make way,' said Harald, and the attendant just peered at him.

'What? Who are you?'

'Spatharokandidatos of the guard. Make way!'

'Who...' Then the attendant stopped and his face went wide, and he bowed fully and deeply. I turned and saw that Zoe had dismounted and climbed the steps, standing beside Harald. She put a gentle hand on his shoulder and pulled him back. 'Thank you for getting me here. I will handle this now. A softer touch is required.'

'As you command, Basilissa.'

Zoe smiled and gestured at the attendant to rise. 'I need to see Patriarch Alexius. Please take me to him.'

As she did, there was movement in the door and the patriarch himself appeared, looking as surprised as the attendant had.

Zoe turned her gaze on him and beamed. 'Ah, Patriarch Alexius. Thank you for meeting me.'

'Basilissa. I was not expecting you while...'

'You have heard the sad news?' Zoe asked.

He bowed his head. 'I have. I am sorry, my empress. What a tragic day.'

'Yes, it is,' Zoe said with a small nod. 'May I come in and speak to you, about the arrangements for the future?'

The patriarch looked like a landed fish, gaping at her and then nervously looking over his shoulder.

Zoe suddenly chilled and her gaze hardened. 'How did you know about the emperor's death, Patriarch? Who is here with you?'

The patriarch's mouth shut and he gave her a slightly defiant gaze but did not speak.

Zoe's expression turned to thunder and she moved towards the door, the patriarch scrambling aside to avoid touching her as she went through with me and Harald at her heels.

She came to a stop in the great vestibule of the church that made up the front of the patriarch's palace, and we saw what she saw.

'Basilissa, what a surprise,' said John with an amused smile.

Zoe looked around in fury, taking in the scene. John was not alone. Standing in a loose half-circle in the great room were thirty or so finely dressed men, all looking confused and surprised, as everyone had been so far to see us.

Immediately I felt that we had interrupted a plot, some sort of treachery, and I moved to Zoe's side with my hand on my sword. Harald clearly felt the same, as he moved in front of her.

'What is this?' he asked loudly, and the threat was coming off him in hot waves so that men even ten paces away looked nervous and backed away.

'Calm yourself, guardsman. There are no enemies here,' John said.

'Then what are you doing, meeting like this in secret on the day my husband died?' Zoe hissed in outrage.

She scanned the room, her brows furrowing in hurt and shock as she looked at all the faces. 'Maurinus, you swore to uphold and protect me. What are you doing here, plotting with John?'

The nobleman she was looking at looked aghast, but could not find the words to reply.

'Or you, Domianus, how could you?'

'Basilissa, I don't understand. I thought...' He looked helplessly at John.

Zoe was practically weeping at the betrayal, truly hurt. These were most of the great men of the city, many of them her allies.

'Basilissa, I thought this is what you wanted?' Domianus said, looking deeply concerned. 'We are here to secure your son's future, and his place by your side as emperor. Is that not what you wished? I...' The nobleman stammered to a halt.

'We were just here reading your husband's final edict, making sure the great men of the city and its patriarchy were ready to carry out his instructions without delay or confusion,' said John with a sickly false smile.

Zoe looked stunned, not comprehending. Then a look of horror came across her face as she understood.

The patriarch came up and smiled gently at her before turning to the small crowd. 'Gentlemen, do not judge the empress. She has suffered a great loss and we are at fault for not informing her about this meeting, which is done in full love and support for her and her son.' He bowed to her, putting a hand on his breast. 'I did not inform you because I knew you would be in mourning, and did not think you would want to be troubled by this formality. I realise that was a grave error, but made with no malice. John made it clear he had your full agreement on this matter, told all of us here that we must support your desire to raise your son to the throne, to cement your husband's legacy.'

Zoe looked at the patriarch drunkenly, and then at John, who could barely contain his glee. She finally recovered enough to make a shaky smile and nodded. 'You are right, Patriarch. I was mistaken as to the intent of this meeting. You understand my concern; this is a difficult day.'

There was a wave of relief around the room as the empress said that, and the patriarch nodded sympathetically. 'I absolutely understand, Basilissa. Please, be assured that we and the great men of the city will support you and your son entirely. There will be no discord or resistance to his ascension, we will ensure it.'

Zoe drew herself up a little and nodded. 'Then I have no concerns to discuss with you, Patriarch. I thank you for your loyalty.'

She turned, and she was shaken enough that she almost stumbled, Harald taking hold of her hand to steady her.

'Take me back to the palace,' she whispered to him urgently. And he nodded.

The men gathered in the room all bowed as we left, the looks of relief on their faces clear to see as I ducked out of the door.

Zoe was weeping, tears streaking her make-up as two guardsmen helped her back into the saddle and Theophilos looked to us in concern.

'Back to the palace,' Harald said with a firm nod, and Theophilos did not push for an explanation of the bizarre incident.

Zoe drew her veil around her, trying to hide her face, and we set off once more towards the palace, even as the city's bells began to toll.

* * *

'That rat bastard!' Zoe shrieked, her careful make-up a complete mess, as she threw a priceless statue to smash against the wall. 'We should have killed him long ago.'

She put a hand to her face and leant against the wall of her chamber while Harald looked on with a hollowed expression.

'I was prepared for his treachery, I readied my people to resist it, but he convinced them all he had given in to me! The fools!' She looked at Harald in despair. 'How did I not see this? He has won. They all believe now that I want my son to be emperor, and there is nothing I can do to change that without completely dishonouring myself in their eyes or looking like a madwoman.'

Harald's eyes flicked around the mess she had made of her own anteroom as if to suggest that they might have a point.

'That cunning little snake,' she said, finally slumping onto a seat. 'He beat me by using my own people and my own words, before there was even a contest. I have no choice now but to go through with it and crown that fucking boy as emperor.' She bit her finger, deep in thought. 'But the patriarch, he knew the truth. I saw it in his face. John bribed him. Not that that should surprise me, for I did the same before my husband's coronation. Bah,

I should have got rid of him years ago. A man who accepts bribes once can never be trusted again. He will pay for this betrayal.'

Harald fidgeted uncomfortably, all his oaths and promises conflicting in a mess even I could not decipher.

'You could leave the city, Basilissa. I have made plans.'

She looked at him in horror. 'The empress of Rome, abandon her city to escape her son before he is even crowned and her husband is buried?' She shook her head miserably. 'The shame of that is unbearable. No. I will not flee.' She raised her hands helplessly. 'I may not even need to, I am so utterly defeated. The whole city now thinks I am raising my own son as my replacement. The entire nobility is behind it, and thus behind John. Am I even a threat to him any more?'

'If that is true, then I can surely protect you, Basilissa, as I always have.'

She looked up at him and nodded, reaching out her hand for his.

She looked at me, the first time she had seemed to see me. 'Leave us.'

'Basilissa.' I bowed instantly. I had no wish to be there a moment longer.

I gave Harald what I hoped was a comforting nod and hurried from the room, leaving my prince to comfort a forlorn empress who had just inherited an empire and lost it in a day.

22

If you have been paying attention to anything I have said, you will not expect that Zoe gave up after that. No. She, like Harald, was incapable from the depths of her soul of giving up on her ambitions. She had no choice but to accept her adopted son as the next emperor, having been so deftly outmanoeuvred by John, but she did her utmost to make sure her own place next to him was secure.

When Michael the elder had become emperor, it had been the very same day that his predecessor had died. Zoe did not allow that, instead declaring the city to be in three days of mourning, with Michael's body paraded through the streets as Zoe walked alongside it dressed in mourning black, holding her dead husband's cold hand at times and weeping.

The city was driven wild by the display of love and devotion to their tragically lost emperor, the hero who had saved the empire from rebellion. Zoe, who had always been popular with the people as the daughter of Emperor Basil II – saviour of the empire – ascended to new heights of public adulation.

It was a clever scheme to make herself impossible to easily remove or push aside, but it could only delay the inevitable. On the fourth day, with Zoe graciously smiling at one side and John at the other, her adopted son was crowned as Emperor Michael V.

Thus began another great hidden war for the palace. John and Zoe wrestled, coerced, bribed and outright murdered each other's supporters and helpers, although it was mostly in the city, not in the palace itself. Harald kept an iron grip on the palace grounds, and anyone found bringing violence or plots inside its walls was ruthlessly dealt with. Bodies hung from one of the sea gates on most days as an example to the rest.

It went on like this for several months, through the end of the year and into the first touches of spring in the next.

Michael was kept busy by both Zoe and John meeting delegations from every theme in the empire, every ally, and many of the empire's foes, and was either blissfully unaware of the struggle or actively chose to ignore it at John's behest.

But little by little, as his experience grew, he became more and more assertive, and Zoe was forced into a distinctly secondary role. It became clear in the third month of 1042 that Zoe was going to lose the struggle for control, and she started more and more desperately begging Harald to intervene on her side, which he repeatedly refused, until she stopped calling him to her altogether.

Harald became simply her guard again, and I think it was an enormous relief to him.

The inevitable culmination of this struggle began in April of the year of our Lord 1042, on a day that began no differently to any other in the palace, with Harald and I on duty in the hall of nineteen as the emperor received delegations from the city's grain merchants, who were complaining of resurgent pirate activity in the east.

When those men were gone, placated by a promise of six ships of the imperial fleet to help patrol the trade route, the imperial business was finished for the day and we prepared to escort the emperor back to his quarters.

'Spatharokandidatos, wait a moment. I need to speak to you,' said Michael, gesturing from his raised chair for Harald to approach. John, who was almost never absent from his nephew's side, stood there impassively as Harald raised an eyebrow at the invitation to stand before the emperor.

My suspicions were raised by that immediately. It was a bizarrely formal gesture, as the emperor and Harald spoke very frequently, and had a cordial relationship that still included sessions of military education.

But Harald nodded and went to stand before the emperor and bowed.

'I hear you have been troubling my chancellor about payment for the guard.'

Harald frowned a little. 'Basileus, I have been politely enquiring as to when the payment your father promised to the guard will be transferred.'

He was referring to the reward of gold that the previous emperor had promised to the guard after our help putting down the revolt of Petar Delyan, as was traditional after the guard came back from a successful campaign. We had not received such a gift since before the debacle in Sicily, and the slowness paying it had caused a deal of resentment and grumbling in the ranks.

Michael looked at Harald with an odd smile and then turned to look at his uncle, who made a sort of helpless gesture of regret.

'I am sorry, Spatharokandidatos, but there must have been some misunderstanding that my father did not resolve before his death. There will be no excessive payment for the guard. All of the funds my father gained from his defeat of the rebels was spent raising churches in honour of the victory in his name.'

Harald's eyes widened a little. 'All of it?'

'I'm afraid not much was gained from the emperor's swift victory,' John added. 'After all, only one minor rebel city was looted, and the rest surrendered without much resistance. I fear the terms were a little generous, when it came to financial penalties.'

Harald visibly bit back his anger. 'Basileus, the guard were promised a reward for their service, by the emperor himself.'

'And are they not paid a good salary?' John enquired with mock innocence.

'Against a high debt,' snapped Harald. 'The understanding has always been that they would earn the extra they needed from good service on campaign in the emperor's name.'

'And did they not have the opportunity for loot and enrichment during that campaign?' asked John with a curious expression. 'I hear that you terrorised vast swathes of the rebel lands, lands that may never host a living being again such was the destruction. They call you the Bulgar Burner,

Harald. Did you forget to empty their purses and homes before you cast them into the fires?'

Harald glared at the smug eunuch. 'Our focus was on victory for the empire. We did not weigh ourselves down with riches.'

'I see. How noble, if a little foolish. And at Skopje, did you not enter that city first? What of its riches?'

'Left with the loyal Greek residents – at the emperor's command, that city was not defiled.'

'Ah, I see,' John said, nodding as if that were news to him. He looked at his nephew. 'A difficult situation, then. I wonder what your father intended.'

Michael looked at John. 'There is no other way we can find the funds?'

John made a good show of considering it, but then shook his head regretfully. 'I'm afraid our treasury is low, after the celebrations of your ascension and the many gifts we gave to secure the full compliance and loyalty of the governors.' He shrugged and held his hands up. 'There is nothing to give.'

Michael nodded and turned to Harald. 'So you see, Spatharokandidatos, my father was mistaken. Perhaps his illness caused a miscalculation.'

Harald's temple throbbed. 'Basileus, I ask you to reconsider. This will cause great discontent in the guard.'

'Are you saying their loyalty might come into question?' John asked, and it was immediately obvious what the purpose of this theft was – to sow doubt in Michael's mind about our loyalty. I stood there fuming with deep-rooted rage.

'Never!' Harald said firmly. 'The question is not of their loyalty or commitment to duty, the question is of recruitment. The guard's numbers are lower than they have ever been, and the thing that draws men to enter its ranks, despite the high cost of doing so, is the golden promise of the empire, that they will be well rewarded for their service. If it becomes known that this promise is not kept...' Harald shook his head. 'We will never be able to recruit more men, and some will leave to seek payment elsewhere.' He gave John a knowing look. 'The guard will wither under such circumstances and lack the numbers to carry out your will and protect you effectively.'

Michael nodded, looking concerned. 'I understand your concerns, Harald, but everyone who comes to visit me needs something. The demands for gold are endless.'

'Quite endless, and the more crucial ones must be met first,' John said with a nod.

'Basileus, I beg you. Do not withdraw the guard's reward for the last campaign. Three hundred of them died for the empire and your father's glory, without question or doubt. Those who survived would do so again for you, whenever you need it. All they expect in return is for fair reward, and the honour of our promises to be kept.'

Michael shifted nervously in his seat, and his eyes flicked between Harald and John, his prior confidence evaporated. 'It does seem... important,' Michael said, and John scowled as he realised his control of the situation he had clearly himself engineered was slipping. It was likely he had downplayed the importance of the guard, or the payments.

'Basileus, I think there is nothing we can do.'

'I need to be protected from my enemies, Uncle. You always say so, and the guard can't do that if they have no men.'

John paused, looking up at Harald spitefully, then he nodded. 'I will go to the chancellor myself, Basileus, and demand that he reconsider.'

Michael broke out into a grin and nodded. 'Excellent.' He turned to Harald, clearly pleased with himself. 'There, Spatharokandidatos, you have a satisfying answer. We will try and find the gold for your men.'

Harald was motionless, not in the slightest reassured by John's obviously empty promise, but unable to argue with Michael's assertion that it was resolved.

He bowed stiffly. 'Thank you, Basileus. The men will deeply appreciate the knowledge that the matter is being addressed.'

That was all he could do, leave the hook embedded that the men would be told to still expect payment, and be all the more bitter if they did not.

'Good. Well, there is another matter to discuss,' Michael said shrilly. 'My future, and securing the empire's inheritance.'

Harald raised an eyebrow. 'I don't understand.'

Michael beamed, brimming with excitement. 'I have chosen a suitable wife, Harald, a woman to sit alongside me and, God willing, to be the mother to my children.'

Harald looked completely blindsided. We had had no indication that the emperor was courting. Contrary to that, we knew from first-hand experience that he was taking every woman he could get his hands on to his bedchamber with no care for nobility or political outcomes. A dozen or so daughters of leading citizens had been lured in to his chambers and been left out in the cold with their reputation besmirched in the past few months.

'Well, that is wonderful news, Basileus, and I congratulate you. Who has the honour?'

Michael looked to the side of the room excitedly and clapped his hands. As with almost everything he did, there was a childish, almost maniacal excitement and lack of decorum. It was disconcerting to witness every time.

The curtain to the hidden door parted and a finely and supremely elegantly dressed woman walked in with two young attendants. She flowed across the marble floor, smoothly and gracefully, the complete opposite of Michael's jerky movements and excitability.

My heart stopped. I heard Harald gasp.

Maria.

Maria Arantios; the only woman Harald had ever truly loved.

She gave us a flourishing smile that passed over us as if we were not there and swept over to Michael, who just gazed at her in wide-eyed adoration and reached out his hand to greet her, rising to an absurd, half-propped knee on his throne like an excited puppy.

'Isn't she wonderful!' Michael exclaimed, looking at us excitedly and finding Harald open-mouthed and speechless. Michael saw that and hesitated. 'What, you don't agree? Wouldn't she be perfect? So beautiful, so elegant. She is a proper noblewoman too. You always counsel me to think politically, Harald. The nobles of the city will have to approve of such an impeccable woman, don't you agree?' Michael sounded almost desperate for agreement, and Harald almost choked as Maria blushed at the praise and looked away, with one hand held to her mouth demurely.

Michael smiled at her again, clearly deeply besotted. 'Oh, you see, she is perfect.' And then he drew her down to kiss him, which she responded to by bending her knees and elegantly pecking him on the cheek before standing again.

'She is delightful, Basileus,' Harald said, as if his throat were full of glass.

'Isn't she!' Michael exclaimed, thrilled to have received Harald's approval and missing that Harald looked like someone had just ripped out his guts with a war axe.

'My love, can you go and wait for me in my chambers while I finish here?'

Maria bowed deeply and smiled, giving Michael her gloved hand to kiss, which he did enthusiastically. She managed to give Harald a sly smile as she turned and swept effortlessly once again from the room.

Michael kept gazing at her as she went and then finally tore himself away to look at Harald. 'She is the right woman, I am certain of it.'

Harald stood there in shock, his face squirming.

'What is wrong?' Michael said, suddenly looking nervous.

'It's just that... Well, she might be a little old to bear your heirs?'

Michael frowned. 'Old? No. She is older than most women marry, it is true, but she is young enough to bear children.' He looked at his uncle for reassurance. 'That is what you told me?'

John nodded sagely. 'The doctors confirm it. She is of child-bearing age.'

I almost scoffed at that. Maria had been at least in her thirties when we met her a decade before. She was magnificent, of that there was no doubt, a beautiful woman by any judgement, but too old to be relied on to bear an heir. I looked at John, my mind racing. What was he up to? Why was he trying to prevent Michael having an heir? I decided that maybe he was leaving the option open to force Michael to adopt another favoured relative, rather than rely on the whims of fate in producing a loyal one himself.

'And anyway, if she cannot bear me an heir, I can adopt a suitable son,' Michael said with a nod. 'As my father did with me.'

You see? I was clever some of the time. I had worked out John's plan, and clearly he had prepared the way with his nephew.

Harald was far ahead of me though, as he always was with such things.

'If she is to become your wife, and thus empress, what of your mother the Empress Zoe?' he said, and his tone was stern.

Michael looked away guiltily. 'I think my mother will understand that I must become the sole ruler. It is my destiny, and she cannot stand in the way of me having a wife, of course. I am sure she will agree, given time and persuasion.'

That was ridiculous. No one in that room believed that Zoe would stand aside for her traitorous handmaid to steal her throne.

John was practically beside himself with glee, and Harald was motionless.

'She knows?'

Michael shook his head. 'I am about to have her told.'

'And what will she do, once she is no longer empress?'

Michael looked confused; he had clearly not considered that. In fact, it was clear that none of this was his idea. He hadn't thought through anything beyond how besotted he was with Maria.

'There is always room in the palace for the mother of the emperor,' John said reassuringly. 'She can manage the household staff, perhaps.' He smiled and nodded as if Zoe would not rather tear her own throat out than be the head of the palace servants for the son she never wanted.

'Yes,' said Michael brightly. 'Something like that. I am sure we will come to an agreement.'

Harald was helpless, completely unprepared for this situation and with nothing he could do about it, not there and then. He bowed stiffly, desperate to retreat and regroup. 'As you command, Basileus. Do you have any further instructions for me?'

Michael looked to John for confirmation, but the eunuch shook his head subtly.

'No, Spatharokandidatos. I will return to my chambers now,' he said with visible excitement. Harald's temple pulsed, because we knew full well what Michael was excited to return to his chambers for.

* * *

'Head of the palace household!' Zoe screeched, staring at Harald in horror when we went to see her later that day. 'That is what that worm suggested!'

Harald nodded forlornly.

'Never, he would never allow it. I will be quietly killed the moment I am replaced.'

'I suspect so, Basilissa,' Harald said gravely. 'I think it is time you leave.'

He did not add what for, we all understood. Zoe looked at him calmly.

'That is now my only option, unless you will finally do what you should have done all those years ago and help me take full control of the throne. But you won't do that, will you?'

Harald grimaced and shook his head. 'I cannot.'

Zoe gave him one last look of deep grief, and nodded, her shoulders slumping and for once, rarely, her full years showing in the lines and exhaustion in her face as she turned slowly away. 'Then it is over. You have a way to take me to safety?'

'I do. I have a ship waiting, and men to take you to the Rus. Yaroslav will welcome you heartily.'

She shook her head. 'To be a gilded prisoner and a tool against the empire.'

Harald grimaced. 'There is little choice, and Yaroslav is the only one I can trust not to hand you back to the emperor.'

She went to go and stand by the window that looked out over the grounds for a few moments and then she finally spoke. 'Then call it. I have nothing left I can do here.'

Harald nodded, turning to me. 'We must be quick. John will expect something and we must be ahead of him. I will go and get Afra and summon the ship. You stay with Zoe. Get her disguised and down to the harbour with a couple of her people, no more. Carry what gold and jewels you can hide under your clothes and armour. No one will notice the sound of clinking metal coming from you.'

I nodded firmly. 'I will.'

'Keep her safe, Eric. I'm trusting you,' Harald said, and then with a last bow to Zoe he jogged out of the room.

Zoe turned to me and she was crying. 'You Northern barbarians and your honour,' she said with a mirthless smile. 'But for it, I would rule the empire alone.'

I bowed my head slightly. 'Without us Northern barbarians and our honour, you would be long dead, Basilissa.'

She stared at me bitterly, then her expression softened and she laughed. 'You are right, damn you. I preferred all these years when you were silent.' She gestured to her loyal handmaid Hypatia. 'I need to get changed, quickly. Wait out here, Varangian. Some things are not meant for barbarian eyes.'

'Be quick, Basilissa. We do not have much time.'

* * *

Zoe was obedient, and it was not long before she returned with Hypatia and one other handmaid, all dressed the same, all the make-up removed from Zoe's face and hands. It was a convincing disguise; I barely recognised her myself. Suddenly I saw before me an old woman, lined and frail, her eyes sunken and mournful.

'Don't look at me like that,' she protested. 'I dislike what your eyes are saying about me.'

'I apologise, Basilissa,' I said with a bow, looking away.

'And don't call me that, I am no longer that.'

'Until you leave these shores, you are, and as such I would die to protect you.'

She gave me an odd glance. 'You really would, wouldn't you?'

I nodded.

'Why? After all that has happened, why? And don't tell me it is an oath, the reason must be deeper.'

I pursed my lips and considered my answer. 'It is because I am loyal to Harald, and he is loyal to you. There need be no deeper reason.'

'And why is he loyal to me?'

I smiled softly. 'For Harald to be loyal to someone there can only be one reason.'

'Why, because he loves me?' she said sarcastically.

I shook my head. 'No, Basilissa. It is because he believes you are worthy of it.'

Her sarcastic look faded and I saw something there, something that had always been hidden beneath the title, the make-up and the power of her personality and words: gratitude. Underneath it all had always been a woman who wanted to be respected.

'Come, Basilissa. The ship will not be long, and it cannot wait without attracting attention.'

'At the royal harbour?'

'No, that would cause questions. We are going to the Julian harbour. It is close, but small, and outside the palace precinct. We will head down past the Hippodrome, there is a small gate there for servants and provisions to go in and out of the palace to the docks.'

'Really? I have never been there.'

'There is no reason you would have, Basilissa. Come.'

We went out of her quarters into the gardens and through the small gate that led into the main part of the palace grounds. The two first bandon guardsmen on duty there looked at me, and then at the three servants I was escorting, and opened the gate without a question. They knew better than to enquire into the details of our comings and goings from the empress's quarters.

'They didn't recognise me,' Zoe whispered as we walked away.

'That is the intention.'

'Am I really so different?' She sounded hurt.

We walked without hurrying and there were dozens of others travelling through the palace grounds, going about their business, and no one batted an eyelid at a Varangian and three palace servants. There was nothing unusual about it at all.

We passed a group of men of the fourteenth bandon, coming back from guard duty, and I simply nodded to them and they saluted as they passed.

They looked at the three women in bored curiosity, but again, there was nothing unusual for them to note.

Behind the kitchens we turned off the main paths and down the long stairs that led behind the base of the Hippodrome that towered above the palace precinct on its near vertical bluff, warned with tunnels.

The area around the base was a hive of warehouses, stores and activity. This was the beating heart of the palace's operations down near the docks, where most of the food, drinks and other supplies came in and were sorted and stored. Everywhere we looked servants, porters and merchants were hurrying to and fro, and no one had the time or focus to look at us as we made our way through the crowd.

Zoe was wide eyed. 'I had no idea this existed,' she whispered to me as I escorted her through the press.

'You wouldn't,' I said softly.

'I should have,' she muttered in wonder as we passed the open doors to a vast tunnel that led under the Hippodrome, where rows of barrels were visible.

She looked up at the wall of the vast arena, towering above us. It was an impressive view, one I was used to but she was seeing for the first time from that angle.

'Come on, quickly, don't stand out.'

She lowered her head and quickened her pace, and we made it through the crowd and down to the lower gate.

The gate was open with a constant stream of traffic, and Vigla guardsmen and Varangians were checking everyone who came in, but only a few who went out. No one really cared what was taken out of the palace, only what was brought in.

We were waved through without a second glance when the guards saw who I was. I quickly looked behind to see if we were being followed through the gate, but the truth was there were dozens of people following us and I had no idea if any of them were doing so with intent.

We went down the backstreet along the seawall until we reached the Julian harbour, which was a simple and workmanlike place, nothing like the royal harbour just a few hundred paces away at the Boukoleon Palace. I swept my eyes over the ships there, and to my relief I saw one just arriving, and then spotted Harald and a few guardsmen in plain cloaks standing on a pier waiting for it.

We wove our way through the tradesmen and porters and walked the last few paces to Harald just as the ship started pulling into the dock under oars.

He looked at Zoe and smiled, giving no indication he was surprised at her appearance. 'This is your ship, Basilissa.'

'Do they know who I am?'

'No, not yet. Do not tell them. Lie and say you are a noblewoman fleeing a jealous husband. Here is a letter for Yaroslav. It will explain everything.'

'Will they turn on me, rob me?'

Harald grimaced. 'They wouldn't dare. They know who I am, at least. And they are well-paid.'

Zoe nodded, looking slightly reassured, and the ship reached the dock.

'Eric?' Harald looked at me.

'What?' I said dumbly.

He raised an eyebrow. 'The empress's jewels?'

My eyes widened, I had completely forgotten. 'Yes.' I reached up and undid the rather fine woven bag that I had slung under my cloak, full to the brim with gold and jewels, everything the empress had had with her.

Harald looked at it disapprovingly and took his cloak off, wrapping it around the bundle and tying it with a strap. Hypatia and the other servant were carrying bags full of clothes and other possessions, and Harald tucked the wrapped cloak between the straps of one of them.

The ship had docked, and a tanned, tough-looking man appeared at the rail, but did not come down. He looked along the dock. Harald waved at him impatiently. 'Come down, help them board.' Harald nodded. 'You know where you are going?'

The mercenary nodded. 'Afra gave us very clear instructions.'

'Did he make it equally clear what would happen if our passenger does not arrive at the other end safe and well?'

He nodded and smiled. 'Do not worry, Harald of the Varangians. I have enough enemies already, and I will not make one of you.'

'Good. Then it is time to go.' He gave Zoe a tortured look and offered her his hand. She took it and let him help her aboard, and then her two servants.

The mercenaries pushed off without any ceremony. Harald looked distraught as the ship floated out into the harbour's waters. Then we heard a rush of footsteps behind us and we turned in alarm as a full fifty guardsmen of the Vigla jogged onto the dock. With them was John, a look of vicious triumph on his face.

Harald scowled and his hand moved away from his sword. We were hopelessly outnumbered.

'You are too late,' Harald spat.

'Oh no, Harald. I am right on time.' He pointed. We turned to see the ship had stopped and the captain was standing on the rail. A dozen men of the Vigla appeared on the deck behind him from where they had been hiding.

Zoe looked around at them in fear, and then her eyes swept slowly to Harald, and they blazed with incandescent fury, although she did not say a word, the radiating power of her anger said it all.

Harald shook his head slowly. 'This was not me,' he called out helplessly to the empress, but she just sneered at him as two guardsmen gently took hold of her and led her down into the ship.

'How did you get to them?' Harald hissed.

'I have known for a while,' John said with sickly joy. 'I was lucky, actually. I wanted to hire them for something else and when I found they were already hired, I grew curious. Well, they got bored, one of their men got drunk and talked to the girl he was fucking to pass the time. That girl worked for me.'

Harald, rigid with anger, slowly pivoted back to land his furious gaze on John.

'Bearded men always think being a eunuch is a sign of weakness, when your cocks lead you into nothing but trouble,' John mused happily. 'Don't worry, not a problem I think you will have much longer. You know, there are only two penalties for treasonous officials, and although execution might be more... final, I will personally be pushing for a smaller cutting. It will be more satisfying to see,' he said, putting a finger to his lower lip and considering it. 'I do remember promising that would happen if you crossed me, a few years ago.'

'And I remember saying I would choke the life from you if you were not silent,' Harald grated, but I could feel his fear under his anger.

'Well, I don't think that matters any more. Thank you for getting Zoe out of the city quietly, it saved me a lot of trouble and I wanted to do it anyway.'

'What?' Harald replied.

John gestured towards the ship. 'Oh, you don't think we are going to kill her, do you? God no, she is far too popular. No, we feel retirement to a monastery is more appropriate, and just out there, in the bay, is the island where her sister Theodora lives as a nun. The sisters reunited. Rather perfect, don't you agree?'

Harald looked at Zoe's ship and saw that it was running out its oars in the harbour's waters, turning towards the island that was distantly visible on the bay.

'Do you know what the most delightful part of this is?'

Harald did not reply, he just stared glumly at the ship as it got underway.

'I gave them part of your Varangian's promised gold to bribe them. I don't think anyone will be expecting payment after their commander is revealed as a traitor.'

He gave us all one final happy glance and then turned away. 'Bring them,' he added casually to the Vigla as he started walking. 'The emperor is waiting.'

23

We were guided, more than dragged, back to the palace. John was clearly intent on avoiding a public spectacle.

Harald looked around like a caged lion, but the Vigla were around us two ranks thick with their hands on their weapons, and they never gave us a chance to think of escaping.

All the Varangians on duty had been removed when we went through the gate, and there were none visible on the short route to the Boukoleon Palace. I had no idea how they had been lured away, but it must have been an order from the emperor himself.

We were taken through the side entrance and up to the shaded veranda that overlooked the harbour. Michael was waiting there with more guards, watching as the ship headed off into the distance towards the island.

'Nephew, I have brought the traitors,' John said with a flourish, walking over to join the emperor where he turned to look at us, the sheer joy of his victory etched into his face with gut-churning clarity. I have never hated a man or a thing more than I hated him in that moment, and I was powerless to do anything about it.

The Vigla had taken our weapons and formed a nearly complete circle around us, enclosed other than for a gap facing the emperor, who was flanked with yet more guards.

Michael looked at John and then at us, and he was smiling. 'My mother is on that ship, you are sure?'

John nodded. 'I am certain. My people have her.'

'I wasn't asking you,' he said, turning to Harald. 'Spatharokandidatos, is my mother on that ship?'

Harald looked confused. The tone of the emperor was odd, almost friendly. John looked equally taken aback.

'Are you still a loyal man of the guard, held by your oaths, Harald, or has everything you ever told me been a lie, and I a fool?'

Harald stiffened and straightened to stand properly. 'I am, Basileus.'

'Nephew, he is a traitor, not a loyal man.'

Michael held up a hand. 'I am speaking.' John looked chastened and closed his mouth.

'You mother, the Empress Zoe is aboard that ship, Basileus,' Harald said.

'And why did you take her to it?'

There was no need for lies now. It didn't matter any more. 'She was leaving for sanctuary in the east, Basileus.'

'Why?'

'Because she feared that John would convince you to have her killed.'

Michael nodded thoughtfully. 'That is true. He tried.'

John looked mortified. 'Nephew, we talked about this. She was always going to be a threat to you.'

Michael turned to John with an odd expression. 'I am not your nephew, John, I am your emperor.' He raised his chin a little, tilting his head. 'You forget that all too often.'

John looked suddenly worried. 'But Basileus, Zoe was plotting against you, she intended to use you for her own ends and when you were useful no more she would have replaced you. You surely see that? I have explained it all.'

Michael nodded. 'In great detail, and I believe you. I agree that she had to go.' John looked deeply relieved, and his smile returned as he bowed and looked back at us.

'But I see no traitor in front of me, John. I see a loyal guardsman who obeyed his empress's wishes, as is his duty and his oath. This man has protected me and my father for over ten years, giving good service and refusing, on many occasions, to betray my family.'

'But Nephew, he—'

'I am not your nephew!' screeched Michael, turning on John in a sudden fury, his hand pointing at the eunuch and shaking. 'Everything you accuse Zoe of plotting is simply something you intended to do to me yourself. You use me, you try to control me, hide the truth from me and feed me lies and deceit. And here, you bring me a loyal man and call him traitor!'

John withered under Michael's sudden anger and power, as shocked as I was, because I had never even seen the timid boy raise his voice before.

'I am not your nephew, I am your emperor, and the only traitor I see in this room is you.'

John gaped, full terror in his face, and my blood was rushing, caught between fear and elation, the joy of watching the unexpected admonishment rushing in my veins.

Michael suddenly flipped back towards us, his anger vanished, his odd, childish smile back on his face. 'I have listened to you, Harald. I have learned. I have absorbed your wisdom about what makes a great man, and a great ruler. I know that you try to advise me, and that you will be loyal to me, not puppet me like my uncle tried to do.' He flicked his fingers at the guardsmen around us. 'Leave them. These men are not my enemy. Back away!' he snapped at the end, his voice rising shrilly. The confused Vigla hurried to obey, backing away across the room and leaving nothing between us and the emperor.

Harald just stared in shock, speechless for one of the first times in his life.

'Spatharokandidatos,' said Michael, pointing at his uncle with a hand that shook with nervous excitement. 'This man is a traitor who plotted against the empress, and to usurp the throne by taking control from me. Execute him.'

John stared at Michael in shock, swaying on the spot. 'Basileus!' he squeaked in protest.

Harald didn't move, his brows sluggishly moving together as if he were not in control of them. We had come into the room just moments ago expecting to be killed, or worse.

'Do you understand me?' Michael said, looking confused and slightly nervous. 'This man committed treason, you witnessed it. There are two penalties for treason and, well...' Michael giggled manically. 'One of them can't apply to him.'

'Basileus, I...' Harald said, trying to regain his composure.

'I, Michael the fifth, Emperor of Rome and ruler of Constantinople, sentence this man to death for treason. Will you carry out my lawful command, Spatharokandidatos?' Michael said, smiling at Harald.

Harald suddenly started breathing properly again and he nodded fiercely, a smile slowly spreading across his face. 'I will. I will take him to the cells to be prepared.'

Michael shook his head rapidly, still pointing a wavering finger at the appalled John. 'No. No, he will find some trick, he will bribe someone, he will cause a revolt. He is too dangerous to let live a moment longer, don't you agree?' He pointed to the floor in front of himself. 'Do it now,' he exclaimed, almost seeming excited.

Harald looked from Michael to John in shock, but then he dipped his head and strode purposefully towards John, whose mouth flapped as he tried to back away, only to find himself bumping into the railing that guarded the twenty foot drop down to the dock below.

'Nephew!' he squealed.

Michael grimaced and turned to John. 'I don't think you listen to me at all, John.'

'Basileus!'

Michael nodded. 'That's better.' But he simply turned away again to look at Harald.

Harald grabbed John by the front of his understated tunic and dragged him across the floor, glaring at him with a wolfish sneer that John was too transfixed to look away from.

Then Harald reached for his scabbard and seemed surprised for a moment to find it empty.

He looked to Michael. 'He had my weapons taken from me.'

Michael shrugged. 'I am sure you are capable of killing a man without a blade, Harald. An experienced soldier such as you. And it saves making a mess. Do it!' he exclaimed with sickly excitement, his eyes wide.

Harald nodded slowly, and then gazed down at John, who was struggling and squirming. Harald smiled deeply, forcing the much slimmer man closer, into a near embrace.

'Do you remember what I promised you, little eunuch?'

John's eyes were pinned wide with fear. 'No. No!' he gasped.

Harald let go of John's tunic with one hand and slowly brought it up, placing his thumb on one side of John's neck and his fingers on the other, cradling the slight mound in John's throat where a true man would have had a proud lump.

Harald started compressing his hand, slowly, his calloused, meaty fingers sinking into John's soft flesh. John's hands and feet slapped and thrashed at Harald, but came nowhere near breaking his iron grasp.

Harald looked up at Michael briefly, with a questioning expression, and Michael nodded frantically, almost spellbound with excitement. 'Do it!' he trilled.

Harald looked back at John and gave him a final smile, and then clamped his fingers together with vicious force, forcing them in behind John's windpipe and crushing it.

John's movements became more frantic and his eyes bulged from their sockets as his face turned bright red, but Harald's grip was unyielding and he never looked away, breathing calmly into the condemned man's face in mockery of his own inability to even draw a final breath.

The thrashing and the slapping slowed and ceased with a few ugly jerks, but still Harald did not release his grip. John's face went slack and his eyes rolled back, unfocused, and still, Harald did not release his grip.

John's body fouled itself in one final humiliation, the effluent dripping from his limp ankles, and finally Harald let go, letting the dead man collapse into a puddle of his own sewage with a thud.

'Oh, he made a mess anyway,' Michael said, looking disgusted.

'It tends to happen,' Harald said, looking at the emperor with an odd expression.

'He is dead? Are you sure?'

Harald nodded.

Michael breathed hard. 'Well, I've never actually... seen that before. It was...' He flapped one hand in a peculiar gesture. 'So visceral.'

Harald kept a stoic expression, but his eyes were full of concern as he watched the emperor's excitement.

'I hear he liked to throw his victims in the Golden Horn,' said Michael, suddenly having a bright thought. He looked at the Vigla guardsmen, some of whom looked distinctly unwell. 'Take care of this,' Michael said, vaguely waving at the mess of eunuch and urine pooled carelessly on the floor. 'Do to his body what he did to those he murdered.' He looked at Harald with bright eyes, looking for all the world as if he had not just had his uncle brutally executed in front of him. 'Come, speak with me in my chambers.'

Harald bowed, his face still a mess of concern and surprise, and we followed the emperor as he strolled from the room.

When we were alone in the emperor's chambers he threw himself down on a chair with a breathless gasp. 'Well, that was remarkable. God, the feeling! I cannot believe it, being free of him, of having my own power!' Michael looked at his hands in wonder as if he had done the deed himself.

'That power, of deciding men's fates... It can be intoxicating, Basileus. And it can be dangerous. You must control it, or it will control you. Use it sparingly.'

Michael looked up at Harald, a little abashed, and he nodded. 'Wise words, as always, Harald.'

'I think it would be wise if you had your mother returned,' Harald said carefully.

Michael wagged a finger. 'No. Sit, Harald, please, before you begin to sound like my uncle. I have made my decision and it will not change.'

Harald grimaced but did as instructed and sat. 'Why?' he asked. 'Zoe is enormously popular. This is a dangerous move.'

'Zoe left of her own free will, to retire to the monastic orders with her sister in grace and tranquillity. That is what we shall say, and I am sure the people will understand.'

'I do not know that they will see it like that,' Harald said carefully.

'Well, I believe they will,' replied Michael with a taut smile, 'and I wish to discuss it no further.'

Harald wrung his hands but there was nothing he could do. He nodded.

'Do not worry, she is perfectly safe. Once the new empress is crowned, and my mother's own position formally voided by the patriarch, I will allow her to return for big festivals, celebrations and such.'

'I don't advise that, Basileus,' Harald said.

'Why?'

'She will not comply peacefully.'

Michael looked at him and then shrugged. 'Fine, it doesn't matter to me. And don't look so shocked, Harald. I had no love for her nor did she for me. She is no more my mother than John was my father.' He giggled to himself. 'I had you fooled, I had you all fooled. They all clambered over each other to control me, but I was learning, Harald. I heard every word you said. Great men do not let themselves be controlled, do they?'

Michael glared at Harald, and it was a very tense question.

'They do not, Basileus, but they do choose and hear wise advice from those they trust.'

Michael nodded. 'You are absolutely right, Harald, which is why you are alive and John is dead. I trust you, and you are wise, but...' He raised a shaking finger and his eyes took on that dangerous, manic look again. 'Never cross the line from advising me to trying to control me. A great ruler cannot tolerate that, you understand?'

Harald nodded stiffly. 'I do.'

Michael gestured towards me. 'Is that what this man is to you? He advises you?'

Harald looked around at me and then nodded. 'He does.'

'But when you disagree with his advice, do you follow your own intentions?'

'I do.'

'And tell me, Varangian,' the emperor said, setting his frantic gaze on me. 'Are you loyal regardless?'

'I am, Basileus.'

Michael nodded. 'Good!' he said and stood suddenly, uncoiling like a snake. 'Go and recover your weapons and continue your duties. I will need to meet with you tomorrow, once you have ensured the palace is secure. I will call for you.'

Harald levered himself to his feet and bowed. 'As you command, Basileus.'

* * *

We were far away from the emperor or any prying ears before either of us spoke.

'I can't understand how all of that, happened,' I said. 'The emperor is...'

'He is mad,' Harald said gruffly. 'Did you see the way he looked at John die? How he enjoyed it?'

'I did,' I muttered darkly. 'So what do we do?'

Harald sighed. 'For now? Our duty.'

'And what of our gold?'

'I will ask him again, when the time is right and now that John is dead.' He shook his head. 'God, that felt good.'

I smiled. 'You kept your word to him, that cockless worm.'

'I always do.'

We were approaching the Varangian barracks. 'Keep it quiet for now, Eric. No one is to know what happened today until it becomes necessary.'

24

We heard nothing from the emperor the next morning, and even into the afternoon. We heard reports from the guards that there were signs of trouble outside the palace, but nothing serious. Finally, I went to Harald's office.

'Heard anything?' I asked.

He shook his head. 'Not a thing from the emperor. I sent for the head of the household, but he has not replied. I don't know if he fled after John died. I'm receiving news of disturbances in the city, it's troubling and I need to see the emperor about it.' He looked up at me. 'In fact, let's go now and find out what is happening. I can't wait any more.'

***

As we left the barracks we saw a commotion over near the Chalke Gate, and a group of thirty or more Vigla headed over there at a jog.

Harald stopped and furrowed his brow. 'We should check that.'

We went to the gate and found a hundred or so men of the Vigla there, armed and armoured and standing around nervously looking through the open gate. Harald spotted the Vigla commander among them and pushed his way through.

'What in hell is going on?' Harald snapped at the commander, who looked around to see who had addressed him like that, his look softening when he saw it was Harald.

'Trouble,' the Vigla commander said with a tense expression.

Harald finally looked beyond the commander and out of the gate. In the background, in the square outside the Hagia Sophia, a crowd was gathered, all standing under the great triumphal column, listening to a speaker who was haranguing them from the raised plinth.

'Who is that?'

'One of the empress's supporters, whipping up the crowd,' the commander said.

'Whipping up the crowd, against who?'

The commander looked at him darkly. 'Against the emperor.'

Harald was staggered. His eyes narrowed and he looked at the crowd again, his features hardening with anger. 'Well why the fuck aren't you doing anything about it?'

The commander looked embarrassed. 'We aren't allowed to leave the walls, Spatharokandidatos. Orders are we are to protect the palace and nothing else.'

'Orders? From whom! I am the commander of the guard, and I gave no such orders!'

The commander looked at Harald in surprise, then shook his head awkwardly. 'You have not heard?'

'Heard what!'

The commander looked appalled. 'You, are no longer the commander, Spatharokandidatos.'

Harald looked at the Vigla commander as if he was insane. 'What? Who told you that? I have the emperor's written command.'

'The previous emperor, Spatharokandidatos,' the Vigla man said apologetically. 'The new emperor has appointed another man, yesterday evening. You were not told?'

Harald went red with anger and humiliation, his teeth grinding. He did not answer, he just looked at the crowd. 'Who is the commander then, and why isn't he doing anything?'

'The emperor has appointed a nobleman, an ally of his.' the Vigla man stuttered to a stop. 'We have not met him, I do not think he is in the palace. We just received written orders.'

'So have you sent word about this trouble?'

'I have not, I was only just informed myself, I got here not long before you.'

'So let's send word.' Harald paused. 'Where do we send a message?'

The commander shrugged helplessly. 'I have not been told.'

Harald was beside himself, agitated beyond reason. 'You don't know how to contact the new commander?'

'No.'

'Fuck.'

He looked at the crowd and then the commander again. 'I will go to the emperor.'

'With respect, my men will not let you through the door, Spatharokandidatos. The emperor has given orders not to be disturbed and he has replaced your men with mine guarding his chamber.'

Harald looked stunned, but he gritted his teeth.

'Then come with me.'

'Spatharokandidatos, please, I cannot countermand those orders.'

'There is treason brewing outside the palace walls!' Harald shouted, pointing at the crowd. 'The new guard commander cannot be found, and you say we cannot even report it!'

The Vigla officer swallowed, trapped. 'I have my orders,' he blurted.

Harald seized him by the tunic as if he could shake sense into him. 'Take me to the emperor before this becomes a disaster!'

The commander finally nodded, although it was hard to tell if it was Harald shaking him by the collar that achieved that effect.

Harald half-dragged him from the formation of his own men. 'Close the gate!' Harald shouted at them as we left, and we ran down the palace thoroughfare towards the inner palace buildings.

We arrived just as Afra came out of the palace, running the other way. Harald and Afra both halted and tried to start talking. 'Harald, I was just coming to you.'

'Where have you been?' Harald said over him, and both men stopped. 'Why have your men been replaced and why didn't I hear about it?'

Afra held up his hands placatingly. 'My men and I were sent out of the palace by the emperor.'

'To do what?'

Afra pursed his lips, looking very nervous. 'I do not know if I can say.'

'Damn all this secrecy, I am the commander of the Varangian tagma, responsible for the emperor's safety, and his safety is in peril, answer me!'

Afra nodded slowly. 'We were sent out to deal with some traitors.'

'Traitors?'

Afra nodded. 'The emperor provided a list, said they were actively plotting against him and had to be dealt with immediately. I asked permission to tell you, but he refused. Said it had to be a secret. I'm sorry, Harald.'

'Who? And where are they, are they imprisoned or...?'

Afra gave him a dark look and then fished a list out of his tunic and handed it over. I saw his hand was flecked with dried blood, which answered the main question.

Harald tore open the list and looked down it, his eyes widening. 'Oh God. These are some of Zoe's foremost supporters, and John's. Saints save us, this is many of the great men of the city.' He looked at Afra in horror. 'They are all dead?'

Afra shook his head. 'Some of them got word and fled, but most... yes.'

Harald looked at him in horror. 'He has started a civil war, from nothing. Was there any evidence of treason?'

Afra nodded. 'Some of them confessed to plotting Zoe's return.'

'Zoe is the empress! It is not treason to support her!'

Afra looked crestfallen. 'Harald, I could not refuse.'

Harald screwed up the list and held his hand to his face. 'What is he doing?' he moaned. 'He hasn't killed Zoe's support, he has brought it out into the open. Did you see the crowd outside?'

Afra nodded. 'It is worse than that, Harald. We saw it in many places through the city. Word spreads quickly, and they found out Zoe's men were being killed. There are mobs in the street, we had to fight our way out of one of them.'

'Oh God. Afra, tell me you were not in uniform. Please.'

'Of course not,' Afra said, shaking his head. 'But they know anyway. We don't exactly blend in.' He raised his hands defensively. 'I told the emperor not to use us, that we would be recognised. He would not listen. That woman Maria was with him, advising him.'

Harald looked at the list dumbly and pushed it back at Afra. 'I have to go and see him, perhaps I can talk sense into him and end this before it gets out of hand.'

Afra nodded. 'That is what I was going to ask you to try.'

Harald breathed in hard and nodded. 'Let's go now then. Afra, go back to the barracks and rouse the guard. All of them. Get them ready to defend the palace if needed.'

Afra nodded. 'Aye, Spatharokandidatos.'

And then we set off at a run into the palace.

It did not take us long to reach the emperor's chambers, but a Vigla guard contingent was standing at the door, and they tried to refuse us entry. 'Out of the way, the emperor is in danger,' Harald snapped.

'No one is to enter,' said the man, looking between Harald and his commander.

Harald raised a fist, his face twisted in fury. 'I don't have time for this, order your man out of the way!' he snapped at the Vigla commander.

'Stand aside,' the commander said to his man, who looked torn.

'It's the emperor's orders sir,' he said fearfully.

'And I will take the blame for breaking them, stand aside,' the commander said in a reassuring tone, stark against Harald's fury.

The man looked around again, and then reluctantly stood aside.

As we reached the door we could hear the moans and gasps of two women from within. Then I realised with a sickly feeling that it was in fact the emperor's oddly high voice, and a woman responding.

Harald opened the door and marched through sweeping aside the curtain.

We went into the emperor's chamber and there was a squeal of protest from the pile of naked flesh on the broad bed. The pile unentwined and part of it raised up, brushing long brown hair aside, and revealed itself to be Maria, who was straddling the emperor and looking at us with an amused grin. 'Aralteg, what a surprise!'

'What, how dare you!' said the emperor, looking around his lover to see us even as another naked girl got up from his side and squealed again, diving for a blanket to cover herself.

Maria made no such move, confident and mocking us, her damp body on full display atop the emperor of Constantinople, who was pinned indignantly beneath her splayed hips.

'Do not look at her!' Michael protested. 'You are not to cast eyes on the empress!'

'She is not the empress,' Harald growled.

Maria turned and put a hand on Michael's chest, patting him coyly. 'Don't worry my love, it's nothing he hasn't seen before.' She shot Harald a dangerous look. 'We were lovers once, a dalliance many years ago.'

Michael froze, and a look of confusion crept across his face. 'You were what?'

Maria laughed a little and bent back down, putting one hand on his face, her breasts pressing against his chest. 'Oh, don't worry, it was nothing, just a little affair to pass the time.' She kissed him on the lips.

Michael sank into the comfort of those lips, and he grabbed Maria's buttocks pulling her in possessively, grinding against her and showing us all that they were still, in fact, fully entwined.

The Vigla commander muttered in embarrassed shock at the sight and turned away.

Harald just looked angrier. 'Basileus, there is a budding uprising in the city. Talk of treason.'

'I know, I sent your men to deal with it,' the emperor mumbled between kisses.

'That did not deal with it, Basileus. It only made it worse. Perhaps it started it.'

The kissing and grinding stopped and Michael propped himself up on one elbow, looking around Maria.

'Then have the rest of the noble traitors killed too. I care not for their poison.'

'That won't work, you can't kill enough people to end this. It's not just the nobles, the ordinary people are starting to go into the streets.'

'Then go into the streets and punish them!' Michael said, exasperated.

'We don't have nearly enough men, Basileus, and that will just turn this into a full uprising.'

Michael groaned in annoyance, patting Maria on one arse cheek and indicating she should get off, which she did with a graphic unveiling of Michael's full form.

The emperor stood and grabbed a glass of wine, drinking from it deeply and wiping his mouth, utterly without self-awareness. I could see now that he was drunk, and his eyes were wild.

'Everyone except Harald and his assistant leave.' He turned to Maria with an odd look. 'You too my love.'

Maria, who had draped herself across the mess of covers, gave a little pout but then complied, standing and walking past us, giving Harald a little smile as she went. Harald's gaze slid down Maria's naked body as she paraded past, only for a moment, but Michael saw it and his expression clouded.

The Vigla commander practically ran from the room, as did the various servants and attendants who had been there, and we were left with the shamelessly naked emperor.

'Who are you to chastise me, Harald?'

'I do not chastise you, Basileus. I am trying to help you.'

'With these problems? If there is trouble, go and deal with it.'

'I cannot, apparently I am no longer the commander.'

Michael looked confused for a moment. 'Ahhh,' he finally said, raising a finger. 'Yes, I forgot to tell you about that.'

'Who have you appointed?' Harald said as evenly as he could. 'I need to talk to them and co-ordinate the response and the security of the palace. I was told an ally of yours, but not who.'

Michael waved his hand dismissively. 'Oh, no. They do not exist. It's me.'

Harald was dumbfounded. 'What?'

'Oh I don't have anyone outside the palace that I trust, you see. They were all John's creatures and most of them deserted me and I had to have them killed. So I made someone up and wrote the orders myself.' He giggled to himself. 'Quite cunning I think.'

Harald's eyes were wide and his mouth was moving like he was struggling to breathe. 'There is no commander? Basileus, I don't think you understand the danger, if you need me to deal with this situation, please, give me the authority back!'

Michael had wandered nonchalantly back to the side table to get his cup, and he turned back to us, swirling it thoughtfully. 'Give all the power back to you? Command of every man in the city?'

'Yes!'

Michael looked at Harald and then pursed his lips. 'I don't think one man should have that power.' He took a slurp. 'Except me, of course. I trust me!'

Harald forced himself to stay calm. 'Basileus, you are somewhat... preoccupied, to be organising the palace security.'

Michael giggled, and then abruptly stopped with a flash of anger. 'So now I hear you know my betrothed so... well. Why didn't you mention that, Harald, when I introduced you to the future empress?'

Harald went still. 'I apologise, Basileus. I was very surprised, and I did not want to embarrass her, or you, with that confrontation.'

'But you had time to tell me privately afterwards. Perhaps when you were strangling my uncle to death, the only man who it seems could keep me safe? Perhaps that was a good time to mention that you have fucked my future empress?'

Harald looked horrified, and Michael giggled maniacally again. 'You used to fuck my mother, you used to fuck my wife, you killed my uncle, and now you want me to trust you with the entire imperial guard? I suppose you were too busy being loyal to Zoe to be loyal to me too. Maybe my uncle was right about that after all.'

'Basileus, that is my mistake not to tell you sooner and I apologise, but I am loyal and always will be.'

'Maybe you want those armed men so you can use this mob to remove me?'

'I do not!'

Michael stared at Harald for a few moments longer and then smiled. 'I believe you, but I had to be sure, you understand?' He laughed a little and returned his cup, suddenly appearing relaxed again. He even picked up a silk gown and put it on. And Harald breathed deeply beside me.

'I will make arrangements for you to get what you need to control the situation, Spatharokandidatos,' Michael said happily. 'As for me getting rid of my potential enemies, perhaps I acted a little hastily, but a great man cannot allow his enemies to roam freely, can he? He cannot tolerate them whispering in dark corners and plotting. No, examples had to be made.' Michael looked at Harald with odd intensity.

Harald grimaced. 'More delicate care is needed, to avoid rousing the anger of the people.'

Michael laughed shrilly. 'The anger of the people? Why should I care? Why would a powerful man care for the anger of that kind of people?' He looked at Harald mockingly. 'I am the emperor, the source of their wealth and safety, they should be grateful! No, let them be angry, I care not.'

'Basileus, they might pose a danger to the palace if that anger goes unchecked.'

'We have walls, Harald, and men to guard them. You, in fact. Now go. Go and organise the men. I will send orders.'

Harald grimaced but bowed his head slightly.

Just as we were about to leave, Michael spun round, his eyes dangerous and flickering again. 'You don't still want her, do you Harald?'

'What?'

Michael waved his hand at the door where Maria disappeared. 'My empress? You don't still want to marry her, do you?'

'Marry her? Basileus I never wanted to marry her, I don't now... I swear it.'

Michael looked at him oddly. 'How could a man not want such an extraordinary woman as her? The devotion she has, the intelligence.' He shuddered and one hand drifted grotesquely to his groin. 'The things she can do with her body.' He went into a sort of trance for a moment and I looked away, beyond disgusted. Then Michael snapped back into the present and shook his head. 'I suppose she never showed you all that, you are only a barbarian, after all, not an emperor.'

Harald bowed his head and smiled self-deprecatingly. 'I suspect that is true. I was just a toy to her.'

Michael nodded jerkily. 'Yes, just a toy. That makes sense.' Then he fluttered his fingers, indicating we should leave, which we did as fast as decorum allowed us.

'Send me the Vigla commander!' he called after us.

* * *

We did not speak before we got back to the barracks, we were both too shocked. The entire guard was assembled, and looked at Harald's obvious distress with concern as we went in. The sounds of the angry crowd outside were audible, even from inside our walls, and the Vigla had closed the Chalke Gate.

'What is happening, Commander?' asked Sveinn, looking nervous. 'I wanted to send the men to reinforce the walls, but I wasn't sure if that was what you needed.'

Harald nodded, trying to give Sveinn a reassuring pat on the shoulder. He turned to look at the massed ranks of the guard.

'I won't try and hide it, there is serious trouble brewing outside. The empress leaving the city has roused her supporters and some violence in the city has put fire into them. I don't know what will happen, but we will defend the palace against any threat.' He looked at Sveinn. 'Send half the men to the gates and walls – I want every entry point guarded. Put another bandon in the sub-floors of the Hippodrome just in case they break in there.'

Sveinn nodded. 'Aye, Spatharokandidatos.'

'Leave two banda here with me. We will respond to any crisis.'

'We aren't going out into the city to deal with the threat?'

'No. It's too late for that and we are too few. We have six hundred men here and it is a city of five hundred thousand. Go. Secure the walls. I will send for the rest of the banda stationed outside the city.'

Sveinn nodded, turning to the men and reeling off a list of orders.

Harald motioned to me and stood to one side. 'We need to get men to the harbour where our ships are and have them brought to the Boukoleon Palace.'

I looked at him carefully. 'Why?'

'In case we need them.'

'To evacuate the emperor.'

Harald shook his head softly.

I understood. 'To evacuate us.'

Harald nodded once.

'I will send a bandon in one of the imperial dromons. There shouldn't be trouble at the port.'

'Good, thank you. And then have them leave the ships in the harbour and return here.'

* * *

The entire guard scrambled into action, and the walls and gates were secured. By midday our two longships had been brought to the royal harbour, an odd sight among the dromons and other vessels there.

The crowds outside were loud, but at that time, not dangerous. So things seemed to settle. I was with Harald in the barracks in the afternoon, going over a new, expanded guard rota in the open courtyard with the various officers when there was shouting at the gate.

We turned to look even as the gates opened and the Vigla commander marched in. We all tensed as we saw that behind him were a hundred of his guardsmen.

Everyone in the courtyard, nearly two hundred Varangians, reached for their weapons.

'Hold!' roared Harald. We were all on edge already and seeing so many armed men march into the courtyard was a spark to oiled cloth.

'What are you doing?' Harald asked the Vigla commander in outrage.

He looked apologetic and nervous, looking around. 'Harald Sigurdsson, by order of the emperor you are to be imprisoned on the charge of plotting an armed rebellion, of attempting to seduce Maria, the emperor's betrothed, and of likewise seduction and corruption of Zoe, the emperor's mother.'

There was utter silent shock around the courtyard. Harald looked at the Vigla commander with a mixture of sadness and resignation, as if he had been expecting it.

The emperor had clearly given in to the insane voices inside his mind, the paranoia that made him lash out against any perceived threat, and had decided Harald was plotting against him. Or maybe it was just jealousy over Maria. Or both. It was impossible to tell with the manic boy emperor.

Someone drew a sword, and the Vigla all drew in return.

'*No!*' Harald roared, holding his hand out towards our men. 'The guard obeys!' he shouted at them, and a few guilty-looking men lowered their weapons.

Harald walked forwards slowly towards the Vigla. 'This order comes from the emperor directly?'

He nodded. 'I had it from his own hand.' He paused. 'I am sorry, Harald.'

Harald nodded sadly. 'You are just doing your duty.' He turned and beckoned to me, unbuckling his sword and passing it to me. 'Look after the guard for me, and prepare for any eventuality.' He leaned in to whisper. 'Get Thorir to get me out if needed.'

'Him too, I'm afraid,' the commander's voice called out, and Harald looked back to see him pointing at me. 'The order is for you and your second.'

I smiled nervously at Harald. 'At least we'll be together.' I started unbuckling my own sword.

25

'Do you think he will execute us?' I asked Harald as we sat in the dimly lit cell in the Hippodrome's sub-levels.

'We should expect it. And from what we have seen, soon.'

I nodded and laughed softly. 'This is not how I expected us to die. I thought it would be in some insane battle you led us into, one unwinnable fight too many.'

'On the contrary – this is the only thing that was ever going to take me down,' said Harald with a smile. 'Betrayal, that is. No one had the courage or the skill to defeat me in battle. Instead, I am killed by an angry, lecherous child.' He laughed deeply. 'It is almost appropriate.'

'He is quite insane. I did not understand the extent.'

'Yes, I didn't realise it until it was too late. I thought he was just nervous. I fooled myself into thinking I could teach him.'

'How could you? He was just a peasant boy with no idea how anything worked.'

'You know, I think you were that too, once.'

'Ah, but you see I still don't know how anything works, otherwise how would I have ended up in this cell with you?' I said with a wry smile. 'This, surely, is proof of my stupidity.'

Harald shook his head, all trace of humour gone, to be replaced with sad affection. 'No, Eric. This is merely proof of your loyalty. I'm sorry it led to this.'

I choked a little at the compliment. Harald never really gave them. 'Look, we aren't dead yet. Afra or Thorir will find a way to break us out.'

'It is true, if anyone can, it will be them. It is just a simple race. Who will reach us first – Afra, or the mad emperor's executioners?'

* * *

We were in that dank room for two days. Only once on the first day were we brought food and water, although it was only the water we really cared for. The small, high window was the only evidence that days were passing. The second day we were ignored completely; even shouting for a guard achieved nothing. Outside, we heard the city in uproar, all day and all night. We wondered if the palace had fallen and we had been forgotten.

Finally, on the third day, we heard the sound of urgent feet, and the chink of weapons and armour.

Harald looked up nervously. 'So now we find out who won the race,' he muttered.

I stood and stared at the door, me on one side and Harald on the other. We had broken the clay pot our food came in and fashioned crude weapons with the shards. It was pathetic really, but we had both agreed we were not going to be executed for the emperor's amusement.

There was a rattle of the locking bar outside being pushed back and then the door opened and light spilled in.

I jumped forwards with a cry and a boot caught me in the chest, pushing me back.

'Stop that, you fools,' came a voice, and I squinted against the torchlight to see Theophilos's annoyed face.

'Magister?' Harald said, holding his makeshift weapon in confusion.

'That was your plan?' the magister said with a tired look.

Harald sheepishly looked at the shard of clay and then discarded it.

'Has the emperor called us to be executed?'

'I don't have a fucking clue what the emperor is doing, no one does,' Theophilos said with a weary sigh. 'He is refusing to see anyone now, but on the first day he was just demanding that we kill all the traitors, ranting about it but not saying who the traitors were. We gave up trying to listen.'

'So who ordered our release?'

'I did. Come. You might be the only person who can save the palace, it is on the brink of falling. The city is in revolution.' He waved us out of the cell. 'Hurry.'

'What of the Vigla? Did you have to fight through them to get me?'

'No, the Vigla told me where you were. They aren't idiots. They want to live too. And most of them are on the walls or holding the gates. Several of the gates have been broken and there has been serious fighting. The Vigla have lost dozens of men to the crowd and they are angry and scared.'

Harald nodded, his mind straight back into action as we hurried through the passages. 'Are the walls secure?'

'Yes, but it won't last for long. We have less than three thousand armed men in the palace, and the mob is endless. When they break through those gates, it will be over very quickly. They already took the Hippodrome.'

'They are in the Hippodrome?' Harald looked above us, as if he could see through the stone.

'Yes, we had to pull back. The upper levels of the Hippodrome belong to them now. We have the tunnels and the imperial lodge with the passages leading to it. We have blocked the internal doors.'

'And the imperial harbour?'

'Still ours, and we have four ships, including your two.'

'Four! What happened to the rest?'

Theophilos shrugged. 'Some people grabbed ships and fled before they could be stopped. It has been chaos.'

We emerged from the Hippodrome tunnels and into the back of the palace.

'So what shall we do?' Harald asked. 'Why do you need me?'

'Because none of us can talk sense into the emperor, nor gather enough authority to command the city and end this. I don't know that you will be able to, but perhaps the Bulgar Burner can try.' The magister gave Harald a wry smile. 'We are a day from being overrun, hours perhaps. You have a certain habit of success in these matters.'

Harald nodded. 'Well, we will go to the first bandon. I need men behind me.'

'Then what?'

Harald gave the magister a grim look. 'Then we are going to speak to the emperor.'

* * *

'Harald! Good to see you,' Afra said with a tired grin when we got to the first bandon barracks.

'Why didn't you come and get me?' Harald said flatly.

Afra gave him a reproachful look. 'Who do you think persuaded everyone else we should let you out against the emperor's orders? I wanted you out without a fight, not to create a new one.'

Harald looked at the magister, who confirmed it with a nod.

'Fine. You did well. Get your men ready, we are going to the emperor.'

'The Vigla won't let you. They are under his direct control now. There are ten of those feckless bastards outside his chambers and they have been told they will be executed if they let anyone through.'

Harald looked at him for a moment. 'So no one can see the emperor, and no one can check what orders he has given?'

He turned to Theophilos. 'Have the mob elected leaders? Made demands?'

'They want Zoe back, in short. There are other demands but that is the gist of it.' He shrugged. 'They don't have leaders so much as some who are louder than others.'

'Fine. Then that is what we will do. Let's go and tell the emperor. We will need his agreement. Zoe and that island are well-guarded.'

'Harald, if you give in to the mob, it might make it worse.'

Harald shrugged. 'Zoe might be able to control them.'

'And what of the emperor? You put those two together, it might be civil war. This can only end in blood.'

Harald's expression hardened. 'One problem at a time. If we don't calm this mob, none of us will be alive to worry about it.'

* * *

We arrived at the emperor's chambers and the Vigla blocked our way. There were more of them than before.

Harald did not address the officer at the front, he just looked at the whole group of them. 'I am here to save the empire, and the emperor. Within a day the walls will fall and the mob will crucify him. Any man who serves the throne, stand aside. Anyone who does not is a traitor, and I will kill him where he stands.'

The tired, nervous-looking Vigla looked at each other, and at the dozens of armed, armoured Varangians packed in behind Harald, and there was a slow shuffle as most of them got out of our way.

Three remained, and the leader turned to curse at his men for their cowardice. Then he turned to Harald with a sneer. 'I'm dead either way, I will not abandon my—'

Harald's fist moved before the man was finished pontificating, and Harald knocked him out with a single vicious upwards blow to the chin, half lifting the guardsman off his feet and dropping him to the floor with a clatter.

The two men behind him, wide-eyed, scampered to get out of the way.

Harald didn't even look at them as he stepped over the prostrate figure and opened the elaborate doors.

We went through into the emperor's chambers and Harald knocked aside a Vigla man who tried to confront him.

The emperor was sitting in a chair with Maria at his side. They both looked up in alarm and Michael scrabbled to his feet. 'Harald? What... what are you doing here?'

'Saving your life,' snapped Harald angrily. 'Though you do not deserve it.'

Michael's eyes were bloodshot and sunken, and Maria looked scared. Her normal confidence was gone.

He looked at Maria. 'Is this what you were hoping for, you foolish woman? A revolution?'

She shook her head softly, looking lost. 'I didn't know this would happen,' she whispered.

'Children, playing with forces they don't understand,' Harald spat, looking back at Michael. 'The only thing that can save us now is Zoe. I need to send for her. I need you to order it so there isn't a fight over her and I cannot spare the men to take the island by force with hundreds of the Vigla guarding it.'

'Zoe?' Michael looked appalled. 'You, you can't! She will kill me!'

'She will not. I will not allow it. I have sworn an oath to you, and I will keep it no matter how worthless you have proven to be,' Harald snarled.

'Harald, do you swear it?' a voice said, and Harald turned to see Stephen, Michael's real father, approaching from the side of the room. 'Can you save him?'

Harald nodded. 'If we act now. Otherwise the walls will fall and the mob will tear us all apart.'

Stephen looked at Harald and then went over to his son. 'Michael, please. Hear reason.'

The miserable boy shook his head, any trace of confidence and regality long gone. 'She will kill me, Father.'

'Harald will protect you. He is capable of great things. Trust me, my son.'

Michael looked at his father imploringly and then at Harald. 'You swear it?'

'I swear it.'

Michael pulled his knees up to his chin and hugged them. 'I didn't mean for this, Harald. I thought I was doing what I needed to do to secure power.' He begged Harald with his eyes. 'Please help me, I promise I will listen this time.'

Harald snapped his fingers at the attendants. 'Whichever one of you writes his orders, come here.'

Several of the white-robed men scrambled to obey as Harald went over to the writing desk and dictated a short order. Then it was sealed with the shaking emperor's ring.

The second the wax cooled Harald shoved it into Afra's hand. 'Go and get the empress. Hurry!'

Afra nodded, limping from the room.

Harald pointed at Michael. 'Clean yourself up. You will need to speak to the people when Zoe arrives and look like their emperor, not a crying boy.'

Michael looked aghast, but nodded.

Then Harald turned to me. 'Let's go to the lodge in the Hippodrome, we need to find out if the mob have leaders we can speak to.'

* * *

We took twenty men to the Hippodrome a short time later, once we had seen that Afra's two ships were on their way to the island where Zoe was being held. We took with us the things we needed for Harald's plan, climbing the grand stairs behind the imperial lodge until we emerged out onto the balcony on the lower level. There were rocks and stones littering the wooden boards from where the angry people had pelted it, and my breath was taken away by the seething, chanting, roiling crowd that was down in the arena in clumps and groups, gathered around fires and listening to speakers.

It was not long before someone saw us and started shouting, and thousands of angry people surged towards us, chanting.

A stone bounced off the wall beside Harald's head.

But he did not flinch or retreat, he just gestured to the men behind us. 'Give it to me.'

One of them passed the rolled banner through to me, and I looked at Harald. 'Are you sure?'

'Yes,' he shouted over the din. 'They can't hear us, but they will see this.'

I nodded and unrolled the banner, letting the black raven fly free and holding it out, displaying it to the crowd.

There was a ripple of shock and pointed fingers, and Harald held both his hands out, shouting at the top of his voice.

The combination of the huge red banner, the famous symbol of the late emperor's victory, and the huge, armoured form of Harald visibly shouting for calm, slowly lowered the fury in the crowd.

Finally, he could be heard a little.

'Bring your leaders to be heard!' he roared repeatedly.

We could not hear what any individual shouted back in reply, but people in the crowd turned to each other and there were intense discussions below. One of the men who had been speaking on a plinth was waved to, and he made his way through the crowd as they chanted.

'Give me the rope,' Harald said to us.

We passed over a knotted rope we had prepared and lowered it over the marble balcony rail, letting it drop down into the crowd. The man saw it coming and looked at it dubiously, testing it with a hand as six of our men held the top of it. He looked at the people around him and they urged him forwards so, reluctantly, he put his feet in the loop at the bottom and clung on to one of the knots as we started to haul him up.

He spun and bounced a little as we brought him up, but soon enough he was at the rail and Harald and I grabbed him by the shoulders and hauled him over.

He got to his feet and slapped our hands away, pulling himself up to his full height and glaring at us all. He was handsome, a bit older than me with greying hair, and the absolute air of nobility that was beyond doubt. Here was one of the elite men of the city.

Harald stepped back and did his best to look welcoming. 'Who are you?' he asked.

'Who are you?' the man asked defensively. He turned his eyes on Harald. 'Are you the Northern barbarian who comes and murders citizens in the night?'

Harald grimaced. 'I had nothing to do with that. I am Harald, commander of the Varangian guard, and all the forces in the palace.'

'Ah, so you are the man who kills our people as we demand justice, taking gold from the traitor son's hands.'

Harald swallowed, trying to maintain his composure. 'I do my duty and defend the palace and the emperor.'

'The false emperor,' the man said with blazing eyes. 'He is no son of the purple. The true empress is Zoe Porphyrogenita, who loved and protected us, and has been cruelly taken from us. Is she alive?'

'She is alive,' Harald confirmed with a nod.

The man's eyes glittered. 'Then we have nothing else to talk about until I am brought to her.'

'She is coming here as we speak,' Harald said, to the man's surprise.

'She is coming here? Why should I believe you? Why did you not wait until she arrived?'

'Because right now, your people and mine are fighting and dying at several gates around the palace. I want the violence to end. Let her come and speak to you, and end the violence until then.'

The man looked at Harald warily. 'How do I know this is not a trick?'

'If it is, you can attack again later. Please, I am here to end the violence that I never wanted, nor started.'

The man glared at him, but I could see he was excited. Then he looked down at the crowd, who were massed, staring up at him.

'I cannot simply order it. I am not in command of the city. No one is. Until this moment I had only a few hundred people listening to me. This monster you created is beyond my control.'

'You could help spread the word that the empress is returning, and we will present her right here, for you to see and confirm, and hear her words.'

The man looked unsure.

'Who are you, citizen?' Harald asked soothingly.

'I am Constantine, and my family name is none of your concern. I have no wish for your killers to come seeking me out if you do not already know who we are.'

Harald nodded. 'Well then, Constantine. An auspicious name. When the empire is in need, men of courage must stand up and serve it. There is an opportunity to save the city, perhaps the empire. Will you take it? I cannot solve this with weapons and violence, as the empire has often needed me to do. This battle will be won with words and trust. Do you have what is needed, Constantine of Constantinople?'

Constantine's eyes flared a little and he rose in stature. 'I believe I do.'

Harald smiled, bowing his head a little. 'Then please, go back down and get to work. We will bring the empress back here before sunset for you to personally meet with.'

Constantine's eyes shone at the promise. Harald had calculated his offer well; no noble man of the empire was going to pass up the opportunity to be presented to the empress as the saviour of the city.

He nodded graciously and then eyed the rope. 'I'm not going back down on that,' he sneered.

Harald smiled and gestured him inside. 'Don't worry – my men will unblock one of the lower doors for you.'

* * *

Zoe arrived on the ship with Afra towards dusk, even as the attacks on the palace slowly faded away as Constantine's word spread. A huge crowd started gathering in the Hippodrome, filling the stands and the arena floor. But the armed crowds at the gates did not disperse, nor did all the fighting end. Some of the rebels were simply too incensed, or did not trust the promises Constantine was spreading.

We met Zoe as she climbed down from the ship, still wearing a nun's habit. A half dozen other women climbed out behind her with the escort of Afra's men.

She saw Harald on the dock and came over to him with a cold and furious expression. 'Aralthes. Take me to the palace and tell me what is happening. I am told it is under siege and the crowd is trying to overthrow the emperor for me?' she asked, getting straight to the issue and leaving her obvious fury with Harald aside.

'Yes, Basilissa.' Harald fell in beside the striding empress, who ignored the palanquin we had brought down for her and simply set off towards the steps.

'Your son...'

'Do not call him that.'

'Yes. Michael has lost control. The people have risen demanding your return.'

'And John? He is not able to stop them?'

'John is dead,' Harald said.

Zoe looked at him. 'Dead?'

'Yes. Michael ordered me to execute him for treason.'

'He did what? The fool! How did he think he would maintain support without him?' Zoe shook her head furiously. 'Not that I am not glad he is dead – I would have ordered it myself this very moment – but what did that idiot child think would happen?'

Harald nodded. 'I have told the crowd that we would return you to the city and present you to them. It seems to have calmed the situation.'

'How did you speak to them?'

'They put forward a representative.'

'Who?'

'A man called Constantine, I don't know his family. He claims to be a supporter of yours.'

'Constantine? Who could that be? Oh, I know – tall, good-looking, older than you?'

Harald nodded.

Zoe scowled. 'Constantine Monomachos. Not a good choice. He is not loyal, he is an opportunist who would support anything he thought gave him position. My late husband exiled him not long ago for a while, and he is desperate for any way back into power.'

Harald looked ashamed. 'I apologise, Basilissa. I did not have another option.'

Zoe waved the apology away. 'It does not matter. Why did it take you so long to free me?'

'Michael imprisoned me,' Harald said with a knowing look.

Zoe stared at him and then shook her head, teeth bared. 'He is too stupid to live. He imprisoned you too? Why?'

Harald nodded nervously. 'He thought I was trying to steal his wife.'

'That whore Maria?'

Harald nodded.

Zoe held up her hand as Harald was about to speak. 'I know, you warned me about her, but I didn't understand the depth of her desperation for power. Let's not speak of it again.'

We reached the steps up to the middle palace, and the path was completely empty.

'You know, you could have prevented all of this by letting me kill that stupid boy,' Zoe said angrily.

Harald started to speak but Zoe held up a warning finger. 'No, I don't want to hear it.'

'Yes, Basilissa,' Harald said meekly.

God, that woman was a force of nature. Here she was, without her make-up, her jewels, her clothes and all the things that symbolised her power. She was just a woman in her sixties in the habit of a nun, and she had Harald absolutely in her command, such was the power of her presence. Truly, she was a wonder.

* * *

We reached the palace and Zoe started to head inside. 'I must change.' She stopped and looked down at herself. 'No, actually, this is perfect. Take me to the lodge immediately.'

'Like this?' Harald said, looking at her plain nun's habit.

'Yes. Let them see what Michael did to me. It will gain their sympathy and trust to look like any one of them, laid low.'

Harald nodded dubiously 'As you wish, Basilissa.'

We rushed her up into the Hippodrome, up the stairs and into the imperial lodge. She paused in the shaded inner room, smoothing her clothes and catching her breath. She looked older, but she looked radiant, confident and regal. It is something that comes from within, it cannot be given purely by clever use of paints and beautiful clothing.

'I am ready,' she said, turning a terse smile on Harald.

Harald opened the ornate door to the balcony and the full volume of the crowd washed over us as they saw the movement – the pulsating, booming, crushing noise of two hundred thousand angry people chanting and shouting. It was a physical force unlike anything else I have ever felt or will ever feel again.

It was power. That is the day I first felt it in its rawest form: true power. I had always thought power was in armies and gold, but those things are just the outer reaches, the useful expression of that raw, visceral living thing that is the will of the masses.

Zoe walked confidently out into that current of raw power and slowly raised her hands, caressing it and amplifying it, reaching for the hood that covered her head and peeling it back with a relieved flourish so that the people could see she was there.

She stood there alone on the imperial balcony, hands clasped in front of her in gratitude, as the arena burst into an outpouring of cheers and joy. Waves moved through the crowd, tens of thousands of people moving like wheat in the wind as they scrambled to get a better look.

She could not speak to them. I could not have shouted to her even from where I stood three paces behind, such was the deafening violence of their adulation.

But Zoe did not shrink from it, did not look around in wonder; she simply turned her look over the entire arena, one section at a time, reaching her arms out in a gesture of love and thanks, and she drank in their love and was exulted in it.

I leaned over the balcony and saw Constantine down by the small side door, and he had a gaggle of the great and the good with him, including the patriarch. I went inside and shouted at my men to open the door and let them through. The guards unbolted the heavy door and ushered the delegation inside. They came up the stairs towards me and made to go out on the balcony to join Zoe, who was still gesturing to the crowd, but Harald's arm snapped out to stop them.

'This moment is for her alone,' Harald said firmly, and they looked annoyed but nodded, waiting wide-eyed while Zoe finished her silent address to the crowd and finally turned to come back in towards us.

The noise subsided a little as she disappeared from the crowd's view and came in to greet the delegation with a beaming smile and a tear on her cheek.

They all bowed to her, but she shocked Constantine by embracing him, almost pulling him into her chest. 'Thank you, Constantine.' She let the stunned man rise again and held his gaze with the intensity of her own, her face screwed up with emotion and gratitude. 'You have always been a loyal servant of my family, and we will not forget this day. The throne is forever in your debt.'

Constantine almost blubbered, overwhelmed, and Zoe gently passed on, to the patriarch who had been bribed to betray her by John.

'Patriarch Alexius. I am so pleased to see you. I have always loved and supported the Church, and always been grateful for your love and respect in return.'

The patriarch beamed and bowed. 'Basilissa. I prayed for your return. We will hold services of gratitude in every church in the city.'

Zoe bowed her head in thanks, kissing the patriarch's hand, who looked so stunned he might have fainted.

She went on like that, through the delegation, greeting each man one by one, until they were all looking at her the way a puppy looks at a returning master.

The flow of power. That is how it works. They had all seen it flow into her, felt it, and they were completely bewitched by its insurmountable force. They were hers, utterly.

'Now, gentlemen, to business.' She gave them a knowing and apologetic smile. 'I never had a chance to explain to you all that my husband never really intended our adopted son to be emperor, but merely to guard the throne at his mother's side while a proper replacement was found.'

They all nodded along like that made sense, no hint of resistance at all.

'My son, though his heart is pure, is not ready for the rigours of the throne, as you have seen.'

More enthusiastic nods. That part, at least, was true.

'So I have returned from my monastic vows, and he will replace me as a servant of the Church while he grows in wisdom and stature.'

'A wise choice, Basilissa,' the patriarch said with a nod.

'I will provide the Church with a generous allowance for his care, of course.'

The patriarch smiled at the proffered bribe and bowed lower. 'We are at your service.'

'Who will replace him, Basilissa?' Constantine said, almost looking hopeful, the deluded little man.

Zoe smiled. 'There is only one choice, of course.' She waved to one of the nuns who had come off the ship with her, one who I had not even laid eyes on.

The nun stepped forwards and pulled back her hood, and my eyes widened as I saw that it was Theodora.

'My sister and I will share the throne, and reestablish peace in the empire.'

The assembled men of the city looked shocked, shocked enough perhaps that one of them might raise the courage to protest.

She held a single finger up to assuage them 'I know – two women cannot be the future of the throne alone. But rest assured, this is a temporary measure until a suitable emperor can be found.'

The worried faces all relaxed, hypnotised again by her demure face. 'Now, it is time that I present my co-empress to the crowd.' She held out her hand vaguely towards the delegation, offering them the final, glowing prize of capitulation. 'Will you accompany us?'

26

Zoe presented her sister to the crowd in the Hippodrome to a wave of support and adulation. A thousand years of tradition was blown away in moments as she and her sister, born in the purple, the last of the imperial family of Rome, took the throne for themselves without an emperor to guide them, and not a soul protested.

It was masterful. The rebellion washed away as if it had never occurred, and Zoe put forth a decree in every public space that all those who had committed violence or crimes were to be pardoned without exception. She paid compensation to the families of the dead, and held a games in the Hippodrome in their honour, sitting alongside her sister, on a very subtly, but noticeably higher throne.

Emperor Michael, without a single ally or supporter left to help him, was quietly ushered away before the day of Theodora's formal ascension, planned for a few weeks later, and, along with Maria, sequestered in the monastery of the Stoudion, in the very room his father had died.

Zoe summoned Harald several days after all the events had finished.

'Basilissa,' he said with a bow after he entered her new quarters, the ones that used to be the emperor's.

'Araltes,' she replied, all the outwards traces of her good humour and appreciation gone. In private, she was bitter and vengeful. Publicly she had forgiven her allies, but away from their sight the fact that they had all abandoned her, even for a moment, was unforgivable.

'Where is the traitor? Is he secure?'

'Yes, Basilissa. He is in the monastery under guard.'

Zoe nodded, her lips curling. 'It is time to end this, Harald, and I will have none of your protesting.'

Harald breathed hard; he had been expecting this.

'You could have another do it, Basilissa.'

'No. This is the final test of your loyalty, Harald.'

'Have I not proved it? I swear to you, I did not know what John was going to do to you.'

'I don't care if you let me be taken by betrayal or incompetence, it makes no difference. If you are loyal, prove it again,' Zoe hissed. 'This entire rebellion, my banishment and humiliation, only happened because you refused my orders.' Her face was lined with anger, her hands tight on the arms of her chair. 'I need your loyalty to be absolute, not conditional. If you want the reward you and your guard never stop asking for, this is the only way you will get it.'

Harald looked at her, his fingers twitching, clenching and unclenching. I knew what he wanted to say, what she did not want to hear. He had sworn an oath, multiple times, to keep the boy alive. But we needed that gold, or all we had done was for nothing.

'What are your orders, Basilissa?' Harald said softly.

Zoe nodded in triumph. 'Go to my son. I want rid of the threat of him.' Her face screwed up in a furious rage. 'End his filthy line forever! Make sure he never sees the light of another day again!' she almost screamed, her hands bunched up in fists and held in front of her as if she were holding the sword herself. 'Today! Now!'

She shook and shivered as the anger passed through her, and then she gave Harald a cold look. 'Do this for me and I will make sure that everything you want is yours.'

Harald looked at her carefully, and then he bent his head, bowing deeply. 'The guard obeys, Basilissa.'

'Swear it, Harald,' she said carefully.

Harald looked at her again and nodded. 'I swear it.'

'Then go and do your duty.' She gave us one last bitter look, then turned and swept from the room.

* * *

Harald strode out of the palace with a fixed expression, anger and revulsion behind those bright eyes. I felt his pain. Zoe had dragged from him an oath he could not carry out without breaking another.

He had reached a crossroads from which no path led that left his honour unstained.

'What will you do?' I asked nervously.

'As my empress commands.'

'Michael is still the emperor. He has not been dethroned. Our oaths to him still stand, your oath to his father!'

'I know it,' Harald spat bitterly. 'Do not lecture me on oaths, Eric.'

I fell to a sad silence.

'Sometimes we must do things we do not wish to, or cannot, because our loyalty demands it.' He looked at me. 'Can you come with me to do this, Eric? Or will you leave me to face it alone?'

I looked at him, aghast that he could think that. 'I will come with you, Harald, of course.'

* * *

We did not share a word as we walked through the city with Afra and ten of his men. Harald was in a stormy silence, and I was miserable.

We reached the Stoudion and went through the guards Afra had posted. Harald ordered all of them to leave the monastery. They looked at him glumly. I think they all knew what was about to happen, and it was their oaths he was forcing them to abandon too.

But Afra quietly urged them, and eventually the monastery was abandoned to the three of us, the monks, and the locked room where Michael and Maria waited.

The three of us went up there in a solemn parade, and the weight of what we were about to do, in a holy place, was crushing to me.

'You don't have to do this, Harald,' I beseeched him.

'It is too late for anything else,' Harald replied bitterly.

We reached the door and Afra unlocked it. We stepped in to find Michael curled up on the bed with Maria at his side. They both looked alarmed and miserable.

'Harald? Oh, thanks be to God. I thought...' He saw Harald's expression and he stopped. 'What is going to happen to me, Harald?'

It was gut-wrenching, no matter what he had done. He was not the emperor lying there, he was a scared boy, looking to the only man he trusted.

'Your title is going to be stripped from you, Michael.'

'That's... impossible,' he muttered. 'I am the emperor!'

'That's not legal,' Maria said, sitting up and looking at Harald in anger. 'It is a title that cannot be taken away except by...' And then her face fell.

Michael looked from her to me, confused. 'What, what do you mean?'

Maria looked at Michael and then Harald, true fear on her features. 'Me also?'

Harald looked at her and sneered. 'You also. Have you ever loved anyone, Maria? Was this poor boy ever more to you than a route to power?'

'Don't talk to her like that, she loves me! She is going to be my empress! My mother will forgive me, she has to! I am anointed by God!' Michael screeched.

Harald turned on him. 'Your mother never forgives, and if John taught you one thing, it should have been that. The second thing he should have taught you is not to let your lust govern you, as it did with this whore.'

Harald looked back at Maria with disgust on his face. 'Do you care about him at all?'

Maria's face screwed up in anger. 'Don't lecture me about what I will do for power, Harald the Bulgar Burner! What would you not do? Who would you not kill?' She snorted derisively. 'So I used you when I thought it would benefit me, so what? I loved you a little too, if that eases your pride, but I loved myself more, as you did.' She flung a finger out, pointing it at me. 'You use this man and others to help you get what you want, so what is the difference between the way I treated you, and the way you treat him?'

She rose from the bed, challenging him with her furious glare.

Harald looked at her sadly. 'Loyalty.'

Maria huffed and crossed her arms. 'Kill us then, and spare me your false sermon. We are no different.'

Harald pointed at the emperor. 'My orders only concern him, so I give you the choice, Maria. Stay with him and share his fate, whatever it is, or leave now with nothing but the clothes you wear and disappear into the city, for if I find you again, I will kill you.'

Maria looked at him carefully, nervous and breathing hard. And Michael reached out for her hand. 'We will face it together, my love. I promise you,' Michael said.

Maria didn't even look at him. She swatted his hand away and got up from the bed in a hurry, gathering the cloak and rushing towards the exit as Michael stared at her in horror.

Harald stepped in front and blocked Maria, and she looked up at him with wide, resentful eyes.

He smiled. 'Thank you for proving who you really are. Run fast, go far. This is my last mercy to you.' He stepped aside and let her through, the sound of her footsteps racing down the hall as Michael cried out her name in pain and loss, leaning over to sob into his knees.

Harald looked at the weeping boy grimly, and he pulled out his knife.

'Harald. Don't do this,' I begged him. 'Zoe isn't worth your honour. She doesn't love you any more than Maria did.'

Harald turned to me, a blank, hollow expression on his once noble features.

'You should leave the room, Eric,' he said, and there was so little humanity in it that I was shocked. He turned away from me. 'Afra, hold him down.'

Afra nodded sickly and went over to grab the emperor and I choked with nausea as the boy started screaming in his shrill voice. I turned and stumbled from the room, overcome by it, and closed the door behind me even as the screams rose to a crescendo.

But they did not stop, they did not slow. The noise was interrupted only for the boy to draw breath and then a noise that might have broken glass emanated from the room, the most distressed and foul noise I ever heard a person make.

The shriek of pure horror faded away, not into nothingness, but into terrible, hacking sobs, and then the door opened and Harald came out, blood spattered across his arms, the bloodied knife falling carelessly from his hand.

'What...' I could still hear the boy sobbing in fear and agony. I looked at Harald in confusion as he passed me, and then at Afra's grimace. The bandit shook his head at me but said nothing.

I peered into the room and my breath caught in my throat. Michael was huddled naked against the back of the bed, pawing feebly with one hand at the bedsheet, two bleeding, terrible hollows where his eyes had once been. The other hand clutched desperately at his groin, grasping the messy wound underneath his blood-soaked organ. On the bed near him were the parts Harald had cut from the emperor's body.

I felt my stomach lurch and I turned away from the terrible sight of the boy scrabbling about in shock for his own stolen eyes and balls, looking at Harald in abject horror.

He was looking at me, and his eyes were flint. 'I did as Zoe commanded. I ended his line and he will never see the light of another day.' Harald shrugged bitterly. 'I have kept my oaths.'

He shouted down the hall towards the gaggle of monks that had been drawn by the noises. 'The boy in there needs you,' Harald boomed. 'Keep him alive.'

Then he reached out to me. 'Come, Eric. I did what I had to do.'

'What do we do now?' I muttered, scrambling like a coward to get away from the awful noises in the room behind.

Harald bared his teeth in anger and disgust. 'I have done my last violence for the vultures that rule the empire. Now we go home.'

* * *

The empress refused to see Harald, once she had learned what he had done. We heard reports of her fury from the palace guards, of her rage and accusations. Harald did not care. He was done with her.

He gathered a few of us in his office the next day – Afra, Thorir, Rurik, Sigurd and me.

'We are leaving,' he said, to varying degrees of shock from our ranks.

'But we haven't been paid,' Rurik said.

'And we won't be. I'm sorry, it was either the gold or my oaths. I swore not to let the boy be killed, and I held to it.'

Rurik nodded.

'Who are we taking?' Afra asked.

Harald looked uncomfortable. 'Well, we can't take everyone. We have room for two hundred men. Priority goes to those who sailed here from the Rus with us.'

'Do we have to go? I mean, can men who wish to choose, stay?' asked Sigurd.

'Of course,' replied Harald. 'It is a free choice for every man.'

'Some will not want to break their oaths,' Rurik said carefully.

'No man will be breaking his oaths. All of us are free to leave with the commander's permission, and I am the commander. I will sign release papers for anyone who wishes to leave. It will all be proper, if a little rushed.'

Rurik looked relieved and nodded. 'Good. What about you? You can't just sign your own release.'

Harald shook his head. 'No. I will send the empress a letter with my resignation. She might claim that breaks my oath, but after all that I have done for her, I do not care.'

'Some of the men might be very angry about this, see it as desertion,' Sigurd said.

Harald shrugged. 'I know, but what can I do? The important thing is that we do not linger. Once word gets out, someone might try and stop us.'

We all knew that someone would be the empress.

'So we only tell those likely to come with us.' He looked at the komes of the seventh, Sigurd. 'Your bandon. Many of them came here with me, or have served with me for a decade. I hope many of them will want to come.' He looked at Rurik. 'Yours too.' and then to Afra, 'And you and your brother – you have many men loyal to you. Offer them places as well. That might make two hundred men, and if so, it is enough.'

We all nodded. We were all going with Harald, there was no question.

'So go and ask your men, quietly. Send them to me, a few at a time, and I will sign them all off from service.'

The rest of them all nodded and left the room. I had no men under my command, so I stayed with Harald as we waited for the first men to come to us.

It did not take long, and soon the first nervous-looking guardsman came through the door. It was Toke, one of the blood-marked, the men who had been with us when we fled Sweden.

'We are going home?' he asked.

'Only if you wish to.'

Toke smiled. 'About time, Prince Harald.'

Harald nodded and reached for his parchment. 'I am glad you are coming with us.'

Then other men of the seventh arrived and came in one by one, finally a nervous looking Ulfr appeared, rubbing the back of one hand in the other.

'I was wondering...' then he stuttered to a stop and looked at the floor, silently cursing himself as his face reddened.

Harald looked up at him from the desk. 'Ulfr, I know you were not with me in the Rus, and we have had our differences, but you are welcome to join us if you wish.'

Ulfr looked shocked and raised his eyes. 'You would have me? After what happened?'

Harald smiled slowly. 'You mean after you got drunk on campaign, disgraced yourself in front of the men, and insulted me and the emperor?'

Ulfr quailed, the shame of it burning in his face. 'Yes,' he said softly.

'You were given punishment for those actions, and you accepted it, and a hundred of your men loved you so much they put their bodies across yours and shared it with you. If I knew nothing else about you, that would be enough to want you at my side.'

Ulfr's jaw sagged open in astonishment. 'Truly, you would forgive me?'

'I did not forgive you, Ulfr. We are soldiers, you were cleansed by punishment and service. I wish I had ten more like you. Come with me, and we will build you again into the great leader you once were.'

Harald stood and his face was warm, almost affectionate. He picked up a paper from the side of the desk and pushed it across. Ulfr looked down in shock and saw that it already had his name on it.

He looked up from the paper to Harald, finally finding his composure and straightening. 'Thank you, Harald. I will not let you down again.'

Harald nodded and reached for his seal with a grin. 'I hope, for Eric's sake, that you do not.'

* * *

Nearly two hundred men collected signed release notes from Harald that day. But of course it could not be kept a secret from the rest of the guard. Sveinn, who had not been with us in the Rus, stormed into the office, barging waiting men aside.

'Is this true?' he shouted, pointing at the half-finished note in front of Harald.

Harald sighed deeply. 'It is.'

'How can you do this?'

Harald looked up and laid the page aside. 'I am sorry you are disappointed, Sveinn. But my time here is over. I never said it would last forever.'

'You are betraying the empress when she needs you the most! The city just had a rebellion, our ranks are thinner than ever, and you are taking hundreds of men! This is a disgrace!'

'We are betraying no one!' I said calmly. 'We have served the empire and we have earned our right to leave!'

Sveinn sneered at me. 'Ah, you too Eric, of course. And don't preach to me about service. Harald did not serve the empire honestly, he used it! He waited until he had earned enough gold and now he leaves, sneaking away like a thief. If this is so honourable, why do you do it in secret?'

'I never made any secret of my aims, Sveinn,' said Harald, wagging a finger. 'I gave the empire ten years of my life. We have killed for the throne, died for the throne, served the emperors and empress loyally while they have done nothing but squabble and try to kill each other. And in return they gave me the gold and experience I needed.'

'And now you take two hundred men. Was that the agreed price?'

'They are free to do as they choose,' I protested.

'Choice?' he looked at me and snorted. 'You, talk about choice? You haven't had a free choice since you arrived here. You just do what he says and follow him like a loyal dog. That is all you are, Eric the Follower. A coward with no mind of his own.'

'Enough!' shouted Harald, coming around the desk and shoving Sveinn into the wall as they snarled at each other. 'You will not call this man a coward or besmirch his name.'

'No,' I said, looking at them. 'Stop this. You are both loyal men, in your own ways.' I put a hand on Harald to restrain him 'He is right, that is who I am – Eric the Follower.' I smiled at him calmy. 'It is a good name, honourably earned.'

I looked away from Harald's surprised gaze to Sveinn's smouldering anger. 'I understand your pain, Sveinn. But this is not betrayal. This was always what was going to happen. Go, go and lead the men who want to remain behind. They will need you, as the empress will need you. But I must go, because I am Eric the Follower, and you are right – I earned that name.'

Sveinn huffed and looked at me and Harald, then spat on the floor as Harald let go of him. He shook his head bitterly and left the room.

Harald watched him go and then looked at me. 'Truly?'

I smiled and nodded, feeling more sure of myself than I had for a long time. 'Truly. I have been afraid of what I am, and what it meant, for a long time. I should embrace it. It is not a mark of dishonour; it was earned in blood and fire.'

Harald smiled and clapped me on the shoulder. 'And I am grateful for it.'

Then he looked at the next man in line. 'Come.'

27

'Harald!'

Harald looked up from his paperwork. There were piles of it on the desk, endless loose ends he was trying to tie up.

Afra came in looking fraught. He had been sent with a hundred men to load our belongings and remaining wealth into the ships.

'What?'

'Our ships have been taken.'

Harald went white. 'What?'

'Our ships were taken from the harbour by men of the imperial fleet after we loaded them. I saw them go, there was nothing we could do.'

Harald's face fell. 'Zoe. Zoe has heard of what we are planning.'

'Can we steal another?' I asked.

Harald just stared at the table. 'I didn't think she would actually stop me. After all I have done for her.'

There was a noise outside and someone else pushed past into the room. It was Admiral Stephen, Michael's father. His eyes were red and his face was drawn.

'What?' Harald asked dully.

'I... uh. I heard what you did for my son,' he said, and Harald looked down, ashamed.

'I'm sorry, Stephen. I really am. I understand your hate.'

Stephen shook his head. 'No, no, you mistake me. I mean to say I am thankful for what you did. I know that Zoe ordered you to kill him, and you spared him.'

Harald looked up at him, shaking his head. 'Stephen, do you know what I did? You would not be thanking me if you knew.'

'I do,' Stephen said, nodding nervously. 'You left my son alive, when no one else would have. Perhaps... perhaps Zoe will still kill him, but I think not. The whole city will know what happened, and she would look a monster if she did anything else to that poor boy now.' Stephen shook his head, tears on his cheeks. 'I know you tried to save him all this time, to guide him and protect him but...' He wrung his hands together. 'He is not a normal boy and I could not prepare him for this life.' The man broke into a tortured sob and Harald dragged himself to his feet and came around the table.

'Stephen... I—'

Stephen got control of himself and pushed Harald away urgently. 'No, there is no time. I did not come to weep with you, Harald. I came to tell you that Zoe ordered me to take your ships. She is calling in forces from outside the city to arrest you, and they will be here tomorrow. She does not dare use the Vigla to confront you in case your Varangians fight them, in case the guard is loyal to you instead of her.'

Harald's eyes suddenly lit up. 'Stephen, my ships. Where are my ships?'

Stephen smiled oddly. 'I was never a brave man, Harald. Nor was I a good admiral like you were a good general.'

'Stephen,' Harald said calmly, putting both hands on the smaller man's shoulders. 'Where are my ships?'

'I'm so incompetent,' Stephen said with a laugh. 'I was supposed to order them away to the island, but I got confused. They are in the harbour on the north side of the city, in the Golden Horn. And my men left them there unguarded.' He shrugged helplessly. 'How foolish of me. Maybe the empress will believe I am merely incompetent again.' He drew in a deep breath. 'Or maybe I will finally have done something brave for my family, who have been destroyed by this cursed palace.'

Harald leaned forwards and kissed Stephen on his balding head. 'Thank you, Stephen. And I am sorry.'

'Go, go now. My mistake will be discovered soon, and you must sail before dark.'

Harald let go of Stephen's head and looked at me. 'We leave now. Everyone who can and wants to. Leave the paperwork.'

I nodded and pushed past Stephen.

'Come with us,' Harald said gently to the broken man.

He shook his head. 'No. I am going to stay here with my son, and care for him if I can.'

Harald nodded. 'You are a much braver man than you think, Stephen.' The admiral left the room, muttering to himself with a satisfied smile on his face.

* * *

'Damn, it's a shame we have to leave without the gold we are owed,' Harald said to me as the men who were coming gathered in the courtyard, surrounded by the glum faces of those who had chosen to stay behind.

'That isn't entirely true,' said a quiet voice from beside us.

We both looked around and saw Thorir and Afra standing there.

'What?'

Thorir looked to Afra for support and Afra nodded.

Thorir looked back at us. 'Well, we anticipated one day needing to leave in a hurry, and wanting to withdraw certain extra funds from the treasury,' Thorir said carefully.

Afra laughed. 'We were planning to rob the palace.' He shrugged guiltlessly. 'If the opportunity ever arose, you understand. The empress owes you money? We can go and get it on the way out.'

Harald stared at him. 'How? The treasury is locked and guarded, and two different palace officials are needed to open it.'

Thorir shook his head. 'No, two different *keys* are needed to open it.'

Harald narrowed his eyes. 'You can't have stolen the keys, it would immediately be reported. What have you done, blackmailed the officials? Bribed them?'

Thorir shook his head. 'They are far too closely monitored for that.' He partially opened his tunic and briefly showed Harald two large iron keys. 'We found the locksmith, and blackmailed him instead.'

Harald's mouth fell open and he laughed, covering it with his hand before we drew attention. He stared at the bandit brothers in wonder. 'We still have to deal with the guards. I don't have any authority over them any more and they will not be overcome with mere threats.'

Afra shook his head. 'I have a written order from the empress that the treasury guards from the Vigla are being replaced with our men today.'

'Written order? Forged, I presume.'

'Yes, but by the time they check and find out, we will be gone.'

A massive smile spread across Harald's face as he looked at them. 'Once a bandit, eh?'

Afra inclined his head slightly and grinned. 'I am famously not a man who changes easily.'

Harald shook his head in wonder. 'But if you come back to Norway with me, and I am king, your ways of banditry will have to cease.'

Afra nodded. 'Of course. And with a suitable retirement fund, and a pardon from the new king, they will. I am too old to be an outlaw any more regardless.'

Harald nodded quickly and stuck out his arm. 'We have an arrangement.'

Afra shook it happily. 'Good. We should go quickly.'

Harald nodded and turned to the men. 'Move out. We are heading down past the senate house, then to the northern sea-gate.'

He didn't tell them why we were going past the senate house. But behind it lay the treasury.

* * *

We got past the senate house without incident and Harald turned and stopped the column. 'Before we leave, we are claiming our promised pay.' He grinned at the men behind us. 'No violence. We are taking what is due to us and we are doing it quickly. Each man take only what he can easily carry. Half of what we take belongs to me, the rest is yours.' He paused and looked around. 'Anyone who wants no part of this, stay here.'

There were wide eyes and smiles in the group of fully armoured men, laden already with their packs and any wealth they already had.

'Let's go.'

Harald simply marched down the path to the treasury building and the thirty or so bored-looking Vigla guardsmen looked at us with nonchalance and then a little confusion. It was an unusually large group of Varangians, but that in itself was no cause for immediate alarm.

He took the forged letter out and presented it to the Vigla officer. 'We are replacing you. There is trouble on the south-western gate again and you are needed.'

The officer raised an eyebrow but took the scroll and inspected the seal, breaking it and then reading it. He looked dubiously at it and then at Harald.

'I don't have all day, Komes. You have your orders. We are to secure the treasury and you need to get to the gate, now!'

Harald's tone didn't brook dissent, and the order must have looked convincing. The Vigla officer nodded and turned to his men. 'Form up!'

They scrambled to get into formation on the path and we made way for them as they marched off.

'Once they reach the gate it won't take long to realise what has happened, so everything must be done quickly now,' Harald hissed, and we jogged to the treasury building's outer gate, throwing it open.

A few surprised clerks looked up at us as we marched in with dozens of armoured men. The treasury official at the table where deposits were made and counted, and payments checked and authorised, stood and gaped at us, trying to articulate a question.

'Tie them up,' Harald shouted, and he and Thorir simply went over to the desk as we swarmed the half dozen or so unarmed officials, binding them quickly as they protested and threatened.

Thorir quickly took the keys out and put them in the two bronze-trimmed keyholes on the huge, heavy doors. He and Harald turned them together and there was a deep clunk from behind the doors, and they unlatched.

Harald shoved the two doors and they started swinging open.

'Bring a lamp,' he said, and one was brought from the desk.

His eyes lit up. The treasury was at least a third full. Ten times more than we would be able to carry away.

'Two men at a time, quickly!'

We filed into the treasury at a jog in a double column, grabbing marked leather bags of gold solidi, each one about ten years' pay for a Varangian guardsman and weighing about ten pounds each. Others grabbed gold bars, ignoring the silver ones because they were simply not worth their weight.

The men started jogging out of the room giddy with delight at the gold they clutched to their chests, stuffed into their bags or slung around their necks.

'Come on, quickly! Don't be picky, just grab something and we will divide it later. Move!' Harald chided them.

The northern gate was the other side of the palace, but we wanted to be long gone when the Vigla realised what was happening.

It did not take too long to get all two hundred men through, and we gathered again outside in an excitable rabble, everyone too awestruck by the enormous wealth we had just acquired to get back into disciplined ranks.

'Back into column, move!' hissed Harald, and we jogged down the hill at the top of the palace, weighed down by all our equipment, loot and belongings.

The last concern was that the gate would be closed and barred, but the Vigla guardsmen there barely raised an eyebrow at a column of Varangians marching out at double time. The officer on watch saw Harald and saluted, shouting at the few other people using the gate to make way.

Harald smiled at the man and returned the salute, and then we were out into the streets.

'He is going to have a very bad afternoon,' I said with a giggle.

We marched quickly to the harbour and found, to our intense delight, that our loaded ships were just lying there ready to go, as Stephen had promised, attended only by a few curious dockyard workers. None of them would have dared touch the cargo. Everyone knew who owned the longships.

Harald looked back along the column as we arrived at the ships. He pointed at Sigurd and Rurik. 'You and your men, in the first ship with me.' He waved Afra over. 'I want you to command the second.'

Afra laughed. 'You are trusting a bandit with half your gold?'

'I am, because you are *my* bandit. Am I wrong?'

Afra grinned. 'You are not wrong, Prince Harald. A pardon in my homeland is worth more than the extra wealth.'

'Good man. Take whoever doesn't fit in my ship and follow us.' He put his hands together and shouted at the whole mass. 'Quickly, stow your equipment and get on benches. I want to go now!'

The men needed no goading. They poured into the two ships with enthusiasm, shoving packs and treasure under benches, dropping weapons in the middle and readying the oars.

Our ship had most of the men we had left Sweden with in it, apart from Afra and Thorir, and we pushed off slightly ahead of the other boat, oars dipping as we turned and headed out into the Golden Horn.

We cleared the harbour without a word being said against us, and made our way into the broad channel that led down into the main waterway at the tip of the city that would take us north.

We were in the stream now, the men pulling happily on the oars. The wind was at the wrong angle to set the sails, so we would row until we reached the main channel and then turn north-east with the wind to power us away.

I looked behind us at the rising mass of the palace hill as we approached it to pass. The spires of the Hagia Sophia rose above the walls and buildings at the top, twinkling in the light.

I smiled, feeling a deep satisfaction as we slid serenely along them, my gaze moving along the walls and...

My smile faded, and I squinted, and my heart fell.

'The chain!' I roared, pointing at the great tower near the entrance to the Golden Horn. 'They are raising the chain!'

Harald whipped around and saw it – the iron links of the harbour chain being swallowed into the tower where the winch mechanism sat. The chain ran from there, down the beach, and along a series of wooden floating rafts with a large gap in the middle, where it sank slackly into the depths.

As it wound up into the tower, that gap would narrow and narrow, the chain rising from the bottom, until it shut off the channel entirely.

Harald turned and screamed at the men. '*Row!*'

He grabbed a spear and started hammering it on the deck to keep time. 'Everything you've got!'

I ran down the central aisle of the ship to the stern, shouting and waving at Afra in the next ship to make sure they saw. Afra waved back from the bow and I heard him also haranguing his crew to speed up.

I looked back at the narrowing gap in the chain. We were angling towards the centre of it, the steersman chewing his lip.

'Are we going to make it?' I asked breathlessly.

The guardsmen nodded fervently. Not making it was not an option.

I looked to Afra again, because their ship was surging now, catching us slightly. That filled me with hope.

But behind them, coming out of another of the city's harbours, were two dromons of the harbour guard, already churning white water under their bows as they gave chase.

'They are coming after us!' I shouted to Harald, and he ran down the ship to join me. He watched the dromons and then looked in front of us. 'They won't make it to the chain before it closes. We will have time to get the sails up and get clear. They don't matter.'

I nodded, more with hope than confidence.

We were almost at the chain, but the gap was narrowing dramatically, the weed-covered iron slowly rising from the water at a shallow angle on both sides of the bow ahead of us, fifty paces away and closing.

'Row, you sons of whores! Row!' roared Harald as we approached the gap, and the men leant into it with everything they had.

We approached the empty water in the middle of the chain and there was a sudden bump near the bow, and then a grinding noise as the bow rode up on the chain and it scraped along the keel. The scraping noise came closer and closer to the stern even as the ship juddered and slowed, oars thrashing the water white.

'Everyone in the stern, get forwards!' shouted Harald as we reached the tipping point and almost slowed to a stop.

We ran madly down the ship, climbing over rowers and benches as our momentum took the middle of the ship up over the chain and the weight of the men going up tipped it forwards, letting us slide off the metal links again the other side with a terrible grating noise.

'Back to the oars!' Harald shouted as the bow of the ship dipped and slewed dangerously under the uneven load.

As we rushed to get the ship back under control I looked behind at Afra's crew.

Afra was standing in the bow as they reached the chain, and he had seen what we had done to get across it. He was holding his hand high in the air, ready to give the signal to rush forwards.

The bow hit the submerged centre of the chain and juddered, the tension pushing the chain above the waterline as the bow crunched into it, raising Afra into the air. Then the chain slipped, disappearing under the water and the keel as the momentum of the ship overcame its resistance and the oars thrashed.

Afra waited as the ship ground over the chain, bow still in the air, and then, as the vessel almost came to a halt, he swept his hand down and roared at his men to run forwards.

Half of them abandoned the rear oars and rushed forwards, scrambling to get the ship to balance over the chain and fall off the other side.

The ship finally went dead in the water, creaking and slewing, poised finely as they strained at the remaining oars.

They had been a few moments later than us, the chain a few fractions tighter, and I watched in horror as their overloaded ship slid backwards into the Golden Horn, popping off the chain, which now sat just at the waterline in front of them, completely barring their escape.

'We must go back and help them!' I shouted, turning to Harald, confused why he had not already given the order.

His face was set in a stony grimace. 'We can't help them, Eric,' he said softly.

I stared at him, not comprehending how he could say that. Then I dragged my eyes around to the beleaguered ship, where even now Afra was organising the men in a futile attempt to back up and try again.

But behind them, desperately close now, the prows of the two dromons loomed. And above each prow, shimmering in the afternoon sunlight, was the dreadful, familiar haze of the dromon's terrible weapon.

'Dear God, no,' I muttered, aghast.

The dromons had prepared their Greek fire.

Harald turned away with a last bitter look, calling out to the men to prepare to raise sail and turn north, and I saw them obey, eyes down, not even daring to watch what was happening behind us.

'We have to help them!' I shouted, railing at these men who were abandoning their brothers, even though I knew there was nothing that could be done to save them.

I felt the helplessness overcome me. The dromons were almost upon Afra's ship, and I saw the crew abandoning their useless oars and Afra shouting orders to get them ready to defend themselves. The few bows they had aboard were already being used pointlessly to decorate the raised protective prows of the Greek ships with feathered shafts.

And arrows flew back in return, by the dozen, and my beloved brothers started falling into the mess of treasure and equipment in the hull.

Afra came to side of the ship nearest me. He stood there, motionless for a few moments, and then he raised his hand at me in a forlorn salute.

I wept like a child as the first wave of fire and death gushed from the prow of the leading dromon, washing over the front half of Afra's ship and dousing the chaotic mass of terrified men within its hellish flames.

I saw the billowing, churning flames reach Afra even as he stood there looking at me, and I swear that even through the tears that clouded my vision, I saw him smiling at me as they enveloped him.

Arrows from the second dromon were pouring into the helpless survivors as they tried to get to false safety in the stern of the blazing vessel, but there was nowhere to hide.

I saw a man I think was Thorir near the steering oar, stripping his armour off and diving into the churning waters as the arrows rained down on the last survivors. But I did not see where or if he surfaced.

I slipped down into the hull of our ship, letting the final death agony of my brothers disappear from view as Harald ordered the sail up and set his flinty eyes on the way north, the way back to his long-lost throne.

He never even turned back to look at the terrible revenge that his lover the Empress Zoe had wrought for his betrayal.

EPILOGUE

There was a stunned silence in the hall as Eric finished the telling of the loss of Afra's ship.

The excitement and interest that had built up during the evening, and the retellings of some of the guard's glorious moments had faded away.

The king looked at Eric with raised eyebrows. 'A remarkable tale, Eric. Considering how famous your devotion to my grandfather was, you seem to have a surprisingly dark view of many of his actions.'

Eric smiled at him sadly. 'I merely tell things as they were, Lord King, and I do not pretend that I think Harald was perfect as a man. But he was, indeed, a great leader worthy of loyalty and love, and fear. Because that is what a great man must inspire in order to succeed. Harald was great not because he sought to make sacrifices to achieve his goals, but because he had the strength to do so when it was needed. He looked ahead in that ship at the path we needed to take, while I looked behind at the things we had lost, because that is the way we both were. It is why he was capable of things that I was not.'

Eric nodded sadly. 'I think some of you assumed my tale would all be of glory and adventure, and there has been plenty of that. But also, it would be a disservice to the true man that was Harald, and those who served him, if that was all I recounted. I seek to have you all understand that those things he sought, the glory he achieved, come with a price.' Eric looked around the room. 'I told you, three days ago, of how a hundred and fifty of us sailed with Harald from Sweden, and that only thirteen returned. And now you know why. Thirteen of us blood-marked were in that ship that escaped the flames of Zoe's wrath, and it was simple chance that only two of us, my friend Afra the Constant, and Thorir the Cuckoo, were in the one that was lost.'

'So Harald lost half of his gold,' Jarl Hakon said with a frown.

Eric shook his head. 'No, not half. Much of our wealth had already been sent to Kyiv over the years, but yes, it was a sore loss of wealth, alongside the far more precious loss of experienced, loyal men. Both would damage Harald's plans deeply.'

'And what of the men who stayed behind? Do you know what became of them?'

Eric nodded. 'I heard from men who returned from the east a few times over the years. Sveinn led the guard for a while, before he too left to go home.' Eric tapped his fingers on the table. 'That bright, young lad Alexios recovered from his wounds, and served with the guard for many years, rising to become its commander too.' Eric smiled proudly. 'The only one of them who could beat me with a sword.' He looked up and his smile faded a little. 'He stayed with the guard until the end, and I hear he was their commander at the great battle with the Turks at Manzikert thirty years after we left, where the strength of the empire's armies was finally broken. He, along with most of his guardsmen, died defending the emperor, who was taken prisoner after they were finally subdued.'

There was a murmur of shock around the room. 'Yes, it is true,' Eric said. 'The guard were defeated in the field, but they did their duty and died honouring their oaths.'

'A good death, then,' the king said, slapping the table. He gave Eric a chilling look. 'May we all be so lucky.'

Eric inclined his head and looked away.

The king rose. 'I thank Eric Sveitungr for his tale, and I raise my ale to our kin, the honourable dead. May their deeds never be forgotten.'

The hall rose and raised their horns and mugs and cheered, drinking with the king.

'And now, let us turn from the past, as my grandfather would have, and celebrate the future, and all the glory it will bring! Bring more ale!'

The king raised his hands to the roar of the crowd, acknowledging it as he swept his outstretched arms around the room.

As the men all crowded at the barrels to get more drink, the king sat down carefully next to Jarl Halfdan and leant in to speak to him. 'I think there is more guile to this Eric than he wants us to believe.'

Jarl Halfdan nodded. 'This is why I sent word to you. I am worried he is preparing the crowd to be receptive if he speaks against your proposed campaign.'

'But why? Why does this old man care so much what decision we make?' the king said, pondering it.

'I don't know. We can prevent him telling the rest of his tale, if you want.'

The king thought about it for a few moments and then shook his head. 'It's too late for that. The men will be angry if they do not get to hear the story of Harald's last campaign from one who was actually there.'

'So what do you want me to do?' Jarl Halfdan said, looking in concern at his king.

King Magnus tapped his forefinger on the side of his mug for a few moments, watching Ingvarr excitedly asking Eric questions. He nodded slowly. 'He won't continue his tale until tomorrow. I will talk to him before. Maybe he is testing me. After all, would the Harald from his tale be overruled by an old man?'

The Jarl shook his head sternly. 'He would not.'

'Well, he calls himself the follower. Perhaps I can get him to follow me.'

'And if not?'

'Harald would not have allowed such disloyalty,' Magnus replied, gazing over the boisterous crowd and sipping his ale. 'And believe me, neither will I.'

* * *

MORE FROM JC DUNCAN

Another book from JC Duncan, *Emperor's Axe*, is available to order now here: https://mybook.to/EmperorsAxeBackAd

AFTERWORD AND HISTORICAL NOTE

And so, Harald's extraordinary adventures in the Byzantine Empire come to a close. For nearly ten years Harald served the rulers of the Roman Empire, and fought in perhaps a dozen major actions, and dozens of lesser ones. He was there at a tumultuous time and had a huge influence on events, far beyond what a mere member of the guard should have had. That is all a testament to the extraordinary man that he was.

You may think that the contents of this book are far-fetched, but, remarkably, a great deal of it closely adheres to what the available records show.

Harald went on the short, vicious and victorious campaign against the rebel emperor Petar Delyan in 1041 with a detachment of the Varangian guard, where he carried his famous raven standard 'Land-Waster' and earned the name in the Byzantine records of 'The Bulgar Burner'.

Why? We don't know. The records of that campaign that survive are not detailed but the battle of Ostrovo was the decisive battle, although no detailed account of it survives so what I wrote is entirely fictional (but, I believe, in character).

The extreme and violent events that took place after his return and before he fled the city are also, broadly, historical. Emperor Michael IV was sick before the campaign started and was so weakened by it that he did die shortly afterwards, probably from gangrenous infection in his legs caused by his various serious underlying illnesses and the exertion of going on campaign.

Zoe and John fought viciously for control of the empire as Michael died, and John forced her to accept his nephew as successor. Michael V is a tragic figure, used and abused by everyone around him as they sought to control him. But he shocked them all by almost immediately having his uncle executed (quite possibly by Harald), having Harald imprisoned on possibly trumped-up charges for trying to steal his mistress (who is recorded simply as Maria), and then finally having Zoe banished.

It was a series of very foolish and inexplicable moves, which I have chosen to attribute (fairly, I think) to some sort of mania or deep personality flaws. It was never going to work, and the people of the city did, indeed, turn on him and demand Zoe's return.

Zoe ordered Michael's blinding and castration in revenge. If you thought I was being over the top, that was actually two common forms of punishment in Byzantine society for the nobility, a deliberate humiliation that ensured the end of that person's influence and family. Again, there is some suggestion Harald himself carried out the sentence.

What is known for sure is that Harald left shortly afterwards. Perhaps he had simply grown tired of the massacres, plotting and death, or perhaps he felt he was rich enough to go home.

He did loot the treasury on the way out, although that is somewhat of a regular occurrence by the Varangian guard when emperors died, a tradition that was tolerated as a sort of payment, a 'congratulations, your boss just died and it wasn't your fault,' bonus.

But whatever the reason for his departure, it is certain he and Zoe had finally and terminally fallen out, as the harbour chain was raised to stop him, and one of his two ships was indeed apparently caught and lost.

Zoe's sister Theodora was put on the throne alongside her, presumably because Zoe thought her sister would be easily controllable. With great irony, Theodora in fact turned out to be extremely forceful in her imposition of her will, and Zoe never attained the sole control of the empire she so desperately desired. To try and force Theodora aside she took a new husband (depicted in this book as the man who negotiated with the crowd), who became Constantine IX. There is a huge, vivid mosaic of the three rulers sitting together in the upper part of the Hagia Sophia, which survives to this day. I have visited that spot where Zoe, in her typically ruthless fashion, had the mosaic depiction of Michael IV's face removed and replaced with the head of Constantine IX.

To stand in the very place where she once stood was a fascinating experience for someone who has spent over a year writing about her and her empire.

Their tripartite co-reign was largely peaceful and prosperous, a new, and short, era of imperial dominance and a booming economy that marked one of the last golden periods in Roman history. The two sisters and Constantine ruled together in a very uneasy alliance until Zoe's death in 1050, Constantine's in 1055, and then, in an ironic quirk of fate, Theodora ruled alone, fulfilling her sister's ambition for a single year until she too finally died in 1056.

But the struggles and successes of the empire after Harald left are not what matters to our story. We leave that all behind in our wake, as Harald did, as the tale heads towards its final chapter, with Harald's return to the kingdom of Norway and his famous invasion of England in 1066.

But for now it is 1042 AD, and the extraordinary prince of Norway has a small band of loyal veterans at his back, a hull full of gold at his feet, and only one thing on his mind: an empire of his own.

ABOUT THE AUTHOR

JC Duncan is a well-reviewed historical fiction author and amateur bladesmith, with a passion for Vikings.

Sign up to JC Duncan's mailing list here for news, competitions and updates on future books.

Visit JC's website: www.jcduncan.co.uk

Follow JC on social media:

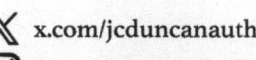 x.com/jcduncanauthor
instagram.com/j.c.duncan
facebook.com/JCDuncanAuthor

ALSO BY JC DUNCAN

The Last Viking Series

Warrior Prince

Raven Lord

Emperor's Axe

Wolves of the Empire

WARRIOR CHRONICLES

WELCOME TO THE CLAN ✕

THE HOME OF
BESTSELLING HISTORICAL
ADVENTURE FICTION!

WARNING:
MAY CONTAIN VIKINGS!

SIGN UP TO OUR
NEWSLETTER

BIT.LY/WARRIORCHRONICLES

Boldwood

Boldwood Books is an award-winning fiction publishing company seeking out the best stories from around the world.

Find out more at www.boldwoodbooks.com

Join our reader community for brilliant books, competitions and offers!

Follow us
@BoldwoodBooks
@TheBoldBookClub

Sign up to our weekly deals newsletter

https://bit.ly/BoldwoodBNewsletter

www.ingramcontent.com/pod-product-compliance
Ingram Content Group UK Ltd.
Pitfield, Milton Keynes, MK11 3LW, UK
UKHW042026230625
6545UKWH00002B/14